"Like an alchemist, Karen E. Olson blends together wildly disparate elements into pure gold. *Dead of the Day* is a delightful dance with the devil—dangerous, dark, and romantic."
—Reed Farrel Coleman, Shamus Award–winning author of *The James Deans*

"Karen E. Olson knows this beat like the back of her hand. I really enjoyed *Dead of the Day*."
—Michael Connelly

"*Dead of the Day* takes the Annie Seymour series to truly impressive territory. Absolutely everything a first-rate crime novel should be." —Lee Child

Secondhand Smoke

"Annie Seymour, a New Haven journalist who's not quite as cynical as she thinks she is, is the real thing, an engaging and memorable character with the kind of complicated loyalties that make a series worth reading. Karen E. Olson is the real thing, too, a natural story-teller with a lucid style and a wonderful sense of place."
—Laura Lippman, *New York Times* bestselling author

"Olson's second mystery hits the mark with setting, plot, and character. . . . Her lovably imperfect heroine charms, and the antics of her coworkers and the residents of 'da neighborhood' will keep you intrigued and amused. Four stars." —*Romantic Times*

"Humor, plenty of motives, and strong character development make this a fast, fun read."
—Monsters and Critics

"Humor enlivens this first-person account. . . . This remains a series with considerable potential." —*Booklist*

continued . . .

"Olson's characters are her own, and her fast-paced plot and great ending make it a perfect read for patrons who like a bit of humor in their mysteries."

—*Library Journal*

"Authentic urban atmosphere, generous wit, and winning characters lift Olson's second outing. . . . Readers are sure to look forward to Annie's further adventures."

—*Publishers Weekly*

"Annie is a believable heroine whose sassy exploits and muddled love life should make for more exciting adventures."

—*Kirkus Reviews*

Sacred Cows

"A boilermaker of a first novel. . . . Olson writes with great good humor, but *Sacred Cows* is also a roughhouse tale. Her appealing and intrepid protagonist and well-constructed plot make this book one of the best debut novels of the year."

—*The Cleveland Plain Dealer*

"In this just-the-facts-ma'am journalism procedural, Karen E. Olson plunges readers into the salty-tongued world of cynical reporter sleuth Annie Seymour. . . . [The story] spins from sinister to slapstick and back in the breadth of a page. Engaging."

—Denise Hamilton, bestselling author of *Savage Garden*

"A sharply written and beautifully plotted story."

—*Chicago Tribune*

"Olson writes with a light touch that is the perfect complement for this charming mystery."

—*Chicago Sun-Times*

SHOT
GIRL

An Annie Seymour Mystery

Karen E. Olson

AN OBSIDIAN MYSTERY

OBSIDIAN
Published by New American Library, a division of
Penguin Group (USA) Inc., 375 Hudson Street,
New York, New York 10014, USA
Penguin Group (Canada), 90 Eglinton Avenue East, Suite 700, Toronto,
Ontario M4P 2Y3, Canada (a division of Pearson Penguin Canada Inc.)
Penguin Books Ltd., 80 Strand, London WC2R 0RL, England
Penguin Ireland, 25 St. Stephen's Green, Dublin 2,
Ireland (a division of Penguin Books Ltd.)
Penguin Group (Australia), 250 Camberwell Road, Camberwell, Victoria 3124,
Australia (a division of Pearson Australia Group Pty. Ltd.)
Penguin Books India Pvt. Ltd., 11 Community Centre, Panchsheel Park,
New Delhi - 110 017, India
Penguin Group (NZ), 67 Apollo Drive, Rosedale, North Shore 0632,
New Zealand (a division of Pearson New Zealand Ltd.)
Penguin Books (South Africa) (Pty.) Ltd., 24 Sturdee Avenue,
Rosebank, Johannesburg 2196, South Africa

Penguin Books Ltd., Registered Offices:
80 Strand, London WC2R 0RL, England

First published by Obsidian, an imprint of New American Library,
a division of Penguin Group (USA) Inc.

First Printing, November 2008
10 9 8 7 6 5 4 3 2 1

Copyright © Karen E. Olson, 2008
All rights reserved

OBSIDIAN and logo are trademarks of Penguin Group (USA) Inc.

Printed in the United States of America

To Liz Medcalf and Kerri Pedersen
Best friends, great journalists

Acknowledgments

I have to thank my editor, Kristen Weber, whose enthusiasm is so validating. I can always count on my agent, Jack Scovil, for his sage advice and droll sense of humor.

Big thanks to John Ferraro and Peter Dalpe, who allowed me to steal memories of their years studying journalism at Southern Connecticut State University, and to Patrick Dilger and Joe Musante in Southern's Office of Public Affairs.

To all my journalist friends who are still in the trenches.

To my fellow First Offenders: Alison Gaylin, Jeff Shelby, and Lori Armstrong. Words can't express how I feel about you guys. And to all the FOFOs: You have made this such a great ride.

First readers Liz Medcalf, Liz Cipollina, and Angelo Pompano, who critique with a great eye even though we're good friends. Mary-Ann Tirone Smith for her friendship; it means the world to me.

To Ranger Wray at the West Rock Nature Center for his patient answers about Judges Cave. There are no community gardens at the nature center like the ones on these pages.

To the drivers of the M bus on my daily commute.

To all my readers who've e-mailed to tell me how much they love Annie and her world.

The "dancing man" is for Jackie Russell.

And a very special thanks to Jan and Stu Hecht of

the former Book Vault for their amazing support. It was a dark day when those doors closed.

I've made up some locations in this book, namely the Rouge Lounge and West Rock School. So don't go crazy trying to figure out exactly where they are. They don't exist.

Last but not least, again, thanks to my husband, Chris, and daughter, Julia, for their unwavering support, love, and hugs. They make all of this so much sweeter.

SHOT
GIRL

Chapter 1

He looked better dead than alive. Can't say that about many people.

He seemed to be merely resting on his stomach on the sidewalk amid some cigarette butts and a broken martini glass, like he'd just lain down for a quick nap but hadn't yet fallen asleep. His arms were twisted underneath him, his knees slightly bent in different directions, and his head was turned to one side; a green olive looked like a growth off the top of his nose.

It creeped me out. But it was like one of those train wrecks people are always talking about—I couldn't stop staring. And as I looked more closely, I noticed what was conspicuously missing.

I tore my eyes away and glanced up and down the sidewalk and across the street, ignoring the police cars, cops, and throngs of people lined up outside the yellow crime-scene tape. I'd managed to stay just inside the tape as the young uniform unrolled it around me. In the pandemonium, no one noticed.

I sidled up to the blond cop in the heavy tweed jacket, a poor choice for a hot summer night. "I heard the gunshots, but where's the blood?"

Detective Tom Behr was listening to me—I knew that only because we had a history and I'd learned how to read his body language, in more ways than one—but he was looking at the body, wondering what the hell had happened here.

"You heard the shots?" Tom frowned; he still didn't look at me.

"I was inside, like everyone else."

I saw his eyebrows rise slightly, the only show of surprise, as he studied the outside of the building in front of us. It was a nondescript reddish brown brick, with a long green and white awning covering a roped-off entranceway.

Anyone could get into the Rouge Lounge, but it liked to give the impression that it was exclusive.

A chuckle escaped Tom's throat as he read the sign over the door: ALL-MALE REVUE, TONITE ONLY, LADIES ONLY.

"You were inside?" he asked, the incredulity charging across his words like a fucking rhinoceros.

I tugged at the black skirt that was too tight and shifted on the red stilettos, all borrowed from my friend Priscilla, who owns such clothes. I could feel the blisters that already had formed on my feet, casualties of the fashionable "no hose" rule. What had I been thinking? With the exception of a tasteful little black dress my mother bought me at Ann Taylor, my closet houses jeans, khakis, button-down shirts, and T-shirts.

I reached for the bag slung around my shoulder—it was small, but I had managed to pack a tiny notebook and a pen along with a few bills and some change—and the strap of the lacy camisole that was doubling as a top slipped down.

As I slid it back up, Tom's blue eyes lingered first on the shoes, then slowly made their way up my thighs to my hips, and finally rested on the V between the lace just over my breasts.

Goddamn but it was hot tonight.

I fumbled with the pen and managed to open the pad. "We heard the shots about five after ten," I said, moving into reporter mode.

"Then you know more than I do," Tom said.

"But I was inside," I repeated.

He couldn't keep the grin from spreading across his

face. "Dressed like that? Does your boyfriend know what you're up to?"

"Jesus, Tom," I snorted. "Believe me, this wasn't my idea."

He snickered. "Whose idea was it?"

I waved my hand in the air at a gaggle of women dressed like me on the other side of the crime-scene tape. "It's a fucking bachelorette party. Renee Chittenden. She's getting married in two days. Everyone said I should go, have fun. Priscilla lent me the clothes. I admit I got caught up in it. Let them dress me up." I shook my head. "Thank God there was a shooting. I couldn't take it anymore."

"Did you see this guy in there?" Tom asked, all business all of a sudden.

I stiffened. How much should I tell him? "Yeah. He was there."

"Do you know who he is?" Tom was watching me, like he knew.

I paused, trying to figure out what I might say. But before I could open my mouth, I heard Tom's name being called. Another detective was motioning him to go inside with him. Tom pursed his lips, nodded, then said, "Don't go anywhere," as he followed his colleague.

I surveyed the body again, but this time had to take a couple steps to get a better view because the forensics guys had begun their work, taking photographs, sifting through the grit on the sidewalk around him. Someone put the olive in a plastic bag.

The eye I could see was open, staring straight ahead at a splatter of bird shit. If he were looking up, he'd see the tree branches over our heads. One of the things I like about New Haven is that it's managed to keep its small-town feel with the trees and grassy areas throughout the city. Unfortunately, the city's nickname of the Elm City doesn't apply anymore because all the old trees died of Dutch elm disease way back when.

I'd hoped that thinking about the trees would distract me, but no dice.

He really did look peaceful, no hard lines in his face from years of living hard. His hair was still full and dark, no monklike bald patch, just a touch of gray at his temple.

I'd heard things, what he was up to, where he was, but I never thought he'd come back to where it all started.

As I studied his face—it had settled into itself as he'd gotten older, making him less awkward looking and more distinguished, sort of like what happened with George Clooney—I waited for some of the old feelings to emerge. But nothing. Time had turned him into a stranger; now he was just another crime victim. Well, maybe I wouldn't go that far. I was glad he looked so good. He would've been happy about that.

One of the forensics guys bumped into me, and I felt myself succumbing to gravity as the stupid shoes I was wearing refused to steady.

"What the hell are you doing on the ground?" Vinny's voice made me smile involuntarily as I tried to get up without showing everyone all my goods. It wasn't easy, and I slipped again. His hands lifted me up, moved me backward, away from the body, and, unfortunately, onto the other side of the yellow tape. I savored the feel of his arms around me before they fell away.

"Shit, Vinny, now I'll never be able to get back over there," I scolded, clutching my small wad of paper, knowing I could still get a story into the *New Haven Herald* if I could find Tom again. It was only ten thirty, and deadline was at eleven fifteen.

"Need my cell phone to call it in?"

I hadn't thought I'd need my phone in the club, so I left it in the glove box of my car in the parking lot. Along with a pair of flip-flops that I could drive in. I shook my head.

"What happened? There was a tease on the news about a shooting. Figured I'd come over here and see if you were okay."

Vinny DeLucia pointed to the TV van parked across the street. Cindy Purcell, aka Lois Lane, was fluffing up her already-big blond curls with one hand, a microphone

in the other; a cameraman scurried around, looking for
the best angle. I shifted a little, not wanting to get in his
shot. There's a reason why print journalists aren't on
TV, and in this getup, I had even more of a reason to
try to be invisible.

Damn, I needed to get my phone and call this in before Dick Whitfield, boy reporter, showed up. I knew he
was on shift tonight.

"Thanks, Vin, I'm okay," I said, hoping he wouldn't
take it personally if I hightailed it to my car. I started
to turn, then realized that in my fall, the skirt had
twisted and was even shorter. I pulled it down as far as
it could go, which wasn't very far. I knew Vinny was
watching me, much like Tom had just minutes before. I
was glad Vinny hadn't seen that. Even though Vinny
and I were a definite item, Tom indicated he still har-
bored hopes, and Vinny could be a typical Italian male
with territorial impulses. Call me fickle, but I liked the
attention on both fronts. Sort of made up for high
school, when I sat home on prom night eating ice cream
and watching *Lou Grant*.

"What happened?" Vinny asked again.

I shrugged. "Beats me. I heard the shots and came
out here. He was on the ground."

I stole another look at the body, but before I could
excuse myself to get my phone, Vinny said, "There's
no blood."

I nodded. "I know."

We mulled that a few seconds.

"So, how was the show?" Vinny asked, his eyes dancing. "I mean, before this."

I rolled my eyes at him. "Awful. Disgusting. Fortunately, because it was so early, we only saw one guy."

"What was so disgusting?"

"He did his little dance, and then he brought Renee
onstage." I shuddered, remembering how embarrassed I
was for her, even though she didn't seem to mind much.
I think it was all those martinis her sisters had bought
her beforehand. "He called himself Jack Hammer."

Vinny laughed out loud, and my eyes strayed over to

Renee and her sisters and girlfriends. They had seemed like they were having a good time. Even when Jack Hammer proceeded to simulate fucking Renee in front of everyone. Even when he sat on her sisters' laps and gyrated. They'd laughed; they hadn't seemed disturbed.

"It's not my crowd," I said. "I shouldn't have gone. I shouldn't have let everyone talk me into it."

"And miss a great crime scene? You? Hell, you'd be here anyway, and you know it." Vinny was only half teasing.

"Yeah, I'd be here, but not dressed like this." I did a little game-show-model wave to indicate my too-tight outfit.

Vinny's smile was more of a leer. "But just think about how much fun we'll have later when you get home," he whispered, his breath hotter than the air against my neck, giving me a chill down my back that was not unpleasant.

Tom came back out of the nightclub, and I gave Vinny a little nudge. "Go home, Vinny. I'll call you when I'm done here and on my way back, okay?"

To his credit, Vinny took a step backward. He knew when to give me space to do my job. Unfortunately, now I had to get into Tom's space and get enough information from him so I could make my editor happy.

The damn shoes made it hard to stoop under the tape, but somehow I managed it, making my way back over to Tom.

"I have to call the paper and give them something," I said. "Was he shot? Was it a drive-by?"

Tom took my elbow and led me up the three steps and into the club. The air-conditioning slapped me across the face, almost burning me with its intensity. Immediately I felt my nipples harden and hoped he wouldn't notice.

Too late.

"You said you'd seen him inside?" Tom asked after a second.

I nodded, eager to distract him. "Yeah."

"He was the manager." He paused. "Anything you want to tell me, Annie?"

I bit my lip.

"You know his name, don't you?" he prodded when I hesitated too long.

"Yeah. I do."

"Coincidence?"

I shook my head slowly.

His name was Ralph Seymour.

My ex-husband.

Chapter 2

Tom thought I was lying. I could see it in the way he stood with his legs apart, his hands on his hips, his head cocked like I was some sort of criminal. Like I should know how Ralph got gunned down in front of the Rouge Lounge.

"Fifteen years?" he asked me for the third time when I told him how long it had been since I'd seen Ralph. "You're sure?"

"He didn't even show up for the court date," I said, my voice loud to match his. "My divorce was really a solo act, not unlike our marriage."

Tom frowned. I knew he wouldn't understand. No one had, especially Ralph. Which had been the problem. And I didn't want to stand here, fifteen years later, and explain the complexities of how I knew after only a year, and at the young age of twenty-three, why I just couldn't stay married to the man.

"The bartender says she saw you talking to him just minutes before he went outside." Tom's voice was cold.

I sighed. "I saw him when I came in." He'd been groping the bartender while she shook someone else's martini.

Tom waited for more.

"Okay, okay, he saw me when I tried to duck into the ladies' room and figure out what the hell to do." I paused. "Jesus, Tom, it had been a long time. I really wasn't sure how to react. It threw me a little."

"But you stood outside staring at his body and didn't bother to tell me who he was."

"So sue me." I studied his face for a second. "He probably talked to a lot of other people besides me. Why aren't you talking to them?"

"Because this is more interesting." A small smile played at the corners of his lips, and I wondered if he had started pursuing that psychology degree he'd considered at one time. "So, what was your conversation about?"

I shrugged. "He said hi, I said hi, he said fancy meeting you here, I said go figure, he said how's it going, I said what are you doing in town?"

A few seconds passed before Tom asked, "What did he say to that?"

I shook my head. "Nothing. The bartender called him over. He said excuse me, we'll catch up later, and walked away. That was it."

"So you don't know why he went outside?"

"No. I was too busy in there"—I cocked my head toward the red beads, à la the 1960s, that separated us from the room where Jack Hammer had been grinding his hips just an hour before—"for the party."

The small smile turned into a grin. "Ah, yes, the party."

My eyes scanned the dark bar, the bloodred art deco round tables and chairs scattered about, empty glasses and beer bottles abandoned everywhere as the customers, ranging from scantily clad young women to women older than me who should've known better, were being interrogated by various uniformed officers. A half dozen reproductions of Warhol's Marilyn Monroe hung side by side across one wall, splashing a startling bit of green and blue and yellow and black. I don't go to clubs—I left those days long behind—but this was a pretty cool place. And it could go either way now: No one would come back because of the shooting, or everyone would come because of the shooting.

It was a crapshoot.

Speak of the devil, if it wasn't Jack Hammer coming toward us. I had to admit the man was buff in all the right places, but he had that sleazy leer and slicked-back hair that made him a great candidate for the sequel to *Donny Does Dallas* rather than the cover of *GQ*.

"Hey, babe," he drawled at me as the uniform cop dropped him off at our side.

I wondered if Tom would arrest me for slugging him.

"This guy says maybe he saw something," the uniform told Tom, stealing a sidelong glance at me and my cleavage, not that there was too much of it, but there was a helluva lot more on display than normal. I couldn't wait to get home and change.

I hoped it wouldn't be much longer now. I could manage a quick stop at my brownstone and maybe even just call in the story to the night news editor. I thought about my cell phone in the car.

Tom saw me looking at my watch. "You're not going anywhere," he hissed, his hand clutching my elbow as he turned to Jack Hammer.

"So what did you see?" he asked him, like I wasn't even there. I was tempted to try to walk away, but I wanted to know what Jack Hammer had to say, too.

Jack Hammer looked from Tom to me and back to Tom. "I was finished with my set"—oh, Christ, was that what he called it?—"and I was outside for a smoke." Connecticut had banned smoking in bars and restaurants a few years ago, which helped my cause when I decided to quit. "Someone opened the door; I saw Ralphie talking to her." He tossed his greasy mane toward me. "Someone handed him a martini and he stepped outside, a few feet from me. He asked me for a cigarette; I gave him one. But I was finished with mine and had to get back for the next set, so I went back in. Next thing I knew, I heard the shots, came back out, and saw Ralphie on the ground."

I was trying to wrap my head around the fact that Jack Hammer was calling him Ralphie. Jesus, he would've hated that.

Oh, yeah, it had been a long time. Maybe he was cool with it now.

"Hey, Tom?"

I looked to my right to see Frank Piscitelli, New Haven's answer to *CSI*'s Gil Grissom, beckoning Tom to come over. Frank was short and squat, what my dad—who is also Italian—would call "a real Guido" from East Haven, who hardly conjured the image of a scientist. Frank spent a lot of time in a small, brightly lit room at the New Haven Police Department, so unlike *CSI* portrayals, it was comical. I was never one for understanding forensics or fingerprinting, but I admit a curiosity about the refrigerators that house the bloody clothing. Or at least that's what Frank told me is in there. It probably contains that day's lunch. Or both. Frank could have a grisly sense of humor.

"Don't go anywhere," Tom warned me again as he walked away.

Jack Hammer, however, did not leave my side. Great. The way I was dressed, he probably thought he could get lucky. But then he surprised me.

"You're Annie, aren't you?"

"Yeah, that's right," I said, frowning. "How the hell do you know that?"

He shrugged. "Ralphie pointed you out earlier." He paused. "He talked a lot about you."

I stood up a little straighter, folding my arms across my chest. "He did?"

"Said you'd been the best thing that ever happened to him."

Yeah, he would say that. And he did say that as I left him and his pathetic lies in New York, where they belonged.

"When did he start working here?" I asked.

Genuine surprise crossed his face as he frowned. "A month ago. You know that."

Before I could respond, Tom came back.

He pointed at Jack Hammer. "Come with me."

I hoped I could finally leave, but Tom was shaking his

head at me. "You have to stay right here. I'm not done with you yet."

That's what he thought.

I glared at him. "At least can I go to my car and get my phone? I've got a pair of flip-flops in there, too." I indicated my blistered feet. "I have to take these things off."

A mix of emotions crossed Tom's face, until finally resignation settled in. "Give me the keys. I'll have someone get the shoes for you." He paused. "But no phone, and I'm not telling you shit."

Even in prison they give you a fucking phone call. I thought about Cindy Purcell outside with her camera crew and wondered if her main squeeze—and my nemesis—Dick Whitfield, was lurking out there, as well. I could only hope that he had the good sense to show up. But he was probably sitting in the newsroom trying to get someone on the phone instead. It was about time for the lottery drawing, and the news editor needed the night reporter to get the numbers off the TV because the copy editors were too busy on eBay and checking their e-mail to get the numbers off the Internet. I regretted not taking up Vinny's offer of his phone earlier.

I hesitated a couple of seconds before I pulled my keys out of my small bag and gave them to Tom. It was too late now. If I changed my mind, he'd wonder why.

"The flip-flops are just on the floor on the passenger side," I said. "Right inside the door."

The keys dangled from Tom's hand as he led Jack Hammer away and out of sight. The minute they turned the corner, I figured it was a good time to see if I could get any information out of anyone else, most likely Frank.

"Detective said you had to stay here." The young cop hovered over me, his shoulders so wide I could use them as an umbrella.

"I just need some air," I tried. He stepped into my path, shaking his head slowly, the frown indicating I obviously did not know how to play well with others. No shit. I glanced around the bar but didn't see anyone who could rescue me. I felt so useless. I hate that.

I pulled a chair up to the nearest table and sat, my shoulders hunched over until I realized anyone standing behind me would be able to see my breasts. I straightened, my back now as stiff as a twig.

Renee and her sisters and friends had been rounded up and were seated at various tables, waiting their turns to be questioned. Renee caught my eye, and since the detective in charge hadn't ordered that she had to stay in one place, she came over to my table and dropped down in the chair across from me. She was better than nothing.

"Wouldn't you know this would happen to me?" She sighed and toyed with her cuticle. "Did Tom say when we could get out of here?"

I fought the urge to remind her that "this" didn't happen to her; rather, it happened to Ralph, who, as far as I knew, was still dead on the sidewalk outside.

"So, you knew the guy?" she asked after a few seconds of silence, realizing I wasn't going to be chatty.

I nodded but was unwilling to offer up any fodder for gossip. I knew telling Renee anything about Ralph would somehow make it over to the *Herald* faster than I could say "Jack Hammer."

"Someone said you were married to him," Renee said, pouting, like it was some sort of race and I'd already beaten her to the altar.

"Long time ago," I mumbled, aware now that one of the blisters on my foot had started oozing some sort of sticky goo. I wanted to take off these shoes in the worst way, but I didn't want to put my feet on this floor that had God knew what on it.

"Looked like you were still pretty friendly with him."

I leaned over to adjust one of the shoe's straps. "What do you mean?"

"I saw you talking to him over by the door, just before he went outside. I saw him kiss you."

Chapter 3

Okay, so I may have forgotten to mention that little detail to Tom. But I was trying to forget it myself. Ralph had caught me off guard. What he was doing barely registered until I felt his tongue probing my lips, because it happened so fast.

"Did you also see me knee him in the balls?" I asked, trying to keep my voice low but unable to keep the anger out.

Renee chuckled. "No. But that would've been funny."

I tried to remember why I'd agreed to attend this little party. It wasn't like Renee and I were great friends or anything. She was ten years younger than me, had come to the paper two years ago from graduate school, following her boyfriend-now-fiancé to New Haven, where he was learning how to be a doctor at Yale. She was the cheerleader, the sorority sister I never wanted to be. I had to admit that she could write, and since her desk was next to mine, we'd managed to have a sort of work relationship that her sisters must have felt was more than it was, because they invited me to this shindig. I had not been invited to the wedding.

I should've questioned that earlier. Why invite someone to the bachelorette party if she's not invited to the wedding?

I didn't have to come tonight. Priscilla had talked me into it.

Priscilla Quinn was my best friend from college and was now at the *Daily News* in New York. She was much more hip than I was, and she convinced me that going to see a male strip show would be a hoot. She was sorry she couldn't come with me—she'd had other plans—but she'd come out the weekend before and brought some clothes with her, knowing I didn't have anything to wear to something like this.

She had no idea she was dressing me for a murder.

Renee held a small bag not unlike mine, and I wondered if she had a cell phone in it. Before I could ask, however, her eyes drifted past me, distracted.

"Hey, there's that guy," Renee said, indicating Jack Hammer, who was coming toward us.

Not again.

Renee did one of those hair-toss things, flipping back her highlighted brown locks and fiddling with her blouse. What was wrong with her? She was getting married, for Chrissakes, and here she was, coming on to Mr. Sleazy.

Jack Hammer wasn't paying attention to her. He scooched down on the floor next to me, leaning in so close I caught a faint whiff of vanilla and maybe cinnamon. Weird.

"Need to talk to you," he said.

I looked at Renee, who looked surprised. Not in a good way. Okay, second strike against me. First I'm married before she is, and now Jack Hammer wants a moment of my time. Alone. Lucky me. I shrugged as she pushed her chair away and marched back over to her sisters, shaking her head as they all looked over their shoulders at me like I'd just agreed to fuck Jack Hammer on the floor in front of everyone. Not that they hadn't wanted to do that just an hour ago themselves.

I liked it better when I thought all Chippendales were chairs.

I turned to Jack Hammer. "What do you want?"

He put a finger to my lips, and I jerked my head back reflexively. Who the hell knew where those fingers had been? "I got it for you," he whispered, slipping something into my hand.

I looked at the business card. My business card. "What about it?" I asked.

"I got it from Ralphie. Just before he went outside. I know you told the cop that you didn't really talk to him, so I figured maybe you had a reason to keep this quiet."

I turned the card over in my hand.

On the back was my phone number. My home phone number. And my cell number. In my handwriting.

"You got this from Ralph?" I asked.

"He told me to put it in the office, in his Rolodex." Jack Hammer bit back a smile. He was still balancing himself next to me—probably all that "dancing" gave him unusually strong muscles. "I won't say anything," he promised.

I tucked the card into my bag and thanked Jack Hammer. Instead of going away, like I'd hoped, he moved to the chair where Renee had been sitting. Jesus. Why did everyone think I wanted company?

"Ralphie was right about you," Jack said.

I didn't even want to know. But Jack was hell-bent on telling me.

"You're pretty hot, even if you are pushing forty."

I glared at him. "Don't look for any dollar bills in your G-string from me, asshole."

He laughed. Really laughed. Loud enough so heads turned. And I had to admit it—somehow it made him less smarmy.

"Why do you do this?" I asked after a few seconds.

"Do what?"

"Get up onstage and pretend to fuck all those women?"

"It's safe sex."

"I guess that's one way to look at it. But it's pretty gross."

"I've got a nice condo on the water, and I drive a Porsche."

Touché.

"So why are you here tonight, then, if you disapprove?" Jack Hammer's eyes were a deep brown, sort of like cows' eyes, with big lashes, and he seemed really interested. Right. He got paid to seem really interested.

"Bachelorette shit. I don't know. Got talked into it."

"You don't seem the type to get talked into anything."

I glanced around. Where the hell was Tom? Last thing I needed was to bond with a male stripper. But that's exactly what was going on.

"Is this a regular gig for you? I mean, here at the Rouge Lounge? Did you know Ralph well?" I asked, ignoring his comment.

He shrugged. "We've been here a few times and at other places around the state. I know Ralphie from before."

"Before what?"

His eyes narrowed. "You know."

I shook my head. "No, I don't know."

He studied my face for a few seconds, then must have decided I was telling the truth, because he leaned back and crossed his arms in front of his chest before saying, "I met him in lockup."

I knew about Ralph's arrest. Priscilla kept up with him and told me. She didn't tell me much else, and only when I asked, which was rarely. Ralph got nailed with two roommates because suddenly their electric bill went through the roof. Cars came and went at all hours of the day and night at the house they'd rented somewhere in Westchester County in New York. A neighbor had complained.

Cops found the basement full of marijuana plants, some almost five feet tall because of the fluorescent grow lights. The cops brought all three of them in, and because Ralph was the only one who didn't have a record, they kept his charge to a misdemeanor and he had to serve only six months of community service. His roommates weren't so lucky.

If he'd been into anything else since then—it was about ten years ago—I didn't know about it.

"What were you arrested for?" I asked Jack Hammer.

"Prostitution."

He said it matter-of-factly, like he was telling me he'd bought a carton of milk at the store. I nodded. "And you and Ralph bonded?" Maybe Ralph and Jack had

some sort of thing going, some sort of Brokeback Jail-
house. But Jack was one step ahead of me.

"Not like that."

"So do you know why someone would gun him
down?" How much did this guy really know about
"Ralphie"?

Jack Hammer shrugged. "Everyone loved Ralphie."

Obviously not. But who was I to mention that?

"You wouldn't by chance have a phone on you, would
you?" I asked before seeing the stupidity of my question. He was wearing a skintight T-shirt and leather
pants that looked like they'd been painted on. Where
would he keep it?

"Sorry, babe," he said. "Back in the dressing room."

Again with the "babe"? Dressing room?

Just as I was about to ask him if he could go get it—
I really needed to make a call—Tom was standing over
me. Where the hell had he come from? One look told
me he didn't have my flip-flops.

"Hey, I thought you were getting—"

"Get up, Annie," he interrupted, glaring at Jack Hammer. "We can't talk here. I've got to take you down to
the station."

"What the fuck's going on, Tom? The station?"

"Just come with me."

"Where're my keys?"

He leaned down and grabbed me under the armpit,
pulling me up. "Just come with me," he said roughly.

I teetered on the damn heels, thought I'd topple over
again. Tom wasn't paying attention. I looked at Jack
Hammer, whose eyebrows were shooting off the top of
his head. I shrugged at him as Tom led me through the
bar and back out into the night, the humidity wrapping
itself around me like a hot, wet towel. It was only the
beginning of June, for Chrissakes.

Tom's Impala was parked at the curb. I could see my
relatively new Honda Civic in the parking lot along the
side of the building. The passenger door was open, and
there were two cops standing sentry next to it.

I looked back over toward the front of the building.

All the people who'd been outside earlier had been herded inside for questioning, and the only ones left were Frank, the coroner, and a couple cops. Ralph's body still lay where it had fallen.

"Can I call my lawyer?" I asked as Tom opened the car door for me.

He handed me his cell phone. "Go ahead."

Shit.

"Dammit, Tom," I said when we were both securely in the car. "Tell me what's going on."

"Call your mother. You're going to need her."

My mother doubled as my lawyer. I stared at him, holding my breath.

Tom's hands gripped the steering wheel, his eyes boring into mine as if he was trying to read my mind. "We found four shell casings in the street. A .22."

The bottom of my stomach dropped out. Okay, so I owned a .22. But it wasn't a secret.

"I went to your car, Annie," Tom said as he started the Impala.

"Yeah?" I tried to keep my voice light, but my throat was dry and it came out as a sort of croak.

The engine purred as we sat idling.

Tom's next question didn't surprise me, considering. "Why did you bring your gun out tonight?"

I didn't answer.

Tom sighed. "Your flip-flops were on the floor, like you said, but one was stuck a little under the seat. When I reached in to pull it out, I felt it."

I'd fucked up. I knew I should never have asked him to get my flip-flops. But my feet had been killing me; I took that risk.

"Dammit, Annie. What was your gun doing on the floor under the seat on the front passenger side? There were six bullets in the magazine."

Even I could do the math. The magazine held ten bullets. If there were only six left, where were the other four?

On the ground near Ralph's body, he seemed to think.

Chapter 4

I woke up my mother. At least I hoped I woke her and didn't interrupt anything. Her voice was a little groggy, and I heard a baritone in the background. Bill Bennett. Publisher of the *New Haven Herald*. My boss. He was living in my house now. Well, it wasn't officially my house anymore, but my childhood shit was still there, my room with the Jim Morrison poster and Elton John albums. It was bad enough my mother had started dating him last year, but to know that he was living there now—must have been in my old room at some point, seeing more of me than any boss should see of his employee—well, that sucked. I couldn't do a damn thing about it.

"Annie, do you know what time it is?" my mother asked.

"About eleven?" I ventured.

"Why are you calling?"

"Well, I'm in sort of a jam, and I need you to meet me at the police station." Understatement of the year.

"What sort of jam?" My mother was wide-awake now; her voice was clear, crisp.

"Well, do you remember Ralph?"

A second passed before she said, "Your Ralph?"

"Jesus, Mother, he hasn't been *my* Ralph for fifteen years. But yes, that Ralph." I paused. "Well, he's dead, and it looks like he may have been shot with a .22 and Tom found a gun in my car, and now he's taking me to the police station for some sort of interrogation and he suggested that I give you a call. Nice of him, wasn't it?" The sarcasm dripped off my lips and from the way Tom pursed his, it had not gone unnoticed.

"I'll be there in half an hour. Don't say a word," my mother instructed, ending the call.

I looked sideways at Tom. "Since I've got the phone, can I call the paper?" It was worth a shot.

"I already talked to Dick Whitfield," he said flatly.

Fuck.

"I didn't give him the victim's name, and he doesn't know about the gun or that I'm taking you in," he continued.

"Taking me in? Am I really a suspect?" I stared at him.

We were stopped at a light on Chapel Street, and Tom just looked straight ahead. I squirmed a little in the seat; the black skirt shimmied up my thighs. As I tried to straighten it, I saw Tom watching. I covered up my legs as best I could with my hands, arms, and little purse.

"No, you don't," I said.

"Don't what?"

"You don't get to look at my legs anymore. You think I'm a murderer."

"Doesn't matter if you're a murderer or not. They're still nice legs," he said with a small smile as the light turned green and he hit the accelerator.

"Can you at least stop at my apartment so I can change? I can't stand the thought of wearing this getup much longer," I said.

Tom's expression indicated he didn't think I should change, and he paused a few seconds. I figured he'd say no, but then, "Two minutes. That's all I'm giving you. I shouldn't even be doing that."

I knew he could get in trouble for this, and I really did appreciate it. I told him as much.

"Just keep your mouth shut about it, okay?" He gave me a sidelong glance. "Although I know how hard that can be."

"Fuck you," I said grimly.

He chuckled.

"What do you think happened tonight?" I asked after a few seconds.

Tom stared straight ahead into the headlights of a passing car. "I don't know," he said softly.

My mother had instructed me to say nothing, and while I don't normally take her advice on things, the situation at hand might call for it.

The Impala pulled up in front of my brownstone minutes later. I scrambled out with Tom hot on my heels. "Hot" being the operative word. I could feel drops of sweat trickling down between my shoulder blades, under my arms, and between my breasts. I'd have to reapply the deodorant.

Once we got into my apartment on the second floor, I made a beeline for the bedroom, but that didn't deter Tom. I stopped him at the door by raising my hand.

"No, you don't," I said.

Tom took my hand and walked around me, around the bed, and to the side table. I took a deep breath as he pulled open the drawer.

I knew what was in there without even looking. A couple of paperbacks, a package of bubble gum, and an empty box of Trojans.

I also knew what wasn't there.

The drawer was where my gun should be. It usually wasn't loaded; the ammunition was next to the gun box in the closet. I kept the .22 here just in case I needed to scare the shit out of an intruder. Both Tom and Vinny told me it was stupid, but it made me feel secure.

I realized that Tom had not agreed to come back here just so I could change my clothes. He wanted to see if my gun was here; if it was, the gun in my car couldn't be my gun. Then I'd be off the hook. Maybe.

He didn't even ask if I'd put it somewhere else. That's what I get for being a creature of habit.

"I'm going to need your clothes," he said softly, indicating the camisole and the skirt. I wasn't stupid. I knew he wanted to make sure there was no blood or gun residue on them.

I couldn't argue. "There are plastic bags under the sink."

He nodded as he slipped out of the room.

My eyes wandered back to the bedside table. I stared at the drawer's contents for a few seconds, wondering in a complete non sequitur if I shouldn't restock the Trojans, but then realized, what the hell, if I'm in prison, I won't be having sex anyway, so why spend the money?

I shut the drawer and pulled the damp camisole over my head, wondering what I should wear to be "taken in." I couldn't imagine there would be a dress code for this. What would Stacy and Clinton of *What Not to Wear* say? I doubted that a tasteful sleeveless blouse, knee-length skirt, and kitten heels would make a difference. To hell with any fashion rules. So I put on my black Sturgis bike-rally sleeveless T-shirt with the skull on it and a pair of black yoga capris. I was in a black mood. And it could be a long night. I needed to be comfortable.

I was about to go back into the living room when I noticed my answering machine winking at me. My heart began to pound.

I glanced at the door—Tom hadn't come back with the bag yet—turned the volume down a little, held my breath, and clicked PLAY.

"Where are you, Annie?" It was Vinny, and that was all he said before the message ended. I let out a sigh of relief.

Another look at the door, and I shouted out to Tom, "I need to use the bathroom."

"Just make it quick," came his muffled response, and his tone told me his patience was wearing thin.

"There's beer in the fridge," I offered. I could've used one, too.

"Yeah, right."

So much for that idea.

I grabbed the phone's handset and went into the bathroom, turning on the water so if Tom wandered into the bedroom, he wouldn't hear the beeps as I touched the keys to call Vinny.

"Annie?"

"Vinny, I don't have much time." Quickly, and as quietly as I could, I explained what was going down.

"Why—"

I cut him off. "My mother's meeting me at the station. I have to go." My voice was flat; I was becoming resigned to spending the rest of my days with Bubba and the gang. Wouldn't you know it would be Ralph who'd be the cause of it?

I stepped out of the bathroom to see Tom glaring at me, the plastic bag containing my slut outfit dangling from his right hand. Jesus, he'd even put the shoes in there.

"We're. Leaving. Now," he growled.

I dropped the phone back into its cradle, slipped on a pair of lime green flip-flops—I own about five pairs; they're cheap at Old Navy—and stumbled out of my apartment, Tom holding on to my arm like I was going to try to make a run for it. Okay, so I thought about it, and since he knew me pretty well, he probably figured I'd try it.

My mother hadn't yet gotten to the police station when we arrived. Without a word, Tom pulled me through the concrete lobby, through the glass doors, and into the elevator. When the doors opened on the second floor, his hand tightened further around my arm and we went down the hall to a small interrogation room. I'd been here before.

The table was still wobbly, the plastic chair just a little off-kilter as I sat. I wished I'd thought to wear sneakers—the air-conditioning was blasting and my feet were cold. I hugged my chest, rubbing my arm where Tom had held me. Maybe it wasn't cold so much as it was foreboding.

"Stay here," Tom ordered, like I had a choice. And then he left, closing the door.

I let my mind wander back a few hours, when I'd seen Ralph at the Rouge Lounge. Ralph. Who was the root of all this.

I didn't always hate Ralph Seymour. I'd kept his

name, hadn't I? Well, that was more common sense than anything else, since I didn't want to be associated with my father, Joe Giametti, casino manager and at times shady character, or my mother, Alexandra Giametti, who was Super Lawyer and had a High Profile in the city.

I leaned back in the plastic chair and remembered Ralph the day I met him, in my first journalism class at Southern Connecticut State University. He wasn't good-looking, but rather geeky. Vinny had been geeky, too, in high school, but this was a different geeky. Vinny was chess club and science class. Ralph was bohemian geeky, wanting to find injustices in the world and fix them by writing about them. He was tall and too skinny, his face mirroring the rest of him, as it was long and thin, his nose too small, his lips pretty nonexistent. He wore his hair back in a ponytail, which I found incredibly sexy at the time, but in retrospect it was all part of the game. His eyes were the only remarkable physical thing about him. They were a soft green that hadn't changed over the years—the first thing I'd noticed when I saw him again—and I wondered how, after everything that had happened, they could still look the same.

Shit, I knew why. Because Ralph was a con artist back then and he was still one now. No. Strike that. He had been one, until tonight.

I got up and peered through the little window in the door, my hand on the knob, knowing before I tried it that I was locked in. I wandered over to the windows and stared through the darkness down to the lights at the train station across the street. A train must have just come in; two taxis pulled out of the driveway in front and a few people made their way furtively down the sidewalk, casting eerie shadows along the roadway.

Ralph and I had cast shadows on the wall of his dorm room that first night as the full moon washed us with its glow. I tugged at the recesses of my memories, conjuring up the faint scent of incense, bedsprings hard against my spine. The mattress was too thin, but it hadn't mattered. I'd fallen for him immediately, a take-no-prisoners sort of emotion that ignored his odd looks and focused on his passion, both for me and his dream of being executive editor at the *New York Times* someday.

I snorted. He fucked up both of those big-time. And now look where he was.

But instead of the anger I usually felt, a sadness rushed through me, a sadness because Ralph really did have talent. To squander that in the way he did, well, that was the ultimate waste.

A knock at the door startled me, and I jumped as my mother stepped into the room. Tom was not with her. She shut the door behind her and handed me a Dunkin' Donuts latte.

"I'm sorry," she said as she gave me a quick hug, and I knew what she meant. She was sorry for Ralph, sorry that I was back in his clutches even though he was dead now. She'd never liked him. Which, I admit, was one of the reasons why I did—at first, at least.

I took the coffee and sat again, my fingers toying with the top of the cup; she sat across from me, taking my other hand in hers. I had to give her credit for not saying anything about my outfit as she forced herself not to stare at the skull on my shirt.

"You have to tell me everything," she said.

So I did.

Chapter 5

It was dawn when I finally walked out of the New Haven police station with my mother. I half expected to see Vinny waiting for me, but he wasn't. When I mentioned it, my mother clicked her tongue.

"You'll see Vinny soon enough. You need to get home and get some sleep."

I *was* tired, but there was too much going on in my head. Tom actually had called me a "person of interest," which pissed me off. He hadn't done the interrogating, though. Conflict of interest and all that shit. So newly promoted detective Ronald Berger got to ask me a million questions about my relationship with Ralph, while we were married and since. I didn't think it was any of his goddamn business, but my mother intervened when I got too worked up, and managed to smooth things over. Nothing against Ronald or anything—he's a nice guy, but just not on the other side of the interrogation table. I'd rather knock back a few beers with him and ask him about other "people of interest."

I strapped myself into the front seat of my mother's Mercedes, prepared for her erratic driving—she'd give any NASCAR driver a run for his money.

"I need to pick up my car," I said as she turned the ignition. "It's back in the bar parking lot."

She sighed, and instead of turning up Chapel, she kept going straight on State Street. The Rouge Lounge was just a block up from Café Nine—another nightspot but without the slick decor—and its parking lot was a rarity in the city, where meters reigned and garages charged way too much for a night on the town.

The yellow crime-scene tape was still attached to a utility pole in front of the bar, but that was the only sign that something had gone down the night before. In the harsh light of morning, the building looked like a hooker who'd put on too much makeup.

My silver Honda Civic, only a few months old, sparkled like a new dime in the dingy lot, surrounded by cast-off Styrofoam coffee cups, cigarette butts, and the occasional syringe. When my 1993 Accord became a crime victim in April, I resigned myself to a new car and found myself loving it. It wasn't one of those hybrids, but it still got good gas mileage and was just as big as my old car. And I finally had a CD player and air-conditioning.

I stepped out of my mother's car, but before I could shut the door, she said, "Wait, Annie."

I leaned down to look at her.

"Be careful," she said, the weariness dripping off her words like the sweat that was slipping down the back of my neck. How could it be so hot so early in the morning?

"Can you go home and get some sleep?" I asked, pulling at my T-shirt and fanning myself with the fabric.

"Don't worry about me," she said, frowning as she stared at my chest.

I had pinched the shirt together at the center of the skull. I waited for a comment about my fashion statement, but it never came. I shrugged. "Thanks, Mom."

She nodded. "That's what mothers are for."

I closed the door, and she took off down the street. I watched until she turned onto Chapel before I approached my car.

It had been searched. Tom had warned me about that as he escorted my mother and me out to the street. Tom also told me I would need to vacuum the car. No shit. While it was still gleaming silver on the outside, as I got closer, I saw the fingerprint dust around the door handles. He'd explained patiently, despite my many outbursts, that they confiscated the gun for evidence, because he—to his credit—was unwilling to believe that I'd actually shot Ralph in the street. It would be tested to see if ballistics could match it with the shell casings found near the body.

My mother told me I could admit it was my gun, and I did so. But she also told me not to say anything else. I didn't.

I opened the car door and wished I owned a Dust-Buster.

However, I knew someone who did.

I reached into the glove box and pulled out my cell phone. At least the cops hadn't taken it and had locked up the car when they were done, so nothing was stolen. I punched in a number and waited as it rang and rang. I didn't even get voice mail. Where the hell was Vinny?

I closed the phone, leaned against the car, and wished I were like Samantha on *Bewitched* so I could just twitch my nose and my car would be clean. I regretted the black shirt and capris; I could feel them getting clammy as the sun blasted heat against me. It was another three-shower day, cold showers at that.

"Did you beat the rap?"

The voice startled me, and I jumped as Jack Hammer came around the side of the building.

"What the hell are you doing here?" I asked.

He held up a black duffel bag. "Left it here last night. We've got another show tonight, up in Hartford."

There was a place in Hartford that had male strip shows? The Berlin Turnpike, sure, but Hartford? New Haven had it all over the capital city for nightlife, restaurants, and theater. I'd been to Hartford after nine p.m., and the streets were hardly bustling. Even the Starbucks closed early.

He held out his hand. "We were never properly introduced last night. John Decker."

I frowned, and he grinned. "You didn't think 'Jack Hammer' was my real name, did you?"

Somehow that moniker fit him better than "John Decker." "John Decker" could be a next-door neighbor, a teacher, one of those "Friends" on MySpace. Okay, so maybe I shouldn't be making any assumptions.

I shook his hand. "Annie Seymour."

"Yeah, I know," he said, holding my hand just a second too long. "Ralphie—"

"I don't really want to talk about him right now," I interrupted. "I have to get home."

He nodded and held up the bag. "Gotta get going, too." But he didn't move. Instead, he said, "You might want to talk to Felicia."

"Felicia?" I asked.

"She works here sometimes. She and Ralphie had a thing."

"Why should I talk to her?"

Jack gave me a lopsided grin. "You never know."

Cryptic asshole.

"I really don't give a shit about Ralph's girlfriend," I said. "Ralph and I were a long time ago."

"Were you?" he asked.

It was the way he said it that made me take pause. He'd said that Ralph talked about me to him. Maybe he'd talked about me to this Felicia, too. My natural curiosity bubbled up, and I couldn't help myself.

"Do you know how to find her?"

Jack shrugged. "She works at bars all over town. Someone probably knows how to reach her."

Weird. I thought a second. "What about you? Do you have a number where I can reach you if I have any questions about this?"

Jack winked. "Don't worry about that. I'll be around." And he disappeared around the corner.

I tried not to think about him as I opened the trunk. I'd done a sweep of my closet and stuck a bag of clothes in there to take to Goodwill. They were strewn all over the place, but I couldn't tell if it was because the cops had gone through them or if they'd just ended up that way after a few quick turns.

I grabbed an old T-shirt, shook it out, closed the trunk, went around the car, and laid it across the front seat. I maneuvered myself on it carefully, trying not to get too dirty, and started the engine.

Before I could pull out of the lot, my cell phone rang. I grabbed it off the center console, where I'd dropped it, and glanced at the number. Vinny.

"Hey there," I said.

"You out?"

"Beat the rap," I said, realizing that's what Jack Hammer had said. "I'm in my car, on my way home."

"Really?"

"Don't sound so fucking surprised," I said.

I heard him chuckle. "I'm just curious, Annie, why they let you go. It seems like there was some evidence to keep you there, even charge you."

I thought back an hour and remembered the look on Tom's face when he told me.

"Ralph wasn't shot to death," I said flatly. "It looks like he just died of a heart attack. That's why there wasn't any blood."

Chapter 6

Silence for a second, then, "You're kidding."

"No, apparently he had been shot at, but whoever shot at him missed him. He died of natural causes. Just collapsed on the goddamn sidewalk."

Tom hadn't been happy that I'd taken my gun out for a ride last night. And he really wasn't happy that I wouldn't tell him any more than that. My mother just kept saying that I had a carry permit, and I was allowed to keep the gun in the car. There was still no proof my gun had expelled those bullets, so she told Tom and Ronald Berger that if they wanted to keep me there any longer, they'd need an arrest warrant.

I couldn't fault Tom for pushing the issue. He and I might no longer be dating, but we had a bond—one that Vinny was all too aware of even if he really didn't have anything to worry about.

So Tom let me go.

I didn't know how long that ballistics test would take, and he wasn't forthcoming with any time frame.

As I replayed the high points of the night to Vinny, my body suddenly felt like I'd taken three Valium, wake me up in the morning.

"I have to get home," I said. "Will I see you later?"

"Definitely," he said. "Glad it worked out okay."

I said good-bye and managed to get to my brownstone on Wooster Square before my eyes started drooping. The red light on my answering machine was winking at me again. I reached out to play the message, then pulled my hand back. I didn't want to do this now, so I ignored it.

The air-conditioning unit in the living room would normally have cooled off the entire small apartment if it were working properly. It was hotter than a fucking furnace, maybe even more so than outside. I stripped off the T-shirt, the capris, and my bra, leaving on only my underpants, and collapsed on top of the bedcovers, wishing for the first time I had an icy water bed. Despite the heat, I drifted off.

When I woke up, the clock read ten a.m. Four hours of sleep. Time to get up. It was Friday, after all, and a workday. I didn't think it would look too good if I called Marty Thompson, the city editor, and said I couldn't come in because I was exhausted from my nightlong interrogation by the police. Especially since now there had been no murder after all.

I didn't bother with a robe as I padded into the kitchen and put on a pot of water to boil. As I reached for the freezer door to get the coffee, I saw the note taped there.

Stopped in, but you were passed out cold. I'm checking on some things. I'll see you later.
Love, Vinny.

I reached into the freezer, welcoming the cold blast against my face and neck, my nipples standing at attention, and pondered the note. This was the first time he'd signed with "Love." For some reason, we never used the word.

We'd been dating almost three months. There were the four months before that when we didn't see each other at all because I was an idiot, and there were three weeks before that when we couldn't keep our hands off each other. And then there were all those years since high school that I didn't even know he was alive until we stumbled across a dead Yalie about the same time and I realized even geeks can turn out pretty sexy.

Vinny had his own private-investigation business these

days, after a few years as a marine scientist studying whales. He claimed that being a private eye was like doing his research, only it was on dry land watching people instead. That said, he still liked to be out there on the water; however, our kayaking expedition a month ago proved that it wasn't going to be one of the top ten things we'd do as a couple—a rather harrowing experience in April seemed to do some damage to my previous water-loving psyche.

I pulled my eyes away from the word and focused on the others he'd written. "Checking on some things" could be code for "I'm checking on what happened last night with Ralph," or worse yet, it could mean he was checking with my mother. Vinny did occasional investigative work for her law firm, and they could be talking about me right this very minute.

I pulled the kettle off the stove, measured four table-spoons of coffee into my French press, and poured the boiling water on it, absently noting the time so I could press in four minutes.

I had enough time to go down and get the paper. I threw on my light cotton Japanese *yukata* and wrapped it around myself, tying it tight.

Just my luck, I ran into my upstairs neighbor, Walter, as he was heading out.

"You know, your boyfriend should pay rent here, he's here so much," Walter said grumpily. Walter was always grumpy. At least with me.

I shrugged, not wanting to get into it. But then I got a little worried. If Walter felt compelled to tell the land-lord about Vinny, maybe he would have an issue with it. And since Vinny and I couldn't even say the word "love" to each other, cohabiting was definitely not an option.

"You really shouldn't let him come in when you're not home."

Walter was still talking to me, even though I had picked up the paper and had my hand on the doorknob. His words made me turn back.

"What?"

"Yesterday. Morning. Said he'd forgotten something. He is a friendly guy, I'll give you that, but it's probably better if he's only here when you are." And with that, Walter made his way down the steps. I watched him, his arms bowing out around his big torso—sort of like that kid in the *Christmas Story* movie who couldn't put his arms down flat—before I stuck the newspaper under my arm and headed back upstairs to my coffee.

Damn. Six minutes instead of four. I pushed the press down and poured myself a cup, opened up the paper, and looked at the front page.

Ralph was above the fold but under a banner story about electric rates going up. I scanned the story; Dick Whitfield had done the best he could with the scant information Tom had given him.

> The manager of the Rouge Lounge was shot and killed in front of the nightclub on State Street late Thursday night.

It had been early this morning , after deadline, when Tom told me Ralph hadn't actually been shot, so no surprise it wasn't in the story.

> Nightclub workers identified the manager as Ralph Seymour, 40. He had worked there only a month. No one could provide an address or any other information about him.
> At press time, a suspect had been taken into custody.

Someone other than Tom had spilled the beans, given Dick Ralph's name, and even told him they were questioning someone. Thank God whoever talked to him didn't know the "suspect" was me.

How the hell was I going to keep this from leaking? I was going to have to talk to Marty. I had to tell him before someone else did. My biggest saving grace was that Ralph had died of a heart attack, so we could just run a few graphs updating the story and that should be the end of it.

Unfortunately, Dick was going to stay on the story; I knew Marty wouldn't let me get within a mile of this one.

The phone rang just as I got out of the shower. I hesitated, not sure if I should answer it, but finally decided it might be Vinny, so I picked up the handset.

"You okay today, Annie?" It was Tom. I took a deep breath, relieved to hear a familiar voice, even if it wasn't Vinny's.

"Yeah."

"I'm sorry about last night, but you know why I had to take you in."

"I know."

"Why didn't you just tell me right away that you had your gun in the car? When you asked me to get your flip-flops." Now that my mother wasn't hovering over me, he was going to do his best to get something out of me. I had to give him an A for effort.

When I didn't respond, he continued. "And when we were at your apartment, you let me look in the drawer for it. You still didn't say anything. Should I be worried about what those ballistics tests will turn up?"

He didn't mention my clothes, the ones I'd last seen in that plastic garbage bag. Probably hadn't gotten to them yet.

I weighed my options about what I would say. "Until I knew Ralph had died of a heart attack, I didn't want you to get the wrong idea. I mean, he was my ex-husband, and we did not have the most amicable divorce."

"You never said much about him," Tom said thoughtfully.

"What was there to say?" I asked, trying to keep my tone light. "We were young, we were stupid. It was the best thing to split up."

"That's all you've ever said."

I had to change the subject. "Do you think Ralph's heart attack was prompted by him being shot at?"

Tom chuckled. "No, Annie, I don't think that. Let's just say that Ralph has heard the sound of gunshots before, and I don't think it would've killed him."

I could hear something in his tone; now *he* wasn't telling *me* everything. "What was up with Ralph? What do you know about him? I know he was arrested once but got off with community service. Too many pot plants."

"Well, he's stayed out of prison," Tom offered, but it wasn't enough.

"That's no answer. What's he been up to?"

"No good."

Everyone's a smart-ass.

"Not a surprise." I thought about what Jack Hammer had said that morning. "What about his girlfriend, Felicia?"

"Do you know her?" I could hear surprise in his voice.

"Not directly." Not at all, but I wasn't going to admit that.

"Well, if you happen to come across her, I'd love to talk to her."

"Why?" My curiosity was more than piqued.

"Let's just say unfinished business."

"What sort of unfinished business?"

"As long as you didn't shoot at him, you have nothing to worry about."

"But someone does, right?" Something was definitely up.

Before I could press it further, Tom said, "So tell me why you felt it necessary to bring your gun out to a bar last night." He was a goddamn broken record. "When was the last time you even went to the shooting range?"

I could still feel the weight of the gun in my hands, the pressure of the earmuffs as I leaned to the left slightly to avoid getting hit in the head with a shell casing. It had been a long time, way overdue—even I knew that. But I wasn't beholden to Tom in any way, and my mother had said to say nothing more.

So I turned back to the only thing that could keep me

grounded: the possibility of a story. Because instinct told me there *was* a story, even if I wasn't getting any answers at the moment.

"So, what's up with Ralph? What's he been into?" I asked again. "Why do you need to talk to his girlfriend? I heard she works at bars all over town." As I said it, I wondered about her line of work. Maybe she was a real "working girl." "What is it she does, anyway? Do you know?"

Silence. Then, "She's a shot girl."

Chapter 7

I arrived at the newspaper half an hour later. My hair was still a little damp, but it didn't matter. The humidity and heat these last couple of days had created a sort of bird's nest out of it, and at least while it was wet, it looked normal.

I didn't want to, but I'd finally checked my answering machine after I got dressed, and it turned out to be my friend Priscilla—who'd loaned me that dreadful outfit the night before. I wondered just how to tell her that Tom had confiscated her clothes. She'd heard about Ralph from Ned Winters, head of the journalism department at Southern Connecticut State University, an old classmate of ours who'd risen to the level of his incompetence. Ned had probably seen the story in the paper. I knew he kept up with both Priscilla and Ralph, but even though we were both in the same city, I hadn't seen Ned since Ralph and I split. A thought crossed my mind: Ned must have known Ralph was back here.

I dropped my bag on my desk and booted up my computer. Renee's chair was empty; the wedding was tomorrow and she was busy with bride shit. Again I wondered why I'd been invited to the bachelorette party but not the wedding. I'd had to buy a present—Priscilla had told me it would be bad form if I didn't bring anything—and I spent as little as I could on some massage lotions I'd found at Bath & Body Works. I guess it was okay I wasn't going to the wedding, because then I'd have to spend more money and I don't like doing that for people I have only a peripheral relationship with.

Dick Whitfield was tapping away on his keyboard three desks away, alternately briefly glancing up at me and then deliberately looking back to his computer.

He must have heard.

Marty had, too, because he was beckoning me to follow him into Charlie Simmons' office. Charlie had come on board as editor in chief only a few months ago, and I'd had some interaction with him then, but I'd tried to keep it to a minimum since. He wasn't going to like this.

I didn't even wait for anyone to ask me to sit. I plopped down in the chair in front of Charlie's desk, stared him straight in the eye, and said, "Yes, I spent the night at the police station."

Charlie, who managed to keep his resemblance to an Elvis impersonator intact by poofing up his black hair in such a way that we almost expected to see him in sequins and blue suede shoes at some point, leaned forward, his elbows on his desk, his fingers knit tightly together.

"What is the connection between you and the dead man?" His voice was low, and I knew I had to tread gently with this one.

"Ex-husband." I looked over at Marty, who had taken off his glasses and was twirling them around nervously. "He died of a heart attack. He wasn't shot. That's why they let me go."

"Why did they find it necessary to bring you in, in the first place?" Charlie asked.

I sighed. "On the advice of my attorney, I can't say." Okay, so my mother might have told Bill Bennett, Charlie's boss, about what was going down last night, but then again, she might not have. I wasn't going to spill the beans if I didn't have to.

"You won't tell us?" Charlie was incredulous; Marty still hadn't said anything.

"All you have to know is that they let me go. I wasn't charged with anything. Ralph was not murdered. There is no problem." I wasn't sure about that last one, but hell, it sounded good.

Charlie didn't think so. He puffed up his cheeks and blew a blast of air out at me. He'd had garlic the night before, no mistaking that. "Well, Annie, I'm going to have to do something you won't like."

My entire body tensed as my stomach dropped.

"I think it might be best to give you a break from the police beat for a while. Dick Whitfield can cover for you. With Renee Chittenden off for three weeks, you can fill her beat until she returns. When she returns, we can reassess the situation."

Marty's face was blank. I wanted him to stand up and say, "No, this wasn't Annie's fault. She doesn't have to be punished." But he didn't. He just sat there, picking at imaginary lint on his trouser leg, not even looking at me. Coward.

Renee covered the social services beat. That meant stories about the homeless and benefits for sick children and dealing with the local clergy. All things that require compassion. I wasn't good at compassion. I opened my mouth to say so, but instead of my voice, I heard Marty say, "Annie will do whatever you want, Charlie."

Within seconds, Marty was pushing me out the door and back into the newsroom, through the sports department, and around the corner toward the cafeteria. He stopped in front of all the plaques declaring various people EMPLOYEE OF THE MONTH. The way my life was going, I'd never see that. I told people it was a stupid award, but secretly I'd always wanted to be recognized for doing a kick-ass job. Unfortunately, my ass was usually the one that got kicked, and I was feeling the pain of that today.

"You will do Renee's job," Marty said softly, shaking his head when I opened my mouth to speak. I shut my mouth and listened. I don't do that much, but Marty rarely looked as concerned as he did right then. "I don't know what's going on, but if you want to keep your job here, you'd better do what Charlie says." He paused, looking around a second to make sure no one was coming, then added, "He wanted to suspend you."

Anger rose in my chest. I hadn't been charged; this was ridiculous. If Charlie had suspended me, I would've had my mother find me a good labor lawyer and sued his ass. Maybe I should just quit.

But then what would I do? I wasn't cut out for doing anything else. Being a journalist was all I knew. This was all I ever wanted to do. And with newspaper cutbacks and layoffs lately, where else would I find a job?

Marty knew what I was thinking—we'd known each other a long time—and he nodded. The anger subsided. He'd gone to bat for me, and I owed him big-time, so much so that I'd have to look deep into my soul and see if any compassion existed there. And if it didn't, I'd have to pretend.

"Thanks, Marty."

"What the hell's going on?"

"Tom found my gun in my car. There were .22 shell casings in the street near Ralph's body. But Ralph wasn't shot." I paused, thinking about what Tom had said on the phone. "Something was up with Ralph, though. Tom was evasive when I asked, said they're looking for his girlfriend. Even though he died of natural causes, something was going on, and it's not over yet."

That got his attention.

"But since I'm not covering cops right now, I can't really get into it." I looked into Marty's eyes. "Can I?"

Marty bit his lip; he was wondering if I could. Finally, "Lay off this weekend, but if you ask around, I don't know about it, okay?"

I nodded. "Know about what?"

He smirked.

We started back toward the newsroom.

"So what should I work on?" I had no clue how to cover social services. The thought of Dick Whitfield finally getting my beat, even temporarily, was getting in the way of finding compassion. I bit back a snide remark.

"Reverend Shaw is working with high school students from the West Rock projects at the nature center there. They've planted a community garden. We need a story for Monday, and I know you're on the weekend shift, so you can work on that today and tomorrow." Marty's eyes conveyed his apologies. "You can do it," he said, and I felt like Rocky when Burgess Meredith was encouraging him to get back in the ring even though he was beat-up and bleeding.

"The good reverend is a fraud," I said quietly. No one knew if Shaw was really a minister; he had no church, appearing out of nowhere a year ago to "give to the community." With a flamboyant air, he crashed into our little city like he was getting Jesse Jackson's speaking fees. He'd become a victims' advocate, a gadfly with a loud voice throughout the city. He fought with the city for money for after-school programs for underprivileged kids and raised hell when it was suggested the cops wanted a lockdown at one of the city projects. No one knew how he made a living; he seemed to have a stream of unlimited cash, but no one questioned as long as he helped. I'd Googled him at one point, after the lockdown rumors, but nothing came up except stories from the *Herald*; it was like he'd never existed before he came to New Haven.

He nodded. "Yeah, I know. But it's a story, and if you do it, you'll redeem yourself."

We walked slowly back to the newsroom, trying to act casual but without any food or drink from the cafeteria, which would've raised red flags if anyone had been paying attention. Dick was still at his desk, Charlie still in his office. The other metro editors were doing whatever they did at this time of day, and no other reporters had come in yet. The business editor was hunched over his desk, the *Wall Street Journal* spread out in front of him, the features editor was on the phone, and the clerk was silently putting mail in everyone's slots along the side wall.

Marty found the Reverend Shaw's phone number in Renee's Rolodex and brought it over to me. He was doing that only because he was feeling like shit.

"Thanks," I said to him again, wondering if I was going to have to keep apologizing forever.

I itched to call Vinny, just to hear a friendly voice, but dialed Shaw instead.

"Yes, how can I help you?" he asked when I identified

myself. His voice was deep, smooth as chocolate. It was
a voice that sounded trustworthy, but I wasn't going to
let myself get sucked in.

"I'm doing a story about the community garden," I
said, my voice stiff. Hell, I can ask the medical examiner
about cause of death, how deep those stab wounds were,
but this was completely unnatural for me. For a brief
second I wondered if I'd been a cop reporter too long.

Nah.

"I was hoping we could get together sometime today
and talk about it." Nothing like perseverance and Charlie Simmons watching me from the doorway of his office.

"We can meet at the garden. How delightful." Who
the hell talks like that? "How about in an hour? There
are several young people I'd love for you to meet."

Yeah, and I'd probably be the fucking highlight of
their day, too. I agreed and hung up, realizing it was
lunchtime and I'd have to get something to eat before I
met with Shaw. I picked up my bag but had one more
thing to do before I left. I'd need a photographer. This
could be dicey, since Ben Riordan, the photo editor,
liked everything scheduled by three p.m. the day before.
Unless it was breaking news, getting a photographer to
actually shoot something without a formal typewritten
photo assignment was like getting management to give
us a ten percent pay increase.

Fortunately, the photo editor was nowhere to be seen.
But photographer/miracle worker Wesley Bell was Pho-
toshopping an illustration for the Sunday health and science page. It was obviously a story about the dangers of
poison ivy, because the young woman in the illustration
was shown from the back, naked except for a trail of
poison ivy from her shoulder to her ass. It was pretty
provocative, but at the same time pretty cool. I wondered how the public would take it while drinking their
Sunday morning coffee.

"Neat picture," I said, looking over Wesley's shoulder.
"Who's the girl?" The photographers liked to use the
rest of us as their guinea pigs for these illustrations. We
had a lot of fun trying to figure out whose eyes were in

the picture for the glaucoma story or whose biceps were accompanying the piece about how to stay fit after the holidays.

"Intern," Wesley said, adding a few more leaves to make sure the girl's ass crack was covered up.

The *Herald* hired college journalism students for the summer as unpaid interns. They would get class credit, but no cash for their efforts. They were like child labor, writing actual stories because our staff was so depleted because of vacations. This girl was hard to recognize, since her face wasn't showing. Her mass of dark hair was pulled up in a makeshift bun. But the one thing that wasn't left to the imagination was the slender body that the swag of poison ivy couldn't disguise.

"Who is she?" I asked. "Haven't seen her around here yet."

Wesley clicked the mouse and said, "She just started this week, but she's only working half-time because she's got some paying job at night. Goes to Southern. Name's Felicia."

Chapter 8

"Felicia" isn't one of those popular names. And a night job? Shot girls work at night.

Because I'm socially inept, Tom had to explain that a shot girl works at a bar, buying shots in test tubes at cost and then selling them independently for the same price but getting huge tips because the girls are usually attractive. They also allow the men in the bar to buy them shots, which means they get shitfaced and, ultimately, pretty friendly with their clientele. Tom also said shot girls are usually college students who can make upwards of three hundred dollars in profit every night.

Nice money if you can stand the work.

I wondered if the *Herald*'s Felicia was Ralph's Felicia.

Damn Tom and Jack Hammer for making me curious about the girl. Tom seemed to have a real reason to try to find her, but why would Jack even bring her up? What did he know? I should've pressed him for his phone number.

But right now I couldn't worry about that. I had to get someone out to shoot the garden. I explained the situation to Wesley, who knit his brow in a frown.

"Not supposed to do that without an assignment," he said.

"Where's Ben?"

"Lunch."

I had a shot. "Come on, Wesley. I just found out about this assignment, and you'd do a great job with it."

I wasn't bullshitting, either. I knew if anyone could make this interesting, he could.

Wesley sighed. "I've got a little time before my next assignment. I could run over there. But if anyone's running late, I won't be able to stay."

I had a feeling Shaw would make sure everyone was there when he said they would be. I nodded and thanked him, stopping by Marty's desk on the way out.

"Going to meet with Shaw in an hour. Wesley's going to shoot something."

Marty smiled. "That's great, Annie," he said, like he was praising a goddamn puppy. "I'll make sure to fill out an assignment sheet to cover our asses with Ben." I knew he was doing that to try to make me feel better that I was being forced into it. I wasn't going to argue with him.

I started to leave, but then stopped. "Wesley says we've hired some intern named Felicia."

Jane Ferraro, one of the paper's three suburban editors, swiveled in her chair so fast I thought she was going to get whiplash. "Have you seen her?" she demanded, but not in a bad way. I liked Jane; she'd been hired about six months before and had the type of Mary Poppins/no-nonsense attitude that was necessary when dealing with bureau reporters just out of college who thought they were the next Anderson Cooper and why-the-hell-did-they-have-to-work-in-this-shithole-for-nothing-wasting-their-talents. Most of them had a long way to go, and Jane was doing the best she could to bring them along and turn them into real journalists.

"I saw a picture of her naked with poison ivy on her ass," I offered. "But that's about it."

Jane shook her head. "We need to pay these interns," she lamented. "Sometimes they show up, sometimes they don't. Felicia was supposed to be at a chamber of commerce meeting this morning in Ansonia but didn't show. Can't get her on her cell, and that's the only number I've got for her. I tried to find her parents in the book, but no dice."

"What's her last name?" I asked, immediately regretting it when I saw Jane's expression change.

"Why?"

I shrugged. "Just curious."

"Kowalski."

"From the Valley?"

Jane nodded. Figured. The Naugatuck Valley was full of people of Polish descent. At least this name was easy to pronounce and spell. Some of them, we just had to wing it. "I'm surprised her first name isn't Sonia."

Jane chuckled. "She told me her mother named her after some character on a soap opera."

I knew immediately what she was talking about. I'd been a *General Hospital* addict for a while back in the late 1980s, and Frisco and Felicia were the new Luke and Laura when that plot got too old. But I wasn't going to admit that to Jane—or Marty, who was listening to the conversation.

"Why the interest, Annie?" Marty asked.

I shrugged. "Someone at the Rouge Lounge mentioned a Felicia. Tom said she was a shot girl."

Jane and Marty exchanged a look I couldn't read.

"She wasn't involved, was she?" Jane asked.

"So our Felicia is a shot girl at night?"

Jane nodded. "Did you see her there?"

I shook my head. "No. Someone told me she knew Ralph, the manager who died."

"I thought he was murdered," Jane said.

I looked at Marty. I didn't want to get into it. "Listen, I have to get going. I need to meet Shaw in less than an hour."

"If you hear anything else about her," Jane said, "let me know. The mayor was pretty pissed no one showed this morning. If she wants to be a reporter, she's got to learn she can't blow shit off just because she might have had a late night."

I thought about what Jane said as I pulled into a parking space on Crown Street. I needed to get a sandwich, and Katz's on Temple served up a bowl of pickles and slaw to nosh on before lunch arrived. I ordered an iced tea and the crispy potato pancake covered in pastrami, grilled onions, tomato, and melted cheese, wondering where Felicia had actually been last night. And where she might be right now.

Halfway through the sandwich, my cell phone rang. Pulling it out of my bag, I glanced at the number.

"Hey," I said.

"Hey, yourself." Vinny's voice was playful. "How are you?"

I told him about my "demotion" and that I was heading to meet up with Shaw. "This sucks," I said, finishing the last of my pastrami.

"You're expanding your horizons," he suggested.

"Fuck you."

"Come on, Annie, it's not forever."

"Yeah, I guess." I downed the last of my iced tea. "You know, there's this girl Ralph was seeing. Tom was really interested in trying to find her, and one of those strippers last night, Jack Hammer—I think I told you about him—he said I might want to find her. I may have a lead on her. She's one of our interns from Southern. And it seems she didn't show up this morning for an assignment."

Vinny was so quiet I thought I lost him. "Hello?" I asked.

"I'm here. You're sure no one's heard from Felicia?"

"No," I said automatically before it struck me. I hadn't said her name. Just as I was about to ask how he knew it, he said, "I'll see you around seven," and the call really did end.

Chapter 9

I tried to call Vinny back, but his voice mail picked up. I put the phone down on the table. How the hell would Vinny be involved with this? How did he know her name? The questions swirled around in my head, landing somewhere unexpected. Why had Vinny been in my apartment yesterday morning when I wasn't there? Walter said he saw him. Even though Vinny and I had exchanged keys, we were pretty respectful of each other's privacy.

I pushed my thoughts aside—there was nothing I could do about it now—and concentrated on where I was heading: West Rock. To get there, I'd have to go through the campus of Southern Connecticut State University, where Felicia Kowalski was matriculated. If I had time after my interview with Shaw, maybe I'd stop over at the journalism department, see if I could find Ned Winters or someone else who could shed some light on this girl. It wasn't like I wasn't familiar with the territory. I'd gotten my journalism degree there—two years after Ralph got his.

My mother hadn't been too happy I went to a state school. She'd had bigger plans for me: Yale, Harvard, Princeton—even New York University would've been more acceptable. But I wasn't smart enough, not in that way you needed to be to get into schools like that. My high school grades were passable, but even then I wanted to be a journalist and spent a lot of my time putting together the school newspaper rather than studying science or math.

I'm sure Vinny would've been happy to tutor me—he admitted he'd had a crush on me back then—but I just wasn't interested in anything else.

I snorted. Wouldn't you know I'd end up with some shit beat because of Ralph. He'd always outshone me. I stayed in the background, letting him be first, allowing myself to wait for my own chance, once he had his. What an idiot I'd been.

I took a deep breath, not wanting to remember. Not wanting to bring it all back. But the emotions that hadn't come while I saw his body on the sidewalk came rushing at me now, and I knew the wounds hadn't healed like I'd thought; maybe that was why I'd been so commitment phobic with Tom and I couldn't use the right words to tell Vinny how I felt about him.

I should get a goddamn Ph.D. for figuring that out.

Ralph had fucked me up big-time. I was glad I'd at least had the last word.

The Reverend Shaw looked like his voice. His skin was a deep chestnut, laugh lines danced around his eyes, and his smooth, shaved head was unnaturally dry in the hot afternoon sun. His fashionable glasses were rectangular with red plastic frames. He wore a dirty white T-shirt, loose jeans, and Birkenstocks. I'd seen photographs of him and had placed him in his fifties, but up close, he was definitely younger. Maybe in his forties, not too much older than me. Either way, his smile was warm, convincingly trustworthy, just like his voice on the phone.

I didn't trust him as far as I could throw him.

Shaw pulled off thick gardening gloves to shake my hand.

"I've read your articles, Ms. Seymour. You're doing a fine job," he praised, his white teeth gleaming. He'd had money at some point for braces. No one had teeth that straight naturally.

"Thank you, but please call me Annie," I said, trying to keep my voice light, like I didn't think he was going to pickpocket me at any second. It didn't matter that he looked like a regular guy—that was the problem. He wasn't a regular guy, but he wanted me to think he was.

"Your photographer is already here," he said, putting the gloves back on and waving his hand to indicate he wanted me to follow him.

I'd parked in the lot next to the Visitor Center, and Shaw had been waiting for me. We walked past the Nature House, which houses a reptile display and tanks that I didn't want to get too close to—I'm not afraid of too many things, but I really hate snakes—and we went around the Ranger Cottage. As soon as we turned the corner, I could see the raised garden beds, and a group of six kids were up to their elbows in dirt. Wesley Bell— never without his bow tie but because of the heat he'd conceded to a short-sleeved button-down shirt with khakis—circled them, his camera hiding most of his face. He wasn't kidding—he was going to get as many shots as he could and get the hell out of there to go to his next assignment.

"These young people are from the projects," Shaw said softly. We were just out of earshot. "They're all from broken homes; they're barely making it through school; drugs and guns and sex are part of their lives. I hope through this project that I can show them there's hope."

Now, this is where my compassion should've kicked in. But with my experience covering the police beat, all I could see when I looked at them was a bunch of dead-beat kids who'd end up like their parents or in my police blotter, either dead or charged with some serious crimes. Even with Shaw's charisma and example, the odds were stacked against them, and most probably couldn't pull themselves out of the hole they were born in. But I was stuck with this, so I might as well try to get what I could.

I made some sort of *mmm* sound to indicate that I understood, sort of like the smile-and-nod you give people when you're not really paying attention to what they're saying.

Wesley was done by the time we reached the garden beds. He shook Shaw's hand, thanked him, nodded at me, and went on his way. I wondered if a picture layout and captions could say a thousand words so I wouldn't have to.

Shaw introduced me to the kids, who gave me only half their attention. No curiosity on their part—the feeling was mutual. Somehow, that made me feel better. I took out my notebook and started writing down everything Shaw was telling me about starting up the garden project, how he'd gone into the schools to find these kids—apparently they were handpicked by the administration—and what sorts of vegetables and flowers were being tended to.

One of the most goddamn boring assignments I'd ever had. And that included the planning and zoning meetings I used to attend as a town reporter years ago. At least at those, someone was always ranting about some injustice—a development was being proposed on wetlands or endangered birds would be driven out if a marina was expanded.

I pretended to be interested and even peered closely at one boy's plantings as Shaw helped a girl who broke a nail while weeding. Tough luck.

One of the plants looked oddly familiar, and I glanced up at the boy, who wore an oversized T-shirt and jeans that hung precariously on his hips with a belt, showing off his boxers. His head was swathed in a do-rag, one of those things that made it look like he was wearing a pair of panty hose, the "legs" wrapped around, tied in the back, creating a tail. He had a smirk on his face, and I knew I was right. I looked around the garden bed and saw a couple more of the same plant.

Jesus. This kid was growing pot.

Now, I had to give him credit. It was dispersed enough between legal plants that probably no one would notice. I wondered if it would show up in Wesley's pictures. That could cause a stir.

I opened my mouth, but the boy put his fingers to his

lips as a smile stretched to his cheeks. He shook his head. "He don't know," he whispered, cocking his head at Shaw.

Yeah, right. And pigs fly, too.

"Bet he does," I whispered back, like we were in third grade.

"No, he doesn't. It's only over here. And every time he gets close, she"—and he indicated the girl with the broken nail, who was now leaning close enough to Shaw so her pert, teenage breast pressed against his arm—"distracts him."

Shaw's face was close to the girl's, and the sun illuminated a slight drop of moisture above his upper lip under his nose.

"What about the rangers? Don't they know?"

The kid chuckled. "Shit, they leave us alone. The Rev, well, he's got some power."

I still didn't believe that Shaw didn't know about the plants, but I did the smile-and-nod thing—I was getting damn good at it—and with one hand pulled my hair up to let a slight breeze cool the back of my neck.

"You go to Hillhouse?" I asked.

The kid nodded.

"What's your name?"

He looked at me sideways for a second. "He already introduced us."

I suppressed a smile. "I meet a lot of people. Remind me."

"Jamond."

"Nice to meet you, Jamond," I said. "So, besides growing plants that get you high, what else are you getting out of this program?"

A flash of fear crossed his face.

I shook my head. "I'm not going to out you. I have to write a story, and I have to quote you to make me look good to my boss."

He digested that a second, then, "It's summer school. Science credits. So I don't flunk out." He said it like he didn't give a shit if he flunked out; this wasn't his decision.

"What grade are you in?"

"Tenth."

"What would you do if you did flunk out?" I asked, dropping my hand with my notebook to my side. He knew I wasn't going to write this down.

"Hang out with my friends."

"Have they flunked out?"

"Some."

"How did you find out about the program? Did you know the Reverend Shaw?"

Jamond shook his head, gave me a sly smile. "Teacher. She hooked me up." From his expression and the tone of his voice, I wondered just what else this teacher had hooked him up with, but before I could ask anything else, he indicated Shaw. "Better go talk to him again." He wanted me away from his crop, so I nodded and joined Shaw, who had moved away from the cute girl with the rack that was threatening to bounce out of her Wonderbra at any moment.

Shaw took his gloves off again. "Sorry, but there's always something to attend to. Did you have a nice chat with Jamond?"

I nodded. "Nice kid," I said absently.

"He's growing pot plants over there." His tone was matter-of-fact.

I nodded. "Yeah."

"He thinks I don't know."

"Why do you let him get away with it?"

"I told them they could grow anything they wanted."

"So you're just keeping your promise?"

He nodded. "It's important." He paused. "And this isn't going in the paper."

I shook my head. "No."

He grinned, his eyes twinkling. "Do you want to talk to the other kids?"

Figured I might as well, and I made the rounds, and even though I carefully inspected the gardens of the other students, Jamond was the only one pushing the limits legally.

Shaw walked me back to my car about twenty minutes

later and shook my hand again. It was surprisingly cool after being confined in the gloves. "Thank you for doing this," he said, and I hated to admit it, but he was growing on me. The kids had nothing but good things to say about him; he was encouraging and not patronizing with them. Jamond might actually stay in school. Well, unless he could cultivate a bigger crop and make a killing. But these gardens weren't that big.

"If you have any more questions, please don't hesitate to call," Shaw said as I climbed into the Civic and he shut the door for me.

I pretended to search through my bag for something as I watched him walk around the building. He didn't look back once, just kept going.

I started the car and began pulling out, but just as I did, a red Porsche careened into the lot and I slammed on the brakes, feeling the car skid slightly as I caught my breath.

I looked out the window at the driver, ready to give him the finger.

He was smiling at me.

It was Jack Hammer.

Chapter 10

I climbed out of the car at the same time he got out
of his.

"What the hell are you doing here?" I demanded.
"You almost fucking hit me."

Jack didn't answer, just reached across his front seat
and pulled out the gym bag I'd seen him carrying earlier
at the Rouge Lounge. He gripped it tightly as he shut
the door and sauntered toward me.

"Hey, there, fancy meeting you here."

"Could say the same about you," I said, cocking my
head at his bag. "Thought that was stuff for your show
tonight."

Jack Hammer looked up at West Rock, the traprock
hill that forms the southern tip of the ridge dividing the
towns of Hamden and Woodbridge. "Hiking gear," he
said.

He was wearing a Patriots T-shirt, baggy shorts, and
Crocs. Something bulky was in the bag, could have been
hiking boots that he'd change into, but I wouldn't count
on it. It was too damn hot to hike, and anyway, even
though the state tried to lure hikers with the promise of
trails and the magnificent vista at the top, West Rock
was more for illicit rendezvous and drug deals.

Oh, yeah, Jack Hammer had a history of the former.
Maybe "a hike" was code. I shrugged. "Okay, sure," I
said, like I believed him.

He started to walk past me, toward the Visitor Center,
but I stopped him by grabbing his arm. It was tight,

muscled, and not unpleasant feeling. I pulled my hand back before he got the wrong idea.

The grin told me his head was full of wrong ideas.

I ignored it. "Can you tell me where Felicia Kowalski is?"

His eyebrows rose slightly. "Still looking for her? Thought you'd find her at the newspaper."

Asshole. He knew all along she was an intern at the *Herald*. "She didn't show up for a meeting this morning," I said curtly.

Something crossed his face, an odd mix of concern and amusement. "She'll turn up."

"Where?" I asked. "Do you know where she'll be working tonight?"

Jack shrugged. "Might want to check Bar. Maybe Alchemy. She could be anywhere; she could hit both in one night." He stared at me a long second, then said, "I have to get going. I'll see you around."

"Do you have a number I can reach you at?" I asked, determined not to let him get away that easy again.

But the lazy smile was back, the twinkle in his eye. "I know how to reach *you*."

What the fuck did that mean? I let him walk away from me and watched him shift the black bag from one hand to the other. There was something heavier in there than hiking boots. I could see jagged ridges jutting out on the sides of the fabric. Maybe it was some sort of rappelling shit—not that I knew anything about climbing, but I've seen the Discovery Channel.

When he reached the corner of the Visitor Center, he looked back and waved with his free hand. I climbed reluctantly into my Civic and started it up, all under his watchful eye. He was hesitant about having me see which direction he was headed, because he didn't move, just stared at me.

As I pulled into the road that led out of the nature center, I saw in my rearview mirror that he'd started to turn the corner, and the Reverend Shaw came up and shook his hand.

*   *   *

I wasn't supposed to see that. Jack Hammer had
looked around behind him at me, but I was peeling out
of the lot, like I had a fucking ambulance to chase. If I
was lucky, he'd think I'd missed Shaw's greeting. I
couldn't figure out the connection between the male
stripper and the preacher, but I doubted Jack Hammer
was there to help garden.

It would be too obvious if I decided to turn around
and ask a few more questions of the good reverend and
his student gardeners. There was no way to get back
into the nature center except the way I'd left, either, and
I didn't want to leave my new car on the side of the
road and hoof it back. This wasn't the best place to do
that. I could taste my curiosity, though, and it was driving me crazy.

I slid the Rolling Stones' *Forty Licks* in the CD player
and found "Mixed Emotions." It matched my mood as
I drove down Wintergreen Avenue toward Southern
Connecticut State University. Might as well follow
through with my plan to find out if anyone there knew
where Felicia might be on a Friday afternoon. Granted,
it was the first week of June—school had been over for
a few weeks and I wasn't sure if summer school had
started yet—so there might not be too many people
around. But it was worth a shot.

I wasn't quite sure why I was trying to track down
Felicia Kowalski. I could probably just wait her out at
the paper—she'd show up eventually. But Tom had said
the cops were looking for her, and given Jack Hammer's
comments, I knew she held some sort of key to something.

I was over in this part of the city anyway, so why
not? Maybe Ned Winters—who had called Priscilla, who
called me—could lead me in the right direction, Felicia-
wise, since he was head of the journalism department. I
was pretty sure he'd have a few things to say about
Ralph, too, but if seeing him could get me some information, then I could suffer through it.

Ned had been Ralph's best friend and roommate. The
three of us and Priscilla practically lived together in

Farnham Hall, although Priscilla and Ned weren't a "couple." They'd had one disastrous night together—Priscilla wouldn't even tell me about it, which made me really wonder what had happened—and decided they'd just be friends.

The only thing about going to Southern that my mother approved of was that I lived on campus—that was not the norm; Southern has always been more of a commuter college—giving me "the college experience," as she put it. I'm not sure cohabiting with Ralph on a regular basis was what she meant by that, but what she didn't know didn't hurt her. And I doubted she'd know what a bong was even if she saw one. It was too bad Jamond hadn't been born yet; otherwise we would've definitely taken advantage of his community-garden crop.

Ned was the pretty boy who had no ambition. He liked being in school, having few responsibilities. After we graduated, he went on to get his master's degree at Columbia in New York City and came back to Southern as an adjunct journalism professor. He'd never worked at a newspaper or magazine, or done anything else that could resemble actual journalism. He was everything I loathed: the professor who pretended to know how it was but had never been in the trenches himself. And to think he was molding young journalistic minds. It was fucking frightening.

When Ralph and I split, Ned called me a few times to "commiserate." By the fourth call, I was tired of replaying the shit and rebuffing Ned's advances. Despite his denials, I also knew he was reporting back to Ralph about my life. I told him to quit bothering me.

Just about a year ago, he called me at the paper "officially" and wanted to know if I'd be interested in teaching a basic newswriting class. I asked him if he was on crack and hung up.

I stopped at the light at Fitch and looked to my right at Connecticut Hall, the dining hall, where the only edible food had been cereal. I was a Froot Loops girl back then. I should've just poured the Budweiser on top of

them; they were mixed up in my stomach most of the
time anyway. Behind the dining hall were the residence
halls. The long walkway over Fitch Street connected the
West and East sides of campus, and I remembered how
damn cold it used to get crossing that bridge to go to
class.

Someone honked a horn behind me. I shook myself
out of my memories and turned left onto Fitch.

The state had been doing a lot of renovation work
here in the past few years. The journalism department
had moved out of Engleman Hall and into Morrill. I
barely recognized either as I pulled into the parking lot
adjacent to both. Engleman was more than double the
size it had been; a sort of mural carved in beige stone
decorated the entranceway to Morrill.

If it had looked like this when I was here, maybe I'd
be like Ned, too, and never want to leave.

I walked into Morrill Hall, and a dozen emotions em-
braced me as the air-conditioning hit me in the face and
I sighed with relief. I hadn't realized how comfortable I'd
gotten with the heat; it was sort of like wearing a heavy
coat I didn't need but had gotten used to, so I kept it on.

I pushed the button on the old elevator, and as the
doors opened, Ned Winters and I both did a double
take; he stepped out and pulled me into a bear hug
before I could say anything.

"Oh, Annie," he said, his breath causing goose bumps
to rise on my neck. "I saw you from my window, so I
came down to meet you. It's just so awful about Ralph,
isn't it? I was worried something like this might happen someday."

Worried what might happen? That Ralph would get
shot? That's what was in the paper; that's what everyone
thought. Why would Ned think this was how Ralph
would end up?

I gently released myself from his arms and took in his
tanned face, hazel eyes, which were blue in one light
and green in another, and blond hair that was spiked up
in an effort to cover an ever-increasing receding hairline.
He'd put on more than a few pounds, and it threw me

for a minute. He'd always been pretty vain about his looks and to see that he'd gained so much weight was a shock. He was nattily dressed in blue slacks and a button-down shirt, his feet clad in brown loafers. Very college professorlike.

Sometimes it was hard to remember we were grown-ups now. Even though those double digits kept getting higher, most of the time I still felt like I had in my twenties. Of course that could have a lot to do with the fact that I was still living my life as I had when I was in my twenties: single and working at the *Herald*.

The gap of differences between my life and Ned Winters' had diminished considerably in just a few seconds of introspection. I felt like Dr. Phil had come around the corner and shouted, "How's that workin' out for ya?" I didn't have an answer for him.

Time to get off the fucking pity pot.

"Well, I know a little more about what happened to Ralph," I started, but Ned took my arm and led me outside, back into the natural furnace.

"Let's go to the student center and get something to drink," he suggested.

We didn't say anything, following the sidewalk. I marveled at the work being done on the library, and as we approached the Michael J. Adanti Student Center, I was struck by how much it had changed here, how time and construction had physically erased what I remembered.

"It was such a tragedy when Adanti died," Ned said as he held the door open for me.

Michael Adanti had been president of the school, on vacation in Italy, when he died in a freak car accident just a couple of years ago. I nodded. I'd skimmed the stories but not much more than that. Our higher-education reporter had covered it.

As Ned pushed open the door to the student center, I could see in his face how comfortable he was here, like he was just going from the living room to the kitchen in his own house. Southern really *was* Ned's life. It had been his life since we'd all gone to school here, and

I wondered what that must be like, to perpetually be in college.

It wasn't the air-conditioning that made me shudder now.

Two iced teas later and seated near windows overlooking the bridge I'd just passed on the road, Ned leaned back and studied my face.

"You look good," he said, like he was surprised.

"You put some weight on," I said flatly.

He chuckled, patted his stomach. "Yeah."

"Married yet?"

"No way."

"Too many coeds to play with?" I asked, but it wasn't a joke and he knew it. A year or so ago there had been some allegations, a pregnant student claiming he was the father. Priscilla told me about it. I tried like hell to get something in the paper—it would serve Ned right—but the threatened lawsuit never materialized and Priscilla said a DNA test had proved the girl's claims false. But knowing Ned, well, I wouldn't be surprised if he *had* been screwing around with the girl.

The scowl turned his face ugly, and more memories rushed back. I pushed them out of the way.

"Priscilla called me," I said, ready to change the subject.

Ned nodded, and the scowl disappeared. "I talked to her, too." He paused. "You said you knew something. Something about Ralph?"

I watched the drops of sweat slip down the sides of my iced-tea glass. I certainly wasn't going to tell him where I'd spent the night. But I had to tell him the truth. "He wasn't shot. He had a heart attack."

Ned let that sit for a minute as he took a sip of his drink. "Was it hard for you to see him like that, though? I mean, I know you haven't seen him in a long time, but it must have been tough."

"How do you know I saw him?" I asked, keeping my voice measured.

Ned frowned. "Priscilla said you were at the bar last night. Didn't you write the story?"

Dick's byline was on the story. I shook my head. "No, I didn't," I said, watching his face but seeing no emotion at all.

"Oh, I just assumed . . ." His voice trailed off as he took a drink of his iced tea.

"Did you know he was in town?" I asked.

He nodded. "He's been back for a while, looking for work. I had him speak to one of my classes this spring."

The incredulity spread through me like a goddamn wildfire. "You let him do that?"

Ned snorted. "Jesus, Annie, he was a helluva reporter once upon a time. He knew his stuff—he was going places."

"And then he fucked it up."

Ned leaned across the table, his eyes boring into mine. "He fucked *you* up."

He was trying to provoke me.

"No, I have a career. He ended up on a goddamn sidewalk on ladies' night."

He sat back again. "You can't ignore the fact that you never got married again, that your job is your life. You never left New Haven after that."

How much had Priscilla told him? I was going to have to talk to her.

"Did you know Ralph was seeing one of the journalism students here? Felicia Kowalski," I said, not wanting to let him get to me.

Ned nodded. "They met that day he talked to my class. She's one of my students." He paused. "She's an intern at the *Herald* this summer."

"Yeah, I know. And she didn't show up this morning for a chamber meeting she was supposed to cover. Do you know how to reach her?"

Ned shrugged. "She's a kid. Who the hell knows? Maybe she's too torn up about Ralph. They got pretty close pretty fast." His tone made me wonder if he wasn't pissed about that. A coed that he couldn't bed but Ralph could.

I wasn't getting what I needed here, and there were too many ghosts. Being with Ned was like being with

Ralph, in a way, and I'd had enough of that. Before I could bid adieu and get on my merry way, however, Ned had one more thing to say.

"I'm surprised you haven't asked about the grand jury investigation."

Chapter 11

Grand jury investigation?

The question must have been written all over my face, because Ned started nodding. "I think Ralph told Priscilla. She didn't tell you?"

I hated not knowing things, and I hated it that he was teasing me, leading me on. "Jesus, Ned, what the hell are you talking about?"

"Ralph got into something serious. I don't know the details. He was pretty vague, and Priscilla said he didn't tell her much, either. Something about a grand jury investigation, possible indictment. He was trying to cut a deal. That's all I know."

I snorted. "My God. Did you know about this when you had him speak to your class? Did you tell your students what he did?"

Ned shook his head sadly. "Get over it, Annie. What happened is ancient history. It killed him to have to give up his dream."

"He made it all up, Ned. He made up those stories. He wasn't a reporter; he was a goddamn sham. If he'd just played it out, done his job the way he was supposed to, he would've gotten to the *New York Times* on his talent, like he should've. He just couldn't wait around; he couldn't be patient." The anger rose like a bubble in my chest. I was barely whispering and my voice was shaking.

"He didn't betray you, Annie. He betrayed himself."

I stood up, pushing my chair back. "He betrayed all

of us," I said as I rushed outside, headlong into the wall of heat that couldn't keep the tears from streaming down my cheeks.

As I sat in my Civic, I wondered how much of this was exhaustion and how much of it was just shit I hadn't dealt with and now it was coming out. I didn't even try to start the car, which was like a sweatbox, but I barely noticed.

Ralph was dead. It was over. But what about this grand jury? And why hadn't Priscilla told me about it? The questions swirled around me until I realized I needed to turn the car on and get some air-conditioning or I'd pass out.

My cell phone rang just as I turned the key.

I dug the phone out of my bag and saw Vinny's number. "Hey," I said as I flipped the cover.

"Where are you?"

"Southern. Revisiting my past." I tried to keep the contempt out of my voice, but I wasn't too successful.

Vinny's silence reminded me that he knew very little about my time at Southern and my history with Ralph. I needed to elaborate. "I know the head of the journalism department. I came by to see him about Ralph—we were all friends once." I paused. "Hey, how did you know about Felicia Kowalski?"

"Did you find her?"

"No. And you didn't answer my question." But before he could, a goddamn lightbulb went off over my head. "Is it the grand jury investigation? Is she some sort of witness or something?"

"Jesus, Annie, how the hell did you hear about that?"

So I was right. And if I didn't know about this, but Vinny did, it might mean only one thing. Which was not good. "Is my mother somehow involved in this? Are you working for her?"

"How late are you working? Can I still pick you up at seven?" Vinny asked, avoiding the question and giving me the answer at the same time.

"How is my mother involved, Vinny?"

"Seven's okay, right? Your shift is over then, right?"

We could go around like a carousel all day.

"Are you okay, Annie?" he asked when I didn't answer. His tone was soft, and I felt myself getting all emotional again.

"I'm fine," I said, but even I wasn't convinced.

"You didn't get much sleep. Can you get a nap in before I get over there?"

I looked at my watch. It was already three o'clock. "Maybe. Can you bring over some takeout from your parents' pizza place?"

"Let's play it by ear," he said after a second or two, and I wondered what was up.

We didn't say good-bye, just both ended the call at the same time, and I turned the car back toward downtown and the newspaper building.

I wanted to write up this community-garden story. At least then I could get it done and over with so I wouldn't be brooding about it all night and I might be able to actually cover something more interesting on my weekend shift tomorrow.

Marty was thrilled with my story about Shaw and the gardens. It was like I was going to get a fucking Pulitzer or something.

"Great job," he kept saying over and over as he pushed his glasses farther up his nose for the umpteenth time. "You're a natural at this." He knew better than to ask me if I wanted to switch beats. It was probably the way I was glaring at him.

"You know, Marty, a good reporter can write about anything," I said, noticing Dick Whitfield was watching the entire exchange. "Did that intern ever show up?" I asked.

Marty cocked his head to one side and took off his glasses. "Why so much interest in her, Annie? Was she just a shot girl at the Rouge Lounge or is there more to it?"

"Someone told me she was involved with Ralph," I conceded. "Did she show up today?"

"No." He chewed on the end of his glasses. "Dick

didn't get much information out of the cops about what went down last night. We're going to run a story updating that your ex died from a heart attack, but there were several witnesses who said they heard gunshots, too. Renee gave us the names of people who were there."

His face showed his disappointment that I hadn't been as forthcoming.

"Shit, Marty, I spent the night at the police station. I wasn't exactly thinking about witnesses and all that crap," I said. "And then you sent me off to see that charlatan and his hoodlum gardeners."

Marty stood up, an imposing figure at six feet four, and led me by the arm to Charlie Simmons' vacant office. Charlie must've had an early Friday night date. When the door was shut behind us, he turned to me.

"Renee told me in confidence that you were seen talking to Ralph Seymour just before he was shot. And that you were seen outside just after he was shot."

I took a deep breath. "Yeah, I did talk to Ralph, and she knows it. We talked about it last night. I was outside because I heard the shots and wanted to find out what happened. There's nothing mysterious about it." I hoped I was convincing enough so he'd leave it alone.

Marty studied my face for a few seconds, and I forced myself not to look away. Finally, he said, "One of her sisters saw you near your car after the shooting."

I knew what he was getting at now. "So you think I shot at Ralph, he keeled over, and then I put my gun back in my car afterward? The parking lot isn't far from where Ralph collapsed."

Marty sighed. "I'm just telling you what's out there." He meant the gossip.

"Tom let me go," I said.

Despite the door being closed, we heard the scanner screech about an accident. On reflex, I put my hand to the doorknob, but Marty shook his head. "No, Annie, Dick's got this."

Through the glass office window, I watched Dick pick a notebook up off his desk. He looked over at us and nodded as he made his way across the newsroom. Dick had been covering courts the last few months—the beat I'd held until I became the crime reporter—and it was possible he'd heard something about this grand jury investigation.

Wanting to ask him about that put me in a compromising position. I would have to be nice to Dick Whitfield, something that was not natural for me. Especially since he was going out to cover *my* story.

Jane Ferraro poked her head in the office and motioned that she needed to speak to Marty. As they huddled together just outside the door, I moved around them and followed Dick's path, catching up with him just as he was about to step outside. I tugged on his sleeve.

"A quick minute, Dick?" I asked.

His eyes were wide, and his expression told me he had no clue how to react. Was I going to yell at him for something, swear at him, order him to let me cover this accident? For a second, I let him wonder as I studied his appearance. He'd begun to abandon his penchant for green clothing, and more browns and blues had joined his color palette. Must be the influence of his girlfriend, TV reporter Cindy Purcell, who was in the newsroom at that very minute, fluffing up her blond locks as she prepared to report for the five o'clock news from Hartford's Channel 9 Shoreline Bureau, aka the *New Haven Herald*.

Dick's eyes were starting to glaze. Might as well get it over with.

"Over at the courthouse, have you heard anything about a grand jury investigation concerning Ralph Seymour, the guy who died at Rouge Lounge last night?" I asked.

The question caught him by surprise, and he nodded involuntarily. "I was going to ask you about that later. I didn't say anything to Marty yet. Especially since this guy was your husband."

I frowned. "Ex-husband. So you *did* hear something? Who told you?"

Dick's pointy ears twitched. I stared unabashedly. I didn't think they could do that.

"I heard it from someone over at the courthouse, a source," he said.

Oh, yeah, Dick had sources. It was hard to believe at first, but I grudgingly had to admit he was getting better at his job. At least he didn't make shit up, like Ralph had. Well, not that I knew of, anyway.

"So what did this source tell you?"

Dick bit his lip, a flush crawling up his face. "He said I should ask you why your mother was representing your ex-husband."

Chapter 12

My mother? Vinny had lied to me. Well, not exactly. He just hadn't answered when I asked about it.

It didn't take a rocket scientist to figure out that he knew something—he did know Felicia's name without me even saying it—and he probably was working for my mother on it. What his exact role was, well, now, that was what I needed to find out.

I sent Dick off to his accident with a wave of my hand, muttering how he'd miss it if he didn't get there right away. He didn't seem to notice I hadn't said anything before he scurried away. But I did catch something in his eye, something that indicated he might just ask me about this again.

Which meant I was going to have to find out about it before he did. And before Marty did.

The clock across the room told me I was meeting Vinny in less than an hour. I sighed, going back to my desk and dropping into my chair, my head in my hands. I'd hoped for a little romance tonight—and some much-needed sleep. If I confronted Vinny with this, we could be up all night, and not in a good way.

I had an insane thought for a nanosecond: Maybe I should call my mother or go over and see her and ask her about this. I could have time before I was supposed to meet Vinny.

No, that wouldn't work. This was a conversation with my mother that would require much more than twenty minutes; she and our publisher, Bill Bennett, were probably sipping margaritas on the back porch of my childhood home, and I really didn't need to see *him* right now, either.

So Vinny it would be. I was not looking forward to this.

Throwing my notebook in my bag, I sauntered over to Marty's desk. "I'm heading home. Do I have an assignment for tomorrow?" The weekend shifts sucked; there were only two reporters scheduled each day, and if news didn't happen, we got stuck covering art shows or, God forbid, community gardens.

Marty studied my face a second. "I thought you'd finish up that Shaw story tomorrow, so I didn't assign you to anything."

He should've known better. I could've written that story with my eyes closed. Practically did.

". . . and since you can't cover your beat—," he was saying.

"Wait a minute. You mean, even if there's a shooting or a murder or a fire or something tomorrow, I can't cover it?"

He shook his head. "No. Simmons made that pretty clear." He shuffled some papers on his desk and pulled one out from under the chaos. When his eyes met mine, they were apologetic. "There's a quilting bee in Branford at the senior center at one p.m." His voice had gotten so quiet, I wasn't sure I heard him correctly.

"A quilting bee?"

He nodded, held out the assignment sheet. I stared at it and opened my mouth to protest, but he held up a hand to stop me. "This'll all blow over soon, Annie."

I grabbed the paper. "I thought since Ralph died of a heart attack, this would be over now."

"But until this thing with your gun is settled . . ." His voice trailed off.

I sighed, but didn't reply, just turned on my heel and walked out of the newsroom.

*   *   *

Vinny was sitting on my stoop.

"Why didn't you go up?" I asked after he kissed me lightly on the cheek.

He pointed up, toward Walter's apartment windows. "I don't think he likes me here when you're not here."

"He told me that this morning," I said. We went through the front door and were halfway up the stairs when I asked casually, "Why were you here yesterday morning after I left for work?"

Without missing a beat, he replied, "Forgot my watch." He held up his wrist to show off the simple Timex. He had a fancier watch, a waterproof thing that he wore kayaking, but this one was his day-to-day. He wouldn't get a ticket from the fashion police, but he might get a warning for it.

The air conditioner in my apartment apparently was still on strike. Vinny opened windows while I rummaged in my hall closet for the big, sturdy fan I inherited from my mother when she had central air installed. I positioned it carefully in the living room and turned it on, but it merely blasted hot air back at us.

"I hate this time of year. Sometimes it's cold, sometimes it's hot," I said, reaching into my fridge for two Heinekens. I handed one to Vinny, then noticed something. "Hey, where's the pie?"

I was starving; he was empty-handed. Well, except for the beer.

Vinny shrugged. "Thought maybe we'd go out."

I took a long drink from my bottle, then said, "Why? I barely got any sleep last night and I'm wiped out. I really just want to go to bed." I also wanted to pick his brain about Ralph, but he was looking damn good at the moment: his T-shirt showing off his swimmer's arms, his "nice" jeans—but wait, something wasn't right. He was wearing sneakers. With socks. He *did* want to go out. Otherwise he'd be wearing flip-flops. And shorts.

And instead of staring at me with that look I'd come to know so well, he was avoiding my eyes, looking at anything and everything except me.

"What's up?" I asked.

Vinny ran a hand through his dark hair and smiled sheepishly. "I just thought it might be nice to go out."

Something was up, but I could tell he wasn't going to let me in on it. He was looking at me expectantly, like I was supposed to say something. Instead, I stood in front of the fan, trying to cool down. "I have to change," I said.

"I'll wait."

He didn't follow me into the bedroom. That was unusual. I grabbed a red sleeveless top that clung in all the right places and pulled on a stretchy black skirt that twirled as I walked. Glancing in the mirror, I saw there wasn't much to be done with my hair, but I went into the bathroom and put on a little mascara, hoping to disguise how tired my eyes looked, dabbed a little blush on my cheeks and gel on my lips. Fairly presentable. Back in the bedroom, I scooched down and reached for the strap of one of a pair of high-heeled sandals under my bed. I managed to find the other one, too, with a little more effort.

Brushing dust off my skirt, I went into the living room, where Vinny was looking out the window.

"Hey, there," I said softly. Maybe with the right moves, I could avoid this going-out shit and we could just go to bed.

For a second, I thought it was going to work. When he turned, he finally had that look in his eye. But then he was all business again, reaching for the door.

"Ready?" he asked, not even commenting on the outfit or how pretty I was or anything. Damn. Our relationship was still too new for him to start ignoring the way I looked.

He followed me down the stairs and opened the passenger door to his Explorer, closing it after me and going around the front before climbing into the driver's seat. I welcomed the air-conditioning, leaned forward, and aimed the vent at myself.

I felt his hand on my thigh through the thin fabric and I jerked my head up. If we weren't already past Olive going down Chapel, I might have been able to change his mind. I slapped his hand away playfully.

"You had your chance," I teased.

Vinny shrugged. "Yeah," he said absently, his eyes locking with mine for a second before they went back to the road.

Again I wondered what he was up to.

We pulled into a lot on Crown Street, next to Louis' Lunch.

"I don't want a hamburger," I said, indicating the small, squat burger joint.

Vinny chuckled. "We're not going there."

We parked, and I had to jog to keep up with him on the sidewalk, but not too far. He stopped in front of the Istanbul Café. Turkish food. I wasn't sure about this.

Vinny saw my hesitation and leaned over, whispering in my ear. "They've got belly dancers tonight."

"Oh, yeah, right, like that's going to entice me," I grumbled. While I wasn't in the mood for a burger, I would rather just have a pizza or pasta. Spicy food had its place, but not when I was overtired and overheated.

I didn't have a choice, however. Vinny opened the door, and he tugged my arm so I had to go through. A tall, dark man greeted us and led us to the back of the small restaurant to a table for two behind sheer orange and red curtains. I rolled my eyes, and Vinny ignored me, thanking the waiter for the menus as we sat. I tried to get comfortable on the pillow on my seat, but if Vinny had thought this would be romantic, he was wrong. I needed a beer, some quick food, and to get the hell out of here.

Vinny seemed oblivious to my feelings as he ordered a lamb dish that we could share, but to his credit, the beer was cold and quenched my thirst. He laughed as I finished it, ready for another.

"Slow down. This is only the first stop."

What the hell?

I barely tasted the food and was happy that our curtains seemed to be a barrier between us and the belly dancer, who had begun to make her way around the restaurant, table by table. I chewed faster, hoping we could finish before she decided we were in the mood for a little entertainment.

Her moves reminded me of Jack Hammer. I wondered again about seeing him with Shaw this afternoon at the nature center. I couldn't make the connection between the two, unless my suspicions about Shaw having some sort of nefarious background were right.

"So where are we headed next?" I asked as our dessert of melted cheese covered with strings of stiff maple syrup was placed on the table. I wasn't sure about it, so I took a sip of the incredibly strong coffee. Jesus. That would wake the fucking dead.

Vinny cocked his head toward the door, his mouth full of cheese.

"Yeah, I know we're leaving, but where to?" I asked. The coffee was doing its job; the beer and sleepy fog had started to lift. I felt like I could run a goddamn marathon.

"Bar."

I glanced toward the window that overlooked Crown Street toward the bar across the street, simply called Bar, like it would be too hard for anyone to remember another name. Okay, the clientele ran a little young, so maybe that wasn't so far-fetched an idea.

"Why?" I asked, but that coffee must have sparked my memory while waking me up, and I remembered. "It's Felicia Kowalski, isn't it? Is she working there tonight?"

Vinny leaned back on his pillow and smiled. "Give the girl a gold star. I was wondering when you'd put two and two together."

"Give me a fucking break, Vin. I had four hours of sleep last night."

"Yeah, but now you're awake, right?"

It had been good strategy on his part. Sometimes I forgot that Vinny was Ivy League smart and almost had a Ph.D. He wouldn't have been caught dead at Southern. But my newfound energy also jolted my memory, and it was time to get to the bottom of what was really going on.

"So tell me more about Ralph's grand jury investigation and how my mother came to be representing him," I said.

Vinny's mouth was full and he choked back his surprise, recovering enough to swallow before a long, slow grin spread across his face. "You mean you don't know everything yet?"

"So what's the deal?" I took my fork and picked at the crunchy syrup until it sank into soft cheese. I tried a taste. It wasn't bad: sweet and chewy and a little sour all at the same time. I took another forkful as I waited for an answer.

"Ralph was into some serious shit." Vinny stared at me a few seconds, then, "He's been buying guns legally out of state but selling them illegally here. For drugs and money."

Chapter 13

The waiter came back, and I ordered another coffee. I'd be up all night at this rate, but I wanted to be alert for this conversation. I sat back on my cushion, letting Vinny's words sink in.

So this was where Ralph had ended up. Back home. Not the Pulitzer Prize–winning journalist he'd dreamed of being, but a criminal.

Vinny was talking. "I knew he was working there. Last night. That's why I was there. At the Rouge Lounge."

His words hung between us for a few seconds.

"So you didn't just see it on TV?" I thought about how he'd caught me as I fell, his excuse for being there that he wanted to see what was going down. To call him a liar, however, would be the pot calling the kettle black.

Vinny sighed. "I was in the bar. I saw you talking to him before he went outside." He paused, then, "I saw that kiss."

Shit. But I asked him what I had asked Renee: "Did you see me kick him in the balls after?"

He frowned, stared at his bottle a second, then looked up at me. "No."

"I did. I kicked him in the balls." I knew the way it sounded the minute I said it: like I was trying to convince myself, too. Not good.

He snorted. "I took a short walk."

To walk off his anger. Yeah, I understood. I tried a

smile on for size. "You should've seen him doubled over."

But he wasn't amused. "Yeah, sorry I missed that." He paused. "I walked around the building. Near the parking lot."

I knew what he was looking for now, but I had to turn this around to something else. "So if you were there, why didn't Tom round you up, too, to question you?"

Vinny studied my face for a few seconds. He was on to me. "He doesn't know I was there."

I hadn't seen him, either, except after, when he was standing behind the crime-scene tape with all the other curious passersby.

"You were in the back room, watching that show," Vinny reminded me, reading my mind. "No men allowed, remember? When I saw you come out and talk to Ralph, I moved out of sight."

"So were you watching me or him?"

Vinny licked his lips, and I could tell he was thinking about lying. But he must have changed his mind, because he said honestly, "Both of you."

"So since you knew he worked there and I was going to be there, were you trying to get some sort of clue about how I'd be around him?" I thought it was a fair question.

Vinny ran his hands over the stubble on his face. Something was wrong, and it wasn't jealousy.

"Jesus, Vinny, did you think I was in some sort of danger?"

It was like someone hit a switch, and the smile was back, his eyes twinkling. "You, in danger? I know you can take care of yourself."

Yeah, right.

The waiter slipped the bill onto the table, and Vinny pulled out his credit card, putting up his hand as I opened my mouth to protest. I usually argued, but decided not to this time. I wasn't in the mood, and the belly dancer was sashaying closer to our table, jingling as she moved. The sooner we could get out of here, the better.

We stepped out of the restaurant and crossed the street, where twenty-somethings were spilling out the door of Bar. I heard the rhythmic thud of a bass from somewhere within. I was too old for this, but the news about Ralph and my curiosity about Felicia had grabbed hold of me, and Vinny had grabbed hold of my arm, and within seconds we were swimming through a sea of firm, nubile bodies.

I wondered if I looked as old as I felt.

"Excuse me, ma'am," I heard from behind as a young man in a Boston Red Sox T-shirt squeezed past.

Yeah, I looked as old as I felt.

I tugged on Vinny's hand. "Let's get out of here. We really don't belong here."

He wasn't paying attention to me. I held his fingers lightly as we wove through the crowd. The music was so loud, I thought I'd gone deaf: Mouths were moving, I saw people laughing, and a chair skidded across the floor, but I heard none of it, my eyes taking in everything, my ears nothing.

I tightened my hold on Vinny's hand, squeezed. He turned to me, smiling, indicating someone behind me. I turned to see a tall brunette with blond highlights wearing a tight camisole and short skirt, legs stretching down into stilettos. I had a flashback from the other night, when I wore something similar. But I wasn't in my twenties. I must have looked like an idiot.

I wondered if this girl was the mysterious Felicia, but I remembered the health and science photo. The hair was the right color, but it was straighter and I didn't remember highlights.

My hand was cold. Vinny was gesturing, talking with the girl, who held a tray of test tubes filled with a clear liquid. He handed over a few bills and took two, handing me one, leaning in toward her, and saying something in her ear before turning to me and shouting, "This is Ashley. She's a friend of Felicia's."

I nodded in what I hoped was a polite way before taking the test tube. I didn't even sniff it; I downed the tequila shot and put the tube back. Vinny and Ashley were grinning at me, Vinny indicating he would buy me another. I shook my head and pointed back the way we came, not waiting for him, moving toward the door, then finally back out into the sauna outside.

A car passed, and I heard its motor rumble as it did. Okay, so I wasn't really deaf. I hoped Vinny was getting some information about Felicia from Ashley. She'd been the only shot girl I'd seen, but then again, I hadn't really been looking too hard.

A couple of guys were standing off to my left, cigarettes hanging from their fingers. That shot had brought back a taste I hadn't had in a long time, and I inhaled the smoke, wondering if one cigarette could get me hooked again. It had been a few years since my last one.

I'd probably have a coughing fit and die on the sidewalk, just like Ralph.

I noticed one of them was looking at me, and I stared back.

"Hey," he said. His hair was spiky, an earring looped through one ear, and he was wearing a black T-shirt with a skull on it.

I should've worn my Sturgis shirt again. Maybe I wouldn't have been mistaken for a "ma'am" then.

Yeah, right.

He wasn't hitting on me, since he was elbowing his friend in the ribs, a small smile on his face. He winked, but it wasn't that sort of a wink—you know the kind. It was a teasing wink, one that questioned what the hell someone like me was doing here on a Friday night.

"Hi," I said, joining him and his two friends dressed almost exactly alike, except their black T-shirts weren't sporting skulls. Might as well make the most of this. "You guys wouldn't know if Felicia's working in there tonight?" I cocked my head toward the door.

They glanced quickly at one another, smiles evaporating. The guy who'd winked frowned. "Who wants to know?"

It seemed pretty damn obvious who wanted to know: me. But I guess that wasn't good enough. "Friend of a friend," I said.

That wasn't good enough, either, since they started shifting from one foot to the other. The guy with the skull dropped his cigarette and ground it with the heel of his sneaker before asking, "What friend?"

I debated with myself for a second, then said, "Ralph Seymour."

"Guy who got killed last night?" the kid asked.

I nodded.

"You think she had anything to do with it?"

He hadn't heard about the heart attack.

"Just want to talk to her."

"You a cop?"

I almost laughed out loud. Tom would have a field day with that one if he ever heard. "No. Ralph was my ex-husband."

Their eyes grew wide and they shifted again, but their eyes indicated curiosity.

"She's not here tonight." The kid who spoke had a high voice, like it hadn't changed yet, even though he had a goatee. "Not yet, anyway."

Shit. Was I going to have to stay here until closing just to see if she'd show up? I stifled a yawn. Where the hell was Vinny? Maybe I could leave him here and go home and go to bed. I calculated the blocks to my apartment. It wasn't too far, although I'd probably have to take the shoes off—I was still sporting blisters from last night—and I wasn't sure walking barefoot on the sidewalk was a smart thing to do.

Before I could make any sort of move, Vinny stepped out of Bar, took my elbow, and steered me across the street.

"She's not here," he said.

"I know," I said, and he frowned.

"How?"

"Kids out front said she wasn't. Where to next?" I put my hand over my mouth to cover up another yawn.

Vinny noticed. "Sorry I dragged you out," he said. "Let me take you home."

"But we have to find Felicia."

He didn't respond as we made our way back to the Explorer. When we were settled in and on our way back toward Wooster Square, I put my fingers on his thigh, lightly tracing the muscle there. He glanced at me quickly, then back at the road. I took that as a green light and let my fingers do more of the walking, and when he looked at me again, I raised my eyebrows and grinned.

He didn't grin back, but he didn't move my hand.

Once the Explorer eased against the curb in front of my building, I felt pretty confident that I knew where this evening was finally headed. Vinny slung his arm around me as we ascended the stairs to my apartment, and when we got inside, he pushed the door shut and put his hand on the back of my neck, pulling my face to his and kissing me.

The heat I was feeling now had nothing to do with the air.

But just as quickly as he'd started, he stopped, staring into my eyes before moving away, pacing across my living room.

Something was wrong.

I let my eyes move around the room, taking in my space, the space I'd called home now for ten years. The Japanese print of Mount Fuji was on the wall behind the rocking chair. Ralph had given it to me as a wedding present. It was the only thing I had from him that I'd kept.

Vinny suddenly stopped pacing. He took my hand and led me to the rocking chair. I sat, and although I couldn't see the Mount Fuji print anymore, I could feel it behind me.

Vinny knelt down in front of me and took my hands in his.

"I was in the bar last night when I heard the shots. I

didn't want to go through the front, but went out the
side door, the one the deliveries come through. That's
where I went after I saw him kissing you." He paused.
This wasn't easy for him. I willed myself not to show
any emotion. "I had a good view of the parking lot."
His voice wavered slightly, and I'd never seen him like
this before. My chest constricted, and I swallowed hard.

"I saw you leaning into the car, the gun in your hand.
You put the gun under the seat."

Chapter 14

This wasn't going the way I expected.

"You're not going to deny it?" Vinny asked incredulously.

I shrugged. "What can I say? You've convicted me already."

"I waited all evening for you to say something, to tell me about last night, but you didn't say a damn thing," he said.

"So you automatically think I'm guilty of something?" I glared at him. "We talked about last night. I told you he kissed me, that I kicked him."

I couldn't look at him anymore, so I took a deep breath, reached back, pulled my hair up, and stretched my neck hard enough I heard it crack as I looked at the ceiling.

It was a light touch at first. The thin scars on his palms tickled my skin as his hands slid up my calves and under the skirt to my thighs. I shifted instinctively toward him as his fingers hooked around my underpants and tugged them down. My breath came faster; I could hear my heart pounding in my ears.

I had no idea that thinking I could shoot at my ex-husband would elicit this sort of a response, but my brain shut down as I felt his mouth on me.

Suddenly, he reached underneath me, yanking me closer to the edge of the chair. My head fell back as the chair rocked forward, slamming it against the rails, but I barely felt it. The wood was smooth under my ass. His hands slipped up under my shirt and unhooked my bra; my legs straddled his hips, grinding against the stiff cloth. His tongue teased my neck before his face shadowed mine, his eyes dark and smoky, a question in them.

He kissed me long and deep, stopping abruptly. I lifted my head slightly to meet his lips again, but he put a hand on my cheek, forcing me back. When he finally spoke, after a long moment, his eyes locked with mine, he said huskily, "Tell me you didn't shoot at him."

I shook my head, uncertain if I could even speak—it was as if my body had completely taken over and there was no room for words anymore.

"Tell me," he said, not willing to let me out of it. "Why did you have your gun?"

I didn't want to tell him. I sorted through the chaos in my head and finally said, "I've been getting phone calls."

Talk about killing a mood. He sat up—when did he have time to take off his shirt?—and I realized our moment was over, hooked my bra, and pulled my shirt back down. My skirt was still hitched up over my thighs, and I left it that way. Wishful thinking. Maybe this wouldn't take too long.

"Phone calls from whom?" Vinny asked.

I shook my head. "I don't know. The phone rings in the middle of the night, I answer, but no one's there. Whoever it is hangs up."

Vinny frowned. "Not when I'm here."

"You're not always here."

We'd tried to keep our nights together to four a week. We had to sleep sometimes.

"So it's deliberately when I'm not here?"

I nodded, grabbing my underpants and shimmying back into them. Moment was most definitely over. Damn.

"Why didn't you tell me?"

"It was only once in a while until about two weeks ago. Now it's every night you're not here."

"Why didn't you tell me?"

"I didn't think much about it until recently," I said.

Vinny's eyes narrowed. "Do you have any idea who it might be?"

I frowned. "Why the twenty questions?"

"So you don't? Have you tried calling star 69 to find out?"

I snorted. "Every time I try it, I can't get shit. Some recording says the number I'm trying is blocked."

"Did you tell Tom about this?"

He wasn't going to let up.

I shook my head. "No."

"But you've been carrying your gun around because of it?"

"Not so much because of it—"

"Jesus, Annie." Vinny stood up and started pacing around my living room. "Why couldn't you just tell me? Why do I have to see you putting a gun in your car?"

I went over to the refrigerator. Two more beers left. I pulled them both out and handed him one. He took it, his eyes looking everywhere but at my face. Okay, so I fucked this one up good.

I walked around the island that divides my galley kitchen from my living room and put my hand on his arm, forcing him to turn so he'd have to look at me.

"I didn't tell you because I knew you'd get all crazy about it. I've gotten this sort of stuff before. It's what I do. I piss people off, and they try to get back at me."

"But you have an unlisted number."

"Some of the people I work with are idiots and sometimes they give numbers out. You know that." I leaned in toward him, ran my finger along his jawbone, felt him tense up. I dropped my hand. "Okay. If it's like that, then maybe you should leave."

He stared at me a second, nodded.

"And did you really think that the only way to get the truth out of me was to seduce me?" I asked his back as he opened the door.

He turned. "I played it wrong." And after a pause, "But you did, too."

It was too hot to sleep. Vinny had been right: I did play it wrong. He had central air-conditioning, and I could be over there, comfortable and getting the rest I needed. In addition to some other things. I shivered despite the heat, thinking about how close we'd come earlier, now frustrated and feeling cheated.

After he left, I finished my last beer and what was left of his, too. I channel surfed awhile, finding *Ice Castles* on Encore. One of the best worst movies ever made. And when the blind skater tripped over those roses on the ice, giving up her secret, and Robby Benson came to her rescue, I cried.

It's a hormone thing.

I climbed into bed at midnight, staying up longer than I wanted, hoping that Vinny would change his mind, that our fight—well, it hadn't seemed like a fight, really, but what else could I call it?—would be forgotten and he could get past what he perceived as my distrustfulness.

I thought again about that note stuck on the fridge this morning. Maybe the word "love" had fucked with my head too much. Maybe that's why I'd been so cryptic with him.

No, it was everything else that had happened. I'd fix it tomorrow. Vinny and I had had to find our way back to each other once before because of my stupidity and stubbornness.

I settled into bed and immediately started tossing and turning.

The phone rang at two a.m.

I sat up and listened to the machine pick up.

I heard my own voice give its command. "You know what to do."

Silence for a few seconds, then dial tone.

As I sat in bed, the glow of the streetlamp slicing across the bed and up the wall, I wiped the sweat from the back of my neck and glanced reflexively toward the window, covered most of the way with the miniblinds. I tugged at the sweat-soaked T-shirt; I wasn't used to wearing clothes in bed—I'd started the practice when the phone calls became more regular.

But I had thought now that Ralph was dead they would stop.

Chapter 15

The buzzer woke me up. I glanced at the clock. I didn't know when I'd finally dropped off, but it was nine a.m. I jumped out of bed and bounded into the living room. Vinny was back.

When I looked out the window, down at the landing below, I saw it wasn't Vinny. I pushed the button to unlock the door.

Tom dropped a box of Dunkin' Donuts Munchkins on my counter and handed me a large iced latte when I let him in. He took a sip from his own hot coffee, a more reasonable-sized cup, before saying, "Good morning. You look like hell."

I started to run a hand through my hair and it got stuck. I might actually have to try to brush it or something. "Thanks," I muttered, taking a drink of my latte, which was ice-cold and immediately gave me brain freeze. I set the cup back on the counter. "Why are you here?"

Tom's eyes were skirting around the room.

I knew what he was looking for. "Vinny's not here. We had a fight."

I don't know why I said that last part. Tom looked at me thoughtfully before chuckling. "We had fights every other day. Why would you be different with anyone else?"

I made a face at him and opened the Munchkin box. They were all chocolate frosteds. My favorite. I picked one out and held it up. "Why the bribe? What do you want?"

"I wanted to see how you were doing."

I shook my head. "No, what's up?"

Tom cocked his head at me and took another sip of coffee. He was taking his goddamn time, that was for sure, and he knew it was driving me nuts. A small smile played at the corners of his mouth, and I remembered how kissable that mouth could be.

Down, girl. Just because Vinny and I had a fight didn't mean I could be looking backward at Tom again.

The way he was looking at me made me wonder if he didn't know exactly what I was thinking. I picked up my iced coffee again, put my lips around the straw, and sucked, bringing back the cold headache, but it made me forget that I was blushing.

"You told me you hadn't seen Ralph Seymour in fifteen years," Tom said, settling in on one of the tall chairs at my kitchen island, his feet firmly on the rung, his hands surrounding his cup as he stared first at it and then back up at me. "Have you talked to him before the other night? I mean, in the past fifteen years."

I slurped my coffee through the straw, my eyes trained on his. "My friend Priscilla has been in touch with him. And Ned Winters, over at Southern, he said he had Ralph come talk to one of his classes this spring. But I really didn't want to hear from Ralph, and he knew that."

"I talked to Winters." And from the way he said it, I knew Ned had told Tom about me and Ralph way back when. "Why don't you tell me your version of what happened with your ex-husband?"

I took a deep breath and another Munchkin, chewing thoughtfully before speaking. How to summarize the collapse of a relationship? "When I found out Ralph had been fabricating stories for the paper we were working for in New York, I knew I couldn't stay with him. He got caught because a copy editor actually tried to get in touch with a charity that Ralph had quoted in a story

about a kid who supposedly had some awful disease; I
don't even remember what it was. But the charity didn't
exist. And the PO box where all the money was going,
well, I do know it wasn't in Ralph's name." I sighed.
"He claimed his source lied to him, that the family lied
to him. But of course the family couldn't be found, either, once the editor started looking into it. Ralph said
they'd called him, said they had to leave town because
of the publicity, but it was his word against everyone
else's at that point." I paused, taking a deep breath.

"He made all of it up. And that wasn't the only story,
either. He was fired. I left him—I couldn't live with
someone who'd done that."

Tom reached across the island and took my hand. "I
wouldn't expect you to."

I looked at his face, searching for a sign that he was
playing around with me, but he wasn't. He was totally
serious. He knew me, and he knew my ethics. I
shrugged, trying to make light of it. "The paper covered
it up. I was working there, too, but ended up getting a
job right away at the *Herald*." And I hadn't updated my
résumé since.

I was as bad as Ned Winters. Seeking solace in my
hometown, never leaving, never even thinking about it.
Maybe I should cut Ned more of a break.

"How is Priscilla involved?" Tom asked.

I told him how we'd all hung out together in school.
How we were all going to get jobs at the *New York
Times*, what we considered our Holy Grail, and change
the world, take down presidents like Woodward and
Bernstein did. I didn't tell him that after seeing *The
Killing Fields* with Sam Waterston, I gave up my ideas
about being a foreign correspondent. There was just so
much I could do.

Instead I ended up covering planning and zoning and
school board meetings. I thought about my interview
with Shaw yesterday and realized just how little I'd ad-
vanced in my career.

Ralph hadn't gone back to journalism. He didn't even
try to rectify anything, salvage what had been his dream.

Priscilla told me he floated awhile, tried to freelance for magazines, but word spread, so he gave up writing altogether. When he was arrested on the drug charges, he'd already started working in clubs, strip clubs. How he got the job managing the Rouge Lounge, I didn't know; it seemed like it was on the up-and-up. Maybe he'd gotten on track a little. But then, of course: "So how long has this grand jury investigation into Ralph been going on?" I asked.

Tom pulled his hand away in surprise, his eyes wide.

"Christ, Tom, Ned told me about it. Ralph told him." I waited a half beat. "And my mother's got a little 'splainin' to do," I added in my best Ricky Ricardo accent. "Guess she's been representing Ralph."

The look on Tom's face told me he didn't have a clue about that. We'd both been duped.

"You didn't know this the other night, when we had you in for questioning?" he asked.

I shook my head and held up three fingers. "Scout's honor," I said.

"She never said anything," Tom muttered.

I chuckled, taking another Munchkin. "She didn't tell *me*, either, and I was married to the guy. But grand jury investigations are secret anyway, and it must be a federal thing, since he'd been buying the guns out of state and bringing them here."

If his eyes were any wider, he'd look like that lemur from *Madagascar*.

"Did she tell you about that?" he asked.

I shook my head. "I haven't even talked to her yet."

He was quiet a minute; he knew Vinny had told me.

"How involved is your department?" I asked.

Tom shook his head. "Our department isn't involved at all. It's all the feds."

Immediately I thought of my friend Paula Conrad, special agent with the local FBI office. And from the look on Tom's face, he was on to me.

"Paula won't tell you shit. If you're going to poke around, it would probably be easier to get something out of Vinny or your mother," Tom said.

I wasn't so sure about that.

"What did you fight about?" Tom asked.

I frowned. "What?"

"You and Vinny. What was your fight about? Was it about Ralph?"

"Sort of, I guess." I thought about Vinny seeing me with my gun. And then I thought about the phone calls. Should I tell Tom? I debated this for a second, but he spoke before I could make a decision.

"You know, we searched Ralph Seymour's apartment. Before we knew how he died." So that's where he'd been while Ronald Berger had been interrogating me.

"I thought you said Ralph's case was federal," I said.

"We knew about the straw purchases." "Straw purchases" was what they called illegal gun sales for drugs or money.

They'd gone in looking for guns, looking for clues as to who would want to see Ralph dead. The feds were probably pissed, but Tom wanted to get there first. He was always an overachiever.

"We were pretty thorough in the search," he said then, his voice changing into his "official" one, the one I've heard when he's interrogating witnesses at crime scenes.

Or me, when I'm a "person of interest."

Uh-oh.

I thought about the implication of what he was saying, and the way he was saying it.

"You dusted for prints, didn't you?" I asked, like I didn't know now what this visit was really all about.

Tom's eyes were dark, and sweat beaded on his forehead. He nodded.

I'd have to come clean.

"Then you probably found mine."

Chapter 16

I knew it had been a mistake to do that story last year about how a suspect is processed. Marty was all gung ho about a first-person account of being handcuffed, Mirandized, fingerprinted, the whole kit and caboodle. At the time I was apprehensive, but Tom and Ronald Berger had made it into a sort of game and we all went out for beers afterward. Tom and I were still dating then, and when we went back to my place afterward, we had a little cop-and-robber fantasy thing going on that now made me blush.

From the look on Tom's face, he wasn't thinking about that. I struggled to push my memories out of the way.

"We put your prints into the system and never took them out after you did that story. Forgot," Tom said simply. "When we went to look for a match for the print, yours came up."

Behind his words, I could hear the question. If I hadn't seen Ralph in fifteen years like I'd claimed, why would he find my fingerprint at his apartment? But he didn't give me a chance to answer. There was more.

"We also found some photographs."

I swallowed hard. "What sort of photographs?"

By asking that, he had his answer, so he continued.

"There are photographs of you."

I took a deep breath. "What sort of photographs?" I asked again.

Tom's eyes were a light blue, and I caught a flash of

cobalt as the sun winked through the windows. "Pictures of you getting into your car, coming up the steps here, going into the newspaper, at that fire last week over in Dixwell."

I could feel my heart pounding inside my chest so hard I was surprised it didn't pop out of my chest like that thing in *Alien*. Tom didn't seem to notice as I took another sip of my iced coffee. It was almost gone.

"So you didn't know about this?" Tom asked.

It was a good question. It would give me a motive to shoot at Ralph. How to explain that it would just be one of many?

"No."

"You didn't notice anyone following you or anything?" Tom asked.

It was time to tell Tom about the phone calls. "I've been getting a lot of hang-up calls. Middle of the night."

Tom's eyes changed slightly, his mouth set into a thin, tight line as he digested this information. "Middle of the night?"

"I never got them when anyone else was here," I said, remembering that Vinny had pointed this out the night before. But I'd been half dressed and sexually frustrated at the time, so I'd been distracted and it hadn't struck me then like it did now.

Whoever was watching me knew when I was alone. It wasn't a random thing.

Tom finished his coffee, got up, and threw the cup away in the trash can under my sink. He turned back around to me. The island was between us, and he ran a hand through his hair. When he raised his arm, I could see the sweat marks on his shirt. It was hot in here, not that I'd noticed at all during this conversation.

"When was the last call?"

"Last night. Around two a.m."

Tom crossed his arms against his chest. "Last night?" His voice was calm, but I knew what he was thinking.

"Yeah, I thought it was Ralph, too."

Those blue eyes settled on mine, and he didn't blink.

"Why? If you didn't know he'd been watching you, why would you think it was him?"

Caught. What should I say? Should I tell him the truth?

Might as well.

"Ralph stalked me after I left him," I said flatly. "Lots of hang-up calls, lots of late-night visits. I caught him in his car across the street from my apartment one night when I got home from a night meeting." I shuddered involuntarily as I told him; I'd changed my phone number five times and still he managed to get it somehow.

"How long?"

"Six months. Then it was all over. I didn't hear anything from him again."

"Why do you think he stopped?"

"I don't know," I said, too quickly.

From the look on his face, Tom knew something was up, but he took a different tack. "Why would you think he'd start up again? After all these years."

What should I say? "Instinct" seemed too silly. "It was just like before, except I didn't see him," I said.

"Did you know he was in town?"

I nodded. "Priscilla," I said simply.

"The calls started after he came back here?"

"Yeah."

"Did you tell DeLucia? About the calls?"

I remembered Vinny asking if I'd told Tom about the phone calls. Why hadn't I told either of them?

"I just told him about it last night. Not before," I said.

"Didn't it worry you?"

I nodded. "Yeah, a little, but if it was Ralph, I knew he wouldn't hurt me."

"How do you know that?"

"He never hurt me before. And he had more reason to back then than he did now."

"Did he?"

The question came at me like a fastball I wasn't expecting. Something in Tom's expression made me catch my breath. I had to say something, and quickly.

"I didn't go into his apartment. If you found my fingerprint, it was on the doorjamb, maybe the doorknob, on the outside somewhere, right? Do you think he thought I knew what was going on? That he was photographing me, or having someone photograph me?"

Tom sighed. "I don't know."

I had another thought. "Did you find anyone else's prints, I mean, besides Ralph's?"

"A couple, but we couldn't ID them."

"Is that why you're looking for Felicia Kowalski? To get her prints? See if any of the ones in the apartment are hers?"

"That, and something else." Tom's lips curled into a small smile, like he had a private joke with himself.

I found myself smiling despite myself. "What? What's going on?"

Tom shook his head, a rumble of laughter spilling out.

"Come on, Tom, you have to tell me."

"No, I don't." I could see, though, that he wanted to.

"Come on," I urged.

He managed to pull himself together after a few seconds, then, "We thought it was funny that a guy would just keel over like that—you know, he wasn't very old." He stopped.

"What?" I prodded.

"We had the medical examiner do a quick tox screen. We thought it was probably cocaine; that happens a lot. A younger guy, working in a business like that, drugs are probably involved, and coke'll cause a heart attack."

His eyes were twinkling, and then he started to snort because he was trying not to laugh out loud again.

"Guy had a fucking hard-on. When we rolled him over, it was reaching for the goddamn sky. And even when rigor passed, it stayed that way."

Okay, so that was weird. And I could see the humor in it. But what did it mean?

He was laughing now. He couldn't help himself. "Jesus, Annie, it was like those fucking commercials. You know, those 'If you have an erection for more than four hours, call your doctor' commercials."

I started chuckling. It was infectious. But I still didn't get it.

Tom was shaking, he was laughing so hard. Finally, he managed to spit out, "Your ex-husband died of a Viagra overdose."

Chapter 17

Viagra? Ralph? From what I remembered, there had been no problem there, but Ralph had turned forty a few months ago and there can be a big difference between twenty-one and forty, sexwise. And we couldn't forget Felicia. He probably felt like he had to compete with those college boys, since he was dating such a young woman.

And then I thought about how I'd kicked him after he kissed me. He certainly didn't have a hard-on then—I would've noticed that. Made me wonder when he took it. Did he really think he was going to get lucky with me?

Tom was trying to stop laughing. I grabbed another Munchkin. Hell, with this heat, I'd sweat off all those calories in no time.

The phone rang, startling both of us, knocking the laughter out of Tom, causing the Munchkin to get caught in my throat. I reached for the handset, but Tom's fingers curled around my wrist.

"Screen it," he advised.

When the machine picked up, we heard my message, then, "Annie?"

It was Vinny.

I picked up the phone before Tom could stop me again, waving my hand at him as I went into the bedroom. He didn't follow me.

"I'm here," I said softly. "I'm sorry." He knew I didn't mean I was sorry about having the machine pick up.

"Yeah, me, too. What's Tom want? He's been there awhile."

I felt a bubble of anger, then pushed it down. "What, are you watching my building?" I asked, then thought about those pictures that Ralph had in his apartment. Had Ralph taken them himself, or did he hire a private eye, someone like Vinny?

"Chill, okay? I was walking over when I saw him pull up. Figured he wouldn't want company." Vinny lived kitty-corner to my brownstone on Wooster Square. My paranoia was getting the better of me.

"Okay, fine."

"You're working today?"

"Yeah." I sighed, thinking about the quilting bee. I didn't mention that I'd be making a stop at my mother's before work. I could try to get some more information out of Vinny about Ralph, but my mother had been representing him and hadn't bothered to mention it, even while I was being interrogated by the police. She owed me an explanation. "I can call you later."

"What time are you done?"

"I'm going in at noon." A quick glance at the clock told me it was ten a.m. and I had to get a move on. Tom would want some more answers before I could leave. The truth was always a good idea, but in this case I wasn't so sure. I wanted to talk to my mother before I was hauled to the police station again. "I'll be off at eight. Dinner?"

"I might be working."

"Felicia?" I asked.

"No one's seen her in two days."

Since Ralph died. "Don't her parents know where she is?"

"Let's just say that she hasn't been on the best of terms with them," Vinny said, his voice tired. Had he gone out looking for her when he left here last night? "Did you get a call last night? I mean, I wasn't there. . . ." His voice trailed off.

I thought about the hang-up. "Yeah," I said quietly.

His silence told me how worried he was. I thought

about telling him about the photographs at Ralph's, but decided against it at the moment. I didn't want to get into it over the phone and with Tom here.

"Hey, I have to get back out to Tom and get to work. Call me later?"

"Yeah, love you," he said, hanging up before I could respond.

I stared at the phone. First the note and now this. Jesus. Like it was something we said all the time.

"Annie?" Tom's voice pulled me out of my thoughts.

He was chewing on a Munchkin when I came back into the living room. "Vinny was just checking in," I said, putting the phone back in its cradle.

"Figured." He pushed his sleeves up farther on his arms, like that was going to make it cooler in my apartment. "So, now do you want to tell me why you lied about being at Ralph Seymour's apartment?"

"You didn't find any of my fingerprints inside, did you?" I asked again, wishing I hadn't finished the iced coffee.

Tom's gaze leveled on my face. "No." He waited. "Why don't you just tell me why you were there?" Now that he'd offered up the revelation about Ralph's true cause of death, he was all official and shit again. I could see he'd been hoping I'd volunteer the information so he wouldn't have to. He should know better by now.

"You're not going to take me in?" I gave him a little smirk, and his mouth twitched, like he wanted to smile, but he didn't.

"You weren't inside, as far as we know. There was no crime, as far as we know." I didn't like the way he kept saying "as far as we know."

I went to the big fan in the window and turned it on. A whoosh of air was yanked out of the room and recirculated. If there wasn't a grate on the fan, it could devour a chicken like those jet-engine tests.

I killed a few more seconds while making myself comfortable on one of the chairs around the island. Tom was being unusually patient.

"Priscilla was here last week," I said, knowing he could be as persistent as me. "She gave me those clothes I was wearing the other night."

His expression changed slightly. I didn't want to give him the satisfaction of asking whether they'd taken a close look at those clothes yet, so I continued with the subject at hand.

"I told her about the phone calls, and she thought it was Ralph, too. She knew where he was living; he'd called her when he moved in. She didn't think he'd start stalking me again or she would've told me sooner about him being back here. But she said I should to talk to him, confront him. I didn't want to, but sometimes with Priscilla it's just easier to go along than argue when she gets something stuck in her head. I made her go with me, though. We went over there—it really wasn't my idea—and we knocked. He didn't answer. I tried the doorknob, but it was locked. We left. End of story."

I wished it were that easy. I wished I could tell him that I'd left my business card—not that Ralph didn't have my phone numbers already, but I wanted him to know that I knew—but I just wasn't ready to tell Tom everything yet. If I told Tom, there would be more questions, and I might feel obligated to answer. As it was, Tom seemed placated, at least for the moment, so I brushed aside any guilt.

"So you didn't see him."

"No."

He studied my face, looking for a clue that I was lying, but he couldn't find it. He nodded. "Okay." He started toward the door.

"That's it?" I asked.

Tom shrugged. "Yeah. For now." But he stopped again in the doorway. "If there's anything else, you should tell me."

I sighed. "Yeah, I know."

He stared at me a few seconds. "Be careful, though, okay? You get any more calls, let me know right away."

I nodded, and he closed the door behind him. I

grabbed another Munchkin and watched him from the living room window as he got into his Impala and drove off.

I took a cold shower, found a clean pair of khaki capris and a white T-shirt. I tied on a basic pair of Keds. Saturday summer work attire. I figured it looked presentable enough for the quilters.

I paused, wondering if I should replace the T with the Sturgis one. Probably not. The skull would freak out the old ladies.

But I realized as I went down the stairs, my bag slung over my back, that it wasn't the little old ladies who were freaked-out.

It was me.

Tom's words sneaked back into my head, and I wondered who the hell had been taking pictures of me. Pictures that Ralph had found it necessary to keep in his apartment. Was it him? Had he been watching me himself? Or, as I suspected as I spoke to Vinny, had he hired someone to photograph me?

I looked both ways as I crossed the street to my car, not so much for safety as for paranoia. Nothing looked out of place. I glanced across the square toward Vinny's building, but I didn't see his Explorer at the curb. He'd probably headed out after he talked to me.

I kept my eye on the rearview mirror the whole way to my mother's. When I finally pulled into her driveway, I sighed with relief, but then caught myself. What did I have to be relieved about? I hadn't noticed anyone tailing me before, either.

I consoled myself with the thought that I hadn't been looking for anyone.

My mother was scrubbing the upstairs bathroom when I arrived. Bill Bennett was nowhere to be seen.

"He's doing errands," she said as she vigorously scoured the toilet with the brush. Her hands were covered in bright green rubber gloves. I recognized them; she'd given me my own pair, but they made my hands sweaty, so I never wore them.

Her hands weren't going to get sweaty in here today. The AC was on so high, icicles could form on my head. While my apartment was way too hot, this house was way too cold. I shivered in my light T-shirt.

"Mom, I've got something important to talk to you about," I said as she stuck the brush back in its little container behind the toilet.

She stood up. I was a little taller than she was, which had been disconcerting when I first began growing. Now I was used to it. Without makeup, she looked her age; lines creased the corners of eyes and her skin had started to get that transparency like crepe paper. A lot of women were getting Botox treatments these days, and I gave her credit for allowing herself to grow older without the benefit of science or surgery. Her hair was as dark as usual, but she'd started to have it colored a few years back. We didn't look alike, but I wondered how my face would change in twenty-five years.

"It's Ralph, isn't it?" she asked, sidestepping past me out into the hall, pulling off the gloves.

I followed her down the stairs to the kitchen, where she had a pot of coffee brewing. She poured each of us a cup and we sat at the table, the sunlight illuminating the bright white room.

I opened my mouth to speak, but she held up her hand to stop me.

"I didn't tell you because grand jury investigations are secret."

"But he was dead," I tried, knowing the lawyer in her was going to win this one.

"We didn't know then that it wasn't murder. I couldn't risk it. It's a federal case."

Again I thought about Paula. I wondered whether she knew about this, and if she did, whether she knew Ralph was my ex-husband. Paula wasn't like Priscilla. I hadn't known her as long and I didn't tell her too much about my marriage and divorce. Maybe a mention in passing— I couldn't remember if I'd even called him by name.

"I still can't tell you anything, and your friend at the FBI can't, either," she said, reading my mind.

I sighed. "Tom told me some things this morning. I have to ask you, did Ralph tell you that he had pictures of me?"

The puzzled look on her face indicated he'd said nothing. "What sort of pictures?"

"If *he* wasn't spying on me, he had someone doing it for him," I said, relating everything Tom said.

Her worried expression concerned me. "You didn't know anything?" I asked.

My mother got up and poured herself another cup of coffee. She held up the pot, asking me without words whether I wanted more, but I shook my head. Between this one cup and the iced latte Tom brought me, I'd had enough caffeine. She carried her cup back to the table. "When Ralph came to me, he didn't say a word about you."

"Why did you take him on as a client?" I asked. "You never liked him."

"I don't have to like my clients."

The words hung suspended in the cold air between us. I gripped my coffee mug a little tighter, warming my hands on it. "So you took him on like anyone else?"

"I took him on as a favor to Ira."

Ira Hoffman was one of my mother's law partners. "Ira? What does he have to do with this?"

"Let's just say it was a favor for a favor for a favor." I could tell by her tone she didn't want me to ask any more questions.

She should know me better than that.

"Whose favor, ultimately, was it?"

She shifted a little in her seat, debating mentally with herself. Finally, "You didn't hear this from me."

Christ, my own mother going off the record. "Okay, okay," I promised, if it would get me some information.

"Ralph was a friend of Reginald Shaw's. You know who the Reverend Shaw is, right?" She didn't wait for an answer. "Shaw came to Ira about it, said he owed Ralph and wanted to get him the best representation he could."

Chapter 18

Shaw? What was up with this?

"What did he owe him?" I asked. "I mean, what did Shaw owe Ralph?"

My mother shrugged. "I don't know. All I know is, Ralph was very complacent, wanted to repent for his 'sins,' as he called them." She emphasized the word with her fingers. "I just figured he'd found Jesus or something like that, and Shaw had helped him."

But that didn't explain why Shaw would owe him; it would have been the other way around.

I thought about my conversation with the good reverend yesterday. If he'd known that Ralph was my ex, he didn't show it in any way. Maybe he didn't know. Why would he?

Although Jack Hammer had. And I'd seen Jack and Shaw looking rather friendly at the nature center. Jack had indicated at Rouge Lounge that he knew all about me. There was no reason why Ralph wouldn't have told Shaw about me, too.

My thoughts were circling the runway, but they had nowhere to land.

My mother was watching me try to work it all out. She cocked her head and lifted her chin. "What do you know?"

I sighed. "I have no idea. I met Shaw yesterday. Doing a story about the community garden program he's working on with some city kids. I hadn't met him until then."

I paused. "Do you know a Jack Hammer? I mean"—
what was his real name? Oh, yeah.—"John Decker?"

She was visibly startled. "How do you know him?"
she asked sharply.

"He was at the Rouge Lounge the other night when
Ralph died," I said. "I met him then, and I saw him
yesterday again at the nature center. After I met with
Shaw. How do *you* know him?"

"I can't say."

Jack was involved somehow in all this shit with Ralph.
"Was he selling guns illegally, too?"

My mother toyed with her mug for a second, then
lifted her eyes to my face. "I'm not at liberty to say
anything about Mr. Decker."

"So the investigation is ongoing, even though Ralph
is dead?"

She shook her head. "The only thing I can say is that
Ralph was not the only one involved in this. He was
cooperating with the authorities; I was trying to help
him."

I knew what that meant: Ralph was naming names to
get a lesser sentence if indicted and convicted.

"I can't divulge any other information at this point,
Anne," my mother was saying. She got up and took her
mug and mine to the sink. "Bill's going to be home
anytime now. Would you like to stay for lunch?"

She knew how to get rid of me.

I slid my chair back and stood. "No, thanks. I have
the weekend shift. Have to get to the paper, anyway."

She came to the door to see me out, and I gave her
a quick kiss on the cheek.

"Oh, by the way, I'm having a barbecue tomorrow.
Would you like to come?" she asked before I could
make my escape.

Shit. One of her parties. That was the last thing I
needed on top of all this. I shook my head. "I doubt it.
I'm exhausted."

She knew I was making excuses, but she didn't call
me on it. Instead, she put her hand on my arm.

"Annie, be careful. I don't know why Ralph had pictures of you—that I can definitely say—but he was into some very serious criminal activity. Please let Tom do his job and find out what was going on with those pictures." She paused, lifted her hand to my cheek. "You might want to keep Vinny close, just in case."

Easier said than done. I tried Vinny on his cell on my way to the paper, but his voice mail picked up immediately, indicating the phone was off. My mother had scared the shit out of me enough so I felt it necessary to tell him as soon as possible about the photographs at Ralph's, and for the first time I didn't think I'd be upset if he insisted on being my twenty-four-hour bodyguard.

I couldn't stop checking my mirrors all the way to work. Even though Ralph was dead, someone was still calling me, so I couldn't say for sure that I wasn't being followed anymore.

As soon as I walked into the newsroom, however, my mood lifted.

"I've got bad news for you." Jane Ferraro was the weekend metro editor, and she truly looked upset. "The quilters had to cancel. The AC went out in the senior center, so they can't meet today."

Darn.

"I'll find you something else to do," Jane said, going back to her desk and shuffling through some papers.

I went to my desk and booted up my computer. While I waited for it, I noticed the red message light blinking on my phone. Instinctively, I tensed up. Was I going to be like this every time I got a phone message? I shook myself out if it and hit my code, then listened.

"Ms. Seymour, this is Reggie Shaw. I just wanted to tell you how lovely it was meeting you yesterday, and if you have any more questions, please don't hesitate to call." Shaw rattled off a number and hung up. I stared at the phone. The number he gave me didn't jibe with the one I had for him, so I replayed the message and scribbled this new one in my notebook. And what was up with the "Reggie"? He hadn't introduced himself so informally the day before.

Jane still hadn't come over with an alternate plan for my afternoon, so on a whim, I Googled Ralph's and Shaw's names together. Nothing. I'd already tried Googling Shaw and came up with a big fat goose egg, so I Googled Ralph and scrolled through a bunch of links to the Colorado White River Rafting Association—they listed a Ralph Seymour as president. I didn't think so. I saw the link to the story from the *Herald* about Ralph's death, but nothing more.

I stared at the screen for a second before Googling Jack Hammer.

I had no idea how popular he was. He was the topic of quite a few blogs about recent male-revue shows, and one of the links would've gotten me in huge trouble with the company if I'd clicked on it, I was sure of that. One of our sports guys had been suspended after visiting porn sites after midnight, when he thought no one would know. It was the same sort of bullshit reasoning as thinking you might be indispensable.

My phone rang, startling me out of my Jack Hammer reverie.

"Newsroom," I answered, making my voice lower than usual so if it was someone I didn't want to talk to, I could pretend it wasn't me.

"Annie? It's Priscilla."

"Hey, there," I said in my normal voice.

"How are you? You never called me back. I talked to Ned. He said he saw you." Priscilla had a habit of answering her own questions, so I didn't have to say too much. But when she paused, I realized it was time for me to participate in the conversation.

"There's been a lot going on," I said, realizing the moment it came out of my mouth how lame it sounded. "Sorry," I tried.

"So what *is* going on?"

Priscilla had actually known where Ralph lived, so she certainly knew more about him than I did. "Do you know why Ralph had pictures of me?" I asked, trying to keep my tone from getting too frosty.

The silence could mean one of two things: She didn't know shit or she did. I waited.

"I have no idea what you're talking about," she said. "What kind of pictures?"

I told her what Tom had said. "You have to tell me if Ralph said anything about me or anything else," I finished.

More silence on the line meant she was digesting this information, either that or she was having her morning coffee. A small sound indicated it was probably the latter.

"Listen, Annie, I don't know anything about any pictures. Do you want me to come out tomorrow?" she asked. "I've got tomorrow off. We can talk about this face-to-face." She paused. "Ned thought maybe we should all get together."

"For what, a fucking wake for Ralph?" I asked, a little too loud because Jane looked up from her desk, frowning. I lowered my voice. "Come on, Priscilla. You guys can mourn all you want, but I really don't give a shit one way or the other whether he's dead."

Okay, so maybe that was an overstatement. I did care, but only because I wanted to find out why he had those pictures, and if he were alive, it would be a helluva lot easier to find out.

"You could ask Ned about the pictures, see if he knew about them. The phone calls, too," Priscilla said.

That made sense, but before I could respond, the scanner started to screech. Priscilla was saying something, but I tuned her out as I listened to the report of a shooting. On the city's Green at one of the bus stops. I glanced around the newsroom. I was the only reporter. Jane was the only other person in the newsroom. She was looking anxiously in my direction. Should she send me or would she catch shit?

"Listen, Priscilla," I said quickly, "I've got to go. If you want to come in tomorrow, let me know." I hung up and jumped out of my seat, going over to Jane.

"You have to send me," I said flatly.

It was bigger than me, and she knew that. The city's annual International Festival of Arts & Ideas had just begun. During the festival's two weeks, there were events on the Green, concerts and theater productions and kids' shows, stuff like that, in addition to events scattered throughout the city. I usually didn't get involved because this was the features department's baby.

Jane was shuffling through the brochure with the festival's events listed in it. When she raised her eyes to me, I knew it was bad.

"There's a kids' concert scheduled there in half an hour," she said, her voice full of tension. "Some rip-off of Raffi, I think."

We were both thinking the same thing: Families had probably been gathering for the last hour or so all over the Green.

We could hear the pandemonium on the scanner. We couldn't ignore this just because I wasn't supposed to be covering the beat at the moment. I was the weekend reporter; I was it. That was all there was to it.

Jane gave a slight nod. "I'll get a photographer over there," she said, making a dash for the photo lab.

I grabbed my bag and a notebook off my desk. Fuck Charlie Simmons.

It was news.

Chapter 19

I had to park on Orange Street, near State. A couple of long blocks away. That was the closest I could get.

I jogged up Chapel, the flashing red lights strobelike against bodies and strollers coming toward me, away from whatever danger was behind them. I shoved through the throngs and managed to make it to the intersection with Church Street. Cops were everywhere, the ubiquitous yellow crime-scene tape taut around the old-fashioned-looking steel bus stops that lined the south end of the Green, hugging Chapel Street across from the old Chapel Square Mall, which now housed a Starbucks, Ann Taylor Loft, and Caffe Bottega.

A glance toward the northern end of the Green caught the huge stage, and colorful balloons filled the air like fireworks, floating on the wind.

A cop with a bullhorn was trying to tell everyone to stay calm, but no one was listening. Piercing screams of toddlers and babies pounded against my eardrums as the mass of people scattered at the edges of the Green to try to reach their cars to get to safety.

It was going to be a goddamn traffic nightmare.

I'd never seen anything quite like it.

I reached the edge of the yellow tape, which was slung from the concrete pillar in front of Starbucks across Chapel Street to a parking sign parallel with Church Street, then wound its way in back of the bus stops, and along the width of the Green.

An ambulance sat in the deserted section of Chapel

Street, its siren quiet. But even if it'd been blasting, I'm not sure anyone would've been able to discern that sound from the others.

No one was watching me, and I ducked under the tape, hoping that whichever photographer had caught this assignment was here somewhere, shooting this.

"You're not supposed to be here." A uniformed cop grabbed my arm and started pulling me away, but then a familiar face peered into mine.

Ronald Berger. I nodded at him. "Hey, what happened here?"

He looked at the notebook in my hand, cocked his head at the uniform, who let me go and scurried off to try to control the crowd.

"You shouldn't have done that," Ronald scolded.

I shrugged. "It's my job," I said. "What happened here?" I was in my element, and Charlie Simmons couldn't take this moment away from me.

Ronald looked over at one of the bus stops. Three cops were leading a guy to a police car. "Fired shots."

I nodded at Ronald, scribbling. "Who is he?"

"No ID. And he won't say anything to anyone. It's like he's a fucking mute."

I looked at the guy's dark face, an earring glinting in one ear, his nose broad, his lips pursed tightly, his shoulders stiff. He wasn't looking at anything in particular, just let the cops push his head down and into the car and allowed himself to disappear.

"Not exactly *Dog Day Afternoon*, is it?" I asked, remembering Al Pacino's loud shouting of "Attica!" "So what happened?"

Ronald took a deep breath.

"Witnesses say he was arguing with a girl, and she shouted 'Fuck you' at him and turned around to cross the street. He pulled out a nine-millimeter Glock and took a couple of shots."

"Jesus, no one was hit?"

Ronald snorted. "A guy and his family were sitting on a blanket nearby, waiting for the concert to start. The guy heard the shots, came over, and fucking tackled the

kid, took him down, got the gun. He was sitting on the
guy's back when the first cop showed up." He paused.
"He was the only one sitting still. By then, everyone was
running. Some people just ran over little kids. Little kids,
for fuck's sake." His arm swept across the air, indicating
the Green. I saw more ambulances farther down Church
and Temple streets, EMTs, and gurneys and all that shit
you normally see on TV.

The adrenaline rushed through my body as I took it
all down. "Do you have the girl, the guy who took him
down? Can I talk to them?"

Ronald frowned. "We're interrogating them now." I
followed his eyes over to a small area to our left, cor-
doned off with three cop cars. A tall man wearing a
Yankees baseball cap was talking to one officer. A little
farther down the street, a young woman in a pair of
shorts that showed off long, slender, muscular legs was
also answering questions. Every cop was watching her.

Something about her looked familiar, but I couldn't
place her.

"What's the guy's name? The shooter?"

Ronald was distracted. "It'll be in the press release,"
he said, moving away.

This wasn't the way it was supposed to happen. And
it wasn't going to, if I had anything to say about it. But
I also knew that I needed to give the cops a little more
time to do their job.

Some people weren't fleeing, I noticed now. There
were a few pockets of families huddling, talking among
themselves, not wanting to miss anything. Maybe they'd
even be on TV. The vans were congregated on Temple,
the reporters and cameramen grim-faced as they taped
their segment, showing their outrage and, of course,
compassion.

A group of young black kids was hanging out near
the yellow tape behind the farthest bus stop. Two of
them were straddling bikes.

I had plenty of people I could get quotes from.

I maneuvered under the tape. While I knew Jane
would want a great story about the guy who tackled the

guy with the gun, I'd start with those kids. They might know who the shooter was. This was a small city, and everyone knew everyone in his own world. I at least needed the shooter's name; it would be easier to get information from Ronald later if I had something to start with. I wondered where Tom was. Maybe I'd missed him.

As I turned to take a look, I caught the eye of the girl being interrogated, the alleged reason why the guy had started shooting. She wasn't too far away, in front of the Ann Taylor Loft. Right away my memory kicked into gear.

It was that shot girl. The shot girl at Bar whom Vinny was talking to when I went outside last night. What the hell was her name?

She frowned at me, then turned back to the cops.

I shrugged off a nagging feeling that this might not be a coincidence. Because what the hell else could it be? There are a lot of college girls in this town; Yale and Southern are not the only schools in the area. But on the off chance that my logic was wrong, I stopped amid the chaos and pulled my cell phone out of my bag.

"Remind me of that girl's name at Bar last night. Felicia's friend," I said, without even saying hello, when Vinny answered. Hell, he knew who it was.

"Ashley Ellis," he said.

"Thanks," I said, but I didn't end the call right away.

"You're welcome," he said, and then he was gone.

He didn't even ask why I wanted to know. He didn't ask me shit.

Damn. He was here somewhere. He had to be.

I pushed it out of my head, concentrating on my job. As I approached the knot of young men, I recognized someone else. Jamond, the kid from the garden yesterday. A stroke of good luck, I hoped. Maybe it could get me in with the group.

"Hey, fancy meeting you here," I said to him lightly.

He still wore that do-rag on his head, the uniform of the day. All five were dressed alike in baggy jeans—worn so low I wondered how they stayed on—and white

T-shirts that had to be extra-extra large. They were all pretty skinny, their clothes hanging on them like they each had been the Incredible Hulk and then suddenly shrank back into Bruce Banner and hadn't had a chance to change yet. The bicycles were a reminder of a story I'd done the previous week about kids on bikes who'd been terrorizing people on the sidewalks, ripping purses and shopping bags out of hands as they sped by. I didn't like to stereotype, and maybe these kids were completely innocent. No one had clear descriptions of the bike riders except that they were black kids. As if they all looked alike. Despite their clothes and slim frames, none of these kids resembled one another. Well, except for the scowls.

If I was to place a bet, I'd say they weren't here for that children's concert.

Jamond frowned at me. I ignored him.

"I'm Annie Seymour with the *Herald*. Did you guys know the guy who was shooting?" I asked.

They all shifted a little, taking quick looks at one another. Who was going to speak first? Was anyone going to?

"We was jus' waitin' for the bus," Jamond finally said when all eyes landed on him.

On bikes? Oh yeah, I'd seen buses with bikes on the rack on the front grille. Not out of the realm of possibility. "With him?" I asked.

More shifting. These kids sure as hell knew who that guy was.

"How do you guys know Ashley?" I asked, indicating the girl and taking a wild guess that they did know her.

This time the shifting was accompanied by some smirks and winks between them. My instincts were right.

"Was she dating him?" I asked. "Is that why he shot at her? What did she do that pissed him off?"

Jamond started chuckling. "Dating him? You mean, fucking him? Yeah, sure she was. And he was pissed, because she fucked him more ways than one."

I knew he was trying to shock me, but he didn't know me. "Fucked him how?" I asked.

More shuffling, but no one said anything.

"Was she cheating on him?" I tried.

Jamond shook his head; the look on his face told me he thought I was an idiot. While yesterday he'd seemed almost friendly, today, among his friends, he wasn't going to let on about our previous encounter.

"How long have Ashley and your friend been together?" I asked. "What's his name again?"

"Listen, Michael don't—"

One of the other guys shot a look full of daggers, and Jamond stopped. Okay, so the guy's name was Michael, but Michael what?

"Michael doesn't what?" I asked, directly to Jamond, who looked me straight in the eye, but a wall had gone up and I knew he wasn't going to say anything else. He was probably going to catch shit from his friends after, and I guess I should've felt bad about that, but I didn't. This was my goddamn job.

I took another shot in the dark. "Do you guys know someone named Felicia, a girl who works with Ashley?"

Instead of smirking this time, each of them tensed, their shoulders raised, backs hunched, heads down, eyes skirting the sidewalk. I'd struck a nerve. "I've been looking for Felicia. Do any of you know where she is?"

More silence.

I sighed. I wasn't going to get anything else out of this group. I pulled a few business cards out of my bag and handed them out. They took them, holding them tentatively as I said, "If you want to talk at some point, I don't have to use your names. It can be off the record."

I didn't wait for a reaction. I knew there wouldn't be one. They'd drop the cards on the ground, make a show of how stupid it would be to talk to me. But maybe, just maybe, one of them would hold on to his card and call me. It was my only chance.

"That was interesting." The voice came from behind me, and I didn't turn around.

"So, how did Ashley fuck with Michael?" I asked. "Did she say anything about a Michael last night?"

Vinny fell into step beside me, his hands in the pockets of his khakis. He was wearing a blue cotton blazer, which I knew without seeing it was covering his gun. He wouldn't wear a sport jacket if he weren't carrying. Even though it was about 110 degrees, he wasn't sweating.

"She got pretty friendly when you went outside," he admitted, looking at me apologetically, but I waved my hand in the air.

"Why wouldn't she?" I asked, and his expression changed; a smile took over his mouth. I wanted to slip my hand into the crook of his arm, but it wouldn't be very professional at a crime scene. Instead, I touched his shoulder, hoping he'd know from that gesture I was happy our "fight" was over.

"She said something about someone named Reggie, not Michael," Vinny said as we walked.

I stopped.

"What?" he asked.

"What did she say?"

Vinny shrugged. "Said something about how unless I was willing to pay for a little more than a shot, she was going to catch shit with Reggie." He snickered. "It was pretty obvious what 'a little more' meant." When I didn't respond, he frowned. "What? What's going on?"

"It may have nothing to do with anything—it may just be a coincidence," I said slowly, "but Reverend Shaw's first name is Reggie."

Chapter 20

The minute I said it, it sounded ridiculous. But Vinny wasn't laughing.

"There has got to be more than one Reggie in this city," I said, trying to convince myself that it was stupid to even make the connection. I had been trying to find something ugly on Shaw ever since he came into town. This would be too easy.

But I didn't have time to ponder it further, because the guy who'd tackled Michael was being escorted our way. He and the cop stopped at a woman holding a little girl who may have been around two or three, her hand on the handle of a stroller that was built like a fucking Hummer. I took a couple of quick strides.

"You're the guy who tackled the shooter, right?" I asked the man, ignoring the cop.

The guy looked at me. He was big, bigger up close than I'd thought, with a thick neck and large shoulders. He smiled shyly, but the twinkle in his eye told me he was enjoying this.

His wife, however, was not.

"Can we get going now?" she asked him, ignoring both me and the cop.

As a good husband should, he addressed her first. "They said they've got some more questions for me." I was taking notes as he spoke. "Can you take Isabella home? They said they'll take me home after."

She didn't want to do it, but nodded, allowed him to kiss her cheek.

"Can I get your name?" I interrupted.

She glared at me, Isabella picked her nose, and he nodded. "Joe Minotti."

"You're kidding." Vinny's voice came from behind me, and he held out his hand. "It's really good to meet you." Vinny turned to me. "This guy was all-American for Notre Dame High School in 1994."

A football player. Great. But I saw the potential for the story. Former high school football star tackles shooter. Fantastic headline.

"What happened?" I asked.

The cop tried to move between us, but I shook my head. "Listen, this'll just take a few minutes. Detective Berger said it was okay." I crossed my fingers under my notebook. Ronald was too busy to keep track of me, and by the time he found out I lied about this, I'd be long gone and the story already filed, probably.

Joe Minotti took off his Yankees ball cap and ran a hand through sweat-soaked dark hair. I could see tufts peeking up over the collar of his T-shirt. "We were just sitting on the blanket, waiting for the concert. We got here late, Isabella was acting up, and we had to sit way back here." He paused, looking at his wife, who was still standing there but wasn't interrupting. He took that as the okay to continue. "I saw them arguing. He was shouting." He leaned closer to me, cupping his mouth, and said, "He told her she was a fucking whore." After a second, he added, "Sorry."

I never understood why it was okay for guys to use the word "fuck" with one another, but they had to get a conscience with a woman. I shook my head. "It's okay. Go on." Vinny was trying not to laugh.

"I saw him pull the gun out from under his T-shirt and take a couple of shots. I had a straight shot—he wasn't standing behind the bus-stop enclosure, just off to the side of it. I was pretty fast in high school, and I haven't slowed too much, despite a few pounds." He patted his stomach, which looked pretty flat to me. I bet he still did a hundred crunches a day. "So I went after him, got him to the ground, and took the gun. It was adrenaline, mostly. Like when I played, you know." He looked at Vinny like Vinny knew what it was like to play football. He didn't know Vinny was a chess geek.

But Vinny was nodding in that male-solidarity shit that happens when two guys are telling their war stories.

"Did you hear what she said to him when she crossed the street?" I asked.

"Last thing I remember, she told him to fuck off. Sorry."

"Listen," the cop interrupted. "The detective still needs to talk to him."

I nodded. "Sure." I had more than enough. "Can I talk to Ashley?" I pointed over at the girl who'd prompted the shooting. She had Ronald Berger's ear pretty good.

The cop shrugged.

With Vinny on my heels, I tried to get past the crime-scene tape, but I couldn't get the uniforms standing sentry to let me go farther. I watched Berger talking to Ashley; he was taking notes, and she was casually braiding her hair at the back of her head like this sort of thing happened every day. All the cops were watching her; the shorts were short, and the legs were long. Too bad she didn't have any of those test-tube shots on her—she'd make a killing with this crowd.

I sighed. "Can't get her now," I said more to myself than to Vinny, who was still beside me.

I scanned the crowd and spotted some people who had not fled because the curiosity factor was too strong. I spent the next fifteen minutes talking to them, getting more color for the story. When I was done, I turned to Vinny.

"I have to go write this up. Are you following me?"

"To your car. You'll be okay at the paper, right? I have some things to take care of."

I nodded reluctantly, wishing my expression had given away that I wanted him to stick by me. The specter of Ralph's pictures hung over me, and the thought of leaving the security of a crowd was giving me heart palpitations. Realistically I knew Vinny couldn't be with me

24-7, and I had to get over it. I told myself that whoever was calling might not have been taking the pictures. The latter had to have been Ralph, and he was dead. End of story. The phone call last night could've been a wrong number.

I had to believe that or I was screwed.

"I'll meet you back at your place tonight at eight, okay?" Vinny said.

As we walked back to my car, I hoped tonight would turn out a lot better than last night did. And if he was with me, at least I wouldn't get another phone call.

That wasn't the caller's MO.

I thought Jane was going to have a goddamn orgasm in the middle of the newsroom when I told her about Joe Minotti and his all-American fucking tackle. She found an old picture of him in the archives, and Wesley had been lurking around the crime scene and gotten a picture of Minotti talking to the cops as well as a shot of Michael being herded into the police car. I'd stopped wondering why I never saw Wesley at any of these places. He knew just how to do it: Get the best shot and get out of there.

I tried to call Berger to see if I could get to Ashley somehow, but no dice. On a whim, I dialed Tom's cell number but the voice mail picked up right away, indicating his phone was off. It was odd, not seeing him at the scene or being able to reach him. I wondered where he was, since he'd been to see me in the morning.

There was no listing for an Ashley Ellis in the phone book. I wondered if Shaw would admit it if I asked him whether he knew her. The comment about "Reggie" still stuck with me.

Ronald had the press release faxed over, and Michael's last name was Jackson. How unfortunate for him. He was charged with attempted murder and illegal possession of a firearm. Bail was set at a quarter of a million dollars, arraignment scheduled for Monday morning.

It was a pretty straightforward story, but Jane wanted more background on Minotti, so she got one of the sports boys to pull something together. I had to weave it into my story, and since most other writers aren't as fast as I am, it was almost eight o'clock by the time Jane gave me the okay to go home.

"You don't think Simmons will have a problem with this?" I asked her.

Jane sighed. "He called. While you were out there. Wanted to know what we were doing. He seemed okay about it, especially when I told him we really didn't have a choice because no one else was here but you."

If I was lucky, this could mean that they wouldn't schedule me on weekend shifts for a while, since having only one or two reporters meant I had to actually cover shit.

But I usually wasn't that lucky.

"He did want me to call Dick," Jane was saying.

"What?"

"I couldn't reach him."

Too bad. He and TV reporter Cindy Purcell were probably away for the weekend or something. I had seen the Channel 9 van at the scene, but I hadn't seen her.

When I stepped outside, it was still bright. The sky over Yale's Harkness Tower hadn't faded yet into pinks or oranges, and I reveled in it. Despite the heat of the last couple of days, I liked summer best of all the seasons because of the light. My usual crankiness settled into a more harmonious mood as the days stretched out like big elastic bands before snapping back into a cold, dark autumn.

Once in my Civic, I turned up Mick Jagger and started singing as I made my way toward Wooster Square, my brownstone, and Vinny.

My cell phone interrupted me, and I pulled over, put on my hazard lights, and glanced at the number on the front screen. I didn't recognize it. A small panic seized me, and I flipped the cover. "Hello?"

"Anne Seymour?" It was a soft voice, a woman, with sort of a Marilyn Monroe thing going on.

"Who's asking?"

"Felicia Kowalski."

Not whom I expected, but I didn't know what to expect. "Yes?" I asked.

"Heard you're asking about me."

Jamond and his friends must have gotten her the message.

"That's right," I admitted. "We had a mutual acquaintance."

"I told him I didn't want to do it," she said, her voice suddenly stronger.

"Not do what?"

"Listen, it's not my fault. None of it's my fault. Just tell the cops that, okay?"

What the hell was she babbling on about? "Why don't we meet at the paper in the morning?" I suggested. "Jane Ferraro's been trying to reach you anyway, wants to know why you blew off that chamber breakfast yesterday."

"I can't do that shit now." Her voice had turned hysterical. It was sort of like trying to deal with that kid in *The Exorcist*. Who the hell knew what would come out of her next?

"What can't you do?" I prodded. "Talk to Jane? I'm sure she'd understand, you know, with Ralph—"

"You know, you're not innocent in this, either." Her voice was tight, accusing now. "So don't pretend you are. I know about you."

"What—"

"Just—"

"Just tell the cops it's not my fault." And she ended the call.

I stared at the small phone in my hand, flipping the cover closed. What did she do? And what wasn't her fault?

The clock on the dashboard told me it was getting closer to eight thirty than eight o'clock now; the sky was shimmering like it does just before dusk starts to fall. I thought about Vinny waiting at my apartment. I wanted to talk to Paula, my FBI friend, alone, without anyone listening, even Vinny. But I also didn't want to talk to her while I was sitting by the side of the road.

Maybe I could get Vinny to pick up some cannoli at

Libby's for dessert. That's right. He'd do that, he'd take the walk, and I could call Paula. I turned off the hazards and started to pull out.

The phone interrupted me again.

This time I recognized the number.

"I'm on my way," I told Vinny.

"Something came up. I'm going to be pretty late," he said.

Even though I wanted him to leave me alone, I wanted it to be only for a little while, not indefinitely. "What's happened?"

"Felicia Kowalski's parents filed a missing-persons report on her a few hours ago."

Chapter 21

"Jesus, Vin, I was just talking to her."

"What?"

"She called me. She said I should tell the cops it wasn't her fault. I'm not sure what that meant."

"She called you? How?"

"On my cell." I wondered for a second how she got the number. From the paper, maybe, or more likely from Jamond. I'd given him my card earlier, and it had my cell number on it. He knew I wanted to talk to her. And obviously he did know where she was.

But something else nudged my memory. Jack Hammer had given me back the card with my phone numbers on it. Ralph had had the numbers, and she had been with Ralph. . . .

Vinny interrupted my thoughts. "Your mother told me about those pictures," he said. "Why didn't you? We were together this afternoon."

"Yeah, and I was covering a fucking story," I said. "It wasn't about me then. I had a job to do."

He chuckled. "Shit, Annie, don't get your panties in a bunch. I know that, and I'm sorry, okay?"

We were apologizing to each other a lot these last couple of days, and I didn't like that.

"Can you give me the number that Felicia called you from?" Vinny was asking.

I punched a couple of buttons on my phone and got the number as the last call received and recited it to him.

"Thanks."

"So, where are you?" I asked.

"I'm going to meet with Felicia's parents. Your mother thinks her disappearance has something to do with Ralph, and Ira wants me to talk to them."

"But the cops are involved now, right? Why you?"

Silence indicated he wasn't going to tell me anything. I left it alone. "Okay. Call me or come by if you're done early."

"Definitely." Another second of silence, then, "Listen, later, when I get there, I want to know everything you know about those pictures. I also want you to be very careful. Go straight home, lock the doors. I'll be there when I can. Don't let anyone in but me, okay?"

"Yeah, sure," I said, trying to sound unconcerned, but his worry was infectious.

"Want me to get you a replacement gun? For the time being?"

"Jesus, Vin, if Tom found out I was carrying again, he'd have my ass."

He chuckled. "Yeah, you're right. But does he have to know?"

"It's not necessary," I said, trying to convince myself as much as him.

"We'll talk about it later," Vinny said. "Be careful."

We ended the call. I found myself back on the road, the sun most definitely setting now. Darkness was moving in quickly, and I had to turn my headlights on.

I thought about Ralph and Felicia, Ralph's death and Felicia's disappearance. I wondered about the connection. How much did Felicia know about Ralph's scheme? As I drove home, Mick Jagger in the background, I started getting really pissed about Ralph and his photographs of me. What the hell had he been up to?

It was easier to deal with anger than with fear.

My stomach growled, reminding me that I hadn't had dinner. Vinny had told me to go straight home, but I was hungry. Where to get something quick?

Thai food was always good, and a whole crop of Thai places had opened up on Chapel Street just beyond York. My favorite was Bangkok Gardens, on the corner. A glance at the clock on the dashboard told me it was enough past the usual dinnertime that I could probably get a seat without waiting.

I parked just down Chapel and walked back up, past the Clare Jones boutique, into which I'd mistakenly wandered at one point and found myself being dressed in some sort of shirt that had to be wrapped every which way by the very effervescent Clare. I knew that without help it would just end up making me look like I was wearing a goddamn straitjacket and I'd be the brunt of too many jokes to actually buy the thing. I ended up with a pair of dangly earrings that were still waiting for their first date.

The waiter led me to a small table in the front corner of the restaurant, and I immediately ordered the pad Thai and a Thai iced tea. As I'd walked up, I'd concocted a plan for after dinner that I'd need to be alert for, and while I wanted a beer, it wasn't a good idea. Vinny wouldn't be happy, but it shouldn't take too long. It was something I needed to do, had to do.

While I waited, I watched the other diners, looked out the window at people walking along the sidewalks. Someone familiar caught my eye; he was waiting at the corner for the light to change.

Ned Winters.

Weird that after all these years in the city together, I never ran into him anywhere, never saw him anywhere. And suddenly here he was, standing at the corner of York and Chapel, just a day after I'd seen him for the first time since Ralph and I split.

A young woman came up to him; his arm circled her waist and he kissed her on the lips. She pulled away from him abruptly. The streetlight illuminated her face, but I didn't recognize her. She was young, thin, streaks of red through short, unevenly cropped dark hair, a white tank top hugging high, pert breasts, a longish, swishy beige skirt leaving little to the imagination, and ballerina flats that kept her at Ned's height. I wouldn't be surprised if she was a student of his.

They crossed the street just as the waiter brought me my food, and I forgot about Ned Winters as I dug my fork into a luscious shrimp, savoring its texture against the crushed peanuts.

I sipped the last of my iced tea, slurping a little, causing the elderly woman at the next table to glare at me. I didn't have the energy to glare back. I was too busy trying to convince myself that what I was about to do was justified. But then, not a lot of what happened recently had been the right thing. Ralph had only himself to blame, though, for what had gone wrong.

We didn't have a big wedding. My mother still hadn't forgiven me for that. Instead, we flew to Vegas and eloped. Part of the reason why my mother never forgave me was that my father stood up with us at the Elvis wedding chapel. Ralph and I both wore jeans and T-shirts. My father wore a frown.

I'd made him promise not to call my mother, and he didn't like Ralph much more than she did. But he did get us a suite at the Tropicana, where he was working at the time.

I had just graduated, and Ralph was already working at the midsized daily near the Catskills in New York State. I'd applied for a reporter position there, and I found out the day after we got married that I'd gotten the job. We would live in Ralph's one-bedroom apartment, and we'd stay there for a couple of years before we could get onto a bigger paper, like the *Times*. We both wanted to work for the *New York Times*.

Maybe I would've made it. Maybe I would've been there now, if I hadn't run home to Westville, to my mother, to where I felt safe.

Staying had become a habit I couldn't break.

I shook off those thoughts as I drove up Whalley Avenue. Instead of turning to my left, which would've brought me into my mother's neighborhood, I turned up Fitch, toward Southern Connecticut State University.

This stretch of Fitch changed from looking like a cute little suburb with one-family houses—but with some crime issues—to apartment buildings and college dorms. I drove under the walkway and continued past campus down to Arch Street, where I turned right.

This area is cluttered with houses right on top of one another, mostly multifamily, some Victorian, some ugly 1960s duplexes, so close you could hear someone in the next house breathe. The old stomping ground from our college days had been where Ralph had last laid his hat, so to speak, and although when I'd come here with Priscilla, it hadn't seemed odd, it did now. Why did Ralph move back here?

The front of the two-family house where Ralph had lived was in pretty good shape, considering. It had been freshly painted a grayish blue color with pale yellow shutters. The house next door was shedding its paint, revealing the dull wood underneath; it was the drab color of white underwear after it had gotten mixed up in the color load. All the houses here had postcard-sized lawns in front; some had wraparound porches. One had wooden patches over its windows and the black scars of fire. I'd covered that one, just a month ago. Had Ralph already started watching me by then, or had he seen me there and begun his surveillance afterward?

As I sat in my car in front of the house, I thought about the phone call last night and despite my best efforts to convince myself otherwise, knew someone was still watching me. Was he—or she, I couldn't discriminate—watching me now? I pushed the thought away, because my curiosity was stronger than any fear at the moment.

I grabbed a flashlight out of the glove box, got out of the car before I could talk myself out of it, and climbed the steps to the front porch. Ralph's apartment was accessible through the door on the left, and there was a white piece of paper stuck to the door and the doorjamb, announcing that by order of the city police department no one was to enter. I'd hoped I could just walk in, but I'd have to break it, announcing that someone had disobeyed. I hoped that all suspicion would be off me at this point.

I touched the doorknob, knowing it would be locked. But this time I had an advantage.

I had a key.

Chapter 22

The paper ripped as the door opened easily. I pulled the key back out of the lock, turned the flashlight on, and shut the door behind me.

Okay, so it was a fine line between this and actual breaking and entering.

I shone the light across the room and felt like I was in the middle of a *CSI* episode. I could never understand why, when they could, they didn't just turn the lights on. But the longer I moved the light around, the more I could see the allure in using a flashlight, the mystery of it. It certainly gave the room an eerie glow. But those *CSI* folks didn't need to hide.

I did.

Ralph's apartment was sloppy. I didn't know if it was from the police search or if he'd never changed his ways from college, when he'd take a piece of clothing off and just leave it where he was at the moment. I played wifey and picked everything up. Idiot.

The living room was barely furnished. A well-worn sofa sat along one wall facing a large, flat-screen TV perched on a long coffee table that looked like it was probably salvaged from the dump or left in front of someone's house for the garbage collector. Ralph had loved picking up pieces of other people's lives. We'd furnished our apartment by borrowing a friend's pickup and driving around neighborhoods.

It didn't seem weird at the time, but now it skeeved

me out. It was either age or another pet peeve about Ralph, probably a little bit of both.

I kicked a couple of T-shirts and a sweatshirt to the side and made my way into the kitchen. The sink was overflowing with dirty dishes—couldn't blame the cops for that one—and Ralph used the tabletop as a cabinet, since there were precious few of them. Three boxes of Cap'n Crunch were lined up as if at attention behind a jar of peanut butter and something in a Tupperware container. I wasn't going to look.

A cursory flash of the light showed me there was nothing here I wanted to see, so I followed the bobbing beacon down the hallway and into a bedroom. A mattress lay on the floor—no box spring, no frame—and the heavy scent of sex hung in the air, mixed with vanilla. A quick flip of the flashlight to the dresser indicated a fat candle sunken in the middle with a black wick. The bedsheets were twisted and halfway off the mattress. Again, there was no way of knowing whether Ralph had left it this way.

Besides myriad shirts, jeans, socks, and underwear on the floor, there was nothing on the walls, nothing on the dresser except the candle. The mattress and the dresser were the only pieces of furniture in the room.

The closet door was open slightly. I didn't want to touch anything—my fingerprints were already on the doorknob outside and I couldn't leave them anywhere else—so I nudged the door open with my toe. More clothes. Nothing but two baseball caps on the shelf above the rack. Yankees. Figured.

A mildew odor permeated the bathroom, and the light reflecting off the mirrored medicine chest made my heart jump for a second. I didn't want to do it, but I picked up the towel off the rack, wrapped it around my hand, and pulled open the cabinet door. Ralph liked prescription medications. Nasonex, Xanax, and Zoloft. Allergic, anxiety-ridden, and depressed. Just what every woman's looking for.

There were so many signs that divorcing the man had been a good idea.

Back in the hall, I saw the door to a second bedroom.
It was halfway closed, so again I used my foot to push
it back. A desk sat propped against the opposite wall.
A dark shade had been pulled down against a window,
but a pile of manila folders had spilled across the desk-
top, scattering papers across it, the chair, and the floor.
I steered my light toward it.

I caught my breath. This was what I'd come for, but
seeing it made it real. Made me take a reality check.

Pictures. Pictures of me. Like Tom had said. And in-
terspersed between them, on top of some of them, were
clips. Newspaper clips, with headlines. And my byline.
Highlighted in yellow.

This was far worse than anything I'd expected. I wondered if there had been more, if the cops had taken
some as evidence.

But evidence of what? That Ralph had a thing for his
ex-wife?

A picture of me and Vinny on the floor caught my
eye, and the light reflected a little, bouncing back into
my eyes like someone had taken my picture with a flash.
I crept closer to it. This picture was taken two months
ago. I knew exactly when, because it was the day we'd
gone kayaking. We were unloading the kayak off the top
of Vinny's Explorer, handing it down to Vinny's brother,
Rocco, who'd come with us.

I shivered. It was cold comfort that Ralph was dead;
what the hell had he been up to with this shit? How
could I have been followed and not notice?

Shining the light closer on the strewn photographs, I
saw myself coming down the steps of my brownstone,
getting out of my car in the parking lot at the *Herald*,
and kissing my mother just outside the door at her house
in Westville.

With each picture, my heart beat faster, and I had to
look away, swallowing hard, blinking back tears from—
well, fear. The phone calls had made me nervous, but
this, well, it was as if the camera lens had raped me.
The photographs taunted me, showing how vulnerable I
was. I wasn't used to being a victim; I was an observer,

an outsider. My hands began to sweat, and it had nothing to do with the heat. The blood pounded in my ears; my knees felt like they were going to give way.

It wasn't a surprise I was so distracted that I barely heard it. But when the front door closed with a distinct thud, my stomach rushed into my throat and I pushed the button on the flashlight with my thumb, bathing myself in darkness. Without the light, I didn't know where to go; my eyes hadn't adjusted, and I could see nothing. I thought about the Xanax in the medicine cabinet; what I wouldn't give to have one of those suckers right now. But I didn't, so as I tried to calm myself, I glanced quickly around the room, looking for a hiding place.

Footsteps moved through the apartment, and a sliver of light crept into the hallway in front of me. I ducked behind the door but was afraid to move it closed for fear it would creak. But whoever it was would smell my fear anyway—I was certain of that.

"Annie?" A hoarse whisper echoed through the hallway.

I didn't recognize the voice.

"Annie?" It was louder now. "I saw your car outside. Where are you?"

I flattened myself farther against the wall behind the door, but the room's overhead light blinded me as the door swung away from me and I found myself staring at Jack Hammer.

"What the hell are you doing here?" he demanded.

I wanted to ask him the same thing. I mean, someone *had* been following me. And he just happens to show up? Seemed like too much of a coincidence. My throat was dry, and I was sure he could hear the hammering in my chest.

"What are you doing here?" he asked again.

I swallowed hard, trying to find some saliva, the ability to speak. Finally, "What are *you* doing here? Are you following me?" I was whispering.

Jack grabbed my arm, and I instinctively pulled away.

"Jesus, Annie, you're not supposed to be in here."

"No shit. And you are?" My voice had come back,

but too loud. Wouldn't you know my smart-ass personality would shine through now.

"I had to get something," he said matter-of-factly. He didn't make an attempt to touch me again.

I stepped out into the hallway, trying to gauge how quickly I could leave the house and get to my car. I regretted that Vinny hadn't suggested replacing my gun earlier, although I might be able to hit Jack hard enough with the flashlight to stun him if he tried anything.

But he didn't. He followed me into the hallway, flipping the switch, so the only light again was from my flashlight.

"Did you know Ralph was following me, taking pictures of me?" I asked, my grip tight on the light as I shone it into his face.

He shielded his eyes. "Shit, Annie, that's too bright."

I moved the light slightly.

"Yeah, I knew," he conceded.

"Did you have any role in this?" I asked.

"I told him he should just call you."

I snorted. Calling me. That was all I thought he was doing.

"You were all he ever talked about," Jack offered before I could say anything.

"But what about Felicia?"

Jack grinned. "Jesus, Annie, she was a good fuck. What else would she have been good for?"

Well, now, I didn't know. "Do you know she's been reported missing?"

Something crossed his face, but I couldn't tell for sure if this was news to him.

"She's a kid. She probably ran off with some guy after she found out about Ralphie and she'll turn up," Jack said, but it was too casual, too, well, something that I couldn't put my finger on.

He had, however, moved very close and put his finger under my chin, tipping my face toward his. I cringed under his touch, every muscle stiffened, and I couldn't move. He didn't seem to notice as he tilted his face back a little to study me for a second before saying, "You have no clue what you're getting into here. You need to stay out of it." And then he dropped his hand and stepped back.

"It's my job to find out what's going on." It was more than that, though, and he knew it.

Jack shook his head. "You're a stubborn bitch, aren't you?"

I was trying to come back with a clever retort when he added, "Just be careful, then. Can you do that?"

I cocked my head in the direction of Ralph's office. "Looks like what I had to be careful about is dead."

Jack Hammer's eyes narrowed. "Don't be too sure."

Exactly what I was afraid of, and I hoped he would elaborate, but he didn't. I had to get my mind off those pictures and get the hell out of here so I could think. I wasn't sure about Jack Hammer, why he was here. I just didn't buy that he had to retrieve something he'd left behind.

To keep myself grounded, to keep the fear away, I had to keep asking questions. "Why are you here?"

"I have to get something," he repeated.

I was about to press him for more, but a red light splashed against the walls. Shit, a police cruiser.

Jack looked at me, put his finger to his lips, then took my hand, pulling me toward the back of the apartment, into the kitchen. Instead of recoiling this time, however, I let him lead the way. Jack twisted the knob on the back door, opened it. I heard paper ripping. The cops had put one of those stickers back here, too. I didn't have time to contemplate that, though, as Jack pushed me outside, then followed me, closing the door quietly behind him. He grabbed my hand again, and we were jumping a short fence that divided Ralph's backyard with the backyard of the house behind his, which fronted another street.

I was out of breath by the time we stopped, two blocks away. Jack was still holding my hand, and I yanked it away.

"What the hell?" I asked.

"Cops."

"No shit."

"We're not supposed to be in there."

"What makes you think they were going there? This isn't a great neighborhood; they could've been going to a domestic or something like that."

"Let's just say I've got an inside track, and I knew they'd show up again. Just didn't realize it would be this soon," Jack said.

Chapter 23

I stared at him. "What exactly were you getting at Ralph's?" I was repeating myself, but determined to do so until I got an answer. "And why don't you think the cops already have it? They've been all over that place. Ralph's death was untimely, and I've got it from the detective in charge that they felt it was necessary to search the apartment."

"He died of a heart attack," Jack said flatly.

"He died of a Viagra overdose," I said, without thinking. A bad habit of mine.

Jack's face showed his incredulity. "Viagra?" he asked, spitting out the word before he doubled over in laughter. "Ralphie?" He shook his head. "No, no, no."

"How can you be so sure he didn't get any help from those little blue pills?" I asked. "I can't imagine that a guy would tell another guy he would need them."

Jack stroked his chin for a second, the laughter subsiding but leaving a smile playing at the corners of his mouth. "You're right about that, I guess. But let's just say I know."

"How?" I couldn't let it alone.

The smile turned into a grin. "Three isn't always a crowd."

I was finding out way too much about Ralph and Jack. I wanted to hit the rewind button and go back to three days ago when my biggest worry was how to get my landlord to fix my air conditioner.

Now all I wanted to do was get my car and go home.

Easier said than done.

Jack and I had walked down the street and turned back toward Arch Street. We were only a couple of blocks away, but we could see all the flashing lights now. We tentatively peered around the house on the corner and looked down at Ralph's. I spotted a tall guy in a Windbreaker with the big telltale FBI on the back. Headlights illuminated his figure, and I recognized Jeff Parker, head of New Haven's FBI office. He was standing next to my car. Another guy came over to him, but this one had the letters ATF on the back of his T-shirt.

I'd never get out of here. But on the upside, I felt safer with the cops there.

"I can give you a ride," Jack Hammer said, startling me out of my thoughts.

I frowned. "No thanks."

"You didn't think this one through," Jack said.

"What are you talking about?"

"Well, when I'm going to break into a house that's been secured by the cops, I make sure I don't park in front."

All right, I was a moron for doing that. But who knew the FBI and ATF would show up? What was left in there? I stole a glance at Jack, who was watching the whole thing like we were in the goddamn movie theater. Were the feds there to get what Jack had left behind?

"My mother said you were a witness in Ralph's grand jury investigation," I said, a little white lie that might get me the truth.

He jerked back, staring at me, startled. "Your mother?"

"She was Ralph's lawyer."

He pondered that a few seconds. "Jesus. She's a fireball." And I could tell by the way he said it that it was definitely a compliment.

"She's my mother, so I don't want to hear about it, okay?" It was disconcerting hearing that from a male stripper. "So, did you know where Ralph kept the guns? Is that why they're there? Is that what you went after tonight?"

"I have no idea what you're talking about." His eyes were wide with what he probably thought looked like innocence, but to me it looked like he was lying through his teeth. "Do you want a ride or not?"

A car slowed down just past us, slamming to a stop. I took two steps to the side and watched Dick Whitfield jump out, his notebook in his hand.

If I'd never been happy to see Dick Whitfield before, I was happy to see him now.

"That's Dick," I said, my voice hoarse. I cleared my throat. "I'll be okay."

"See you around, then."

He turned to go, but I grabbed his arm. "Wait." I paused, then, "Why did you meet with Shaw at West Rock? Is he involved?"

Jack shrugged. "I was going hiking. I thought I told you that."

"Listen, I might want to talk to you again. How can I reach you?"

He shook his head. "I told you. I'll be around." He winked. "When you least expect it."

That was what I was afraid of. But he walked away, and I stood there for a second. I was just about to follow him when—"Annie! What are you doing here?"

Dick had come back to his car. I sauntered over to him, like I was covering the damn thing, just like him. I held the flashlight behind me, hoping he wouldn't notice it.

"Heard about it," I said vaguely. "What about you? You're not working tonight, either." I had to turn the tables on him so he wouldn't question me any further.

"I got a call from a source. They're looking for guns and drugs. This was—well, you know who lived here, right?"

I nodded. "The city cops were all over this place yesterday. Do the feds really think they missed something?"

Before he could answer, two figures came down the steps. To my surprise, however, they were coming out of the apartment next door to Ralph's. Who lived *there*?

The men were carrying black duffel bags, not unlike the one I'd seen Jack Hammer carrying just yesterday at West Rock. I glanced behind me, but he had vanished like the ghost he was.

"What the hell are you two doing here?"

Dick and I turned to see Tom coming toward us, his eyebrows knit with anger.

"Can't keep shit quiet in this city," I said. "Figured we'd see what was up." I cocked my head at the house. "Who lived next door to Ralph?"

Tom looked at Dick for a long second before turning his eyes on me. He stared at me for what seemed like minutes before saying, "I'm not at liberty to say."

"Shit, Tom, it has to be connected to Ralph. I mean, hell, he lived here, too. So who lived there?"

"Even if you don't tell us, we can find out anyway," Dick said without realizing how stupid it was to threaten that.

"Then go ahead," Tom said, confirming my suspicions that he'd call Dick's bluff. He turned to me. "Someone broke into Ralph's apartment." He said it like he knew it was me. But he couldn't prove it.

"How do you know that?" My voice actually sounded normal. Like I really was here covering this.

"We put up a seal, and it was broken." Half his face was hidden in the shadow, the other half illuminated by the streetlamp. I couldn't completely see his expression.

"Why would someone break in?" I asked, trying to act nonchalant.

"I don't know. Why don't you tell me?" Tom said.

"How the hell am I supposed to know?"

We glared at each other for a few seconds. Dick, to his credit, didn't say anything until, "Can you give us anything about what's being confiscated from the apartment?"

Tom shook his head. "This is the feds' game here," he said. "You can ask them, but I bet they won't say anything."

"If it's the feds' game, why are you here?" I asked.

He didn't like that, narrowing his eyes at me, studying my face until I was happy it was dark because then he couldn't see me flush.

I was still holding the flashlight behind me, and I shifted a little. I had left my bag in the car on the floor of the passenger side, but my keys were in my pocket. I didn't have a notebook out, like Dick. Tom noticed, but instead of saying something about it, he just tossed a "Stay back until we're through" before walking away.

Dick looked at me, his eyebrows all furrowed together like a fuzzy caterpillar. "You shouldn't be here," he said, as if he'd finally figured that out. He was so slow on the uptake.

"Don't worry, I won't write about it," I said. "You've got the whole thing." I made it sound like I was handing him everything on a fucking platter, like he was completely competent.

Sad thing was he believed me and grinned. "So you're just here to check it out?"

"Don't tell anyone, okay?" I asked conspiratorially.

"Mum's the word," he whispered.

It was way too easy. But no one ever confused Dick with the sharpest knife in the drawer.

My car was parked just behind the first cruiser. I said good-bye to Dick and pulled my keys out of my pocket, shifting the flashlight and tossing it in when I opened the door. It rolled under the seat just in time.

"What was that?"

Tom was behind me. I didn't turn around, just twisted my neck so I could look at him. "What was what?"

"What did you put in your car?"

I pointed at my bag on the floor in the front. "My bag."

"Someone saw a light in the house. Like a flashlight. When we got the call, I recognized the address and decided to check it out." He was trying to trip me up.

I forced myself not to move, to keep my expression neutral.

"Why are you really here?" His breath was hot; I

could feel the whisper of his day-old growth of beard just underneath my ear.

I shivered.

"Cold?" he asked softly, moving closer, his fingers circling my wrist so I couldn't move.

"No."

"How did you get in?"

"In where?"

"In the house."

My eyes moved up toward Ralph's place of residence. "I don't know what you're talking about."

"Will I find your fingerprints inside this time?"

"No." I wasn't lying. I'd been careful.

"If anyone finds out you were in there, I won't be able to help you."

I was trying to figure out a response when another car pulled up just behind mine. It was a long, sleek Jaguar, one of those cars I always thought about, but even if I could afford one, I knew I couldn't ever take it to a crime scene.

Apparently, the Reverend Shaw wasn't as practical as I was.

Chapter 24

Shaw stepped out of the car, pressing a button on his key fob, and all the doors locked. Like that would keep anyone out in this neighborhood.

"Thank you for calling me, Detective," Shaw said, his hand outstretched and taking Tom's. He saw me and smiled. "And the lovely Ms. Seymour."

Tom's eyebrows shot up into his forehead, but he shook Shaw's hand firmly and didn't say anything.

"I'll give you any information you might need about my tenant," Shaw said.

"Your tenant?" I butted in. Tom gave me a look, but he should know by now that I don't stand on ceremony at crime scenes.

He couldn't stop Shaw from saying, "I own this property."

He did? I began to wonder about land records. I was a bit rusty with hunting them down, but back in the day, when I was covering towns, one of the things I had to do on a daily basis was check land records at town hall to see who was buying what and if anything was worth writing about. When a reporter is covering a town of only about ten thousand people, she'll go anywhere for a story, and land records proved to be a gold mine when it came to learning about new developments and shit like that.

If Shaw owned this house, what else did he own? A quick visit to city hall might tell me. Or maybe just a call to Kevin Prisley, who covered the mayor's office and spent time in the city clerk's office, too.

Tom was leading Shaw away from me, toward Jeff Parker. I knew better than to follow them. Shaw had forgotten me as he was introduced. More hand shaking was going on. I watched for a few seconds, then looked back at my car. Shaw's Jag was close, but I thought I could get out. I was the goddamn Queen of Parallel Parking. I climbed into my Civic and maneuvered the wheel so I just squeaked by the cop car in front of me and without even getting close to Shaw's Jag.

My head was a jumble of thoughts as I made my way back down Fitch to Whalley Avenue toward downtown. The conversation with my mother intruded somewhere between Jack Hammer and the black duffel bags carried out of the apartment.

Shaw had asked Ira Hoffman to represent Ralph in the grand jury investigation. Shaw owed Ralph one, my mother had said. What did he owe him?

I couldn't wrap my head around it. Ralph was living in Shaw's house. That still seemed more like Ralph owed Shaw.

When I reached the end of Whalley where it merged into Elm Street in the midst of the old Gothic buildings that are Yale University, I realized I might have dodged a bullet tonight. I didn't trust Jack Hammer, but if he was the danger he'd warned me about, he hadn't acted on it when he could've. Granted, there were cops everywhere, and all I'd had to do was scream. Now going home alone scared me more than being at Ralph's.

That was fucked-up.

I thought about going to Vinny's. Even if he wasn't home yet, I had a key; he probably wouldn't mind if I let myself in, and then I wouldn't have to deal with any middle-of-the-night creepy calls.

Without stopping in front of my brownstone, I turned left around Wooster Square and pulled up across from Vinny's building, which was similar to my brownstone. It had more perks, however: Besides the central air, there were two washing machines and a dryer in the basement.

Before I got out of my car, I glanced in the rearview

mirror but didn't see any headlights anywhere around
the square. The clock on my dash told me it was ten
thirty—had I been over at Ralph's that long? It seemed
like only minutes—and the lights in Vinny's third-floor
apartment were off, so he still wasn't home.

I sat in the car for a few more seconds with all the
doors locked. I had no clue whether anyone was still
following me. The only person who kept showing up
unexpectedly was Jack Hammer. It seemed my presence
at the house tonight surprised him, too, and he'd expected the police to show up. His warning to be careful
made its way through my head. He knew more than he
was saying.

My heart began to pound in an unfortunately familiar
way as I opened the car door. On impulse, I grabbed
the flashlight. It could do some damage if I had to hit
someone with it.

A shadow crossed the street as I made my way to
Vinny's building. My heart sped up even faster, my feet
skipping more quickly, but then I realized a cloud had
just passed over the bright moon for a second.

I took the steps two at a time and slid the key into
the lock at the front door, opening it and making sure
it was shut securely after I got in. As I climbed the
stairs to Vinny's apartment, relieved I was locked inside,
exhaustion spread throughout my body. I hadn't gotten
much sleep the last couple of days, and I was ready to
pass out.

When I opened the door to Vinny's apartment, I was
hit with a familiar scent. My mother used to take me to
swimming lessons at the YWCA on Howe Street when
I was a kid.

Vinny's apartment smelled like a pool.

It was all the cleaning products. Vinny was neat, really
neat. No dust bunnies at his house, unlike mine, where
I had started to feed them and give them names until I
realized how quickly they would multiply. But it still
didn't get me to pull out the vacuum more than every
few weeks.

Vinny's place, though, well, you could eat off the floor.

The kitchen gleamed. No crumbs on his counters. The bathroom was spotless, not even a drop of toothpaste or one small hair in the sink.

When I'd first met him, I wondered if he was gay. But the kisses quickly assured me otherwise. He was just neat.

I unlaced my sneakers and walked barefoot through the dark living room, knowing I wouldn't run into a pile of newspapers like I would at my place. I also knew that every book was alphabetized by author on the shelf, and even the tops of the picture frames on the walls would be free of dust.

Vinny's king-sized bed beckoned, but I went into the bathroom first after dropping my bag on his couch. My toothbrush was in its slot next to his. He'd made a big show of buying me one to keep here, even though I lived just a block away. I was so nervous it would get all clotted with toothpaste and look out of place that every time I brushed my teeth, I spent ten minutes cleaning it afterward.

The idea of cohabitation scared the crap out of me. I could visit this life every now and then, but I didn't think I could live with it every day. It was another reason why the "love" that had popped up so suddenly was giving me angina.

I pulled my T-shirt over my head and slipped off the capris, carefully folding them and placing them on Vinny's dresser. I unhooked my bra and stuck it between the shirt and capris. A glance in the mirror reminded me that maybe I needed to start working out now that I was almost forty. But the idea of sweating on purpose was about as alluring as cleaning my apartment, so I quickly dismissed it.

While I liked being naked in Vinny's apartment when he was here, I wasn't sure I was comfortable about it when he wasn't. This was the first time I'd let myself in without him already being here, and now I wondered if I shouldn't call him to warn him he'd find me in his bed.

I took one of his T-shirts out of a dresser drawer and slid it over my head. My bag was still in the living room, and even though I could use his phone, I would call him on my cell before turning it off.

I still hadn't turned on any lights, made a detour for the fridge, grabbed a Corona, and started toward the couch.

The phone rang.

I froze.

As the sound echoed through the room, I told myself I was being ridiculous. This was Vinny's apartment; whoever was calling was calling him. I debated a second about answering. If it was his mother, she certainly wouldn't be happy if I picked up the phone. She and I were not on the best of terms. On the other hand, if it was his brother, Rocco, I'd have someone to talk to for a few minutes while my heart started beating again.

I heard a click. Too late. The machine picked up.

"Talk to me." We may have been at opposite poles regarding cleanliness, but we had the same taste in answering-machine messages.

A second passed, then, "Vinny?"

It was a woman. A woman with a breathy voice. A woman with a goddamn sexy breathy voice. It wasn't Rosie, his ex-fiancée. I unfortunately knew her voice too well. No, this was a stranger. And despite my noncommittal feelings, jealousy intruded, even though I tried to tell myself it could be a client. Vinny dealt with a lot of divorce cases when he wasn't tracking someone down for my mother's law firm.

"I just missed you. I'll try you on your cell."

The machine clicked off. I grabbed a pen out of my bag, writing down the number listed on Vinny's caller ID.

And immediately felt guilty. But I pushed aside the guilt and went to Vinny's desk, where his laptop sat. I had a cheap Dell laptop; this one was a fancy Apple PowerBook. I turned on the small desk lamp, brushing the room with a soft yellow. The chair was cold from the central air, and I shifted a little so the T-shirt was farther under my butt.

I opened the laptop and found the power button. I

knew I shouldn't be doing this, but Vinny had access to an account where he could find out the name of someone living at a particular address using a reverse directory. I'd asked him to help me a couple of times when the cops wouldn't oblige. This time, though, I was on my own.

I had to hook up to the Internet. Vinny had given me a short tutorial at one point, hoping I'd abandon my PC, so I found the little triangular thing up at the top left, clicked on it, and clicked again and there I was—the wireless AirPort was ready to go.

I found Firefox in the little bar across the bottom of the screen and clicked on it. Damn Mac, no right click, just one click. Vinny swore by the thing, but the price was still prohibitive for me.

Fortunately, his sidebar listed all his bookmarked places and I found the reverse directory site easily and clicked again.

I typed in the address of Ralph's house and hit Send.

Immediately, the screen popped up with the information. Damn, but it was fast. I would have to think about getting DSL or cable Internet. My dial-up really was a pain in the ass, and I couldn't download shit or watch videos or anything and I had to be tethered to the phone line.

The house listed the owner: Reginald Shaw. Okay, so that wasn't a surprise. But it didn't give me who lived there.

I hit the back arrow and found myself at the start of a new search. I typed in the phone number of the woman who'd just called. I told myself it was in my own best interest to do this.

It didn't come up as residential or business, so I hit "cell phone" and hit pay dirt.

Ashley Ellis. The shot girl at Bar. The one whom Michael Jackson had shot at earlier today on the Green.

Chapter 25

My first thought was not what you'd expect, which should've been why Ashley Ellis and Vinny were playing phone tag. That was my second thought. My first thought was that I could call Ashley, get a few quotes from today's shooting, and still make deadline for the final edition. I shut down the computer and closed the cover before rummaging in my bag. I pulled out my cell, a notebook, and a pen. I punched in Ashley's number.

"Hello?" The voice wasn't as breathy this time; she obviously didn't recognize my number on her screen and probably thought I was a wrong number.

"Ashley Ellis?"

"Yes?"

"This is Annie Seymour, with the *Herald*. I saw you this afternoon, after the shooting. I was wondering if you could answer a few questions for me."

The silence was long enough for me to wonder if she'd disconnected the call. My pen was poised above the notebook, waiting.

"Hello?" I asked.

"Yes, I'm here." She paused again. "What do you want to know?"

"Michael Jackson, the guy who shot at you, what is the nature of your relationship with him?"

"What do you think?" she asked sarcastically.

Fair enough. "What were you arguing about when he pulled the gun?"

"Is this going in the paper? I don't want anything in the paper," she said.

I wished now I'd paid more attention to her last night when I saw her at Bar with Vinny. "Where do you go to school?" I asked.

The change of subject threw her, but she sounded relieved when she said, "Southern."

"What year?"

"Senior."

"What's your major?"

"Education." She seemed more comfortable now.

"How long have you and Michael been dating?"

"We're not dating or anything. He's still in high school." She spit out the last two words like they were poison.

"Why did he feel it necessary to shoot at you?"

"He, well, wanted, well . . ." Her voice trailed off. "I really don't want anything in the paper."

"Witnesses said you told him to fuck off." She hadn't hung up yet, so I figured I could keep firing questions at her.

"He was annoying me."

And if she was stupid enough to keep answering, I wasn't going to stop. "That's pretty strong language for mere annoyance."

"Okay, listen, but you can't put this in the paper. Okay?"

I figured I could eke something out of this conversation on the record, anyway. "Sure. What happened, Ashley?"

Silence for a second, then, "We met a couple months ago at Bar when I was working. He looked older—he didn't tell me how old he was. We went out a few times. But he thought it was serious. I didn't." Her voice was flat, her words sounding scripted. It was probably the same speech she gave the cops this afternoon.

"So that's why he shot at you?" I tried. "Because you didn't want to get serious?"

"Yeah."

"Someone told me that you screwed him over on some deal." It was a little bit of a stretch, but I wanted to see where it went.

"I, well, I don't know what you mean."

I switched gears again. "I saw on the press release that his address was listed over at Brookside, the housing project." Brookside was just on the outskirts of the Southern campus. The city was trying to clean it up over there, closing a lot of it down because of the crime and trying to renovate. Problem was, the same people were moving back in; they were just moving into nicer places. I didn't like covering anything at Brookside. There was just one road in and out. "There's a lot of drug activity over there. Was Michael involved in that?"

"I'm not going to comment. I have to go." I could hear her anxiety.

"Just one more thing, okay? Nothing to do with Michael," I said quickly.

She was quiet a second, then, "What?"

"Felicia Kowalski. I know you're a friend of hers. You worked with her. She's missing."

"I know. I'm really worried about her." The anxiety was more pronounced now.

"You don't know where she might be?"

"Last I saw her, she said she was heading for Rouge Lounge."

I took a breath. "When was that?"

"Thursday night."

The night Ralph died. "Was it to see Ralph Seymour?"

"Yeah." Pause. "Hey, didn't you say your name was Seymour?"

Okay, so she wasn't stupid. But I wasn't going to be stupid enough to answer her. "How serious was their relationship?" I asked.

"Pretty serious."

"I heard she wasn't on good terms with her parents."

Ashley snorted. "That's an understatement."

"Did she live on campus?"

"Until about three weeks ago, when school let out."

"Where did she move to?" I asked.

She was quiet again. Damn.

"Ashley, do the police know where Felicia was living?" I prodded.

"With me." Her voice was so soft, I barely heard her.

"You're roommates? Where do you live?" I wondered again about who lived in that apartment next door to Ralph.

"It's a really nice place. We're in a condo at City Point."

City Point was on the water. The condos there were pretty snazzy, gated and all that shit. I wondered how a couple of college students could afford that. Even college students who made a killing by being shot girls.

"Are you renting?" I asked as casually as I could.

"Oh, yeah." But the hesitation in her voice made me wonder.

"Did you call the cops when Felicia didn't come home?" I asked.

"I guess I didn't think too much about it, until her parents called looking for her. I guess she was supposed to go to some family reunion or something and didn't show."

Like she hadn't shown for that chamber of commerce meeting.

"So you have no idea where Felicia might be?"

"No. I wish I did."   .

A lightbulb went on over my head. "Michael Jackson, he knew Felicia, too?"

Again I thought I'd lost the connection; she was so quiet.

"Ashley?"

"What happened today had nothing to do with Felicia," she said. "Michael's just, well, wound a little too tight sometimes."

Seemed like an understatement, but who was I to argue?

"Have you talked to Vinny DeLucia tonight?" I asked, switching gears.

"How do you know about him?" She paused. "Oh, shit, you're the one who was with him last night, right, at Bar? That's you, right? That's why you're asking about Felicia. He's looking for her."

"Yeah," I said. "Did you talk to him tonight?"

"No. I can't reach him. I've tried. He left a message for me. Listen, I have to go," she said. "I'm getting another call."

The connection ended.

I punched in the weekend late-night editor's number at the paper.

"I've got some quotes from Ashley Ellis, the girl who was shot at this afternoon on the Green," I told him. "Can we still get it in?"

I dictated the stuff about Ashley and Michael dating briefly and her breaking it off. That was as far as I could go, I knew; otherwise she could sic a lawyer on me. With my luck it would be my mother. I could hear the night editor's fingers on the keyboard. "Great," he said when I was done. "Thanks."

I put the cell down on the coffee table, folded my legs underneath me, and ran a hand through my hair. That was the easy part.

I looked around Vinny's apartment and wondered if he knew Ashley and Felicia were roommates. I snorted. Of course he did.

I thought about their condo at City Point, and Jack Hammer squeezed back into my thoughts. He'd said something about a condo on the water. I wondered if he lived over at City Point, too. He knew Felicia, probably knew Ashley.

I sat on Vinny's sofa and stared at the shadows on the walls. I had no clue where Vinny was, no clue what time he'd come back. Suddenly I wanted to go home. Sleep in my own bed. To hell with any mysterious caller. I'd take my trusty flashlight and beat the crap out of anyone who tried to get close to me on the way. I glanced at my watch. It was midnight.

I took off the T-shirt as I went back into the bedroom and tugged my clothes back on. The mirror told me I'd put my shirt on inside out; the tag was dangling in front of my neck. I didn't bother fixing it as I picked up my bag and touched the doorknob.

It turned without me giving it any effort.

Fuck.

I stepped back to let him in.

Chapter 26

Vinny saw the tag first, a small smile on his lips. "Fancy meeting you here," he said, then made a big show of looking around. "Since it looks like you got dressed in a hurry, is there something I should know about? Someone hiding in the closet?"

I punched his bicep playfully. "You asshole."

He chuckled, his arm snaking around my waist, his lips on mine, and I dropped the bag. It landed with a thud on my foot, but I kicked it aside as Vinny's tongue ran down my neck, his hand now caressing my skin under the shirt, his fingers slipping inside my bra and teasing my nipple. I groaned.

But "tease" was the operative word here. As quickly as he'd pulled me to him, he pushed me away. The smile was still there, but a tenseness had settled around his eyes.

"What're you doing?" he asked.

I wondered what I should say, decided the whole truth might not be a good idea, so I simply said, "Leaving?"

"I see that." The smile was gone now. He crossed the room and ran a finger along the top of the laptop on his desk. There was nothing I wanted more right at that second than to be that laptop, but his mood had been broken. Me, I was still hot and bothered.

"I came over here because I didn't want to get another call," I said truthfully.

Vinny came back over to me and traced my jawbone with his finger. It was my turn to get tense; it reminded me of the way Jack Hammer had done that, too, not less than two hours ago.

"What were you doing there?" he whispered.

No more hot and bothered, but definitely sweaty and nervous now. "Where?" I tried to ask casually.

"Jesus, Annie. I'm tired of playing twenty questions. What were you doing at that house with that stripper?"

Jealousy at any other time might be cute. But anger bubbled up through my chest. "You're spying on me now?"

"I didn't think I had reason to, but your mother—"

"Oh, fuck. My mother asked you to watch me, didn't she?" I narrowed my eyes at him. "You've been watching me all along. You were watching me at the Rouge Lounge, too."

"I was there to watch your ex, not you."

"But I just happened to be there, and you just happened to see me."

Our voices had gotten louder, and Vinny put a finger to my lips. It was dry and cold now, but it lingered, and I couldn't help myself. I had to stop this conversation, and I knew how. I opened my mouth and ran my tongue along his finger until I had the whole thing in my mouth, my hands at his belt, unlocking the cold metal, freeing him in one swift move.

Talk about mood swings.

His other hand slid inside the back of my capris, cupping my ass. I undid my own zipper and shoved the fabric down to my ankles, kicking it aside. We teased each other with our tongues for a few seconds before I locked one of my legs around his thigh, and he lifted me up, sliding my back against the smooth wall and slipping inside me so quickly and completely that I couldn't help but cry out. But in a good way. To hell with the neighbors. If they were going to hear something, they were going to *hear something*.

It was over in what seemed like seconds but long enough to leave us both breathing hard, the sweat slick under my shirt. Vinny's mouth lingered against my neck; one of my hands was plastered against the wall, the other in his hair. He let me down slowly, reluctantly, both of us knowing we needed more time—hours—in bed, out of bed, on the floor, everywhere.

Vinny pulled my shirt up over my head, and I exorcised everything from my mind except what I was expecting next. But it never came. As quickly as the shirt came off, it went back on, but this time with the tag in its proper place.

"Put on your clothes," he said gruffly, pulling his jeans up from his ankles.

I touched his cheek, feeling the stubble under my fingertips. He covered my hand with his for a second, then shook his head. "Later," he said simply.

So I did as I was told, and he handed me my bag. "Where are we going?" I asked when he opened the door.

"City Point."

As Vinny started up the Explorer, I asked, "Are we going to see Ashley Ellis?"

The SUV had started moving. "She told me she talked to you."

I remembered she hung up because she was getting another call. Couldn't pull one over on Vinny.

"Yeah. She called." I didn't tell him I hadn't answered his phone, that I'd taken her number down from his caller ID, or that I'd updated my story for the paper. "You think it's so urgent to talk to her that you have to go see her now?"

"I do." He stopped the Explorer abruptly at a light, and I jerked against the seat belt.

"Shit, Vinny," I scolded.

"Listen, Annie," he said firmly. "I didn't think I needed to explain my job to you, but Ira Hoffman wants me to find Felicia Kowalski. Going to her condo is part of that job. Talking to her roommate is part of that job."

We were swinging wildly between emotions these days.

"Do you think they're both involved with Ralph and the guns?" As I was asking, I knew it was a stupid question. Ashley was in it up to her elbows. Michael Jackson had wanted her dead because she'd screwed him on a deal.

Vinny didn't answer. He knew it was a stupid question, too.

"Does she know I'm tagging along?" I asked.

"No." He stared at the road in front of us.

"She might not be happy to see me."

"Might not be."

"She knows I work at the paper. She might not tell you shit with me there."

"Might not."

"So you're taking that chance?"

He gave me a sidelong glance. "I left you alone earlier and look where you ended up. At your ex's apartment. With that stripper."

I knew it was his clue that I should say it. But I wasn't going to say it unless he said it first. And not as an afterthought. Writing it in a note didn't count, either.

I leaned toward him and ran my tongue around his ear. "You've got nothing to worry about," I whispered. It was the closest he was going to get, and he knew it, from his expression. But he also gave me a lopsided grin and chuckled.

"Okay, it's not just that, either. I'm worried about those calls you're getting, the pictures Tom found, and those feds didn't take toys out of that apartment tonight."

"Who lives there?" I asked, figuring since he knew goddamn everything, he should know that, too.

But all he did was shrug, indicating that he might not know, or if he knew, he wasn't going to tell me.

Story of my fucking life.

The Explorer was the only vehicle on Sargent Drive. We took a few turns and found ourselves in front of the City Point condo complex. The guardhouse was tall and rectangular with a Victorian design. A cupola would've been at home on top. The flicker of a TV illuminated the interior, but I didn't see a guard, and no one came out to greet us. The gate was up, almost like it was waiting for us.

"Maybe he's out on his rounds," Vinny said softly as we drove past. "Keep an eye out for Section B." We bounced in our seats as we went over a couple of speed bumps.

"You haven't been here?"

"Felicia's parents told me where she was living, but the cops were here earlier and I figured it wouldn't be a good idea to show up then."

I thought about how Jane Ferraro hadn't been able to find Felicia's parents to see where she was yesterday morning. "I thought Felicia and her parents didn't get along."

He glanced at me. "She's a college kid. She still thinks she's smarter than they are. But that doesn't mean they're not worried about her."

Headlights approached, and I squinted through the windshield. The car was going as slowly as we were because of the speed bumps. As it passed us, I saw it was a police cruiser.

"Maybe that explains where the security guard is," I thought out loud, thinking it was probably a domestic. The cop would file a report, and the press release would get faxed—to Dick. But I didn't have too much time to contemplate my future at the *Herald* as I spotted a sign indicating Section B was to our left. I pointed. "Turn there," I said.

The speed bumps were closer here, and the SUV was crawling between them. Signs with numbers on them were on either side, as were the tall buildings. I looked out the window and counted what I figured were the different units. Looked like about five stories.

Parking was underneath the buildings. Vinny eased the Explorer into a spot under one of them and shut off the engine. We got out at the same time, and he pushed the button on his key fob and the doors clicked locked. He took my hand as we made our way toward an elevator, shimmying between a BMW and a Jaguar. Which reminded me of something.

"Shaw. What's his role in this?" I asked.

Vinny shrugged. "I don't think he's got any role."

"But he wanted Ira to take on Ralph's case. Why?"

"Beats me. That's not anything I need to know about."

That seemed so 007, somehow. And as I turned it over in my head, it was pretty sexy. I laced my fingers through his. "What about what Ashley said about the guy Reggie?"

"Annie, I don't know anything about that." His tone was teetering on patronizing. I took my hand back.

I didn't have any time to argue the issue, however, as the elevator doors opened and we stepped inside. Vinny pushed the button for the fourth floor. It was a jerky ride up—for what these folks were paying to live here, they should at least have a smooth elevator—and the doors opened onto a landing.

Vinny studied the sign and started toward the right. From the outside, it had looked like an enclosed building, but up here, we were on a wooden walkway lined with hanging flowering plants. A couple of walkways stretched out to one side, leading to units. Vinny kept walking. The farther we went, the more I could see the black water just beyond us, the moon casting a glow, shimmering in the darkness.

We stopped at a door right at the end of the walkway. From our vantage point, I could tell that this unit must have a spectacular view of the water, because Long Island Sound was just on the other side of it.

Vinny pushed the bell, and we could hear it echoing inside. Even though there was a window to the right of the door, no light was emanating from within. I wondered how big this condo was.

After a few seconds, Vinny pushed the bell again, and again we could hear it. But no footsteps approached.

"Damn," he muttered. "She said she was home. She told me which unit."

He reached out and turned the doorknob. It moved easily, and the door swung open. I looked at Vinny, who shrugged and stepped inside.

From somewhere, he'd pulled a small Maglite. Jesus, I was in another episode of *CSI*. I should become a cast member.

"I guess you've got your gun, too?" I whispered.

He chuckled softly. "Always be prepared."

"I don't think Boy Scouts carry guns."

"Neither do reporters."

Chapter 27

No one was home.

We tiptoed through the foyer, Vinny flashing his light into the kitchen before we made our way into the dining room and then the living room. Huge windows overlooked the edge of New Haven Harbor and out across Long Island Sound. A small deck wrapped around the front, and the glass door leading out to it was to the left and wide open. I stepped outside to hear waves lapping against the pilings under the building.

Vinny's hand slipped around my waist, I could feel his body against mine, and I struggled to stay professional, to keep my mind on the fact that we were in Felicia and Ashley's condo and no one was here.

"Where is she?" I asked out loud.

The hand disappeared, and he stepped away. Vinny looked out over the water. "Maybe she changed her mind."

"Why was the door unlocked?" I asked, a shiver tickling my spine. Something was off here.

We went back into the living room. Vinny's Maglite landed on an oversized beige sofa, a glass-top coffee table with nothing on it, a comfy-looking side chair, and empty built-in bookshelves. Ashley had said they'd just moved in a few weeks ago, which would explain the sparse furnishings. But if you move into a place, there are usually packing boxes. I didn't see any as the light scanned the room.

I banged my knee into the coffee table. "Shit," I said.

"Ssh," Vinny said, moving away from me and down the hall. I followed him, stopping a couple of times to rub my knee.

A king-sized bed dominated the master bedroom, but the selling feature again was wide windows overlooking the water.

"Cool place," I murmured.

While it looked like no one lived in the other rooms we'd seen, in here, the floor was littered with clothes: miniskirts, tank tops, workout shorts, and a couple of sports bras. The closet door was open, revealing even more clutter and more pairs of shoes than I could count.

"It's like at your place."

I thought he was kidding, but he never broke a smile.

I nudged him. "You know, someone could go into your place and think no one was living there—it's so fucking clean."

"Nothing wrong with cleanliness, Annie. You could vacuum now and then."

I pointed at the dresser that stood in the corner. "I shouldn't touch anything. My fingerprints are on file."

"So are mine," Vinny said, whipping out a pair of surgical gloves and slipping them over his hands. He reached back into his pocket and gave me a pair.

"You already opened the front door," I said.

"And I'll wipe it clean when we leave," he said.

We bickered like an old married couple who were used to breaking and entering together. How fucked-up was that?

The top drawer held what could've been a display at Victoria's Secret. Lots of lacy pieces of string that wouldn't cover anything, but then, that was the point.

Vinny picked up a red thong. "Why don't you wear shit like this?"

"Because it's uncomfortable?" I slapped the thong out of his hand and back into the drawer. "Anyway, I prefer to be unhindered by fabric while I'm fucking someone."

"Is that it?"

"Yeah."

He flashed the light up to my face, almost blinding me. I shielded my eyes with my hand. "What the hell?"

"You think we're just fucking?"

He was serious. "I'm not sure this is the time or place to be having this discussion."

"Maybe it is," Vinny said. "We're here, alone, no one to bother us, and we can't get distracted."

He should speak for himself. "No," I said, trying in vain to keep the frustration out of my voice. "You know we're not just fucking."

"Yeah, *I* know. But do you?" He'd moved closer now, his breath hot against my cheek. "What the hell did he do to you?" he whispered.

Tears sprang into my eyes, and I blinked a few times to keep them at bay. "Let's just move on here, okay?" I said, my voice husky.

Vinny touched a curl at my cheek; his lips found mine and brushed them lightly. "Okay," he said.

I swallowed hard as he left the room. I stood for a few seconds, getting a grip on myself, before following him through the living room and into a den. He was checking out the phone on a wide desk, and the address book that sat next to it.

"You know, if you had caller ID, we'd be able to find out who was calling you," he admonished.

We'd been through this before. But I had considered it, especially in the last weeks, and I told him that.

"Too bad you didn't set it up. We'll call the phone company on Monday and do it," he said.

"Yeah, but if the star 69 tells me the number's blocked, won't caller ID?"

He didn't answer as he tugged at the bottom drawer, the biggest one, but it wouldn't budge.

"Don't you have lock picks or anything like that, Mr. Private Eye?" I teased.

"Jesus, Annie, that's on TV. Who do you think I am, Magnum?"

"You've improvised before," I reminded him.

"Stay here."

The light bounced off the walls as he left the room. It was creepy in here, standing in the dark, but not as creepy as it had been at Ralph's. The light came back into the room before Vinny did, and he was holding something in his other hand.

"Tweezers?" I asked as he started to go to work on the drawer.

I wandered across the room, the light landing on a set of double doors that probably led to a closet. In my head, I went over the layout of the condo and figured that this closet was side-by-side with the one in the master bedroom.

I walked closer, my sneakers slipping a little on the hardwood floor, like it had just been waxed. Tugging at the latex gloves to make sure they were secure, I reached out and used both hands to grab the two door handles. I yanked them open.

"Vinny," I said.

"I've almost got it."

"I don't think it's important."

"It's locked for a reason."

"Some things aren't locked up."

Maybe it was the tone of my voice, but Vinny got up from his crouch and turned, pointing his flashlight in my direction.

A couple of misshapen wire hangers dangled from a rod that ran the length of the closet, which was the size of a small room. But that wasn't what bothered me.

What bothered me was the blood that the light illuminated.

Vinny's voice was measured. "Stop there," he warned.

"Too late." I couldn't keep the waver out of my voice. I indicated my feet. "I slipped in it. It's on my sneakers." So much for thinking the floor had just been waxed. I was going to track blood through the condo if we left now. The light moved up against the walls and across the closet, showing more blood splatter.

"Holy fuck," I said, glued to the floor.

"Don't move. Not an inch."

No shit. I stared straight at the closet; through the corner of my eye, I could see the light bobbing behind me until it was dark in the den, the only light filtering through the window from the half-moon outside over the water.

In what seemed like hours but was really just seconds, the light was back.

"No blood anywhere else," Vinny announced softly. The flashlight showed that the only blood was right here, where I was standing, and in the closet.

"So why not?" I asked.

"Beats me," he said.

Vinny's Maglite crossed the floor, into an area with no blood. "Take off your shoes," he said. "Do you think you can step far enough over here, where there's no blood?"

I'm not the most flexible person, except in certain circumstances that Vinny was intimately aware of, but fear was a good motivator. "Sure," I said, even though I wasn't. I stood one-legged like a flamingo as I wrenched off one shoe, then brought that foot down as far away as I could. I'd managed it. It was like playing a grisly game of Twister. How the hell was I going to get the other shoe off and that foot over where the bare one was?

"Toss me the sneaker," Vinny said, and I did. He held it by the back, then placed it carefully on the floor upside down, the bottom facing the ceiling.

Vinny's hands were under my armpits somehow, and he lifted me up. "Keep that foot raised," he ordered, and I did as told.

I fell on top of him on the floor just beyond the splatter, my bloodied shoe high in the air. He wiggled out from under me and wrenched off the shoe. It joined its mate on the floor.

I stayed on the floor for a second as he sat, his knees under his chin, breathing hard. I knew it wasn't because I was too heavy—or so I told myself—but because of the stress. "Gotta call the cops," I said softly.

"When we're gone," Vinny said, picking up my sneakers and handing me the Maglite, which guided us back out the door.

He remembered to wipe the knob with the tail of his shirt.

We went to the elevator, trying not to make any noise, trying not to attract attention. I turned off the flashlight as we emerged in the parking area; the dim lights led us to the Explorer. I walked gingerly on the pavement, sand and small stones and, I think, a cigarette butt clinging to the bottoms of my bare feet. Vinny opened the back with his key fob. "There's a towel," he said, and I knew what he wanted. I grabbed it and spread it in the back. Vinny dropped my sneakers in the middle and covered them with the towel.

"What are we going to do with them now?" I asked.

He didn't answer me, just indicated I should get into the Explorer. I brushed my feet off before getting in. He backed out, and we moved back to the little road that would lead us out of the complex. Finally, after going over the second speed bump, Vinny spoke.

"We went in there without being invited. It puts us in a compromising position."

No shit. "But we still have to call the cops."

"Do you want to spend another night being interrogated by Tom?"

He had a point. "So what do we do?"

Another vehicle was coming toward us. He had his brights on, and I shielded my eyes, peeking out underneath my hands. It was a red Porsche convertible. Swanky, just like the complex. The driver looked at us as he passed, and I did a double take.

It was Jack Hammer.

Chapter 28

"Fuck," I said softly.

Vinny sped up. He recognized him, too.

"He said he had a condo on the water. Maybe it's just a coincidence," I suggested as we passed the guardhouse. This time, the guard was leaning back in his chair, watching the TV we'd seen earlier. He sat up and looked out at us, but Vinny floored it and we ricocheted off the last speed bump, out of sight.

"It wasn't a coincidence," Vinny said as we turned down Howard Avenue.

"How can you be so sure?"

We stopped at a light, and Vinny turned to look at me. The streetlight shone on his face, and I could see the concern in his eyes.

"When I saw you at the house on Arch Street"—Ralph's house—"I followed him back here. That's why I didn't get home earlier."

"When you were on Arch, had you been following me or following him?" I asked.

"Him."

"I thought you were meeting with Felicia's parents."

"Had a change of plan." He didn't elaborate.

"But you didn't know how to find Ashley's unit. You said you hadn't been here."

"I couldn't get in before. I saw him drive in, but the guard was here. The guard let him in."

"So does he live here?"

Vinny sighed. "No. He lives in a condo in West

Haven. On the water." He said it like he knew it for a fact, which he probably did.

So Jack hadn't lied. But why would he be here, then?

"The guard let him in," I said. "Which means either he knows Jack, or Jack was expected. Probably the guard knows him, since he just got in now and we know Ashley isn't there to ask."

Vinny could see the question at the tip of my tongue. The light turned green, and he turned right onto Sargent Drive. "I don't know why he's gone back there."

"Maybe he's going back there to clean up the mess he made," I said, too flippantly, considering.

"Maybe." Vinny's tone indicated my statement might not be off the mark.

"But why would he kill Ashley?"

"Who says it was Ashley?"

The question hung between us.

"You think maybe it's Felicia?" I had another thought before he could answer. "You don't think Ashley was setting you up, sending you over there? I mean, I called her on a cell phone—she could've been anywhere."

Vinny didn't speak for a few minutes, then, "It's time to call the police."

I could see where he was going with this. Call the cops and maybe they'd find Jack Hammer with a scrub brush and some bleach. But there was a flaw with that plan. "He saw us," I said flatly. "He might have taken off."

"Yeah, but either way we have to call."

I reached in my bag for my phone, but his hand covered mine. "No. Not that way."

"What way?"

"You'll see."

We'd just turned the corner on State Street and Vinny pulled into the lot across the street from Café Nine. A couple of stragglers were outside, smoking. It was late, almost one thirty. Worst thing about Connecticut is that bars close at two a.m. and no one can buy liquor or beer or wine on Sundays or after eight p.m. the rest of the week.

Vinny found a pair of flip-flops in the back of the Explorer. They were too big, but I managed to curl my toes around the tops and they didn't fall off when I walked.

Vinny talked the bartender into giving each of us a Scotch on the rocks, even though the lights had come on, indicating last call. It was a scary time at a bar; everyone was drunk and making last-ditch efforts to hook up. Vinny just needed a phone.

He borrowed one from some guy who'd just thrown up in the restroom. At least that's what Vinny told me. And then he went outside and called 911.

We sat at the bar as the bartender put myriad glasses into racks to be cleaned.

"Do you really think Felicia's dead?" I whispered.

Vinny swished the liquid around in his glass. "I don't know."

I took a drink of my Scotch, let it burn all the way down my throat. "Whoever's dead, do you think Jack Hammer did it?" Thinking about being alone with him earlier in Ralph's apartment was starting to give me another panic attack.

He looked at me then, his eyes piercing into mine, but not in that good way.

"Not out of the realm of possibility."

"Do you think he's the one who's been stalking me?" I asked.

"He followed you to Arch Street," Vinny said. "He was downtown, on Chapel Street. I saw you leave Bangkok Gardens, get into your car. He was three cars behind you. I followed the two of you there." He paused.

"It wasn't a coincidence that he showed up at that house."

We went back to Vinny's apartment after our drinks and went to bed. No teasing about Victoria's Secret. No fondling. No tongues.

I waited to hear his familiar snoring, the soft sounds that he made when he slept. But I fell asleep without his white noise.

The next thing I knew, I heard voices. Vinny's. And a woman's. Out in the living room, maybe the kitchen.

The clock told me it was already ten as I pulled the sheet around my naked body and got out of bed, peering through the crack in the door to see who it was.

She walked by the hallway, and I pulled back, tightening the sheet around me. Damn. Vinny's mother. She didn't like me very much; she loved Rosie, Vinny's former fiancée. I wasn't Italian, even though my father—really my stepfather—was Joe Giametti, well respected in the community. But my mother was Jewish, and Vinny's mother was uncomfortable because she had no idea who my "other people" were. Talking about my biological father, whom my mother divorced when I was a toddler and who apparently died in some sort of construction accident not long after that. Joe Giametti was the only father I'd ever known, and it didn't matter if he was related to me genetically or not. I even went to St. Anthony's High School, his alma mater. Going to Mass every morning, I felt, was enough induction into the Catholic faith as anything. But not to Mary DeLucia.

I stood in the middle of Vinny's bedroom, wondering what I should do. Perhaps I could just wait her out. However, there was one problem. I had to go to the bathroom. Really bad. And to get to the bathroom, I had to go down the hall. Granted, just a short ways, but enough so that I could be seen.

I heard water running, which made my situation worse. I threw off the sheet and put on my clothes.

I poked my head back out into the hall. I could hear them talking, but I couldn't see them. If I couldn't see them, I figured, they probably couldn't see me.

I figured wrong.

Halfway down the hall, Mary DeLucia's small frame loomed large in front of me, her eyes dark and piercing.

"Good morning," she said, and from the tone of it, she certainly didn't think it was very good.

I still had to go to the bathroom, but I couldn't very well do that now. I willed myself to hold on for just a little longer and, as boldly as I could, met her at the end of the hall and followed her into the kitchen, where

Vinny handed me a cup of coffee without a word or any expression at all.

His mother had started "stopping by" in the mornings when she thought I might be there. I had no idea why, except to make us uncomfortable.

It was working, at least on me. Vinny ignored it. He had disappointed his mother before—he became a marine scientist instead of offering to run the family's pizzeria business and then dumped Rosie despite a two-year engagement—and had decided not to allow his mother to bother him.

My problem was that I wanted her to like me. This was completely foreign to me, since I didn't give a shit what anyone thought of me, but I really wanted this woman to like me. So she unnerved me. And I acted like an idiot in front of her. Which made her dislike me more.

"It's nice of you to come by and have breakfast with my son," Mary DeLucia said coldly. She always pretended that she didn't know we were sleeping together.

"Thought he could use some company," I said, looking at Vinny for help here.

I didn't appreciate how he quickly turned to the stove, where he was scrambling eggs, a small smile on his face.

I couldn't last any longer. "Excuse me," I said as I fled down the hall and into the bathroom. I sat there a lot longer than I needed to, trying to get my bearings. I needed to get some stuff done this morning, but now I was going to have to make small talk with Vinny's mother.

As I emerged from the bathroom, I heard my cell phone ringing in my bag in the living room. I bypassed the kitchen and went to answer it.

"Hey, there." It was Priscilla. "I just got on the train."

Shit. I forgot. She was coming today.

"I talked to Ned," she said. "He really wants to get together."

Great.

Obviously my silence conveyed my feelings, because

she said, "Listen, Annie, it might not be that bad. He lost his best friend, and you know how he thinks college was the best time of his life. There's really no harm in spending a little time together. I know he regrets having to take sides when you and Ralph split."

I took a deep breath. Might as well try to get used to the idea. I knew Priscilla, and once she got something in her head, you couldn't get it out. And Ned, well, I might as well suck it up. He *did* lose a friend, and we *had* been friends once. I'd just try to make this "get-together" as short as possible.

"What time are you getting in?" I tried to make my tone light.

"Should be there by noon."

"I'll pick you up at the train station." At least I had a good excuse to leave now. I needed to go home and shower. "Call me when you get to Milford, and I'll meet you out front when the train gets in." From Milford, it was about fifteen minutes to New Haven.

I closed the phone and picked up my bag. I shuffled back into those oversized flip-flops of Vinny's and went back into the kitchen, where he was scraping eggs onto plates. I shook my head. I wasn't going to stick around and risk dribbling food on my chin. His mother looked at me with daggers in her eyes.

"Priscilla's on her way in from the city," I said.

Vinny frowned, and I shrugged.

"She wants to get together with Ned Winters. I guess talk about Ralph or some shit like that."

Mary DeLucia's eyebrows rose with the utterance of the word "shit." Shit. I'd forgotten to watch my language. Another strike against me. Like I had anything going for me at all.

Vinny walked me into the hall, closing the door partially behind him so his mother couldn't see us. He cupped my cheek with his hand and kissed me for what seemed like hours but was just seconds.

"I'll call you in a little bit," he whispered.

I nodded. "Should I call Tom?"

"About the condo?"

"I might be able to get some information."

"How will you say you know about it?" Vinny asked. "We weren't there, remember?"

I shrugged. "I'll think of something."

"Be careful," Vinny said. "Keep an eye out."

I nodded, knowing he probably wouldn't be too far behind me, anyway. I kissed him again, still unwilling to say those words I hadn't said in years to anyone. I hoped the kisses were enough.

It was hotter today than it had been yesterday. The heat rose off the sidewalk, and I jogged across the grass in Wooster Square. I looked back at Vinny's about halfway across the square and saw him watching me from his window. He waved, and it made me feel safe. I wiped the sweat off my forehead as I reached my brownstone. On my way up the stairs to my apartment, I picked up the paper, shaking it out as I got inside and spreading it out on my kitchen island. The story about the shooting on the Green was the lead story on page 1. Wesley had gotten a great shot of Michael being herded into the cruiser. I scanned the story and saw the quotes from Ashley were all there.

I flipped through the rest of the paper, looking for Dick's story about the raid at Ralph's. I finally found it, buried on page A4 at the bottom.

> The FBI and ATF raided an apartment on Arch Street Saturday night, apparently in connection with the death of Ralph Seymour, manager at the Rouge Lounge, Thursday, sources said. No one would comment on what they took out of the apartment, which was next door to Seymour's.
>
> The Rev. Reginald Shaw owns the two-family house and said the apartment is currently vacant.

I wondered who the "sources" were and thought about how the apartment raided was "currently vacant" as I shed my clothes and made my way to the bathroom, where I turned on the shower. I stood under the cool water, knowing the minute I stepped out, I'd be uncomfortable again.

There was no mention in the paper about anything connected to the condo at City Point. It was long after deadline when we'd called 911, so it wasn't surprising.

Priscilla had just gotten on the train, so I had some time and stayed a few extra minutes in the shower before getting out and rummaging for a pair of khaki shorts and a tank top. The back of the shirt was drenched by my heavy, wet hair within seconds but provided no relief. I rarely put my hair up, but found a big hair clip in the drawer where my gun should be. I gathered up my locks and twisted them around and clamped the clip around them, leaving a sort of silly ponytailed look. But it was cooler, so who was I to give a shit what I looked like?

I heard my cell phone ring in the depths of my bag, performing a duet with my stomach. I was hungry; I should've had those eggs at Vinny's.

As I flipped the cover on the phone, I gazed into my refrigerator, savoring the coolness but cursing its emptiness.

"Hello?"

"Are you the lady reporter?" His voice was young.

"Yes. And this is?"

"We met at the garden. And then yesterday. On the Green."

"Jamond?"

"I know you be askin' about Michael, and I saw the paper. Ashley, she lies. She the one who got Michael in trouble, not the other way around."

"Got him in trouble how?"

"Those guns."

Chapter 29

I let the two words settle down before I asked, "What guns?"

"The ones she be sellin'."

I thought Ralph was selling guns. "She sold Michael guns?"

"She didn't, well, herself, but she hooked him up."

Ashley could be in on the straw purchases with Ralph. I wondered about Felicia. Did her disappearance have anything to do with this?

"Did she hook him up with Ralph Seymour?" I asked.

"Who?"

"Who did she hook Michael up with for the guns?" I asked.

"Some white dude. His name ain't Ralph, though."

"What is it?"

"Said it be Johnny."

John Decker, aka Jack Hammer? I immediately thought back to the duffel bag he was carrying. The snapshot of his face as we drove by him last night at the condo complex had imprinted itself in my memory. Had he killed one of those girls or both to cover up his role in all this? Why was he following me?

"Do you know how I could reach this Johnny?" I asked Jamond. If Tom hadn't rounded him up last night, I wanted to make sure he'd be able to find him.

"I don't know." But by the guarded tone, I was certain he did know but wasn't going to tell.

"He doesn't have to know you told me." I made a lot

of empty promises in my job, but this one wouldn't be hard to keep. There were enough people involved so Jack wouldn't have to find out a fifteen-year-old kid had ratted him out.

"Listen, I ain't no snitch."

"No one has to know," I promised again.

He was quiet a few seconds, then, "I really don't know." It was all I was going to get out of him.

Damn. "What about a phone number?"

"Michael had that."

Double damn. Michael right this very minute was spending the weekend at the Whalley Avenue jail. Where I couldn't ask him anything. "Jamond, how involved are you in all this?"

"Not too. Michael got shit for luck, though," he said.

"How so?"

"He jus' turn eighteen."

And was no longer a juvenile. He no longer had the protection of the system. If he managed to get himself out of this somehow, it would be on his record.

"Jamond, you shouldn't be involved. Listen to the Reverend Shaw." Christ, what was I saying? Shaw was as much a charlatan as Ralph had been, as Jack Hammer was. But the kids obviously looked up to Shaw, as much as I didn't trust the man. "I'm sure he's trying to help you."

"True dat."

I needed to hang out in the hood a little bit to get the jargon right, but like most places it just wasn't my scene. Sort of like going to Istanbul Café to see belly dancers.

"I need to go," Jamond was saying.

"Wait—" But he'd already hung up.

I stared at the phone after I snapped it closed. I thought Ralph was out of my life forever, and here he was, dead and making my life and the lives around him miserable.

My stomach growled again. I needed to get something to eat. But something light. Priscilla would undoubtedly want to have lunch somewhere, since she'd arrive around

noon, so maybe I could get something at Atticus to hold
me over. I felt safer going somewhere where there'd be
more people around.

I furtively looked around for signs of anyone following
me but saw no one. Not even Vinny.

Atticus was not that crowded, and I sat at the counter
and ordered a bagel with cream cheese and a latte. I
was halfway through the bagel when he sat down next
to me.

"Ms. Seymour, what a pleasure." The good Reverend
Shaw was always so polite. Even last night, when his
property was being raided by the ATF and FBI.

Since I'd just been talking about him with Jamond, it
seemed more than merely a chance meeting, but I
chalked it up to the bad karma that had surrounded me
ever since I'd seen Ralph last week.

I smiled as pleasantly as I could while still having nagging negative thoughts about this guy. "Good morning,"
I said through the cream cheese that had stuck to my
teeth. I ran my tongue around my mouth to try to pull
out all the poppy seeds. When I thought I'd been successful, I put the bagel down and said bluntly, "Isn't this
church time for you?" I knew Shaw didn't have a parish
of his own, which seemed odd to me.

Shaw's wide smile looked like he was auditioning for
a toothpaste commercial. "I've just come from church,"
he said, indicating his suit and tie. He'd looked as im-
maculate when I saw him in his gardening clothes.

"So what did the feds find in your house?" I tried to
ask nonchalantly.

He knew what I was after, and the smile never wavered. "I'm not responsible for my tenants' activities,"
he said simply.

"But you said the apartment they raided was empty.
At least that's what was reported in the paper," I said,
taking a sip of my coffee, keeping my eyes trained on
his face to see any type of reaction.

"That's right. I have no idea who was storing anything
in that apartment." He was smooth—had to give him
that.

"What about Ralph Seymour? What was your connection to him? What did you owe him that you felt it necessary to hire one of the best defense attorneys in the city for him?"

Shaw's face quivered slightly, and if I hadn't been looking for it, I might have missed it. My question had thrown him, even though he recovered quickly. "Ralph and I met some years back. We had both been in trouble. We helped each other spiritually."

Ralph had never helped anyone spiritually in his life. He was a goddamn atheist.

"I understand you were married to Ralph at one point," Shaw was saying, and a tone had entered his voice that told me he didn't like questions that he didn't want to answer, so he was going to try to turn the tables on me.

I took another bite of bagel and nodded.

"When will the story about the garden be in the paper?" Shaw asked, switching gears again.

That was supposed to be my job: throwing him off the subject. But I can be as flexible as the next guy. "Tomorrow," I said.

"Did you get what you needed from the young people?" It was as if we'd had no other conversation until this point, and it told me that he wasn't about to tell me shit about what went down the night before.

I nodded.

"The boy, Jamond, I hope you'll protect him in the story." He was referring to the pot plants, and I nodded again. Felt like a bobble-head doll.

"Seems like a nice kid, but he runs with a fast crowd," I said after I swallowed.

Shaw frowned. "What do you mean?"

"The kid who was arrested yesterday for shooting at that girl downtown, he was a friend of Jamond's. I saw Jamond afterward."

"Did you talk to him?"

"Yeah."

"Was he helpful?"

Shaw was fishing for something, but I couldn't pinpoint what it was. "Yeah, I guess you could say he was helpful." He didn't need to know about the phone conversation just half an hour ago.

"I saw in your story this morning that you spoke to Ms. Ellis."

"Ashley?" I asked. "That's right. Do you know her?" I thought about her comment about "Reggie" when Vinny was talking to her at Bar.

"Yes. She's the one who recommended Jamond for the community-garden program."

My confusion must have been written all over my face.

"She was his student teacher this past semester at Hillhouse," Shaw explained patiently, as if to a small child. I didn't like being condescended to, but this was interesting shit. Jamond had never indicated that he knew Ashley outside Michael and the guns. I still had his number in my phone. I was going to have to give him a call back.

"So you've met Ashley?" I asked.

Shaw nodded, and for the first time his eyes looked behind me instead of at me. "She was lovely. Very caring. A good teacher. She wanted to do right by Jamond, saw his potential."

That's for fucking sure, if she was hooking him and his friends up with guns.

Shaw's eyes sank back into mine. "I don't know what was going on yesterday, but those young people are the reason why I'm here. Someone needs to show them that people of color do not need to resort to crime and violence."

If he didn't watch out, he'd break his own arm from patting himself on the back. And from what I'd seen of Ashley Ellis, she wasn't Mother Fucking Teresa. I pushed my plate and cup back and looked at the check, but before I could pick it up, Shaw's hand had covered it. "Let me buy you breakfast," he said, the gleaming smile back.

I shook my head. "My boss wouldn't like that very much. I can't have sources pay for anything for me."

"I'm not a source. You did me a favor, writing that story. I'd like to repay that."

I looked more closely at him. "I would prefer it if you didn't." I pulled the check out from under his hand and got up, slinging my bag over my shoulder. "How many guns did they find in that apartment last night?" I asked casually.

He looked me straight in the eye. Didn't flinch.

"Twenty-five."

"Had Ralph bought all of them?"

His stare never wavered. "I don't know." He paused a second, then said, "I know you're suspicious of me and my relationship with your ex-husband. But he was trying to do the right thing after doing the wrong thing. He was paying penance for his sin."

I snorted. "Ralph never paid penance for shit. He did what he wanted to do and to hell with everyone else. He was just trying to save his ass and send someone else to prison longer than he'd have to go. What I want to know is, who was he giving up to the feds?"

He didn't take the bait. He continued to smile at me. "Have a lovely day, Ms. Seymour. And I'm pleased that Jamond was such a help to you, for both stories. He's a good boy. I have hope for him."

I was dismissed. I pretended I wasn't as pissed as I felt as I went up to the cashier and handed him the money for my food. While I waited for my change, I felt someone behind me and turned to see Shaw leaning down.

"Watch your back," he whispered in my ear before disappearing out into the sunlight.

Chapter 30

I stepped outside and looked up and down the sidewalk, but Shaw had disappeared. Watch my back, he'd said. Yeah, right. Someone had been watching it all right. It was time to call my friend Paula Conrad, a special agent with the local FBI office. I'd waited too long as it was.

I found myself back in my car and heading home. This conversation needed to be had in the confines of my own living room, on my landline. As I eased the car against the curb in front of my brownstone, I glanced over toward Vinny's place, but his Explorer was nowhere to be seen. I wondered if he'd followed me downtown, if he was following me now.

I still wondered how I could call Tom and ask about the condo, the blood, what might be going on, without letting on how I knew about it.

Maybe I could let Dick Whitfield do my dirty work, somehow get him to find out. But I couldn't do that without some plausible story, and one just wasn't coming to me at the moment.

When I got into my apartment, I hit the top of my air conditioner a couple of times to see if it would start working again, but it just whirred loudly and spit out more hot air. The big fan might be too much, so I rummaged in my closet and came up with a smaller one, setting it on the floor in the living room before plugging it in. I sat on the couch in front of it, and it managed to do a mediocre job of cooling me off.

I picked up the phone handset and dialed Paula's home number.

"Hello?" She sounded perky; she would, since she had central air in her house.

"Hey, there," I said simply.

"I was wondering when you'd call. Jeff Parker said he saw you last night on Arch Street. Wanted to know if I'd talked to you. I told him I hadn't, that you hadn't heard about this from me. Who'd you hear about it from?"

"Another source," I lied easily. "I heard you guys found twenty-five guns in that apartment."

"Jesus, how did you hear that?"

I chuckled. "You know better than to ask me that."

"And you know better than to try to get information out of me." She paused a second. "Really, Annie, this is big. Your ex was into some serious shit."

"So they *were* his guns." I said it as fact.

"Don't trick me into telling you anything more." By saying that, she confirmed it. It was easy, too, for him. Use the apartment next door for storage. I wondered if Shaw really didn't know, or if he had just been closing his eyes to it.

"Can you at least tell me when you started this investigation?" I pushed further.

"No."

"Come on, Paula. Off the record." I hated saying it, but I didn't have a choice.

"No."

"How about Ashley Ellis? I hear she was hooking up kids with guns."

"How the hell do you get your information?"

So Jamond was right.

"What are you guys doing about that?"

"I can't tell you shit, Annie."

I had another card to play. "What about Felicia Kowalski? She's missing. Was she involved with this, too?"

"What do you know about her?" Paula's question came quickly, too quickly.

"She called me. Said to tell the cops it wasn't her fault. What wasn't her fault, Paula?"

"She called you?"

"Yeah. On my cell. If you answer my questions, I can give you the number she called from."

"Fuck you." But it was said halfheartedly; she might be persuaded by my little bribe.

"What wasn't her fault?" I tried again.

I could almost hear the wheels in her brain whirring. She didn't say anything, though.

"She was involved with Ralph, right? With the guns? Her and Ashley?" I couldn't stop pushing. I needed to know.

"It's not been verified, but they have been identified as possible accomplices." Sometimes Paula got way too official with me.

"So they helped him sell the guns?"

"I can't say. This is all part of a grand jury investigation." She paused. "As you may know, those proceedings are secret until an indictment is handed down."

"Fuck that shit," I said.

"Okay, listen. The minute we can release anything, I'll call you first. But can you give me that number? We need to check it out."

I gave it to her, again caught between a rock and a hard place about that condo. Paula should know about it, too. But with my luck, Tom and Paula might actually join forces—against me if they knew I'd been there and not fessed up immediately.

"What about Reggie Shaw? What does he have to do with this?" I asked.

"Why won't you let up? I can't say anything." She was getting pissed. I didn't care.

"Did you know Ralph was stalking me?"

That stopped her. I heard her catch her breath. "What?"

"So you didn't know about the pictures of me in his apartment?"

"Damn." She was silent for a few seconds, then, "Listen, Jeff Parker's been asking me a lot of questions about you. I wasn't there when they raided the place, but now the questions make sense to me."

"Questions like what?"

"Like, how much do I know about your relationship with him? You know, I really don't know anything."

"There's not much to know," I lied. I was getting good at lying, feeling more comfortable with it these days. That wasn't a good thing, but it was necessary for the moment. "We weren't married too long—it just wasn't going to work out." I'd told Tom more than that, but somehow having the feds know what really happened didn't sit right with me. And telling Paula was telling the feds, friend or no.

"There's got to be a story—," she started, but the buzzer interrupted.

"Hey, Paula, someone's here. I have to see who. I'll call you later." I hung up before she could say anything else.

I probably should've just stayed on the phone. Ned Winters was standing on my stoop. I didn't want to let him in, so I picked up my bag and locked the door behind me before making my way downstairs.

For someone I hadn't seen in years, I was certainly getting my fill of him.

"Hey, Ned," I said, but his presence unnerved me. "What's up?"

Ned leaned toward me and air-kissed my cheek. His eyes were downcast. "I'm sorry about getting all worked up the other day." His voice was soft.

I actually found myself feeling sorry for the guy. "That's okay."

His eyes lifted and rested on my face. "Priscilla called. She said she's on her way in and I thought we could pick her up together." He indicated a red Jeep parked in front of the building.

"She was going to call me when she hit Milford," I said.

"She just called me."

"Huh?" Why hadn't she called me? That had been the plan. I tried to shrug off my discomfort.

"She said your phone was busy."

Oh, yeah, I was talking to Paula. But why didn't she try my cell?

Ned opened the passenger door to the Jeep, and I climbed in reluctantly. I wanted to drive. I didn't like the idea of not having my own car. At the first light, I turned to him.

"How did you know where I live?" I asked.

Ned shrugged. "Priscilla told me you lived over here."

I didn't like it that Priscilla had told Ned anything. It felt like there had been a lot of talking going on behind my back, and it creeped me out.

"I thought maybe we could go out to lunch, the three of us. Downtown somewhere," Ned was saying.

I was still a bit uncomfortable about getting too chummy with Ned, but on second thought, Ned and Ralph had remained friends. He knew about Felicia and the grand jury investigation. I wondered what else he knew.

Ned stuck a Springsteen CD into the player on the dash. I wanted to turn it up to discourage conversation, but he turned it down so we could barely hear it. Why he even put it in in the first place, I didn't know.

"I talked to Ralph's parents yesterday," he said.

So maybe this wasn't such a great idea. I stifled a yawn. "You know, I'm just doing this for you and Priscilla," I said, staring out the window. The Jeep didn't have air-conditioning, and I was glad I'd put my hair up. We stopped at another light, right near the station, and I fought an urge to jump out of the Jeep and hightail it back to my place. Even though I might get some questions answered, I didn't want to mourn Ralph. He didn't deserve it.

But I stayed in the Jeep, and we pulled up in front of the train station just as a throng of people came out. The train must have just arrived, and I saw Priscilla step through the doors.

She was like a goddamn walking rainbow.

Priscilla was a head shorter than me, with close-cropped, spiky red hair that would've been darker if she didn't frequent the salon every month. A row of silver earrings framed each ear, and the sleeveless yellow T-shirt showed off the baby blue butterfly tattoo that draped over her shoulder. She wore stretchy gray capri sweats, and the platform flip-flops that gave her a little more height were orange. An army green messenger bag was slung across her upper body, accentuating the breasts she always tried to hide. It didn't matter that she had amazing cheekbones that gave her face a pixie look despite the few extra pounds she'd put on over the years. No one looked at her face. Women pay good money for breasts like that, and Priscilla lamented that she couldn't just give them away to a needy flat-chested girl.

Priscilla leaned in the window and gave me a kiss on the cheek and nodded at Ned before climbing into the backseat.

"Hey, there," Priscilla said, greeting both of us. "I'm starved. Where to?"

Again I wished Ned weren't there, that Priscilla and I could just go to Clark's Dairy and get a turkey club and hang out.

"Union League Café," Ned said. "My treat."

The fancy French place on Chapel Street that served foie gras and duck confit and individual French coffee presses was one of the most pricey restaurants in the city.

Priscilla was reading my mind as we both shook our heads, indicating that neither of us was dressed for it. Ned just smiled condescendingly, putting a hand on my knee and caressing it slightly. "You look great," he said quietly. Then, as an afterthought, he looked back at Priscilla. "Both of you."

Priscilla frowned. "Bullshit."

"Come on, it's not dinner. It's lunch, and the Yalies dress worse than that," Ned said.

"But they don't eat there," I said, slapping his hand lightly. He pulled it away.

"You're both fine," he said.

Priscilla and I exchanged a look. We weren't going to change his mind. Screw it. It wasn't worth arguing.

*   *   *

The ornate decor of the Union League Café intimidated me, but I wouldn't let it show. I was already starting to try to figure out my escape. I could get a phone call from work; Vinny could need me; Tom could want to arrest me again.

Anything would be preferable to this. Sitting at a table with my best friend and my ex-husband's best friend and staring at one another, no one saying anything until we'd ordered food that was too expensive. Ned wanted drinks "to celebrate our friendship," but I said no and just ordered Pellegrino water, even though they both ordered Bloody Marys. Ned and Priscilla exchanged a look; I ignored it.

"So how about those Red Sox?" I asked, trying to joke around, but it went over like a fucking lead balloon.

"You know, Annie, Ralph still cared about you. Even now," Ned said.

"Yeah, and he liked stalking me, too," I said. "Did you know that?"

The waiter stumbled a little as he poured Pellegrino into my glass, but discreetly left before he could overhear anything else.

Ned frowned. "What do you mean?"

I settled back in my seat, which wasn't easy because the chairs were a bit stiff. "He had pictures of me. Either he or someone else was taking pictures of me. Tom found them," I said, unwilling to let on that I'd seen them for myself.

"This sounds like it was worse than before," Priscilla told Ned.

"Before what?" Ned asked.

Since I hadn't been in touch with him, I'd thought Priscilla might have told Ned about the stalking, but his question made me realize she hadn't. I gave Ned the short version. He took a sip of his Bloody Mary.

"You're sure about that?" he asked.

I nodded. "Yeah. But this time is definitely worse." It was time to see if Ned knew anything at all, and I asked him, "How serious was this relationship with Felicia?"

Ned snorted. "For him, not too serious. But for her, well, he had her wrapped around his little finger." The same ugly tone came into his voice as I'd heard the first time I'd asked him about Ralph and Felicia. Again I interpreted it as jealousy.

"She's one of your students, isn't she?" I asked, adding the proverbial fuel to the fire and wondering how far I could push him. "What kind of student is she?"

Ned fingered his fork for a second. "She was very ambitious. She wanted to go the distance." He paused. "You didn't see her at the *Herald*?"

I shrugged. "She just started, right? I don't pay much attention to the interns." Understatement of the year. I didn't even pay attention to Dick until he started getting in my face. "Although she did pose for the poison ivy art for the health and science section."

"I thought that was her," Ned said thoughtfully.

"Do you know Ashley Ellis?"

"She and Felicia are roommates," Ned said, taking a sip of his Bloody Mary.

"I hear they've got a fancy condo over at City Point."

Ned snorted. "They're just renting, although they got it for a song. That's what happens when the owner is a friend."

"Friend? Who's that?"

"That preacher guy. You know the one—Shaw's his name. He's everywhere these days."

Chapter 31

The Reverend Shaw certainly was everywhere. And he owned interesting properties in New Haven.

"You know Shaw owned the place where Ralph lived, too, right?"

This wasn't news to him. "How do you think Shaw met those girls?"

"What was Ralph's relationship with Shaw?"

Ned chuckled. "That was one thing Ralph kept close to the vest. I asked him the same thing, and he wouldn't tell me."

I mulled that a few seconds before saying, "Felicia's been reported missing. Did you know?"

His eyelids flickered for a second, but it could've been the sneeze that followed. Then, "No, I didn't know. What do you know?"

"Very little. Just that her parents reported her missing, no one's seen her in two days." And there just so happened to be a pool of blood in her condo. But I didn't enlighten him about that.

Ned looked from Priscilla to me as a small smirk crossed his face. "Why the twenty questions? What do you think I know?"

"You knew about the grand jury investigation," I said, then turned to Priscilla. "You, too."

Priscilla at least had the decency to blush. "I'm sorry I didn't tell you. He made me promise not to tell."

"And you honored that promise? Even though you and I—"

"I've stayed in touch with him, Annie," she said, cutting me off. "You know that."

Ned pushed his chair back and stood up. "I'm going to the men's room." His face was white.

"He knows something," I said as we watched him cross the room.

Priscilla snorted. "Of course he does. Ralph told him pretty much everything. Me, not so much everything."

I believed her. I had to. Or our long friendship had just been a sham. And I didn't want to think that.

"But how do we get him to tell us what Ralph told him?" I asked.

Priscilla shrugged. "I don't know. It's not like either of us has been *that* close to Ned. Not like you were with Ralph."

"But you went out with him that one time."

A small chuckle escaped. "Oh, shit, that's right."

The smile was contagious. "What happened that night? You never told me."

Priscilla glanced across the restaurant to make sure Ned wasn't coming back yet, leaned across the table, and whispered, "He was a lousy lay."

I couldn't help but laugh. "You never told me it got that far."

She made a face, rolled her eyes. "You really don't want to know. We were much better friends. But speaking of getting it on, how are things with you and Vinny?"

I felt myself flush.

"That good, huh?"

I was about to tell her about Vinny's note and the "love" reference, but saw Ned swaggering back from the bathroom. "He always thought he was hot shit, didn't he?" I asked, not really expecting an answer.

She surprised me. "He's really broken up about Ralph, Annie. Cut him a break, okay? I know how you feel, but can you put it aside for a little bit? It means a lot to him to have us here."

Ned slid back into his seat; the color had come back into his face, and he took a drink from his Bloody Mary.

The waiter came with a tray full of food. I had ordered

only an appetizer of foie gras and a spinach salad, but Priscilla and Ned were salivating over their meals of steak and fries.

Before I could stop them, they started tripping down memory lane, stories about nights at the Keg House and all-nighters putting out the school newspaper, and, inevitably, Ned came full circle to how Ralph and I had come back from our wedding in Vegas with Elvis dolls for both him and Priscilla.

I glanced at my watch.

"Catching a bus?" Priscilla asked, a smile in her voice.

This was a lot easier for them than it was for me. While they'd been talking, I'd let my thoughts drift back to last night and that condo. I'd ignored it long enough. My curiosity was getting the better of me. I knew what Vinny and I had done was wrong. It could even be called obstruction. We should've called the police the instant we'd discovered the blood. We should've been there so we could have told them Ashley wanted Vinny to meet her there.

We panicked. Not surprisingly. We *did* call 911, but it was time to come clean. I had to talk to Tom. And leaving this little party wasn't going to be a hardship.

I took the last bite of my foie gras, had one more sip of my Pellegrino, pushed my chair back, and stood.

"Listen, guys, it's been fun," I said. "There's some stuff I have to do." I looked at Priscilla, whose expression did not mask her confusion. "Sorry, but this is important, and this"—I waved my arm in the air across the table—"is just too fucking weird for me right now." I looked pointedly at Ned. "Don't think we're going to be best buddies now, okay?"

"What about—," Priscilla started.

"Ned can take you back to the train. I'll call you later, okay?"

My flip-flops echoed as I left the restaurant, leaving them with their mouths hanging open. When I stood outside the sidewalk, I took a deep breath. I felt like shit leaving Priscilla with Ned, but I hadn't gotten any information and I couldn't stand another minute of it.

                              *   *   *

The heat didn't bother me as I walked up Chapel
Street toward York. If they were going to try looking
for me, they'd look for me at my place, which was in
the opposite direction. It was just about two o'clock, and
I jaywalked across Chapel to the art gallery and sat on
the steps. I wanted to tell Vinny first what I was going
to do, so I punched his number into my cell. I only got
his voice mail. I left a message asking him to call.

From my vantage point on the stairs, I saw Priscilla
come out of the restaurant just a block up, Ned right
behind her. I didn't want them to see me, so I scurried
into the art gallery.

The cavernous concrete decor fit my mood, and I wandered until I found a spot where I could sit and stare at
the Chinese scroll paintings. But Ralph even interfered
in my appreciation of those, as they reminded me of the
Mount Fuji print he had given me.

I thought about seeing Shaw this morning and wondered what his warning had been about. Had he known
Ralph had been following me? Did he know about those
late-night hang-ups?

I had lived all these years seemingly invisible. No
listed phone number, so no listed address. Renting, so
I wasn't in land records. None of it made a damn bit
of difference.

I wondered about Felicia, her phone call to me yesterday pleading with me to make sure the cops knew "it"
wasn't her fault. What wasn't her fault? And why had
she called *me*?

I wanted to put Ralph down, lay him to rest, but he
was haunting me through his girlfriend, through his best
friend, through *my* best friend.

I wondered why Vinny hadn't called back. He
wouldn't like it if I called Tom without telling him first,
but I couldn't put it off any longer. When I checked my
cell phone, however, I didn't have any bars in the gallery. How did they do that?

I'd have to go outside, back on the street.

I hovered just outside the entrance and checked to

see if there were any messages or missed calls. Only two of the latter. Priscilla. I punched Tom's cell number into my phone.

"I figured I'd hear from you," he said without saying hello first. "I'm surprised you're not here yet."

Huh? "Where?"

A couple of seconds of silence, then, "You don't know, do you?"

"Know what?"

I heard him sigh. "We found a girl's body a couple hours ago. On the grounds at West Rock School. She was beaten to death."

Chapter 32

I started walking the few blocks home so I could get my car. It was Sunday, I wasn't dressed for a crime scene, and I wasn't supposed to go anyway because I'd been banned from my beat.

But Tom had said Felicia Kowalski's student ID was found with the body. Her face was so battered, however, she was unrecognizable from her picture.

I flashed back to the blood on the floor at the condo. Despite my best intentions, I didn't ask Tom about it, and he didn't say anything. He sounded a little busy at the moment.

West Rock School was very close to Southern, Felicia's stomping ground, at the base of West Rock, obviously. The city was full of magnet schools that catered to kids who wanted to be in the arts or the sciences, but West Rock School was an old-fashioned neighborhood public school that took kids from kindergarten through eighth grade. After that, the kids went to Hillhouse High. Of course the school wasn't in session over the weekend—and it was pretty secluded.

No one from the *Herald* was at the scene, Tom said.

Someone had to cover it. But I had to cover myself. So I called Marty as I walked.

"Cops found a body of a girl at West Rock School," I told him when he answered. "I just talked to Tom."

"And I just talked to Dick," he said. "He's on his way. Simmons'll have my ass if you go. I saw your story today about the shooting at the Green yesterday. That

was great, and I talked to him about it. He understands
why you had to go, but this has to be Dick's story. If
you go up to West Rock School now, Simmons could
get you on insubordination."

"Tom says it's Felicia Kowalski," I said.

"What?"

"The body. Felicia was reported missing yesterday.
Tom said her student ID is there."

"Jesus," he said softly.

I thought about everything I'd learned while on my
double-secret probation. "I think she had something to
do with the grand jury investigation."

"That story about your ex and the straw purchases?
You think she was involved?"

"They were dating. She disappeared the same day
Ralph died. No one's seen her. She was reported missing." The words hung between us.

Marty was quiet a couple of seconds before, "Get over
there and see if you can find out anything. Work with
Dick. He's going to have to have the byline, but you
know more people than he does. Help him, but don't
do the story, okay? You can't."

Being Dick Whitfield's assistant wasn't my idea of a
good time, but at least I could go out there and maybe
not get fired.

The phone rang just as I got to the car. I climbed in
and put on the hands-free headset. It would take me a
little while to get up to West Rock, and I could multitask
with the best of them. I'd thought it was Vinny calling
back, but I recognized Priscilla's New York number.

"Sorry I left," I said.

"What's wrong with you?" Priscilla was pissed. "I've
been trying to call you, but I haven't gotten through."

"I've got to get to a crime scene."

"I thought they pulled you off that."

"I'm back on as of now. I can't talk."

"What the hell's wrong with you?" she demanded
again.

Now, that was the million-dollar question, wasn't it?
"Listen, I don't have time to get into it. You and Ned

have a nice afternoon. I'm sure you guys can talk all about Ralph and me and all this shit without me there."

"But I came to see you." Her voice was quieter now. "I've been worried about you, since, you know, Ralph—"

"I don't want to talk about it, okay? Have a nice day with Ned, and I'll call you later."

I hung up without saying good-bye. I tried to get the headset off, but it got caught in the damn clip at the back of my head. I had a tangle of wire hanging down across my cheek, and at the next light I yanked it out, pulling about a handful of hair with it. Hurt like a sonofabitch.

I had to drive through the Southern campus again, down Wintergreen, to West Rock School. I turned on my scanner, but didn't get anything new. Just before the intersection where I'd turn left to get to the school, two police cruisers were blocking the road. I pulled over, grabbed my bag, and jogged over to them, waving my press ID.

"You can't drive in there," one of the uniformed cops said.

Three TV vans were parked just beyond the cruisers. Usually they were fashionably late, but today, they were punctual. Must be a really slow news day.

"But I can walk in, right?" I asked the cops, not waiting for an answer but barreling past them.

As I approached the TV vans, I saw Channel 9 reporter—and Dick Whitfield's girlfriend—Cindy Purcell primping, wiping her forehead and applying a little powder to pretend she wasn't ready to jump into a cold shower. A bead of sweat dribbled into the cavern that was Cindy's cleavage, her breasts bubbling over a white lace camisole under a hot pink blazer. I grinned at the cutoff jeans shorts underneath and her sandals. They were probably just going to do a waist-up shot.

"Dick here?" I asked, going up to her, trying not to stare at the bright, unnatural pink adorning her thick lips that looked like she may have had some sort of collagen treatment, but don't quote me on that.

She looked startled that I asked her a question, then nodded. "I didn't think you were supposed to be here."

It wasn't a statement that needed any sort of response, but as I turned to go, I felt a hand on my head. I jerked away. Cindy held my hair clip.

"It was falling out. Let me help you," she said, and before I could stop her, she had my hair twisted up on the back of my head with the clip securely fastened. "There. It won't come out now."

I felt it with my fingertips. No, it probably wouldn't. How the hell did she get my hair twisted that tight? I wished I had a mirror.

And then I remembered I didn't give a shit how I looked.

I mumbled a "thanks" and hightailed it up the paved road and turned up the driveway to the school. The parking lot to the right was crowded with an ambulance, two more police cruisers, and what looked like Tom's Impala, as well as the coroner's van. Just beyond the vehicles was a flat field surrounded by trees at the foot of a hill that ran up West Rock. That's where she was.

I sidestepped the cruisers. Crime-scene tape ran in a yellow circle, cordoning off an area about fifty feet away. Frank Piscitelli and his crew were doing their thing with collecting evidence, but they were in the way and I couldn't see the body. I spotted Tom beyond Frank; he'd abandoned his usual sport jacket and wore jeans and a Yankees T-shirt. When I'd switched boyfriends, I'd inadvertently switched teams. Vinny was a Red Sox fan. I personally didn't care, but New Haven was divided, not only by the Sally's versus Pepe's pizza question, but by Yankees versus Red Sox. Both were taken very seriously.

Tom's gun sat at his waist, his gold shield glistening as the sun caught it. He looked damn sexy. What is it about a guy with a gun?

The sun beat down on the small gathering, and I wished I hadn't left my sunglasses in the car.

I spotted Dick sort of kitty-corner to me, and Wesley was snapping pictures every which way. They had gotten as close as they could. Cindy Purcell and her cameraman still hadn't come up the driveway; maybe they'd do their newscast from where I'd seen them. No grisly bodies on the five o'clock news, just Cindy's pearly white teeth set in a grim line as she reported the gruesome news.

Dick frowned when I approached.

"What are you doing here?" he asked. "I thought you were staying away from this beat."

"Marty said I could come," I said, happy to burst his bubble. "Said I could help."

Dick didn't like that, but he didn't question authority. That was one of his problems.

"She's pretty beat-up," Wesley muttered, his camera shutter clicking.

"How bad?"

Wesley peered out over his camera, his eyes unusually dark. "Her face doesn't look like a face."

That's what Tom had said. Beaten beyond recognition. I looked around us, seeing some poison ivy just next to the nearest tree, and remembered the photo illustration Wesley had done with Felicia, the one where the poison ivy was snaking down her back. It would be the worst irony if she died in a bed of it.

"Tom says it's Felicia Kowalski," I said softly. "She's been missing, and her ID was with the body."

Wesley frowned and shook his head. "No. I don't think so."

"You don't think so what?"

"It's not her."

"How the hell would you know? You just said her face doesn't look like her face."

"Yeah, but I got some shots of her body. This one doesn't have a tattoo on her hip."

"What?"

"Felicia Kowalski has a tattoo of a rose on her hip. I saw it when I photographed her for the illustration." Wesley took a deep breath. "I saw a lot of her when I took that picture, and that tattoo was pretty memorable. If the cops think it's Felicia, they're wrong."

Chapter 33

On one hand, I was happy that the mysterious Felicia Kowalski was not the girl on the ground. But if it wasn't her, then who was it? I thought back to the blood at the condo, felt my heart start to pound. Had anyone seen Ashley Ellis this morning?

While I still hadn't told Tom about my nocturnal visit to the condo, I did have to tell him now that this girl wasn't Felicia.

I raised my arm and started waving at him. He spotted me, but only after everyone else did and one of the other cops nudged him. He frowned, but he made his way over to us.

As Tom ran a hand through his short blond hair, I could see the wet circles surrounding his armpits. Maybe I should give him one of those little personal fans as a birthday present. He moved his head to look around me, and I turned to see what he was looking at. It was just the school building behind me. But then he touched my hair. The clip.

"What the hell is this?" he teased, like we were the only two there.

Dick's eyebrows rose, and even Wesley grinned.

I yanked my head away from his hand. "Haven't you ever seen a fucking hair clip before?" I asked.

"Not on you," he said.

Tom's gaze came back to my face, and I flushed, telling myself it was the heat and not the intense blue of his eyes. Or the gun at his hip.

"It's not Felicia," I said quickly.

"What do you know?" he asked.

I glanced at Wesley, whose smile had disappeared. "You might as well tell him," I said.

Tom's eyes now locked on to Wesley's face. "Tell me what?"

"Felicia Kowalski has a tattoo of a rose on her hip. This girl doesn't."

Tom was quiet for a second before asking, "And how do you know that?"

Wesley tapped the top of his camera. "Zoom lens. And I photographed Felicia last week."

Something crossed Tom's face and he nodded. "That picture, the health and science picture. That was her, wasn't it?"

Wesley was nodding. "I saw a lot of Felicia that day. There was a tattoo. I Photoshopped it out for the illustration. This girl, though, there's no tattoo."

"Who found the body?" Dick suddenly found his voice, and it was a damn good question. I was sorry I hadn't asked it myself.

Tom stiffened, putting his cop armor on. "Body was found this morning at ten a.m. We got a 911 call."

"Who called it in?" I wasn't going to let Dick ask all the questions.

"Anonymous. No one was here when we got here."

"Did you trace the call?" I asked.

"Cell phone number. Not in any system. Probably a disposable."

"Do you think it was the person who did this?"

Tom shrugged. "No idea. Could've been a jogger."

Not around here. The field was secluded enough behind the trees lining the road that a body wasn't going to be noticeable unless you came up into the driveway and into the parking lot. Tom knew what I was thinking. "Or a hiker," he suggested then, indicating West Rock, where there were myriad trails. But it was the same story. In order to see anything here, you'd have to be pretty close. On school grounds.

"A student?" I asked. "A teacher?" Ashley Ellis, student teacher, popped into my head again.

"Maybe."

"Time of death?" I asked.

"Sometime between midnight and nine a.m."

"Was she killed here?"

"No," Tom said. "Looks like the body was dumped here."

I was quiet a second. It was time to tell him about last night. Because if this body had Felicia's ID, it seemed like a no-brainer that whoever it was, was close to her. Like Ashley. I opened my mouth, but before anything could come out, I heard Tom's name being shouted, and he jogged away toward the body.

I took a deep breath, running everything I knew through my head, trying to sort it out and make sense of it.

Ashley and Felicia were involved with Ralph, with his gun scheme, according to Jamond. Ralph had been under investigation; he was cooperating with the feds to get a lesser sentence. Whom was he going to sell out? Did that person find out? Figured Ralph would die before he could do right. The only thing he managed to do was to get a hard-on. And he'd needed a little blue pill to help him out with that.

Shaw had gotten Ralph his attorney. He'd given him a place to live. He'd given his girlfriend a place to live. Somehow he had to be involved.

I couldn't forget about Jack Hammer. How he was going toward the crime scene last night as Vinny and I left it. What was his role?

And then there was Felicia, who hadn't been seen since Thursday night.

I had an idea. I waved at Tom, who shook his head, but I waved even harder. He wasn't happy, but he came back over.

"Listen, Annie—," he started.

"No, I have to say this. I don't really know shit, but Felicia had a roommate, Ashley Ellis, the girl who got shot at yesterday on the Green." I stopped, struggling to find the right words that wouldn't piss him off too much when he found out what I'd been hiding.

Something crossed his face, but I couldn't read it. "That's right," he said slowly. "You interviewed her for the paper about the shooting yesterday."

"She was mixed up with the guns," I said quickly, hoping I could get out of this without even getting into it. "I heard that from a source. He said Ashley was hooking kids in the projects up with guns." The minute the words came out of my mouth, I realized what I was saying. She was a goddamn teacher. She should've known better.

I was stalling.

Tom's gaze unnerved me, and I braced myself for an interrogation.

"Who's your source?" he asked before I could speak again.

I shook my head. "I can't say. I haven't gotten it confirmed, but that's what I've heard." I paused. "Oh, but I do know Reverend Shaw owned the condo that Felicia and Ashley were renting at City Point." Once I started procrastinating, it got easier.

Tom's eyebrows shot up. "You know a lot for someone who doesn't know shit," he said.

As Jamond would say, true dat. I shrugged.

Tom's eyes searched my face for a second. It was like he knew without me even telling him. But he was going to make me.

"I heard something might have gone down at that condo last night," I said as evasively as possible.

He nodded slowly. "How did you hear that?"

I tried indignation on for size. "You know you shouldn't ask me."

He wasn't buying it. But he bit his lip a little, off to the side, before saying, "If you hear anything else, I'd appreciate you telling me."

I nodded. "Yeah, sure."

I watched him walk back to the knot of people surrounding the girl's body, feeling like a coward.

Dick Whitfield approached. "What was that all about?" he asked.

My cell phone started to chirp, saving me from having to answer. I flipped it open. I looked at the number on the screen. "Hey, there," I said to Vinny, walking out of Dick's hearing distance.

"Hey there, yourself. Sorry about my mother."

"Yeah. Sorry I had to leave."

"Are you still with Priscilla and Ned?"

I looked around me, the cops bustling, the coroner's van backing up now into the field, the body ready to be moved. "No. Girl's body found at West Rock School." I told him what was going on.

He didn't say anything.

"Felicia's ID was under the body, but it's definitely not Felicia. You know, she wasn't killed here—," I started.

"You think she was killed in the condo." Vinny finished my sentence for me. "You think it's Ashley."

When I didn't say anything, he asked, "Are you going to the paper to write it up?"

I looked at my watch. Three o'clock. Since this was really Dick's story, I didn't have to go to the paper now. "No. Dick's here. I'm not supposed to cover crime." God, that sounded so pathetic.

"So you're leaving now? You're going home?"

"Yeah, guess so. I probably should call Priscilla and see if she's left town yet." I told him I'd abandoned her with Ned Winters. "She probably hates me."

"Oh, Christ, Annie, all that girl shit is supposed to go away when you grow up."

"It never goes away, Vinny. That's the curse of being a woman."

"I thought the curse was—"

"I'm hanging up now," I interrupted, ending the call and flipping the phone closed.

I found Dick hovering just before the yellow crime-scene tape. "You've got this, right?"

"You're not sticking around?"

"You can handle it."

A look of genuine appreciation crossed his face, and I realized that I'd crossed a line. I'd told Dick Whitfield that I thought he could do this job without me. I was fucked.

"And if you screw it up, don't come crying to me," I said, hoping to save my ass, but it was too late.

I left him there, trying to get someone's attention for more information. He wasn't exactly having a lot of luck at that. Too bad. Cindy Purcell and her cameraman had finally emerged up the driveway and were making their way across the parking lot. I nodded as I passed, but didn't say anything.

The two cops I'd seen on my way in were leaning against their cruisers in the same spot. No one else was trying to get in, so they were shooting the shit. I held up my hand in a little Queen Mother wave as I passed. One of them lifted his shades, squinted at me. Jesus, just because Tom and I had dated didn't mean the uniforms could ogle me like I was the bearded lady at the circus.

I had just slipped the Rolling Stones' *Forty Licks* into my CD player when the phone rang again.

I didn't even look at the screen as I flipped it open.

"What do you want now?" I asked playfully, sure that it was Vinny.

"Annie?"

I didn't recognize the voice. "Yes?"

"Annie, it's John Decker."

It took a moment to register. "Oh, right. You." Jack Hammer. Why couldn't I think of him by his real name? Because he was a goddamn male stripper, that's why. And then it dawned on me that Jack Hammer was calling me. I glanced at my phone. I finally had a phone number for him, especially now that he was No. 1 Suspect in my book. I had to act casual. "What do you want?" I asked, even though my heart had started to race.

"That girl. I know you probably think I killed her. I didn't, but I think I know who did, and you're in a lot of danger."

Chapter 34

"What kind of danger?" I asked, the first question that popped into my head. And then, without waiting for an answer, "Why do you think I think you killed her?" Two more questions squeezed into my thoughts: How the hell did he know about the dead girl? Was he here somewhere?—I didn't get a chance to ask them since he was saying something.

"You were at the condo last night. I saw you. You and your boyfriend."

He saw us like we saw him.

"So what happened there?" I asked. "Was this girl killed there? Was it her blood in that room? Is it Ashley Ellis?" His flat tone pushed me over the edge, and I wanted answers. Now.

"I can't talk." His voice got softer, his tone more rushed, like someone else had come into the room. "I'll call you later. We have to talk face-to-face." And the call ended.

I tried calling back, but I didn't even get voice mail. Shit.

What the hell was Jack up to? And why was I in danger?

I realized it was the second warning I'd had that day. The first from Shaw. Who knew Jack. Maybe they were in cahoots. Maybe they planned to kill me next. But then why would they both warn me?

I sighed. I had to tell Vinny about this, but I didn't want to. He already felt threatened by Jack Hammer, even though there was no need to be. But while he made fun of the "girl shit," there was also guy shit that was coming into play here. Men and women were totally fucked-up in so many ways. It was a wonder we managed to have friends and procreate at all.

I was so caught up in my thoughts that I didn't even notice them creeping up behind me.

Okay, so "creeping" might be an exaggeration. I mean, they were two uniform cops, so "creeping" was not totally possible.

"Ms. Seymour?" one of them asked. It was the guy who'd stared at me. He was young, probably just out of the academy, from the looks of it. The shades had disappeared altogether and he'd taken his hat off, showing off a buzz cut that reminded me of a trim, white-blond lawn, but he quickly slipped it back over his head.

"Yeah?"

"Detective Behr asked that we detain you until he can get here."

Tom? Detain me? I looked behind the cops and saw him jogging toward us, his face scrunched up like he'd sucked on a lemon. When he reached us, his back was wet with sweat, and he wiped his brow, flinging little droplets onto my shirt.

"Sorry," he said, taking my arm, nodding at the two uniforms, and walking me out of earshot.

"What the hell, Tom?" I asked.

"I just got an interesting phone call patched through to me." Tom's eyes were dark, his voice low. "A guy named John Decker tells me you broke into a City Point condo last night."

My heart jumped up into my throat, and I tried to swallow it without him noticing. I shrugged, not trusting my voice to keep my secret. Why the hell did Jack have to call Tom? What was he up to?

"You knew about that 911 call last night, didn't you? That's what you were trying to tell me, right? You really *were* there." His voice was barely above a whisper, but there was as much force behind it as a goddamn hurricane. "I was over at that condo most of the night, Annie."

When I didn't say anything, he took a deep breath. "Fuck it, Annie, what the hell is going on? Why are you breaking into condos? Why are you carrying your goddamn gun around?" His voice had gotten louder. The uniforms were trying not to obviously eavesdrop as they shifted from foot to foot, exchanging little smirks.

"I already told you—"

"Yeah, right. The fucking phone calls." I'd never seen him so pissed. "But I want the truth. I want to hear you say it. Was this guy telling me the truth?"

I tried to make my face go all innocent. "Who is he?" I asked.

"Jesus, you know who he is. He's that stripper, your ex's friend."

"You believe him?"

Tom studied my face before answering, squinting in the sunlight. I felt his eyes run across my cheeks and down to my lips before they settled back on my eyes. "I'm tied up here at the moment, as you can see," he said, waving his arm toward the crime scene. "But I'm going to have an officer take you home and wait there with you until I can get there."

"So you *do* believe him?"

"I want to talk to you. I want you to tell me what's going on."

"I've been getting phone—"

"Yeah," he cut me off. "I know. The calls. Maybe if you're straight with me, we can figure out what that's all about and who it is. And who's been taking pictures of you. In the meantime, Officer Riley has offered to follow you home."

Mighty big of him. "I get to drive my own car?" I asked, unable to keep the sarcasm out of my voice.

Tom ignored it and cocked his head toward the guy with the lawn for a head.

"Yessir?" the officer asked.

I could see Tom was eating up the respect. He certainly didn't get it from me.

"Once you escort Ms. Seymour home, I'd like you to make sure she stays there until I get there." He paused then, having another thought. "Follow her inside. If anything's out of line, take her immediately to the police station and call me." Tom turned to me. "Okay?"

Something was up here. If he believed Jack Hammer, why ask this cop to check out my place? Was he protecting me from something? Had he told me everything Jack Hammer had told him? Jack had said I was in danger. Did he tell Tom that, too?

As I looked into his eyes, I saw more than anger there. I saw fear. Jack *must* have told him.

However, I was feeling like a prisoner rather than protected, which made me think of my father. In his world, if you were getting protection, it certainly wasn't going to be from a young cop but from some guy in a dark suit and a fedora, a cigarette hanging out of his mouth. Someone who looked like Robert De Niro or Harvey Keitel or Ray Liotta. Someone who knew Joe Pesci was just around the corner with the baseball bat.

Tom's voice pulled me out of my thoughts. "I'll be there as soon as I can, Annie."

Riley went to his cruiser. I turned to my car but felt Tom's hand on my shoulder. I twisted my head to look at him, and he cupped my cheek and stared at me a long second. "Don't do anything stupid," he said softly.

I made a face at him. "Who, me?" I asked.

Riley pulled up and indicated I should get in my car. I did so, noticing that Tom kept looking back at me every few steps or so, before he was out of sight. I pulled away from the side of the road and started back up Wintergreen, with Riley on my ass. To his credit, he didn't turn on the lights, but he might as well have. I got a lot of looks as he followed me all the way back to Wooster Square.

I half expected to see Vinny on the steps when I eased against the curb in front of my brownstone, but no. A few people meandered through Wooster Square, some sitting on the benches, a few dogs playfully bouncing between the trees. Just another normal summer Sunday in New Haven.

Until the cop got out of his cruiser behind me.

"Your keys, ma'am?" Riley asked, his hand out. He was taking this a little too far, but, hell, who was I to stop him?

I dropped them in his palm, wishing Tom had made it clear that I wasn't a "ma'am." I was feeling my age a little too much these days. "Second floor," I said simply, indicating which apartment was mine.

Riley skipped up the steps and unlocked the front door, and I followed him up the stairs. When we reached the apartment door, he held up his hand. "Just a minute, please. I have to check it out."

I watched Riley let himself in, his right hand touching the top of his revolver in the holster at his hip. Reminded me that my gun was still MIA.

Riley disappeared down the hallway to my bedroom and bathroom. I closed the door behind me and stood in the middle of the living room, uncertain how to deal with this situation. Riley came back out a few seconds later, his arm now hanging loosely at his side, relaxed.

"Everything's all clear, ma'am," he said.

"Annie."

"What?"

"Just call me Annie. Do you have a first name?"

"Jonathan."

"Do you want a soda?" I asked. I wanted a beer, but figured he was still on the job and a Coke would have to do.

He looked slightly uncomfortable, but it was probably because it had just struck him that it was hotter in my apartment than it was outside. "Sure," he said.

I went to the fridge, took out a Heineken for me, a Coke for him. We drank silently for a few seconds, and I began to regret being so social. I didn't know what to say to this guy, so I busied myself with the big fan, trying to get it to circulate some air.

"Air conditioner broken?" Riley asked, indicating the unit in the window.

I nodded. He went over to it and pulled off the front before I could say "heat wave."

"Filter's filthy," he said, pulling out something that looked like a dead cat. He took it over to the trash bin and shook it out. It looked slightly cleaner after that, and he went to work on the innards of the machine. I decided it was time for a bathroom break.

When I came back, the air conditioner was whirring like it was brand-new.

"How'd you do that?" I asked.

Riley blushed and smiled shyly. "Thanks for the soda." He raised the can in the air, nodded, and went out the door.

I stood by the window in front of the air conditioner, savoring the cool air that was actually spouting from it. Damn. It was too bad he was so young. He'd be useful to have around. Neither Vinny nor Tom had ever been so useful. Well, not in that way.

I took a long drink of my beer, but nearly choked when the phone rang, startling me.

I stared at the handset from across the room. Should I answer it? It might be Tom to tell me he was on his way. It might be Vinny. It might be Priscilla, still mad at me for leaving her with Ned.

I waited so long that the answering machine kicked in. "You know what to do." My voice echoed through the room.

A click indicated that whoever was on the other end had hung up.

Chapter 35

I looked out the window. Riley was tapping the steering wheel, keeping time to music that he might or might not be actually listening to. Someone knew I was home, had probably watched him escort me up and then go back down alone.

Jack Hammer's warning ricocheted around in my head like a fucking pinball.

Even though Riley was just outside, I went to the door and locked the dead bolt and put on the chain lock. I thought about the fire escape platform just outside my bedroom window, and I made sure that window was locked, as well.

Becoming agoraphobic was looking really good right about now. I could get pizza delivered; Vinny could bring groceries. I could get DSL or a cable modem and start e-mailing stories to work; I could do all my interviews by phone.

The more I thought about it, the more I realized it could be done. I would never have to leave the confines of my own apartment. I could exist here until I grew old and died. All I'd need was about fifty cats and I'd be that crazy lady who scared small children on Halloween.

I looked away from the window and stared at my apartment, which, thanks to Riley, was getting a lot cooler. I finished my beer and was debating another when the front buzzer scared the shit out of me.

I looked down at the stoop and saw Priscilla, barefoot and holding her shoes, Riley holding her arm.

I buzzed them in, unlocked the chain, and opened the door.

"She says she's your friend," Riley said.

I nodded. "That's right."

He flashed a smile at her, tipped his hat at me, and went back down the stairs. I closed the door as Priscilla flopped down on the couch. An odor had come in behind her.

"Who's the bodyguard?" she asked.

"Where's Ned?" I asked.

She tossed her head and flung her shoes on the floor. "He got some urgent phone call and had to leave. He put me in a fucking cab. *A fucking cab.*"

"You're the one who wanted to be friends with him," I said grimly. "Did he at least pay for it?"

She snorted. "No fucking way."

"But he paid for lunch?"

"And the drinks at the Playwright after."

That's what I smelled. The booze. She was drunk.

"Where did Ned have to go that was so important?" I asked.

Priscilla shook her head, but it was too much for her. She jumped up and ran down toward my bedroom. I heard the bathroom door slam shut. From the recesses of my apartment, I could hear Priscilla getting sick. Damn. She wasn't going home tonight. I couldn't send her home.

I finished my beer and sat on the couch, my head back, my thoughts spinning out of control. If Tom didn't show up soon, I'd go crazy just sitting here. I tried Vinny's cell, but didn't get an answer. I hit END without leaving a message.

Priscilla was moaning. I found her on the floor, her head hanging over the toilet. She'd flushed. Thank God.

"What the hell were you thinking, getting drunk?" I asked. I didn't care that she was sick. She brought this on herself.

Priscilla managed to raise her head slightly and snorted.

"And what the hell is up with Ned?"

"Even though I hate him right now, I really don't hate him. He just wants to be friends again. He misses us."

Yeah, and I missed him like the fucking prom.

"Are you finished here?" I asked, indicating the toilet.

She shook her head, and I went to the linen closet for a washcloth. I soaked it in cold water and came back into the bathroom, putting the cloth against the back of her neck. She made a soft sound, sort of like a cat purring. "Thanks."

I heard my cell phone ringing. Maybe it was Vinny. "I'll be right back," I told Priscilla, who'd moved closer to the toilet again. I shut the door, trying to shut out her sounds.

The cell was in the bottom of my bag. I looked at the number; something about it looked vaguely familiar.

"Ms. Seymour?"

"Jamond?"

"Something bad has happened."

No shit, Sherlock.

"I don't know who else to talk to."

"Define 'bad,' Jamond. Growing pot plants in a community garden can be bad. Your friend shooting at Ashley is bad. Is this worse?"

"Hell, yeah." But he still wasn't forthcoming.

"Listen, you called me. Why don't you tell me?"

"I'm in trouble, and I can't go to the cops. But you know them. Maybe you can talk to them."

I sighed, knowing Jamond was at the bottom of the priority list when it came to society. "What are you in trouble for?" My voice was soft as I thought about this kid who had nothing going for him. Jesus, my compassion gene must really have kicked in. God knows it wasn't any sort of biological-clock thing. That alarm had never been set.

"I know you been lookin' for her."

"Who, Jamond?" Butterflies started crashing against my insides.

"Felicia. I found Felicia. But someone else got to her first."

*   *   *

How the hell was I going to get out of this apartment without Riley seeing me?

Jamond said he'd found Felicia's body up at Judges Cave at the top of West Rock. He said she'd been shot; the gun was next to the body. Problem was, he'd touched it before taking off, and now he was too scared to go back or call the cops.

Okay, so maybe he did shoot her. The thought did cross my mind. But why call *me*?

I told him he had to talk to the police. However, I didn't want to turn him over to Riley downstairs. I had to take him to Tom myself. He agreed that if I went with him, he'd tell the cops everything he saw, take them to the body. I couldn't have him come to the apartment; I'd have to meet him somewhere.

So I told him to meet me somewhere familiar to both of us. At the old student center on the Southern campus. It was a decrepit building now, but I remembered it in its heyday, when we'd all gather around and watch that new music phenomenon, MTV. Who knew that music could be *seen*?

We could never have imagined YouTube.

I tried Tom's cell, but I got his voice mail. He was probably still working the scene at West Rock School. As I thought about it, it couldn't be a coincidence that Felicia's ID was found with that body, especially if her body was just up the ridge.

I left a message telling Tom he might want to check out the Judges Cave, there might be another body there, and he could reach me on my cell about it.

As much as I wanted to protect Jamond, it was my civic duty to at least tell Tom what he'd told me. It was the least I could do after not coming clean with him about the condo last night. I would do damage control later.

Priscilla was on my bed, the cold, wet cloth covering her eyes. I sat down next to her, accidentally bouncing the bed in a way that was not soothing for a person who'd just tossed her cookies.

"Mmmmm" came out of her throat as her stomach rumbled ominously.

"I have to leave," I said.

She was still as a statue, her arms at her sides, her bare feet pointed toward the ceiling. "Where?" she managed to croak.

"I have to meet this kid, Jamond. He says he found Felicia. She's dead."

Her fingers twitched. She loved a good story, too, and this one was a doozy. "You've got that cop watching you."

I was eyeing the window that I'd locked so carefully before, the one from which I could step right out onto a fire escape and climb down into the alley between my brownstone and the buildings that lined Wooster Street. "I've got a plan."

Priscilla raised her arm and carefully lifted the cloth off one eye. It did not look happy with me. "Do I want to hear this?"

"Yeah, in case I don't come back," I quipped, but only halfheartedly. I told her about going to Southern. She was dubious.

"Why don't we call Vinny? He can go meet that kid for you. You really should stay here until Tom gets here."

I'd thought about that, but he still wasn't picking up his phone. I'd left a message this time. "He knows where I'm headed," I said as I laced on a pair of sneakers.

I went into the living room and grabbed my bag before going back to the bedroom. I went over to the window, unlocked it, and lifted the glass. It was one of those old-fashioned storm windows with a screen in it, drafty as all hell during the winter. I slid the two buttons on the bottom at the same time and pulled up the screen.

Peering out at the fire escape and the ladder that descended from it, I felt a little dizzy. I'm not much for heights. But it wasn't one of those fire escapes you see in the movies, where the ladder slides down and you have to drop about six feet to the ground. No, my landlord had actual stairs built up to my apartment and Walter's upstairs.

Looking at it from this angle, I was surprised I'd never been burgled. It would be so easy.

"You're not really doing that, are you?" Priscilla had taken the cloth off her eyes completely and was propped up on her elbows, the butterfly tattoo stretched wide on her shoulder.

"Yeah, sure," I said, but I wasn't convincing even myself.

"Stay and wait for Tom," she said again.

"I promised Jamond," I said. "He's scared."

"Doesn't he have anyone else to call?"

I thought about that. What about Shaw? Why hadn't Jamond called *him*? But then again, maybe he knew something about Shaw. Shaw was mixed up with Ralph in some way, and maybe Jamond knew how. Jamond knew about the guns, knew about Ashley and Felicia.

"Everyone knows where I'm going." I justified it to myself as well as to Priscilla. "I'm just going out the back way."

I swung my leg over the windowsill and stepped out onto the landing. My bag was slung over my shoulder, across my chest. The wall of heat slapped my skin, and I realized just how cool my apartment had gotten since Riley had fixed the air conditioner. "Close the window and keep the air inside," I instructed Priscilla as I headed down the stairs. She was back to being prone on the bed, though, the cloth covering her eyes, so it might be a while before she got to it.

The next problem was my car. So I hadn't thought this through. The car was in front of the building, in front of Riley's cruiser. How the hell was I going to get out to Southern?

New Haven does not have taxis trolling every block, looking for people to pick up. You have to call one to come get you. And it could take a while. New Haven also does not have a subway system or a local train system.

It does, however, have buses.

I had no clue about bus schedules.

I maneuvered through the alley and ended up on Wooster Street in front of Sally's Apizza. A white clam pie and a beer sounded pretty good right about now, but they weren't open yet and I had other plans. I'd seen buses go down Chapel Street, and maybe, just maybe, I could walk up Olive and over to Chapel without Riley seeing me. His cruiser was on Chapel, in front of my building, pointing in exactly my direction. He wasn't expecting to see me a block away, so perhaps I could get away with it.

I jogged over to Chapel, glanced up the street, saw the cruiser, but couldn't see Riley inside. I started down the sidewalk and jaywalked. I'd have to catch the bus on this side of the street.

I spotted a bus-stop sign and hovered beneath it, my back to the direction the bus would come from because I couldn't risk Riley spotting me. I glanced at my watch, wishing a schedule were posted on the sign—I had seen that on bus-stop signs around the Green. Wouldn't you know they'd make it tough if you were out of the loop, so to speak?

I shimmied around a tree with a trunk so thin it wasn't a satisfactory shield, but it would have to do. I didn't want to walk farther; it was too damn hot.

I thought about whoever had been watching me, taking those pictures. If it wasn't Ralph, was I being watched right now? I reached inside my bag and curled my fingers around my keys. They were the closest to a weapon I had. I should've put a kitchen knife in my purse, but with my luck it would've stuck out the side and stabbed me or some other unsuspecting person on the bus.

Speaking of which, I finally heard a rumbling behind me. The hulking blue monster stopped, the doors opening for me. Go figure. Public transportation.

I'd slung my bag over my shoulder and pulled out my wallet as I stepped up into the bus. My nose caught the scent of body odor and diesel fuel. I had a dollar bill in my hand, uncertain what to do with it.

The bus driver frowned, pointed at a silver box. "It's a dollar twenty-five," he said. "Exact."

I slid the bill into the machine and found a quarter and dropped it into a slot.

"What bus do I take to Southern?" I asked.

The bus driver looked at me with that look you give people you think are total losers. "The B1. You'll need a transfer." A ticket popped up out of the silver box and he indicated I should take it, so I did. "You get off at the Green and then pick up the B1 there."

He pulled away from the curb, causing me to lose my balance a little, but I grabbed on to the railing next to him and surveyed the bus for a seat.

I was the only white person. Not that anyone was really paying attention except me.

I slid onto the first seat I saw and glanced around me, careful not to look at anyone too long, but long enough to notice the three kids in the back of the bus whose excessive use of the word "fuck" might have been a little too much even for me; a gray-haired, stout woman with a faux-leather bag who was trying to ignore the kids in the back; and a scruffy guy with googly eyes and dread-locks who creeped me out for no reason except I was pretty sure he was crazy.

We were at the Green in no time. I clutched my transfer ticket and got off, wondering how long I'd have to wait for that B1 bus. A B2 came by, but I didn't think that would be right. The driver had been careful to say B1.

I had to wait but a few minutes, however. The B1 slid to a stop, its sign announcing that it was, indeed, heading to Southern. I stepped up through the door, put my transfer ticket into the little slot, and found a seat, feeling quite proud of myself.

Not that I was going to be taking the bus ever again, but at least I knew how it worked now.

I barely had time to sit down when I heard my cell phone ringing in the bottom of my bag. I dug it out and glanced at the number before flipping it up.

"Hey there," I said.

"Where the hell are you?" Vinny was pissed.

"I'm on the bus." I had to talk loud because I could barely hear myself over the engine. A few heads turned and looked at me. I pretended not to notice.

"The bus?"

"You have to speak up. I can't hear shit." The last word got me a dirty look from the elderly woman who'd followed me off the Chapel Street bus and onto this one. I looked at the floor. "I'm headed to Southern."

"Why are you on the bus?" Vinny shouted.

I held the phone away from my ear a little and figured everyone would be privy to my conversation, so I should be somewhat discreet. "I couldn't take my car because of the cop in front of my building."

He was quiet a second, then, "I'm not even going to ask. So how did you get to the bus?"

"Snuck down the fire escape."

Silence again. I thought I lost him. "Hello?"

"Yeah, I'm here. You're fucking crazy, you know."

"You're not the first one to tell me that."

"You're going to meet that kid?"

I'd left him a pretty detailed message, telling him about Jamond's claim about Felicia.

"Yeah. He says he saw Felicia up at Judges Cave. He said she was dead."

"How are you going to get up there if you don't have your car? It's quite a hike from the campus."

I *really* hadn't thought this through. But I had an idea. "You could meet us there, and we could all go together." Sounded like a party to me.

"I . . . st . . . you."

"What? You're breaking up."

And then I really did lose the connection.

Chapter 36

Vinny's words resonated as the bus jostled me around in the incredibly uncomfortable seat. There was a spot of something brown on the seat next to me, so I tried not to shift too much. We stopped every now and then, people getting on, people getting off, and while it wasn't my scene, the air-conditioning was pleasant, no one made eye contact, and I didn't have to think about driving. Someone else was doing that.

But what *would* I do when I got to Southern? I hoped Vinny had heard me before we were disconnected and would be there to meet me. Otherwise Jamond and I would have a long walk.

I tried Tom again and again got voice mail. I hoped he was checking messages and sent someone up to West Rock.

I thought about the Judges Cave, the landmark where two judges, Edward Whalley and his son-in-law William Goffe, who'd signed the death warrant for England's King Charles I, hid out after fleeing persecution by Charles II. Two major city streets were named after the judges, and the cave, which sports a nice little plaque commemorating its historical value, was a common destination for school field trips and hikes.

Personally, I wouldn't let a kid go up there. I'd written enough stories about the prostitution and drug deals going on at the West Rock summit that it wasn't exactly on my *1,000 Places to Go Before I Die* list.

I stared out the window. We were moving at a pretty

good clip up Whalley Avenue—yes, that Whalley—and I realized we were going through Westville, my mother's neighborhood. She had a car.

Okay, she might not like it if I took the Mercedes up to West Rock, but did she really need to know where I was going with it?

I pulled the yellow cord, which made a *ding* sound, and the STOP REQUESTED sign lit up.

When I stepped out of the bus, the heat held me in a bear hug and I was sorry I'd dissed the mass-transit system. Maybe I should have stayed and gone to Southern, but it was too late now. I was only a few blocks from my childhood home. As I walked, I tried to concoct a realistic story as to why I was visiting on foot and why I needed to borrow the car.

Oh, hell, she wasn't going to believe me.

I stopped on the sidewalk, sighing, wondering what I was doing, and wishing I'd taken one of those schedules from the front of the bus. Maybe another bus would be along at some point.

As I stood there, alone, I suddenly felt like I was being watched. The bus adventure had been just that— an adventure—and I hadn't had time to think about my mysterious caller or those photographs. But now I was in a deserted neighborhood. I saw no people. Not even a moving car. I couldn't shake the feeling. I willed my feet to start walking again, now with a wider stride, toward my mother's house, and reached into my bag for my phone.

I turned the corner to see a car idling just ahead. It was a Porsche. A red Boxster. Not totally unusual in this neighborhood, but what was unusual was that it wasn't in someone's driveway covered with a tarp to keep the birds from shitting on it.

I didn't move as the engine died and the door swung open.

Jack Hammer stepped out into the street.

I caught my breath and willed my feet to move faster. I had to walk past him to get to my mother's. I had no choice.

"Annie, I have to talk to you," he said as I approached.

He didn't seem to notice I didn't slow down, ready to go into a jog or even run if I had to. My mouth was too dry to say anything. I sent out telepathic messages for some cars to drive by.

No such luck. The streets were abandoned. Everyone was inside, basking in central air.

He fell into step beside me, and I found my voice. "What the hell are you doing here?"

A smile slid across his face, his eyes twinkling. "How did you get away from that cop?"

My chest constricted, and my face must have changed, because he laughed. Really laughed.

"Oh, shit, I was on my way to see you, I saw that cop out front, and then when I turned back down Chapel, I saw you get on the bus. Figured I'd find out where you were going."

"I'm going to my mother's," I tried to say casually, although my throat felt like I'd swallowed a spoonful of sand. "She lives up the block."

"You couldn't tell the cop that and just take your car?"

"Maybe all that global-warming shit made me realize that I could take the bus to my mother's and save on gas and help the environment," I spit out, shocked that I could even form a coherent sentence.

Jack's mouth twitched. "Come on, Annie, you were making an escape. Don't bullshit a bullshitter."

"I really am going to my mother's," I insisted.

"Then let me take you the rest of the way." He indicated the Porsche.

Yeah, right. I'd get in the car and never be heard from again. Dick Whitfield would get my beat, Vinny would move on with his life, and I'd be the next body Tom would find in the woods. No, thank you.

I shook my head. "It's just around the corner."

"Then I'll just walk the rest of the way with you. You shouldn't be alone."

No shit. I shouldn't be with him, either. I wondered how fast I could run if I needed to. I made sure I kept an arm's length away from him, and he didn't move any closer. At least not now.

"What happened in that condo?" I asked. If he had any ideas about abducting me, I was at least going to find out what was going on.

"I have no idea. I found what you found." He paused but didn't look at me. "I passed the cops on my way out."

"So you didn't hang around to talk to them?"

"You didn't."

Okay. He had me there.

Then he surprised me. His expression grew more concerned. "You need to know something." He paused. "Someone's gotten too close to you. You have to be careful."

I snorted. "Yeah. I know about the stalking. Old news, Jack."

"It's more than that."

"What is?"

"He thinks you know more than you do." He'd slipped on his sunglasses while we walked, and now he took them off, his eyes piercing mine.

"How do you know what I know?"

Jack grinned. "I know a lot more than you think."

That's for sure. And that's exactly what I was concerned about.

"So is it you?" I asked defiantly. "Are you the person I should be afraid of?"

He chuckled. "You should be so lucky, but no. It's not me."

"And I should take the word of a stripper?" I don't know why, but for some reason, I believed him.

"Male dancer," he emphasized. "I think I'm growing on you."

I didn't want to go there. "What does Shaw know?"

"Shaw?"

"Yeah, Shaw. He warned me, too. This morning.

What's his connection with all this?" Maybe because I'd found out about his properties, Shaw thought I was finding out more about his mysterious past.

Jack Hammer stuck his hands in his pockets and kicked a stone out of his way, watching it skitter across the sidewalk. "Ralphie trusted Shaw," was all he said before we turned the corner and my mother's big white house loomed in the next block. I could feel the tenseness in my shoulders melt away. Just a few more steps now. What I hadn't counted on were the cars along the street and in the driveway. Shit. The barbecue. I'd forgotten.

A low buzz of conversation reached my ears from the backyard. The scent of steak hung suspended in the hot air. My stomach growled.

"Smells like something's cooking," Jack said, grinning.

"Thanks for the escort," I said, aware that the side door next to the garage was opening, and wanting him to get the hell out of there and leave me alone.

"Annie?"

It was my mother. In the doorway. She was dressed immaculately in a pair of khaki Bermuda shorts and a sleeveless button-down blouse, her hair swung up behind her head sort of like mine was. But that was where the resemblance between us ended.

Except maybe for the frown. At Jack Hammer.

She closed the door behind her and came toward us. "What are you doing here?" she asked Jack. It was almost as if I didn't exist.

"I walked Annie here from the bus stop."

Now I most certainly did exist. Her eyebrows shot up into her forehead as she turned to me. "The bus? Where's your car?"

This wasn't going to be easy. I opened my mouth and hoped something smart would come out, but all we heard was my cell phone ringing in my bag. I pulled it out, relieved to have the distraction. The number was familiar.

"Hi, Vinny," I said, turning around, leaving Jack

Hammer to my mother's questions, which I could hear her asking quietly as I stepped away.

"Where the hell are you? The bus came and you weren't on it," he scolded.

"I thought I might borrow my mother's car, but she's having a barbecue and she's not totally happy I'm here, I don't think," I said quickly, barely above a whisper so she wouldn't overhear. I didn't want to tell him about Jack Hammer. That wouldn't go over well.

"Well, that kid Jamond, he's not here, either. No one's here. It's summer break, it's a commuter college, and the campus is dead." Not a great choice of words, but accurate, as I remembered.

"I hope he's okay," I said.

"I can come get you," Vinny offered. "I'm not far."

My mother was giving me the evil eye.

"Hold on a few seconds, okay? I'll call you right back."

He'd started to say something, but I didn't hear it as I closed my phone and joined my mother and Jack Hammer again.

"You are welcome to stay, Annie, but I've told Mr. Decker he has to leave," my mother said, her voice measured and hard as steel.

Jack shrugged, his lopsided grin back on his face. "No problem. I'll see you around, Annie, okay?" He started back to his car as my mother and I watched. When he was around the corner, my mother turned to me.

"What are you doing?" she demanded.

I sighed. "Please don't ask me any questions."

She was shaking her head like she used to do when I would come in at four in the morning, drunk or stoned or both. She always pretended she didn't know, and she never said anything. But this time would be different.

"Do you know about him?" she asked, tossing her head in Jack Hammer's direction. "He knew about Ralph's gun scheme, but he won't say anything. We can't prove he was involved, but my gut tells me he knew about it—he knew that those guns your ex-husband bought killed two innocent kids in Hartford three months ago."

Holy shit.

"Ralph was ready to roll over on whoever was heading up this operation," my mother continued. "Of course he was stalling, trying to get the best deal he could for himself, and I had the feds ready to grant him almost full immunity. But then he died."

I thought about Jack Hammer and our cryptic conversation. I didn't want to worry her by telling her Jack had been warning me.

"Do you think Jack—I mean, John Decker—is the guy?" I asked. "The guy you're looking for?"

My mother sighed. "I don't know."

I thought about it a few seconds. Jack Hammer had had plenty of opportunities to harm me—he'd been alone with me last night at Ralph's, he'd just walked me those desolate blocks to my mother's. He hadn't hurt me. He'd told me to be careful.

He did say it was someone who'd gotten close to me. Maybe he was setting me up.

Shaw was still one big question mark. Jack hadn't said anything that could've let him off the hook, either. And both Shaw and Jack were tight with Ralph.

As I opened my mouth to ask my mother about Shaw, the question melted on the warm breeze when the door opened behind her. I froze, not wanting to see Bill Bennett, my boss, the publisher of the *New Haven Herald*, in a pair of shorts and a T-shirt with an apron sporting some sort of grilling pun.

But it wasn't Bill Bennett.

It was Dick Whitfield.

Chapter 37

I couldn't speak for a second, then managed to sputter to my mother, "What the hell is he doing here?"

"He came by to talk to Bill about something."

She didn't have time to tell me anything else, because Dick was walking up to us, a big grin on his face. "Hey, Annie," he said, like he hung out at my mother's house, my boss' house, on a regular basis. His keys jangled from his fingers. "Gotta have some of those steaks, they're great." He faced my mother. "Thank you so much, Mrs. Giametti."

"Alex, please."

Oh, Christ, now my mother. Dick Whitfield was going to plague me in my personal life now, not only at work. I was screwed.

"Alex, thank you."

My mother shot me a look that said, "See, he's not that bad." If she only knew.

Dick paused in front of his Toyota Prius and gave a short wave. As he opened the door, an idea popped into my head.

"Dick, can you give me a ride?" I asked.

Both he and my mother looked surprised.

"Vinny's up at Southern. I need to meet him. Can you take me up there?"

Dick shrugged. "Yeah, I guess so." But he didn't sound so sure.

I didn't give him any time to change his mind, though.

I leaned into my mother's face and kissed her cheek. "Maybe I'll get back later, okay?"

Her face was dark—she didn't know what I was up to and she didn't like that—but she nodded. "Okay."

I pulled open Dick's passenger-side door and climbed into the Prius. I'd been in the car once before, and it was just as neat as it was the first time. When he started the car, Michael Bublé crooned at us.

"Do you have anything else to listen to?" I asked, pulling open the glove box, but not seeing any CDs in there.

Dick leaned over and shut the box. "No," he said firmly.

"So, what were you doing at my mother's house?" I asked. "She said you came to see Bill about something."

Dick's eyes were planted on the road ahead of us, his hands at that perfect ten o'clock–two o'clock thing they teach in high school driver's ed class. "Bill asked me to come over," he said.

"Why?" I wasn't sure I wanted to know.

He glanced at me out of the corner of his eye and then looked back to the road. "I'm going to be employee of the month next month."

Oh, fuck. Fuck, fuck, fuck.

I knew I couldn't say that out loud, so it went around and around in my head for a few seconds. "Oh," I managed to spit out. "And so he invited you to my mother's annual barbecue to celebrate?"

"I can't tell you any more," Dick said, although now I knew there *was* more. And I knew I wasn't going to like it.

"Sure you can." I tried to keep my tone light, like I wasn't ready to strangle him. "I won't tell if it's a secret."

He shook his head rather violently, like he had Tourette's or something. "It's nothing, Annie, okay?"

I didn't want to press it, because I didn't need anything else to bring me down. Instead I punched Vinny's number into my cell. It rang several times and then his voice mail picked up. He must be on the phone. I left a message that I'd meet him in front of Engleman Hall.

The rest of the trip was spent in silence, although Dick kept stealing glances at me, little furtive glances, sort of like a ferret. When we pulled into the parking lot at Southern just near Engleman Hall, I opened the door and thanked him for the ride.

"Where's Vinny?" he asked.

I looked around for the Explorer, but didn't see it. He always checked his messages, though, so I was sure he'd show up here if he wasn't here right this second. "I'll be fine," I said, even though I wasn't totally sure.

Dick didn't argue—although for the first time I wanted him to, despite the bad karma in the car—and he left me on the sidewalk in the June heat. I watched the Prius peel out of the lot and careen down the street. I didn't think he wanted to get rid of me *that* bad.

As I stood alone, exposed, I had that feeling again. The one that I was being watched.

There was no one there.

Literally.

A beat-up Corolla was at the far end of the parking lot, but besides that, there were no cars. No people.

A shiver tickled my spine, and I took a deep breath, deciding to get a little closer to Engleman Hall. Within a minute or so, I was standing near the doors, looking out over the abandoned campus.

Even though Vinny had said Jamond wasn't near the old student center, I needed something to do. Something to keep my mind busy. As I walked across campus, I wished again that Tom hadn't confiscated my gun. Or that I hadn't been stupid enough to leave it in a place where he'd see it. But how was I supposed to know he'd have to reach under that seat?

I thought about those four expelled bullets.

The ballistics test was supposed to come back tomorrow, I remembered Tom saying.

If Ralph died of a heart attack, though, could the cops issue a warrant for attempted murder?

I should've asked my mother that. I should've stayed at that barbecue. Even though I would've had to make small talk with Bill Bennett. Even though I'd have to suck it up and pretend I was happy for Dick Whitfield and his employee-of-the-month award.

Fuck.

I think those kids on the bus had an effect on my language.

Not.

Someone was moving over near the student center, which was surrounded by a barbed-wire fence. Parts of the brick were falling off; a window was broken on the second floor. The building would be taken down, but it was probably full of asbestos, so it might take a little while.

I felt like I was getting ADD; I couldn't concentrate on one thought for too long. Didn't they have drugs for that?

Drugs reminded me again of Jamond. Maybe he was late, like I was. Maybe he took the bus, too.

My cell phone rang, startling me. I flipped the cover, still glancing around to see if anyone was lurking around the building, but there was no more movement.

"I told you I'd come get you at your mother's, and I'm here, but she said you left with Dick Whitfield." Vinny sounded like my mother.

"I told you I'd call you back."

"And how long ago was that?" he admonished.

"I left a message. You didn't answer."

A second passed, then a quiet, "Shit."

"I'm at Southern," I said, my voice way too loud. I took it down a decibel. "I said I'd meet you here in my message. Can you come get me?"

"I'll be there in about ten minutes. Don't go anywhere this time, okay?"

"Promise. I'll be in front of Engleman Hall."

"Which one's that?"

"Just come up Fitch and pull into that big parking lot. You can't miss me. There's no one else here."

But as I flipped the phone shut, I realized I was wrong.

Chapter 38

A shadow crossed my path, and a hand wrapped itself around my wrist so tightly that I dropped my phone. I twisted around to see Jamond, still holding me, bend down and pick it up. When he stood back up, his expression was unreadable.

"Took you long enough," he said.

"Let go of me," I demanded. "Give me back my phone."

He studied the new phone I'd gotten when I renewed my contract last month. "I don't think so," he said.

For a skinny kid, he sure had a strong grip. I tried to wrench free, but his hand was like a vise. This wouldn't do. I yanked up my arm quickly and then back down again. Shock crossed his face as he realized he'd lost hold, and I pulled my hand away. I backed up a few steps, ready to run.

"Give me back my phone, Jamond," I said.

He shook his head. "Sorry about this," he said, smashing it to the pavement. I watched as little pieces of my cell phone skipped along the sidewalk like stones skimming along water.

Double fuck.

I was going to have to wash my own mouth out with soap.

"What the hell, Jamond?" I demanded. "Listen, what's wrong? Did you make that shit up about Felicia up at the cave?"

Jamond slipped a gun out from under his T-shirt. I stared at it, like it was some sort of illusionist's trick.

"Felicia's up there, all right," he said, waving the gun at me. I took another step back. "Stop moving," he added.

My feet wanted to run, but I stayed put. "What are you doing?" I asked him.

Jamond was shaking his head. "I changed my mind. I don't want your help. Fuggedaboutit. You have to forget we even talked."

I clutched my bag, which was still slung over my shoulder. "What is this, the Mafia?" I asked. Little did he know that I had some experience in that area. I wished I hadn't ignored the creepy feeling that had sneaked up on me. Was Jamond the person who'd gotten too close to me that Jack Hammer had warned me about? Had he killed Felicia and wanted to lure me here to kill me, too? Did this have to do with Ralph's guns? I tried to remember what Jack had said, something about how the person watching me thought I knew more than I did. Jamond just might think that, considering our previous conversations about Ashley and Felicia.

"Listen, if Felicia's dead up on the summit, we need to call the cops," I said.

"Too late for that," he said, indicating my phone.

I tried to think quickly. Maybe I could talk my way out of this. "Yeah, like you don't have a phone. All you kids have them. All that text messaging and shit." His eyes grew wide with each sentence, like he thought I was a moron because I was over thirty and I shouldn't know about that. "I've got a friend who's a cop. He'll listen to you. We can get in touch with him; he'll help." I paused. "I don't have to tell him about the gun."

The smirk indicated Jamond didn't believe me.

I threw up my hands. "Then what the fuck are we going to do here?" I asked. "You're holding me at gunpoint, you destroyed my phone, I don't have a car, it doesn't look like you've got one, so what's the plan?"

"What's going on?"

The voice came from behind me, and I whirled around to see Ned Winters standing behind me. I hadn't even heard him approach. I took a deep breath, relieved to see someone I knew, even if I didn't think of him as "a friendly face."

Ned's eyes were trained on Jamond and the gun. "What's going on?" he asked again.

Jamond stared at him and shrugged. "Lady dropped her phone," he said.

I opened my mouth to argue the point, but then closed it again. Ned was staring him down. No one said a word for a couple of seconds, but I couldn't stand it anymore.

"Jamond asked me to meet him here, but what he wanted to say, well, he changed his mind," I told Ned, whose eyes flickered from Jamond to me, back to Jamond.

In an instant, Ned had moved in and grabbed Jamond's wrist not unlike the way Jamond had grabbed mine just minutes before. Ned took the gun as Jamond's fingers went slack.

An ugly smile crawled across Ned's face. "Changed your mind?"

I could've sworn Jamond's face went white. Granted, that wasn't exactly possible, but the expression told me that if he were as white as I was, he would've gone even paler.

Ned dropped Jamond's wrist, the gun dangling from his own fingers at his side. He finally took a long look at me. "Shall we call the cops?"

Jamond took advantage of the moment and became Speedy Gonzalez as he shot off around the corner of the building. Ned thrust the gun at me; I clutched it as he jogged after Jamond, out of sight. I waited a few seconds, feeling a bit helpless, but then Ned emerged. I could hear him panting as he got closer, his body half doubled over. That extra weight and the heat must have thwarted him.

"Disappeared," he said between breaths, his hands on his knees as his back rose and fell; he was trying to suck in as much air as possible. "What the hell happened here? What was he saying about Felicia?" he asked after a few seconds.

"You heard that?"

Ned waved his arm in the air to indicate the empty campus. "Voices carry, especially when the air's still like this." He paused. "I heard your voice and something crash. Must have been your phone." He pointed to its remains at our feet.

"Yeah." The gun was heavy in my hands. A Glock. I wondered if it was one of Ralph's. Even if it wasn't, Jamond hadn't gotten it legally, I was sure of that.

"So what about Felicia? Did anyone find her?" Ned was asking.

"Jamond said he saw her body up at Judges Cave." I put my hand on his forearm as Ned stood up straighter. "Thanks, Ned. I don't know what Jamond planned to do."

Ned flashed a smile at me. "What are friends for?"

I chuckled. "You know, you aren't Dirty Harry or anything. Never were."

"But I got rid of the bad guy, didn't I?"

His words reminded me. "Vinny's on his way over here now; I should go out to the parking lot and meet him." I indicated the Glock. "And we have to do something about this."

Ned reached for it, so I gave it to him. "We can call the police," he offered.

I'd been trying to do just that for hours now, but Tom wouldn't return my calls. And I was sure Riley wouldn't be happy that I'd skipped out on him. I sighed. "He's just a kid."

"A kid with a gun," Ned said firmly. "We have to call the police. Let's go inside to my office and use the phone there."

"Why don't we wait until Vinny gets here?" I suggested. "Vinny will be really worried if I'm not out waiting for him."

"It's so fucking hot out here," he complained. "That running, well, I don't do that very much. At least it's air-conditioned in my office. And I have a phone."

He wasn't going to let it go. He *had* come to my rescue. But I didn't want to miss Vinny. Ned could see I was debating with myself.

"My office window looks out over the parking lot and the sidewalk," he said. "Remember? That's how I saw you coming up the other day."

Reluctantly I followed him. I didn't see the Explorer anywhere as we reached Morrill Hall, even though I was sending Vinny telepathic messages.

"How's Priscilla?" Ned was asking, the Glock swinging at his side. It had looked so large when Jamond held it, since he was shorter and a lot skinnier. In Ned's hand, it looked almost like a toy.

"Drunk as a skunk and getting sick all over my apartment." An exaggeration, but he didn't need to know that. "Hey, why did you put her in that cab? Why did you leave her in that state? You could've at least brought her to my place."

"I had to go." Ned had turned slightly, and I couldn't see his face. "You know my dad's been sick."

I shook my head. "No, you never mentioned that."

His face fell. "Oh, I did. At lunch."

I actually felt a little guilty for not paying attention. "I'm sorry," I said lamely.

I heard something then: a car, no, a bigger vehicle. Vinny? I ignored Ned's surprised look—he'd already opened the door and was waiting for me to walk in—as I jogged back to the sidewalk. The familiar Explorer skidded to a stop just a few feet from me. Vinny jumped out and came over, giving me a quick kiss.

"You're harder to track down than anyone I've ever known," he scolded playfully.

Ned had come up behind me, and I turned and introduced them. "Vinny, this is Ned Winters. Ned, this is Vinny DeLucia."

Vinny started a bit when he saw the gun in Ned's hand. "Long story," I said.

"But you're going to tell me, aren't you." It wasn't a question.

Ned's eyebrows rose and his lips tugged into more of a grimace than a smile as he interrupted. "Ah, the love of your life." He held out his free hand, and Vinny took it.

I wondered if I could blame my flush on the heat. It was that elusive word again. Vinny didn't seem to mind; in fact, he seemed to revel in his new title. He grinned.

"Nice to meet you. I don't know much about Annie's college days, but I'm learning a lot more about them all the time."

"I could tell you some stories—," Ned started, but I put my hand up to stop him.

"Listen, we can save those stories for another time. Vinny, I need your phone to call Tom."

"Where's yours?" His eyes settled on my bag, which usually carried all my essentials.

I sighed. "It's part of the long story. I'll tell you after I make the call."

Vinny unclipped his phone from his belt and handed it to me. I held it hesitantly. "Why don't we get in the car and I can call from there? It's hot out here," I said. I didn't want Ned to start telling Vinny those college stories while I was distracted on the phone.

When Ned's eyebrows shot up, I added, "We need to get back to my place and see if Priscilla is okay." I looked at Ned. "Someone got her drunk and dumped her."

Ned indicated the gun in his hand. "What about this?"

I really didn't want to stick around much longer. While I was grateful for Ned's heroics, I was hot and hungry and tired. I also realized that if Tom knew what had happened here, I'd again have to give a statement and go through all those shenanigans. I wasn't in the mood. "Can you hold on to it for the time being?" I asked. "I'll call you in a bit, once I get in touch with Tom."

"Whose gun—"

I stopped Vinny by putting a finger across his lips. "I'll tell you in the car."

Vinny shrugged. "Nice meeting you." He nodded at Ned, who looked at me as if he were losing his best friend all over again. I owed him for what he'd done. And for not paying attention about his father. That compassion somehow kicked in just when I least expected it.

I put my hand on his shoulder and leaned in, kissing him on the cheek. "Thanks, Harry." I smiled. He smiled back, and I felt a surge of our old friendship. We'd been there for each other a long time ago, and knowing that he would still be there for me now, even after all that shit with Ralph—well, let's just say that even though I'm not a warm and fuzzy kind of person, it was oddly comforting.

Vinny slung his arm around my waist and gave Ned a short wave as we made our way to the Explorer. Ned watched us until we were inside, and then turned back toward his building.

When we were safely strapped in and my fingers about to punch in Tom's number on the phone, Vinny's hand wrapped itself around mine, stopping me. "Okay, you're telling me everything. Now."

I sighed and related the whole story. Vinny's eyes grew wide when I got to the part about Ned grabbing the gun from Jamond, but he didn't say anything. Just listened until I got to the part where he showed up.

"Well, I don't know what his angle is, but the kid was lying to you, that's for sure," he said when I was done.

"Felicia's alive."

Chapter 39

I stared at him a few seconds and realized he was serious. "How do you know?" I asked.

Vinny chuckled. "You don't trust that I can do my job right? I find people for a living, remember?"

I thought back to someone he hadn't found, and he read my mind. "Okay, so I miss one every now and then. But Felicia, she's okay."

"Where is she?"

"In a safe place."

I frowned. "Is she in danger?"

"Why do you think she disappeared?"

I snorted. "Don't be a smart-ass. So tell me about it. Where is she? How'd you find her?"

We were heading down Fitch Street, and my stomach growled before he could answer. It was dinnertime; that measly spinach salad I'd had at the Union League was hours ago.

"Food. Let's get some food," he said.

"The Japanese place on Dixwell. The one that used to be Hama but is something else now. I want some sushi," I said, even though the longer I was away from my apartment, the more pissed Tom would be if he found out I wasn't actually there. Now that I was away from the situation, I must have been suffering heatstroke to think about calling him about Ned and Jamond and the Glock.

Vinny wrinkled his nose. He hated sushi. I thought that was sort of funny, a marine biologist who hated fish.

"You can get something else there," I said. "They've got all sorts of cooked food, too, you know." I paused. "And you made me go to that Turkish place."

He conceded that it was my turn to pick a place, and it wasn't far from where we were, so he made a couple of turns and soon we were pulling into the back parking lot.

The new owners of the restaurant hadn't changed the interior much. It was typical Asian stark design, and its popularity was still running high. We were told we had to wait about fifteen minutes. Even though I was dying to ask Vinny about Felicia, he didn't seem to think that was too important at the moment, because he asked, "Are you okay?"

I knew he was asking about the whole Jamond episode. I thought about it a few seconds before nodding. "Yeah," I said. "It happened so fast, and it was sort of like in slow motion at the same time. Know what I mean?"

Vinny nodded. "But it can catch up to you."

I understood what he was saying, but this was different. "I wasn't really afraid," I said. "I know Jamond had a gun and all, but I didn't really believe that he'd use it. It seemed more like, well, a prop. Something to scare me with, but that's all. And he really didn't put up too much resistance when Ned took it away. He just took off."

"Think someone put him up to it?" Vinny's dark eyes bored into mine, and I nodded.

"Yeah."

"Who?"

"Jack Hammer, maybe?"

Vinny nodded slowly, and I could see those little wheels in his brain turning. He had something he wanted to say, but his cell phone interrupted. He pulled it off his hip and answered it, then handed the phone to me. "It's for you."

I frowned, said, "Hello?"

"I've been trying to call you," Priscilla admonished.

"Where'd you get this number?" I asked.

"Jesus, Annie, it's in your book here on your desk. When I couldn't reach you on your phone, I figured maybe Vinny knew where you were."

I told her about Jamond and losing my phone and Ned.

"And here I was thinking he was an asshole, but what he did was amazing. Didn't think he had it in him," she said. "Listen, can I stay the night? I don't feel like taking the train back."

"Want me to bring you some miso soup? We're at Hama."

"That would be great. But isn't it called something else now?"

Even though I was standing in the doorway waiting for a seat, I couldn't remember the name of the place. "Yeah. I don't know how long we'll be."

"Don't worry about me. I borrowed a T-shirt and your sweats and I'm watching TV."

I thought about my best friend sprawled on my couch, then took a look at Vinny, who was looking pretty sexy with a five-o'clock shadow.

"I could stay at Vinny's, and you could have my bed," I offered, punching Vinny in the shoulder as he shot me a grin and a leer.

"Like that wasn't the plan already. See you later," she said, and we signed off.

"Are we having a sleepover?" Vinny's lips tickled my ear, and I shivered a little, but just shrugged.

The hostess finally took us to a table for two and took our drink order. Despite the crowd, it didn't take long to get our Sapporos and order some food.

I took a long drink of my beer as I waited for my sushi and Vinny to get around to telling me about Felicia. His hand wrapped around his glass and swirled his Sapporo for a second before he looked at me.

"She was at that stripper's place."

It caught me off guard.

"Jack Hammer?" My brain raced in a million different

directions before it stopped on one thought. So that's why Vinny had looked so curious about me thinking Jack Hammer was in cahoots with Jamond. "He knows I've been looking for Felicia."

Vinny made a face at me. "So you think the smarmy bastard was going to tell you?"

"How did you find her?" I asked, ignoring his question.

"I went to his condo. I thought maybe he's the one who's been following you, making those calls."

Him and me both.

"He wasn't there, but she let me in."

"That was pretty serendipitous, wasn't it?"

"I wasn't totally surprised to see her."

"Why not?"

"When she called you? She was calling from Decker's phone."

I let that sink in for a few seconds. "Okay, well, did you ask her about Ashley Ellis?"

"I told her a body was found at West Rock School. That her ID was found with the body." He paused and took a drink of his beer. "She got hysterical when I told her. Said it had to be Ashley, that she hadn't seen her or talked to her since last night. She said she was scared—she didn't know where to go."

"Where to—" I stopped. Jack Hammer. She was staying with him but felt compelled to go somewhere else. Felicia suspected him. Damn. Was I right that he was behind what happened with Jamond? If so, he'd really been screwing with my head this afternoon. He'd had me almost believing he was innocent in all this. I had to remember that playacting was his business. "So you gave her a place to go?"

Vinny nodded. I could see from his expression he might not want to tell me where she was. Sometimes it was damn tight between that rock and hard place.

He had put his cell on the table, and I picked it up, punching in Tom's number again, but still got the voice mail. I left another message. What was up with this? I had another idea and punched in Dick Whitfield's cell number. I should've thought of this when I hitched that ride with him earlier.

"Yes?"

"Dick, it's Annie."

"What do you want?" His voice was high, nervous.

"Did you get an ID on that body at West Rock School?"

"Not yet."

"Have you talked to Tom?"

"Listen, Annie, you're not on the story. You said that yourself. You also said that I could handle this, and I am."

I didn't like it that Dick was getting uppity. It was easier when he was submissive. But I didn't have Cindy Purcell to blame this time. I had told him he could handle it, that it was his story. It was my own fault. I'd created this monster.

"Dick, I'm not trying to take the story away from you. I was just wondering if you had an ID and if you've talked to Tom." I tried to keep my voice light. It wasn't easy.

"I talked to Tom about half an hour ago," he conceded.

"Did he say anything about a report of another body?" I'd left the message about hearing about Felicia's body up at Judges Cave.

"Another body? No." Dick's tone told me he was confused. "What's going on? Is there another body?" He was worried that he'd missed something. I was sorry I couldn't indulge that worry and confirm it. "I haven't heard anything on the scanner, and when I talked to Tom, he didn't say anything." His voice got higher with each word.

"No, no, Dick, there isn't," I said, although maybe I shouldn't allay his fears so quickly. But I was tired and hungry and the waitress had just set my sushi down in front of me. "So there's no ID on the body yet?" I asked again.

"No, Annie," Dick said. "What do you know?"

"Nothing more than you," I lied easily. I heard a familiar sound in the background: a police scanner. "Are you at the paper?"

"Yeah. But not for long." Silence for a second, then, "If you hear anything else about that other body, you'll tell me, right?"

Jesus, he was paranoid.

Oh, right, I had egged that on. I smiled to myself. "Yeah, sure, but there's no news there," I said quickly, then closed the phone and handed it to Vinny, whose mouth was full of beef teriyaki. He was frowning at my yellowtail and salmon sushi.

"How the hell can you eat that shit?" he asked when he swallowed.

"Tom hasn't given Dick an ID yet," I said, ignoring him. "So where did you hide Felicia?" I savored a piece of sushi. Vinny didn't know what he was missing.

Vinny drank some more of his Sapporo before answering, and I could see he was thinking about this carefully.

"Like I said, in a safe place."

Even though there were a lot of things I really liked about Vinny, sometimes I really hated him. But just as I was about to push the issue, he added, "She's at Rocco's." His brother. Vinny grinned. "Rocco was all over it, thinking he could get something for his next book." Rocco writes best-selling crime novels and is always angling for a new plot idea. He's got a condo in Ninth Square.

Rocco was a good idea; I had to give it to Vinny. No one would even think to look for Felicia with him, since the players in this game most likely didn't even know he existed. I could vouch for Rocco's sleuthing and bodyguarding skills, since we'd spent some time together on a story in April. There might be only one problem.

"So when Rocco got a good look at Felicia, he probably started drooling," I said, stuffing the last piece of sushi in my mouth.

Vinny finished his beer before speaking. "She cut her hair and colored it. I guess it was her idea of how to camouflage herself."

"So she doesn't look as hot; is that what you're telling me?" I asked.

"She's okay. Not my type." His gaze was intense, and I felt a hot flash that landed right between my legs. He knew, too, and waved the waitress down. "Time to go," he said.

I nodded, but then remembered the miso soup I'd promised Priscilla. When the waitress brought us the check, I asked her to bring a to-go container. When Vinny raised his eyebrows, I said, "It won't take long to drop this off. And you probably want to check in with Rocco, anyway. Make sure he hasn't eloped with Felicia or anything."

We were halfway to the Explorer in the parking lot when Vinny's cell phone rang. He answered it, then handed it to me. "Tom," he mouthed.

I took the phone. "So you don't return calls anymore?"

"Christ, Annie, it's been a long day. And last I knew, Dick was on this story."

"I've left you like a billion messages."

"I called your cell but got your voice mail. Then I got this latest message saying you wanted me to call this number. What the hell is going on? Why are you calling me about Felicia Kowalski's body up at Judges Cave? There's no body up there."

"I know. I made a mistake." I paused. "That girl at West Rock School, any ID yet?"

"Who wants to know?

What the hell? "What do you mean?"

"Are you asking officially for the newspaper or are you asking for another reason?"

"It matters?"

"Yeah. It matters."

I mulled that a couple of seconds. "Okay, no, it's not for the paper." For me, saying those words was akin to Vinny actually swallowing sushi.

But if I could get an answer off the record from him, I could always try to confirm with someone else and call Marty with it.

You can take the girl off the beat, but you can't take the beat out of the girl.

I should have a goddamn bumper sticker made up.

"So what's the reason?" Tom was asking.

"Reason for what?"

"The reason why you're asking for ID? Anything I should know?"

I watched Vinny's face as I answered. "It's Ashley Ellis, isn't it?"

I heard him catch his breath. It was so slight that if I hadn't been paying attention, I probably wouldn't have heard it.

"I also know where Felicia Kowalski is."

Vinny wasn't happy I said that. His eyes narrowed, getting darker. I shook my head. I had to offer up something, and I still wasn't sure why Vinny would hide her from the cops.

"Where?" Tom was interested.

"First, I need you to confirm on the record that the body is Ashley Ellis."

"Will you tell me then where the girl is?"

I thought a second. "Why do you want to know so bad?"

"I can't tell you that."

We were at an impasse. I wasn't going to tell him anything if he wasn't going to tell me anything. He knew that, but he also hadn't played all his cards.

"If you don't tell me where she is, I can have you arrested for obstruction," he said.

The surprise must have shown on my face because Vinny leaned forward, wearing his curiosity on his sleeve.

"Obstruction?" I asked, and Vinny's eyebrows shot up. "What the hell do you want her for?"

"How much do you really know about your ex-husband's activities, Annie?" Tom asked. "Am I going to have to arrest you tomorrow when I get those bullet ballistics tests back? How come you're hiding his girl-friend? How involved are you?"

"Have you found whoever took those pictures of me?" I demanded, my voice too loud.

"I'm coming over," Tom said.

"Over where?"

"To your apartment—where else?"

"Oh, shit," I muttered.

"What?"

"I'm not there." I said it so quietly I hoped maybe he wouldn't hear.

"What do you mean, you're not there?" So much for not hearing. "Riley's sitting out in front of your building. He said your friend came by, that you guys haven't left."

"Well, Priscilla is still there. . . ." I let my voice trail off.

"Where the fuck are you?" I had never heard him this angry.

"Hama. Just leaving. I can be there in twenty minutes."

"If you're not, I'm issuing a fucking warrant."

He ended the call.

Vinny frowned. "What's up?"

"Tom's going to arrest me if I'm not back at my apart-ment in twenty minutes." I filled him in on the rest of the conversation as we got into the Explorer. "He wants Felicia. I don't know why."

"Maybe because she and Ashley were part of the straw purchases," Vinny suggested.

We were already zipping down Putnam toward Whit-ney. Vinny was taking Tom's threat seriously.

"Why are you hiding Felicia?" I asked.

We stopped at a light. Vinny turned to look at me.

"Your mother asked me to."

Chapter 40

"Why does my mother want you to hide Felicia?"

Vinny shrugged. "I don't know. She pays me. I do what she says."

"Oh, come on. You're not stupid, and you're not just a thug. What's going on?"

"Your mother told me to hold on to her until tomorrow morning, and then I have to take her to your mother's office." He sighed. "I really don't know more than that."

I had put the cell phone in the center console, and I grabbed it, punching in my own phone number. The answering machine picked up, and I waited until my short message was played. "Priscilla, it's me." I said.

But no one picked up.

"Why are you calling her?" Vinny asked.

I waited a few more seconds, then ended the call. I rubbed my forehead. I was getting a killer headache. "Why didn't she answer?" I asked myself, staring out the windshield.

I punched in Priscilla's cell number, and it just rang and rang until the voice mail picked up. "Something's wrong," I said.

The Explorer was now at the corner of Putnam and Whitney, and Vinny turned right to head downtown. "What's going on?" he asked softly.

"I was going to tell her to head Tom off," I said. "I want to go to my mother's and talk to her about this. But if Priscilla isn't answering, something's wrong."

"She might be asleep."

"She sleeps really light," I said. "Especially when she's not in her own bed."

I felt the Explorer take on a little more speed, and we were turning down side streets until we hit State, then careened up over the Grand Avenue Bridge next to the satellite train station.

When we pulled up in front of my building on Chapel Street, we saw Riley and Tom waiting for us. Riley wore his hat. Tom wore a frown.

I sped up the steps.

"Annie!" Tom's voice was menacing, but I ignored him as I heard Vinny talking to him.

My apartment door was wide open, and I ran inside, looking in every room, but it was empty. When I came out of my bedroom, Tom, Riley, and Vinny were waiting for me.

"Where's Priscilla?" I asked Riley.

A sheepish look crossed his face. "She left."

"Alone?"

He shook his head. All eyes were on him, and he shifted uncomfortably.

"Who did she leave with?" I demanded.

"Some guy in a Jeep. A red Jeep."

Ned Winters. What the fuck? Why had he come over here?

Tom picked something up off the kitchen island. "A note," he said simply, reading it and then handing it to me.

Ned came by. Said he could take me to the train, so I decided to go home. Talk to you later. P.

I took a deep breath of relief, but I was curious why she left a note rather than just calling me on Vinny's phone like she had earlier. Or maybe she had, while I was talking to Tom. I'm not very good with the whole call-waiting thing—or anything else technical. I tried to remember if I'd heard the telltale beep, but I'd been so upset with Tom I hadn't noticed. And if she was on the train, that could explain why she didn't pick up her cell. Sometimes it was just too loud on the train to hear it if it was in a purse.

Tom was still glaring at me. Shit. I was in trouble.

"Where's Felicia Kowalski?" he asked.

I tried not to look at Vinny, but I glanced at him for a split second, and Tom noticed, turning to him. "You both know. Where is she?"

Vinny's expression didn't change. "I can't tell you, but I can tell you that you can call my employer and see if you can get it out of her."

Tom knew Vinny was talking about my mother. He looked at me. "Your mother's involved in this?"

"Maybe you should just tell us why you want Felicia so bad. Isn't she more important to the feds than the locals right now?" I asked. "She knows, doesn't she? She knows everything, right?"

Tom leaned in toward Riley and whispered something to him. Riley looked at me a long second. He was probably pissed that I'd sneaked away on his watch; I'd made him look like an idiot in front of the chief of detectives. After he'd fixed my air conditioner and everything. I just shrugged at him; what could I say? He shifted his eyes away from me and nodded at Tom, stepping outside, closing the door behind him.

Tom ran a hand through his hair; his eyes were underlined by dark circles. He had gotten about as much sleep as I'd had the last couple of days.

"Okay, listen, but this is all off the record."

Maybe. "Okay," I said.

"She was seen with Ashley Ellis last night." He stopped, letting the words sink in.

"Before Ashley was murdered?" I asked.

He continued as if I hadn't even spoken. "They left Bar together. A man had approached them; he had his arm around both girls."

I butted in. "Let me guess, it was Jack Hammer. I mean, uh, John Decker."

Tom allowed himself a slight smile. "The description fits."

I thought quickly. When I talked to Ashley last night, she hadn't mentioned she was with anyone. She said she hadn't seen Felicia. Vinny followed Jack Hammer from Ralph's apartment to the City Point condo, and then we saw him driving back in when we were leaving. Vinny found Felicia at Jack Hammer's place.

Maybe Jack had picked the girls up at their condo and brought them to Bar. Somehow Ashley got back to the City Point condo and Felicia ended up at Jack's. If the two girls were together, Ashley had lied to me about seeing Felicia.

"The dead girl was Ashley, wasn't it? And you need Felicia because she can fill in what happened between the time they left together at Bar and the time of Ashley's death, right?"

"She might have more information about her friend's death," Tom conceded, confirming that the body at West Rock School definitely was Ashley Ellis.

"Who told you this?" I asked Tom. "I mean, who's the witness who told you about Jack leaving with Felicia and Ashley last night? Some stupid kid who might have gotten it wrong?"

"No."

I could see he was reluctant to say anything, but I pressed him. "Come on, Tom, off the record, remember?" I crossed my fingers behind my back.

"It was Reggie Shaw. Shaw saw them last night."

Chapter 41

My first thought was, What the hell was Shaw doing at Bar?

And then I knew I had to tell Tom I'd spoken to Ashley. I told him what she'd said to me.

"So between the time you talked to her and the time Shaw saw her, she found Felicia and they met up with John Decker," Tom said simply.

"Or she was with them when I talked to her and lied about not having seen Felicia," I said. "Why was Shaw there?" It was nagging at me.

Vinny was quiet through this entire exchange, but I could see him thinking the same thing.

Tom shook his head. "He said some kid had called him, needed to talk to him about something. He was reluctant to give us the kid's name, but he finally did. I can't find him, but that's no surprise. He lives over at Brookside."

"Was the kid's name Jamond?" I asked.

Tom looked startled. "Yeah," he said before he thought about it. "How do you know?"

"I met him at the community garden on Friday for a story. It's Shaw's project. And let's just say that I had sort of an altercation with Jamond just a little while ago."

"What kind of altercation?"

I had to come clean. I told him about how Jamond had called me, how I'd sneaked out of the apartment, taken the bus, and ended up at Southern, where I found out Jamond had lied to me for some reason and he broke my phone and held me at gunpoint.

"Did he try to take your purse?" Tom asked.

"I don't think it was a mugging. He set me up for something, but I don't know what." I took a look at Vinny and sighed. I'd left out the part about seeing Jack Hammer near my mother's. So I told them about that, too.

Tom and Vinny both wore worried expressions.

"Do you think it's Jack?" I asked. "Do you think he's the one responsible for everything?"

"He seems to turn up at the right times," Tom admitted.

"So does Shaw," I said. "I saw him at Atticus this morning. He told me to be careful, watch my back."

"He warned you?"

I nodded. "How would he know about me being stalked?"

Tom sat on one of the chairs at the island and put his head in his hands. Vinny didn't move. We stayed like that for a good couple of minutes, all of us thinking about what was going on and no one having a clue.

Finally, Tom got up and looked at Vinny. "Okay, listen. You have to take me to Felicia. I need to question her." He looked at me. "Riley's going to stay outside. You have to stay put this time. No going out the back way. We have to go on the honor system here. You're being stalked; people are warning you; a kid is threatening you. Is that enough to keep you here?"

I felt like a prisoner and totally helpless. "Can't I come with you to see Felicia?" I asked.

Tom snorted. "Jesus, Annie, no." He turned to Vinny. "We can call Alex on the way, so she knows you're being coerced into it. She might want to meet us there, and that would be okay, too." He started toward the door, then stopped as he realized Vinny wasn't following him.

"Can you hold on a minute?" Vinny asked.

Tom looked from him to me and nodded, going out and pulling the door behind him but not shutting it completely. Vinny's arm snaked around my waist as he pulled me to him. I laid my head on his shoulder, could feel his heartbeat on my breast. My breathing slowed, and I drank in his scent as I felt his five-o'clock shadow brush my cheek.

"Please do as Tom says and don't go anywhere," he whispered. "I don't know what I'd do if something happened to you."

He kissed me then, long and slow, and my body didn't want him to go. *I* didn't want him to go. I wanted that sleepover—without the sleep, of course.

Finally, Vinny pulled away, but his face was inches from mine. He gazed at me as if he was memorizing me. "I love you," he said simply, then let me go and walked out of my apartment without a look behind him.

I waited for the claustrophobia to settle in, but it didn't come. All I felt was warm all over, and I decided a beer just wouldn't do as I took the bottle of cognac out of the cupboard and poured myself a short one. I carried the glass with me to the window, where I saw the tail end of Tom's Impala moving down the block, Riley in his cruiser in front of the brownstone.

Where was the freak-out? He'd told me he *loved* me. It was that word. The one I hadn't used in a very long time. The one I hadn't heard in a long time because I went out with men who were as emotionally stunted in the commitment area as I was.

Vinny had been with his former fiancée, Rosie, for five years. Five years. I couldn't imagine that. I hadn't even been with Ralph for three years. But I had loved him, loved him with every part of myself. Until he screwed up.

Maybe finding out that I hadn't really known him at all was what had done it for me. Finding out that he was a con man, that I'd been conned. It demeaned what I thought we'd had together, and he actually thought I'd go along with it at first.

"Come on, Annie," he'd said. When I closed my eyes, I could see him in front of me, that crooked smile.

"We'll take the money, go somewhere, start over. No one has to know. It's easy, you know. You can just write anything and they'll believe it because it's in the paper. Jesus, people are stupid."

Had he thought that all along? Had he been planning this con from the get-go? I never knew. He did think I was so blinded by the love goggles that I'd forgive him. And obviously from his behavior at the Rouge Lounge, he thought he had another chance. I couldn't believe his arrogance. But it had been there at the start; I had just chosen not to see it.

He was probably sorry no one made a movie about him like the one about Stephen Glass or that he hadn't gotten a book deal like Jayson Blair.

I swirled the brown liquid in my glass, and a tinge of something hit me. I couldn't put my finger on it, but knowing that Vinny wasn't going to screw up, he wasn't going to be like Ralph, was somehow comforting.

I sipped my brandy as I watched the streetlights come on around Wooster Square. The long day had started to settle into its short night, twilight bleeding into darkness. I wanted to be with Vinny and Tom right now, seeing Felicia, finding out what the hell was going on. But I was stuck here, with a bodyguard who could fix air conditioners.

I wondered if there was anything else around the apartment that needed fixing.

And then the phone rang.

I glanced at it, decided to screen. My voice seemed too loud. My hand shook slightly as I waited for the response that never came.

Silence for two seconds, then dial tone.

Whoever it was, was still out there. Calling me. Knowing that I was alone. Maybe he'd seen Tom and Vinny leave. But surely then he had seen Riley in the cruiser.

I moved away from the window. The lights were out, and it was darker now. If I turned the light on, whoever was outside would be able to see me. I sat on the couch in the dark, sipping my drink, wondering if I had enough to last the night.

The phone rang again.

My whole body stiffened, the liquid swishing in the glass as my hand started to shake. I heard my voice again, the beep, and then:

"Annie? It's Ned. Ned Winters. If you're there, pick up."

Chapter 42

A flood of relief washed over me, and I picked up the handset. "What's up, Ned? You took Priscilla to the train?"

"Oh, well, she decided not to go home after all. Why don't you talk to her?"

Not even a second passed and I heard, "Hey, Annie."

"Hey there, girlfriend. What's going on? It's not like you to change your mind a million times. That binge must have really hit you. We brought you soup." I saw the take-out bag still sitting on the island, and I got up to put it in the fridge. "I can't believe Ned came to pick you up after abandoning you. What's up with him?"

"Ned talked me into staying. We're at the Anchor. Since you already had dinner, how about a drink?"

"Didn't you have enough earlier?" I asked, sounding like her mother. But she *had* been throwing up in my toilet all afternoon.

"Oh, I'm not drinking. You kidding me? After today? But it would really be great if you could come have a drink. I'll stay over at your place after all. I can get a ride home with you."

I was about to say I couldn't, I had to wait for Tom, when Priscilla whispered, "Listen, Annie, I can't handle Ned alone. He's a wreck, about Ralph, about his dad. I really could use the reinforcements."

I sighed. "I've got that cop out front."

"Oh, him?" Priscilla giggled, her voice back to her normal tone again. "He's a cutie."

"If you're a cradle robber maybe. But what I'm saying is, I can't leave. If I climb out the window again, Tom'll have my ass."

"Oh, hold on, Ned wants to talk to you."

"Annie? Why don't we come by and pick you up? The cop knows me from before, and if you tell Tom you're just going out for a drink with us, he can't be upset about that, can he?"

There was an odd logic to it. I didn't want to stick around here. Granted, I'd be stuck with tripping down memory lane again, but it was preferable to just waiting for Vinny to come back. And since I'd abandoned Priscilla with Ned earlier, I felt like I owed her one for that.

"Yeah, sure, okay," I said. "I'll meet you out front."

I hung up and grabbed my bag, locking the door behind me. Night had fallen now, and the streetlamps glowed against the silhouettes of the trees around the square. The heat and humidity had not dissipated but hung like a wet cloth. I went over to the cruiser, which was running. Riley rolled down his window, and the blast of cold air hit my face.

"My friends are picking me up. You know, Ned, the guy with the Jeep, who picked up my friend Priscilla earlier," I said. "I'll call Tom and tell him we're going to the Anchor for a drink."

Riley shook his head. "You're not supposed to leave."

"Listen, are you on duty? This is a total waste of taxpayer money to sit here in front of my apartment all day."

"I've got orders," he tried.

"Do you have a cell phone I can use?" I asked. "I'll just call Tom and tell him what's going on."

"Don't you have a cell phone?"

I thought about the bits of plastic on the sidewalk over at Southern. "Not at the moment," I said.

Riley reluctantly handed me a cell phone, and I punched in Tom's number.

"Are you okay?" His voice was anxious, like I shouldn't be.

"Priscilla and Ned are at the Anchor and they're coming to pick me up and take me over there, too. I tried to tell Riley here that it was okay, and he doesn't have to babysit me anymore." I paused. "How's Felicia?"

He was quiet so long I thought I'd lost the connection. "Hello?" I asked.

"Yeah, I'm here. Okay, I'll meet you at the Anchor."

"So what's up with Felicia?" I asked again.

"She's not here."

"What do you mean she's not there?"

"She gave Rocco the slip."

"Jesus, what are we, in a Humphrey Bogart movie? What do you mean, she gave him the slip?"

"Just like I said. You know how you got out of your apartment earlier? Well, she had the same idea. With the same success, apparently." The exasperation dripped off Tom's words.

"So you don't know where she is at all?"

"No sign of her. Listen, I need to talk a little bit more with Vinny and his brother. Vinny and I will meet you at the Anchor. Stay put there, okay?"

"Sure."

"Let me talk to Riley."

I leaned against the side of the cruiser, ignoring Riley's frown, as he talked to Tom. When he was done, he stuck his head farther out the window. "I'll stay until he picks you up."

I nodded, but I wasn't totally paying attention. My car was right there. I'd missed it today, riding that damn bus and then riding with Dick. If I drove myself, then I could bring Priscilla home after just one drink, leaving Ned behind.

But just as I was about to look for my keys, the red Jeep came toward me. It eased to a stop in front of my building. Ned waved. I gave a wave back, then nodded at Riley before I crossed the street and climbed into the Jeep.

"Where's Priscilla?" I asked.

"She's saving the table for us," he said, pulling away from the curb.

"I'm surprised she didn't go home," I said. "She was pretty sick."

"She's better now. She had something to eat," Ned said, his eyes trained on the road. He wore wire-framed glasses.

I chuckled. "Guess our eyesight isn't going to be getting better from now on, right? I didn't know you wore glasses."

"Just for night driving," he said, but I could tell his thoughts were somewhere else.

"Thinking about your dad?" I tried to grab at some of that elusive compassion.

He shrugged.

The Jeep went around Wooster Square and turned back, going in the opposite direction it had come from on Chapel. Ned didn't seem like he wanted to talk, so I didn't say anything else. He kept looking in the rearview mirror, however.

"Something wrong?" I asked.

He shook his head. "Probably nothing."

"What do you mean?" I twisted around in my seat and saw a set of headlights behind us. "Is someone following us?"

"I don't know. But those lights were behind us when we went around the square, and they're still there. Didn't you say someone was stalking you?"

My chest constricted with each word.

Ned took a right onto Church Street.

"Where are you going?" I asked. The Anchor was just off Chapel Street, which was the road we'd been on.

"I'm going to lose him," Ned said, glancing up and down between the rearview mirror and the road in front of him. He stopped at the light at Elm, in the middle lane, then swerved quickly to the right, turning down the one-way street, ran a yellow light at Orange, swinging fast to the left.

The headlights stayed with us.

And the farther north we went, the farther from the Anchor we were. Tom would be pissed if I wasn't there. But Priscilla was.

"Give me your phone," I said.

Ned shook his head. "No."

"Jesus, Ned. I'm going to call Priscilla. Tell her why we're not there yet."

"Hold off a little. This shouldn't take long."

The car swung around through the back streets between Orange and Whitney. This was Yale grad-student territory, big old houses split up into apartments, no yards, just a patch of green in front, some with flowers, some overgrown. I'd thought about moving here at one point, but my neighborhood was less dicey, a little more tended to.

Ned turned up Edwards, ending up on Munson, with a little maneuvering. The headlights continued to tail us. I knew where Ned was heading now; when he turned up Crescent, around Beaver Pond Park, it was clear.

Soon we would be at Fitch Street, where Ned felt more comfortable—at Southern Connecticut State University.

We were a long way from downtown New Haven at this point.

We'd turned down Fitch when I realized the headlights behind us were gone.

The Jeep slowed to a stop. Ned hit his hazard lights and cocked his head toward me.

"What?" I asked. "What's going on?"

Ned shifted in his seat. His face was clouded in a shadow, so I couldn't read his expression.

"How did you get a key?" he asked softly.

"What?"

"How did you get a key?" Ned asked. "Only Ralph and I had keys to the apartment. But you let yourself in."

I swallowed hard. How the hell had Ned known I was there the other night? I tried a small chuckle, but it came out as sort of a twitter, inhuman almost. "I don't know what you're talking about," I said, although not too convincingly. I certainly wouldn't have believed me.

Ned's hand snapped around mine and held it tight before I could even think about getting out of the Jeep. "Did he give you the key? He wasn't supposed to do that. It wasn't supposed to happen that way."

I stared at him a second, this person I'd once been close to, this person who'd once been a best friend. This person who had come to my rescue just this afternoon. We'd shared a lot together—kid stuff, stupid stuff. We'd shared dreams. And I should've suspected something earlier. But sometimes when the obvious is right in front of us, we don't see it.

Jack Hammer had said it was someone who had gotten close to me. Couldn't get much closer than this.

"You've been helping Ralph stalk me, haven't you?" I asked. I wondered why my voice was so calm, why my heart wasn't beating a million miles a minute.

"Why did he give you the key?" Ned sounded like a goddamn broken record.

I thought back to three nights ago. Had it been only three? It felt like a lifetime.

Seeing Ralph had thrown me for a loop. It had been a long time, but I could never have forgotten his face, despite the tug of time around his eyes, his mouth. When he kissed me, he'd pressed the key into my hand.

"You know where to find me," he'd whispered. "Tonight. We can pick up where we left off."

I hadn't had time to give it back; he was gone, groping that bartender who looked at him like he was the best thing since sliced bread. I'd recognized myself in her, the girl I'd been, the one who'd fallen so hard for this man. But he hadn't been a man; he'd been a stupid kid, worse than Dick Whitfield, because even though Dick was a boob, he would never make shit up. He had ethics. The one thing I'd thought Ralph had but the only thing he didn't have.

How could I have been so wrong about him?

I found myself nodding slowly as Ned's fingers dug into my wrist. "He wanted me to meet him that night," I admitted.

Ned laughed then, a sort of fake laugh that reminded me of that creepy Chucky the doll from those horror movies. "You think it was because he wanted to fuck you?"

Okay, yeah, that's what I thought. But I wanted to

know what Ned thought, because maybe I was wrong. I'd been wrong about Ralph before. I shrugged.

His fingers tightened.

"Dammit, Ned," I said harshly. "What's going on?"

"You're not even frightened?" he asked. "I don't scare you?"

Funny. He didn't.

He reached under the seat and held a gun to my head. "What about now?"

Chapter 43

Okay, so maybe he'd gotten a little scary. Feeling that barrel on my forehead jump-started my heart.

"What do you want from me?" I asked after a second. My voice didn't crack; I actually sounded pissed. What was wrong with me? Here I was, a gun to my head, and I was being cocky. I should be shitting in my pants.

Maybe now that Vinny had said he loved me, I had a death wish. It would be the easy way out.

Not.

It was really just that I couldn't wrap my head around the fact that this guy whom I used to get stoned with on a regular basis was holding a gun on me. A Glock, for God's sake. It could be the one he took from Jamond earlier. Who did he think he was, Rambo? No one who got stoned that much could be violent. At least not on weed. The weight gain I could see. The gun, well, not so much.

Ned's hand wavered slightly, then steadied. "You really don't know, do you?"

"Ned, I've seen you more in the last two days than in the last fifteen years. How should I know why you've got a gun on me?" I reached up and grabbed his hand, the barrel of the gun moved toward the window, and an explosion rocked the Jeep.

I slammed into the seat so hard my head snapped, not that I could hear it. The world had gone silent, a ringing echoing through my head. I opened my mouth and tried to make a sound, but nothing penetrated my ears. From the look on Ned's face, he was experiencing the same thing I was.

So now I knew the reason they made me wear those earmuffs at the firing range.

Ned's mouth was moving, but it took a few minutes before I heard snippets: "what," "like," and "shit." But not in that order. I shook my head, trying to tell him I couldn't make out his words, but he must have misunderstood because he lifted the Glock toward me again.

"If you try anything like that again, or try to get out of the Jeep, I'll shoot you."

I heard that, but it was like I was in a tunnel with cotton in my ears.

"You fucking shot your windshield, Ned—what the fuck?" I said, although my new hearing impairment made the words sound as if they were coming in from somewhere over Rhode Island.

Ned's face was expressionless, like he'd been taken over by the pod people. Or like he was getting my voice signals from space, too. The latter was more likely. He set the gun in his lap, pointed at me, and put the Jeep in gear, skidding away from the curb too fast for me to regain any sense of self-preservation and make a jump for it. I also believed he might just throw caution to the wind, decide he'd be deaf for the rest of his life, and shoot me.

I knew now that the headlights behind us had been nothing, just another car that happened to be going in the direction we were, and that Ned was the one all along. The ringing in my ears reminded me of those initial phone calls he made after Ralph and I split, the more recent call about teaching a class. I thought about how he'd never outgrown college—or Ralph. Ralph could tell him to jump off a fucking bridge, and he would've done it.

But how to get out of this. My thoughts swirled around like scrambled eggs, no answers, just one big mess. Priscilla was back at the Anchor, no clue what was going on. Vinny and Tom would show up there. She wouldn't be able to tell them a damn thing. Riley watched me drive away with Ned, and he might be the one who would be quoted in the paper as "the last person to have seen *Herald* reporter Annie Seymour alive."

Oh, fuck. Dick would write the story. The humiliation alone made me happy I would be dead, so I wouldn't have to read it.

Ned drove up Fitch, past the buildings at Southern, turned down Wintergreen. Toward the projects. Or West Rock. I figured I could take my pick. If he shot me and left me at the projects, that would make sense. I could be just another victim. West Rock, well, my body could be up there for days, weeks maybe, and I'd be so decomposed that I could be difficult to identify, like Ashley Ellis. Dental records wouldn't be a help. I hadn't been to the dentist in years. I didn't have a dentist because the idea of going to one gave me a panic attack. My thought, which I believed valid, was that if nothing in my mouth hurt, why should I voluntarily get poked with a metal toothpick, causing unnecessary pain? I flossed regularly in the hopes that I could keep my teeth until I was fairly old.

"Old" was looking dubious right now.

But I'd been in dubious situations before, and with people I didn't know as well as Ned. Okay, so I didn't know enough about him to know that he might want to stalk me, but I had known him back in the day. It might be time to give a shit about Ralph; it might buy me a little more time and maybe I could figure out just why he was doing this.

"So, have you had issues with me for a long time, or did they just start recently?" I asked casually.

The gun was still balanced nicely on his lap, within reach if necessary. I could see Ned's smirk as we passed under a streetlight.

"You don't know, do you?" he said again.

"Jesus, Ned, why would I ask if I did?" I was alternating between nervous, scared, and pissed off. It seemed as if right now I was pissed. "I mean, we haven't seen each other in a long time."

He snorted. "That's what you think."

Something in the way he said it made me take pause. Had we seen each other and I just didn't remember? That was likely, being as self-absorbed as I could be.

"You wanted me to teach that class—," I started.

"You think teaching is beneath you," he interrupted. "Like what I've done with my life is fucked-up, and what you've done is all fucking glorious and let's save the world."

He couldn't have been farther from the truth—except that I did think his life was fucked-up. But now wasn't the time to admit that. So maybe he was harboring hate for me outside of Ralph's influence.

"Listen, Ned, I admire teachers," I said. "I couldn't do it, which is why I turned you down. I couldn't stand in front of a bunch of kids and tell them how to write a goddamn news story. I just do it. You're the one who shows them how." Okay, so that was a bit of a stretch. We'd had a couple of Ned's students as interns along the way, and they weren't exactly going to end up at the *New York Times*. He didn't have to know that, though. Not with a gun aimed at me.

"And I'm not sure that spending my career at the *New Haven Herald* is all that glorious," I admitted. "We all had dreams back then, you, me, Ralph, and Priscilla. Actually, of all of us, Priscilla is probably in the best place. I mean, she's in New York—she's working for a paper that still has some respect, well, if you don't think about those tabloid headlines. She works at a paper that actually had its own fucking reality show on Bravo."

The Bravo show was actually pretty interesting. I was jealous of the reporter who took the subway to crime scenes. Of the newsroom where the editors seemed to want news, real news, not stupid animal stories or stories about community gardens.

"Why did you start asking all those questions when that student said I got her pregnant?" Ned demanded.

Oh, shit.

"You know, I got into a lot of trouble over that. I was on probation—they almost fired me. All because of your questions."

Telling him it was my job would be lame. Because he was half-right in his suspicions. I'd wanted to stir something up. I'd had no idea, though, that I'd succeeded to any extent.

"I really didn't mean—," I started.

"You didn't mean to try to ruin my career?" He snorted. "You can be such a bitch. I didn't completely believe what Ralph said about you until then."

That really pissed me off.

"What the hell did he tell you? That I was a bitch for not saying making up stories was okay? For not sticking by him when it all fell apart after the story about the sick kid?" I thought a second, wondering how much Ned knew, then decided: Screw it. "He set up a fake post office box and took most of the money that was donated. I don't know exactly how much, but the stories he wrote went out on the wires and people from all over sent in donations."

I thought I was going to go through the windshield even though I was strapped in by my seat belt. But Ned had stopped so suddenly, the Jeep screeching to a halt by the side of the road. He picked the Glock back up and aimed it at my chest.

"What?"

He hadn't known. No one had. I was the only one, and I'd never told. I got Ralph to stop stalking me when I threatened to tell the cops where the money was, that he'd taken most of it, turning over only a pittance and saying that's all there was when he got caught.

I told Ned the little I knew. I had no idea what Ralph did with the money in the end. He hadn't tried to contact me again, although he did know where I was and he kept tabs through Ned and Priscilla. I didn't mind that, as long as I didn't have to see him or talk to him. I closed that door and locked it. Until he showed up again.

Ned was making *mmm*ing sounds during my story. He hadn't looked like a psychopathic killer before, despite the gun, and he really didn't look like one now. He just looked like Ned, college professor, with a tight grip on a Glock.

It reminded me of that test when we were kids: What in this picture doesn't belong?

The blow to my jaw knocked me for a loop. I hadn't seen it coming. I'd started daydreaming and was gazing out the bullet hole in the front window of the Jeep when I felt the gun's impact. Intense, immediate pain spread through the left side of my face. My jaw felt like it must be in a million pieces, but when I instinctively reached my hand up and touched it, nothing moved or seemed askew. I shifted my mouth a little, probed with my tongue to see if my teeth were floating around somewhere. Oh, Christ, would I have to go see a dentist now?

No, it seemed like everything was in its place.

So much for not thinking Ned could be a psychopath.

"What was that for?" I managed to sputter, the movement of forming words sending needles into my face, even though I knew the answer. I'd been able to walk away from Ralph, the spell broken, but Ned never did.

"Does there have to be a reason?" He spit the words out at me—literally, as I could feel the droplets land on my chin. I suppressed an urge to wipe them off, not wanting to make him any angrier and afraid that touching my face again would cause more pain. I could already feel my jaw swelling.

"He knew you wanted to get back at me, right?" I asked. "That's how he got you to go along with helping him. Jesus, Ned, Ralph used people. He used me; he used you. He was a goddamn criminal." I paused. "I don't know what he wanted out of me now—maybe he wanted to prove that he could still charm me. Is that what it was?"

Ned didn't say anything, just floored the accelerator, and the Jeep shot back out into the street. We spun around to the left, past the Brookside projects, and up the road leading to West Rock. The gate was wide open. I thought they closed it after sunset. That's what the sign said, at least. Someone was asleep on the job, which did not bode well for me at all.

I didn't ask where we were going, since I pretty much

knew. We spiraled around to the summit, where the Judges Cave sat primly just back from the road. This was where Jamond had said he'd seen Felicia's body. A flashback of how Ned had saved me from Jamond popped into my head.

Going over it now, a few hours out and with more perspective on Ned's state of mind, I realized that perhaps Ned hadn't been so gallant after all. When Jamond told Ned that he'd "changed his mind," he'd looked scared. And the way Ned had looked back at him—I knew now that Ned had set me up. Vinny's arrival thwarted the plan, but then he had a new one. Get Priscilla to get to me. Easy.

So fucking easy it would make my head spin if it weren't already spinning with the pain from my jaw. I tried opening my mouth, but it was almost locked shut; I could feel a pulsating just in front of my ear.

But even though I could make sense of Ned's fierce, misplaced loyalty to my ex-husband, I still didn't know why Ned would stalk me, want me dead.

"Why?" I managed to say between clenched teeth. "Why are you doing this?"

"You tried to kill him."

I stared at Ned. "Tried to kill who?"

"Ralph. Don't deny it. You had your gun—you shot at him."

"No, Ned. I didn't shoot at Ralph."

"You had your gun at your car. I saw you. Your boyfriend saw you. You shot at Ralph."

If my mouth didn't hurt so much, it would've hung open. "Jesus, Ned," I sputtered. "I went to my car to get my flip-flops. They were behind the gun under the seat, and I had to take the gun out to get them out. I heard the shots but didn't see anything. I froze and didn't put the gun back until after the shooting started. I stuffed the gun back into the car, didn't have time to change my shoes. I went back into the bar through the back door and then went out the front, where Ralph was on the ground." I paused, touching my tender jaw for a second, instantly regretting it, then added, "Someone might have shot at him over his gun deals. I had no reason to shoot him."

"He was stalking you," Ned said flatly.

"Why?" I wished there were more light; I wanted to see his face.

"Does it matter now?" He poked the gun into my left breast. "Get out," he said. "Don't try to run. There's nowhere to go up here."

No shit.

I opened the Jeep door and got out, sorry that my questions hadn't elicited an answer. That's the way it is with reporters: Sometimes you get answers; sometimes you don't. Not that Ned would know that, being in a classroom all day.

He grabbed my arm with one hand while still holding the gun on me and pulled me back around the Jeep and toward the cave.

The large boulders that made up the Judges Cave looked like they had been precariously placed against one another, as if they would at any moment go tumbling down the hill on the other side. The slices of space between the rocks were black holes, and the "cave" was more of a lean-to. I'd read somewhere that the judges, Goffe and Whalley, had been sleeping in the cave when they saw a panther staring at them from outside. It frightened them so much they took off and didn't return to their hiding place.

I heard something in the crevice, but it wasn't a panther. It was moaning. Oh, shit. I'd rather have a panther. Some drug-addict hooker probably had a john up here and they were going at it. I stopped, and when I did, Ned jerked forward, but not enough to lose control of either the gun or me.

"Maybe we should leave them alone until he can pay her and they can leave," I suggested.

Ned chuckled. "But we're going to join them," he said.

Chapter 44

I wasn't too far off on the "John" part. It was John Decker, aka Jack Hammer, but he wasn't exactly enjoying himself. He was on the ground, on his side, a dirty bandanna stuffed in his mouth, and he was tied up like a pig at a roast, with a rope around his wrists that led to his ankles.

Ned used to throw parties at the beach out in the little suburb he grew up in on Long Island Sound and he could tie a pig like no one I knew. But how he managed to overcome Jack was questionable, until I saw her step out from the shadows, from behind one of the boulders.

It had to be Felicia Kowalski. Vinny's description of her hair fit. He was wrong, though, that she wasn't hot anymore. She was hot like Uma Thurman in *Kill Bill*, the gun completing the picture. It wasn't a Glock—her hands were small—this looked like a .22, like mine. And then a memory kicked in. Ned standing on the corner while I had my dinner at Bangkok Gardens, a woman meeting him. It was Felicia, but I hadn't recognized her because of the hair.

The moaning was coming from Jack Hammer. I stood corrected: This was not the kind of moaning Vinny's neighbors had heard last night. This was an uncomfortable cry for help.

"He won't shut up." Felicia kicked him in the back, and he grunted louder. She waved her gun at me. "What the fuck do you think you're doing with *her*?"

Guess I wasn't part of Felicia's plan. But from the

nudge in my side with the Glock, I could tell I was most definitely part of Ned's.

I surveyed the environs: Jack strung up like a pig—I could make a snide comment, but it didn't seem fair to kick him again while he was down—the entrance to the black hole in the center of the boulders lit only by a candle perched precariously on what looked like a sort of natural shelf, protected by a "ceiling" so its flame stood still as a soldier at attention despite a breeze that touched my face. A spiderweb tickled my ear and neck as Ned pushed me forward. I wanted to brush at it, but wasn't sure how that'd go over, so I just took a deep breath.

Bad idea, as the strong scent of urine filled my nostrils. Someone had pissed here recently.

Ned chuckled. "Don't worry." While I'd been concentrating on Felicia's gun, Ned had somehow gotten hold of another rope. I saw the makings of a small fire then, wood stacked together, ready for lighting. Ned snapped the rope, and I snapped my head back at him. I could only guess that I'd be the next one trussed for the roast.

Problem was, I didn't much like that idea.

"I thought it was just going to be him." Felicia indicated Jack Hammer, who let out a loud moan, his eyes wide.

"Don't worry," Ned said again. He looked around. "Where's the kid?"

Felicia shrugged. "Took off. Said you had something else for him to do."

Kid? I thought again about Jamond's role that afternoon. Sounded like he'd been asked back for an encore.

"He was supposed to wait," Ned said, but he didn't seem too worried. Jamond wasn't innocent in this, either, so he'd have no incentive to tell the cops anything. I was screwed.

"Okay, Ned," I said through my clenched jaw, trying to keep the pain at bay but having a fucking hard time of it. "You have the upper hand here"—nothing like saying the obvious—"but I just want to know why. Why the hell are you doing this? Is it really that you think I tried to ruin you professionally or that I tried to shoot Ralph? Christ, Ralph wouldn't have stuck by *you*. He would've sold you up the river. I mean, he *used* you, knew how you felt about me, got you into this shit in the first place. What did he really want from me, Ned? What was the point of the stalking? What did you get out of it?"

The candle flickered as the breeze changed direction. Now in addition to the piss, I smelled rain coming. That summer rain, the kind that we used to run around in when we were kids, the kind that took the heat away— even for a little while.

When he didn't say anything, I cocked my head at Felicia. "What about her? Where'd she get that .22? Someone shot at him with a .22. Ned, maybe her? Maybe she saw him kiss me—maybe she was jealous." I was grabbing at straws, but as I said it, it sort of made sense.

Felicia shifted a little, but didn't say anything. Ned's face was unreadable; another breeze, a stronger one, had rolled through and the flame almost went out, clinging to life with a faint glow before gaining momentum after a second or two.

Jack Hammer moaned again, like he was trying to say something.

"What about him?" I asked. "Why is he dressed up for a clambake? What are you going to do with him?"

Ned snorted. "He was in the way."

"How?" I ignored Jack's louder moan. If I let myself feel the fear that was creeping up my spine, I'd lose it. Asking questions was my job; it kept me grounded.

"He saw me," Ned said, glaring at Jack.

"Where?"

"Watching you."

"When?" Jack Hammer's warnings to be careful now made a lot more sense. But if he knew Ned was watching me, why didn't he just tell me?

"Tie her up," Felicia said. Maybe I'd hit a nerve with the jealousy possibility. Maybe I wasn't off base. And maybe because I was shooting off at the mouth, I might end up dead. With Jack Hammer by my side. Talk about indignity in death.

Ned didn't like taking an order. He frowned at her— I could see that clearly; my eyes had grown used to the dark, sort of like I was a cat, or maybe a panther—but he grabbed my arm. He fumbled a little with the rope, and I gauged the distance between Ned and me and Felicia and that gun.

Maybe three feet. Jack Hammer on the ground between us. We were just outside the entrance to the "cave." Surveying the small space, I wondered how the hell those judges hung out here for so long.

"What are you going to do with us?" I asked. "Take us somewhere, shoot us, leave us dead?"

The words didn't scare me, sort of like by saying them out loud I was exorcising the fear. Jack's moan now sounded rather inhuman. I wanted to tell him to buck up—I couldn't help him if he was going to lie there and cry. Jesus, it was like something Dick Whitfield would do.

There was something seriously wrong with me. Because I just couldn't see Ned killing me, even though he'd hit me, so I was in total denial about all this. It didn't matter that he was making some sort of fancy knot in the rope, that the Glock was within his arm's reach on the rock where he'd put it.

A flash pierced the sky, and a second later, a crack of thunder rumbled across the ridge. The patter of rain followed.

I had an idea.

Ned had taken my wrist and was wrapping the rope around it, pulling on my other arm to get that wrist in line so he could string them together. I stared out over his shoulder, at the cave's entrance. Just one more. I just needed one more.

I'm not one to pray. I don't promise God all sorts of shit so I can get shit in return. I don't believe in that. But I do believe in fate, that everyone has his or her time, and if it's not your time yet, you're not going to die.

It wasn't my time yet. I felt that so strongly, so when the next flash of lightning momentarily stopped Ned's hands from moving over mine, I shoved him back with every bit of strength I had and ran into the summer rain, the thunder crashing into my ears as I went around the boulder to my right and stumbled down the hill as fast as I could.

A shot rang out as I ran, and I felt a searing pain not only in my jaw now but in the back of my thigh, the adrenaline pushing me past it, like I was outside my body, watching myself run in the dark through the woods. My feet pounded against boulders embedded in the ground, slipping slightly as I left the hard surface onto a softer, more pliable one.

He was following me. But unlike before, I knew it now. I heard the crunching on the dried leaves behind me—the rain might make the leaves slick, good in that it might slow Ned down, bad in that it might slow me down—Ned yelling, "Annie, for fuck's sake, you can't get away."

Something was dribbling down my leg. Somehow I knew it wasn't rain, but I didn't stop. The rope was still dangling from the one wrist, and as I glanced down to try to pull it off, I fell, rolling across something prickly and hard, fast enough so that when I hit the tree, it knocked the wind out of me.

This was all Ralph's fault. I pulled the anger up from inside my gut and dragged myself to my feet. I had to get out of the woods and get some help for Jack Hammer and sic the cops on Ned and Felicia.

The sky lit up like the fucking Fourth of July, and Ned's silhouette was coming toward me, his arm raised, the gun pointed—not at me. I don't know what he saw, but he thought I was about a hundred yards away. I scrambled behind the tree I'd hit, my footsteps covered by the clap of thunder that rolled across the ridge and down into my chest.

So many questions cluttered my head, but I couldn't think about them now. My eyes hadn't moved from Ned's figure, which was standing still as he surveyed the landscape, looking for me. I hoped he couldn't hear my heartbeat, which was louder than a goddamn drum.

The lightning cracked static across the sky, breaking the darkness into sections. I waited for the rumble that followed and ran farther down the hill. I felt like I'd been running for hours until my feet finally touched pavement. The road. It wound farther down. I glanced behind me but didn't see Ned, didn't hear anything except the rain, which was coming down even harder now. My hair was dripping down my back; my clothes felt as if they'd been plastered on. Yeah, I was one big fucking papier-mâché project.

Even though I couldn't spot Ned, I didn't want to take any chances and crossed the road into the woods on the other side, hoping the brush and trees would help shield me. It was as if my feet couldn't stop moving even if I wanted them to; I just ran.

Until one of the trees in front of me reached out and grabbed me.

Chapter 45

A tall black man standing in the woods at night could be mistaken for a tree. Really, he could. That's just what I'd done. Mistaken him for a tree. And as I stared into the face of the Reverend Reginald Shaw, I wondered if I shouldn't have just let Ned shoot me. I didn't like the look on Shaw's face.

"What the hell are you doing?" he demanded, his face close to mine, his grip on my arm even tighter than Ned's had been.

I jerked back and shook my head, breathing so hard I was unable to speak.

I'm not used to any sort of exercise. I figured this was my quota for the next five years.

To my surprise, Shaw let go of me, and I fell back, not realizing he'd been holding me up. I sat on my ass in the wet leaves, staring up at him, wishing I could have a time machine and go back and start over. From Thursday night, when I'd seen Ralph for the first time. I would've handled everything so differently if I'd known.

Yeah, right. Probably not. In retrospect, everything seemed easy.

"It's not safe out here," Shaw scolded, his voice loud.

I caught my breath and struggled to get up. He held out his hand and pulled me so I was standing. "Shush," I said, a finger at my lips. "They'll hear you."

Shaw glanced around. "Who?" he asked, and to his credit, he did lower his voice, but it still rumbled like the thunder that seemed to be over. Even the rain had let up a bit, and the heat had started to squeeze its way back, penetrating the chill that had temporarily air-conditioned the ridge.

"Do you have a phone?" I whispered. I had no idea what he was doing out here, skulking in the woods, but I didn't have time to stop and interrogate him about that now. If he was in on any of it, he'd probably deny having a phone.

But Shaw produced a BlackBerry—of course—from his pocket and handed it to me without question. If this was a trick, he was good.

I punched in Tom's cell number, heard it ring, then, "Hello?"

That's right, he wouldn't know it was me; it was Shaw's phone.

"Tom?"

"Annie? Where are you?"

"West Rock." I quickly told him about Ned and Felicia and Jack Hammer, the whole time more than aware of Shaw's eyes watching me.

When I was done, Tom said, "Shaw's with you?"

"Yeah."

"Can I talk to him?"

I handed Shaw the phone. "He wants to talk to you."

Shaw nodded, taking the phone, and turned slightly away from me as he listened to Tom. After a few seconds, he punched END and stuck the phone back in his pocket. "He said—" But he was interrupted by an explosion that slammed against our ears.

Ned was coming down the hill and had spotted us. Shaw took my hand and pulled me behind him as we went deeper into the woods. Ned obviously didn't give a shit anymore; we heard more shots ring out, then tires screeching against wet pavement.

"Get in," we heard a female voice shout—Felicia—and then she gunned it, the Jeep skidding down the winding road until the sound faded and finally disappeared.

We stopped; Shaw dropped my hand.

"They got away," I said softly.

"John's up there?" Shaw asked, cocking his head up the ridge.

I nodded. "Ned was chasing me. I don't think Felicia could've gotten him in the Jeep. He must still be on the ground up there." I knew we were going back up there, but I also knew I had to call Tom again.

Shaw was one step ahead of me. The phone was in my hand before I could ask for it, and I thanked him as I punched in the number again.

"Annie?" Tom asked.

"Ned and Felicia, they're in a red Jeep, Ned's red Jeep—you can probably get his license plate. They're on their way down the ridge. We're going up to get Jack," I said.

"I told Shaw—" But I hung up before he could continue.

I nodded at Shaw. "Let's go."

We'd stood still long enough so that my legs felt a little wobbly. I reached down to my right thigh and felt something sticky, something that wasn't rainwater. I lifted my hand close to my face and saw a darkish hue. Shit.

The pain came back like a hot poker against my skin now that I had a few seconds to remember it. "I think I got shot," I said disbelievingly, and with those words, my jaw clicked and sent another rush of stabbing pain into my face.

Shaw studied my face, then stooped down and looked closely at my thigh. I had no pride left.

"How bad is it?" I asked, unable to twist around far enough to see.

He stood. "Flesh wound. It looks like it just nicked you on its way somewhere else."

"But it's bad enough so it's bleeding."

"It's not bleeding anymore; it's clotting nicely."

"I thought you were a preacher, not a doctor."

Shaw smiled, and I could see those straight teeth even in the dark. "You haven't done your homework. I'm disappointed."

I didn't have time to respond. He started off without

me, and I followed, wondering what the fuck he was talking about. He had to know Google didn't recognize him. LexisNexis showed nothing. He was a goddamn ghost, or, if the city fathers were to be believed, a guardian angel for the downtrodden.

Speaking of which . . .

"Jamond," I said as I limped up next to him. Now that I knew I'd been shot, or at least grazed by a bullet, it was affecting my brain and, by extension, my ability to walk properly. Just minutes ago I was flying through these woods like there was no tomorrow.

Of course I had thought there might not be a tomorrow, so the incentive was there.

"What about Jamond?" Shaw asked, not stopping.

"He was up here. Ned played him. I think he might be in danger, too." I told him about Jamond luring me to Southern and his change of heart, which seemed to anger Ned. And then how Ned had asked Felicia about "the kid." "Was Jamond involved with the guns, too? Did Ned know that? How much did Ralph tell Ned?"

"Why do you think I know anything about any of this?" Shaw asked softly. We were walking at a healthy clip, and the humidity was clinging to us, but he wasn't even breathing hard. He was a cool operator, that was for sure.

"Because you're here." As I said it, the butterflies flew up into my chest. He was involved somehow, maybe not with Ned but with something else. "Why *are* you here?" I asked.

He didn't stop, looked straight ahead. "Jamond called me. He said I should come up here. I didn't know any more than that until you ran into me. I make it a point not to ask questions of the young people. I don't judge them. They learn how to trust that way."

I turned his words over in my head. "So Jamond's okay?"

"He's laying low. His words."

Jamond had called for help. Not the cops, I'd been right about that, but the one person he felt he could trust. Maybe he really would be okay after all.

We could see the outline of the Judges Cave now

against the sky, which had brightened as the moon began to emerge from behind the storm clouds. The muscles in my legs felt like they were stretched too tight, the wound in my thigh just another place I hurt.

"What was between you and Ralph?" I asked. "What did you owe him?"

Shaw stopped then; a smile filled his face. "You thought the worst of him."

No shit.

"He wanted to win you back. He knew once you found out about the charity money that you would never return to him."

Again, no shit. I waited as Shaw sighed deeply.

"He gave the money to me."

I let his words sit for a second. "When? Why?"

"We met that night he was arrested. I was there, too. That's when we met Mr. Decker."

"The three of you? In lockup together? What were you there for? I know about Ralph and Jack." I couldn't wrap my head around "Mr. Decker."

Shaw had resumed hiking up toward the cave, but at a slower pace as he contemplated what he was going to tell me. Finally, "Drugs. Worse than Ralph. A lot worse. But we shared something there—I knew he'd lost his dream."

I snorted. I couldn't help myself. Shaw gave me a nasty look. Even in the dark I could see it.

"He lost his dream, his wife. He wanted to purge himself."

He fucking purged it all right.

"So he gave me the money. But on one condition. That I use it to educate myself." Shaw paused. "So I did."

"Give me a break," I said. "That's all it took to turn you around? You didn't take the money and go out and buy more drugs? Were you a dealer?"

"He didn't give it to me right away. We'd become friends."

"You can't tell me he hadn't spent that money before that."

Shaw stopped, studying my face. "He had it in a separate account. He knew he had no right to it."

No shit.

"Did you know what he was up to? I mean, with the guns?" I asked.

"I was trying to help him, but he got in over his head. Once he was in, he couldn't get out." He stole a glance at me. "He wanted to see you."

He saw me all right—through a camera lens. "Did he even think he could justify stalking me?"

Shaw sighed. "He didn't know how to approach you. I told him he should just call you."

While I could see Shaw might have been trying to talk sense into Ralph, it obviously hadn't worked.

He was talking again. "But he knew it was too late once those kids got shot in Hartford. Someone went to the authorities, gave them Ralph's name."

"Who? You?"

"It was Mr. Decker."

Jack? Really?

"I thought Jack was involved," I said. "He had that duffel bag at the nature center the other day, the one that looked like the others the feds took out of the apartment."

Shaw chuckled. "He went hiking. He was no more involved than I was. We both wanted to help Ralph. He didn't know Mr. Decker was the one who'd turned him in. But Mr. Decker and I talked to him, and he finally agreed to cooperate. He was repentant."

I didn't have a lot of sympathy for Ralph. He'd never been sorry for what he'd done to start this roller coaster; how could I believe he'd be sorry for anything after that?

Shaw was nodding. He knew what I was thinking.

"I know. He'd spent his entire life pretending to be a victim. He saved me, but I could do nothing to save him. The least I could do was to get him a good lawyer." Shaw's tone was full of regret.

The story didn't explain how Felicia and Ashley got so mixed up in this, why Shaw had given them a place to live, and I was about to ask about that, but we'd reached the cave. I pushed the questions aside as we circled the smaller boulders around to the entrance, which was dark, the candle no longer flickering. But even in the dark, we could see.

Jack Hammer wasn't there.

Chapter 46

I stared at the empty spot where Jack Hammer had been moaning not too much earlier. Did Felicia untie him, set him free? Or did she just untie his feet and make him get into the Jeep, and now he was being held captive somewhere else? We'd passed no one, heard no one else in the woods, as we came back up the hill.

"You're sure he was here?" Shaw asked.

Under normal circumstances, I'd get pissed that I was being questioned, but since Jack wasn't here and I'd said he was, I couldn't blame Shaw for his confusion.

"Yes. He was right there. On the ground. Tied up." I glanced around. "Felicia had a gun on him."

"Felicia Kowalski is a troubled young woman," Shaw said quietly.

"Yeah, like I couldn't figure that out," I said sarcastically. "Listen, what else do you know about all this, I mean, really? That was a nice story and all about Ralph and his bullshit, but Felicia and Ashley Ellis were involved, too. You must know more. Ashley's dead—someone killed her in your condo."

"I'm aware of that. I spent most of the afternoon with the police."

"Why did you rent the condo to them?"

"They needed a place to live. I needed a tenant. There's really nothing sinister about that."

Guess not, if you looked at it from a purely business point of view.

"So who killed Ashley?" I asked as a siren sounded in the distance.

"Ralph got your friend Ned involved in things he shouldn't have," Shaw said grimly.

"He's not my friend. Anymore," I added. "He killed her?"

"I didn't say that."

"So Ned didn't kill Ashley?"

"Ned introduced Ralph to Felicia. Ned knew Felicia had connections with the young people in the projects. He knew what Ralph needed for his scheme. He helped set it all up. But he was just a pawn." Shaw was so damn calm about all this. Why was he making me figure it out when he obviously knew everything that was going on? He wasn't my goddamn shrink.

"Someone else was involved, right? Someone Ralph was working with. Did Ned know about this other person?"

Some of the puzzle pieces had started to fit, but I still didn't have the whole picture.

Shaw didn't have an opportunity to answer. The siren had gotten louder, and the cruiser swung around just beyond the picnic table that sat on a small patch of dead grass in the middle of a paved circle. A uniformed cop stepped out of the car and approached us. As he got closer, I recognized my new best friend, Officer Riley.

"Hey there," I said casually.

He flashed a light across my eyes, then across Shaw's, stopping on Shaw's face. "You," he said simply.

I felt a slight tension hanging in the air amid the humidity. Could be racial tension. Riley hadn't seemed that way earlier, but then again, I didn't know him too well.

The light scanned the cave after a few seconds.

"Thought someone was tied up here," Riley said.

I shrugged. "Was earlier. No clue where he got off to."

"Detective Behr said you're both to come with me."

I wondered where the other cops were. I mean, I'd told Tom about Ned and Felicia and Jack Hammer, but he only sent one guy? I asked Riley about that.

He was still eyeing the cave as he said casually, "The Jeep didn't make it too far. We stopped them at the corner of Wintergreen and Fitch. They sent me on ahead to pick you up."

He herded us into the backseat of his cruiser, and we started down the road. I watched the back of Riley's head as Shaw stared out the window like we were on a Sunday morning drive.

The drive down made me a little dizzy, sitting in the backseat and all. I never did well in the back. I figured I could keep my questions for Tom, even though it was driving me crazy that I didn't know everything. I thought about Shaw and his claim that Ralph's stolen money turned his life around. Could it be true? And why didn't Ralph turn his own life around?

"He knew he couldn't," Shaw said, startling me. I hadn't realized I'd spoken out loud—or, at least, whispered it to myself.

"Why not?" I asked.

"He liked making up that story. He liked the con," Shaw said flatly, watching me carefully. "He was good at it—conning people."

I snorted. "Yeah, he was."

Shaw sighed. "I was the impetus for getting him back here. I thought maybe by coming back to the scene of the crime, so to speak, he could sort it out, sort out what happened with you and, by extension, what had happened to him all those years ago. Instead, he managed to get involved in something worse."

The words scrambled around in my head. Shaw kept talking as if he didn't notice my confusion. But I was learning that not much got past Shaw.

"He met a cop who got him started with the gun purchases," Shaw said, his eyes lifting up toward the back of Riley's head. "The cop wanted drugs. He gave Ralph the guns for a trade, plus a little monetary incentive. It was easy. Really easy."

Riley's ears perked up at that. He cocked his head back a little, listening to us without even pretending he wasn't.

"My mother said Ralph was going to spill the beans, tell the feds who was in on it with him. Did you have something to do with that?" I asked.

Shaw nodded. "But then he died."

"Who's the cop?" I asked, more than aware that Riley had slowed down now, waiting to hear what Shaw had to say.

"He's been closer than you think."

With a lurch, the cruiser slammed to a stop. I hit the back of the front seat with my forehead. I hadn't bothered strapping myself in. Shaw had landed with more of a thud than I had; his head was bigger.

"What the fuck?" I muttered, sitting back and looking up at Riley.

But I didn't see him.

I saw the barrel of a gun aimed at my face. I remembered Jamond telling me how "Johnny" had supplied guns to his friend. Riley's first name was Jonathan.

"Get out," Riley growled.

Shaw had already opened the door, and I scurried out after him, ignoring my hurt leg.

"That way," Riley ordered, cocking his head toward the woods. Major déjà vu. He nudged us forward, staying just inches behind, hitting each of us in the shoulders every now and then with his service revolver to make sure we wouldn't look back at him.

"When I say so, I want you to run," he said. "To me, you're Ned Winters and Felicia Kowalski. I didn't realize that they'd already been caught."

Of course I can't keep my mouth shut. "But you said—"

"Detective told me to come up here before I heard on the radio that they'd gotten the Jeep."

So he was going to kill us and get away with it with that story. Shit, it would probably work.

"You both think you're so fucking smart," Riley said. He pushed Shaw forward. "How long would it be before you told the feds who the cop was?"

Riley shoved me as Shaw stumbled. "And you, you have to show me up and climb down your fire escape?

I'll probably get written up for that." He snorted. "Looks like I can get rid of two problems for the price of one."

I had no doubt that I was just in the wrong place at the wrong time, even though he'd obviously been jonesing for me since I made him look like an idiot. And I had no doubt he'd shoot us. Shaw didn't, either, but there was something about the way Shaw was jogging, the way he was holding himself, that made me wonder if Shaw had a plan.

I certainly hoped so, because I didn't. I was all out of plans. I was tired and hurting and my stomach growled in hunger. I thought about Vinny and that I'd been too scared to tell him I loved him. I thought about Tom and how I would always care about him, but not in the same way as I cared about Vinny.

Jesus. My life really was flashing before my eyes. Well, pieces of it, anyway.

Ned hadn't worried me like this. Okay, so he did shoot me, but he was a lousy shot and just grazed me. Riley was a cop. He was trained in this shit.

"Annie, listen to me." Shaw's voice was barely a whisper. "When I say so, run to your right. You'll meet up with the road. Just keep going down the hill."

I didn't have time to think. Out of the corner of my eye, I saw Shaw bend down, pull something out from under his pant leg.

"Run, Annie," he hissed, and the gunshot bellowed through my ears, deafening me as I did as Shaw said: I ran to the right, another shot and then another echoing across the ridge.

We were closer to the entrance of the park than I'd thought. I stumbled through the trees and hit pavement just as a car swerved to miss me, its tires screeching as it skidded across the road. My sneakers betrayed me and I slipped, rolling on my shoulders until I came to a stop just inches from the car.

Tom stared down at me. "Who's shooting?"

I pointed up the hill. "Riley. He shot at us. Shaw has a gun, too. But he's the good guy." I could barely spit out the words; I'd managed to land on my face, the side where Ned had hit me, and now every part of me was throbbing.

A cruiser came up behind Tom's Impala, but he was already gone. I told the two uniforms what was going on, and I was alone again. I pulled myself up into a sitting position, leaning against the back bumper of the Impala, the heat of the tailpipe searing my skin without even touching it. I couldn't move.

I heard another shot ring out somewhere above me, but I couldn't even lift my head in its direction. My hair was still damp from the rain; my clothes were stuck to my skin with sweat, my sneakers squishy. I felt like someone had put me in the washing machine and then hung me out to dry.

Shaw's words filled my head: Ralph, coming back to purge himself of his sins and getting involved in something worse than before. He couldn't stay away from trouble; it was too alluring. More alluring than that dream of writing for the *Times*. More alluring than me.

Ned had made everything even easier, even if he didn't realize it at the time. He introduced him to Felicia, who introduced him to Ashley, who introduced him to Michael Jackson, and that's where he found the drugs for Riley. Jesus. Riley. There was a story there, and I thought about Dick Whitfield. Maybe Marty would let me on it, at least a little. We didn't have to tell Charlie Simmons. Did we?

And then I knew. Riley had killed Ashley. I flashed back to last night, when Vinny and I passed the cruiser at the City Point condo complex. The cop had kept his head turned, so I hadn't been able to make out who it was.

I had spoken to her before that. Maybe she knew him and told him she'd spoken to me. I had a hard time believing she'd known he was a cop, but maybe she did. Either way, I knew he'd killed her. Felicia had gone into hiding. If she'd been there, she probably would be dead, too. Instead, she ran first to Jack Hammer, but Vinny convinced her that Jack was involved, so she then ran to Ned, who wasn't much better, but the only thing he was really covering up was the fact that he'd helped Ralph stalk me.

I heard the rustling first, then saw movement in the woods, the flashlights bobbing. As they approached, Riley was handcuffed, walking. My eyes skirted around, looking for Shaw, and spotted him with Tom, behind the rest of them. Shaw had saved my life. Like he claimed Ralph had saved his.

Eye for an eye, maybe?

No. I had to admit that I was wrong about Shaw. He *had* tried to warn me after all.

Tom leaned down and gently took my arm, pulling me up. His face was close, his expression concerned. "Are you okay?"

I nodded. "Sure. Million fucking bucks." My jaw was clenched, and I thought I'd keel over from the pain from just those few words.

Another vehicle arrived, but I wasn't paying attention as I watched Riley get pushed around by his pals. You get what you deserve, I thought grimly. I knew what it was like to be in bed with Ralph Seymour; now Riley knew, too. It wasn't the best place to be.

I was so entranced by the scene before me that I didn't hear him coming up behind me until his hand circled my waist, a familiar hand that pulled me into his chest. I laid the good side of my face on his shoulder, breathing in his scent. I closed my eyes and melted into him.

"I love you, too," I said softly into Vinny's ear.

Chapter 47

Jack Hammer was eating it up. I sat next to his hospital bed, my notebook in my hand, but I wasn't taking notes; it was a sort of comfort thing for me. Jack was grinning at the nurse, a gray-haired woman older than my mother who fussed over him like he was goddamn George Clooney or something.

"Thank you so much, Wilma," Jack said, his eyes twinkling. "And can I get some fresh ice water?"

Wilma patted his shoulder, careful not to disturb the bandages that covered it, took the plastic pitcher off the tray table, and waddled out of the room with what she probably thought was an enticing smile.

I slapped him on the leg when she was gone. "You should be ashamed of yourself," I scolded.

He chuckled. He shouldn't be in such a good mood. He wasn't totally off the hook. A cop stood sentry outside the door. Jack had admitted he'd seen Felicia put something in Ralph's martini at the Rouge Lounge, but he didn't say anything. When I told him how Ralph had died—from the Viagra overdose—he knew what had gone down. But he'd stayed mum.

Felicia had gotten the Viagra from Ned. I remembered not seeing any in Ralph's medicine chest, even though there were plenty of other drugs.

Felicia had slept with Ned before she got involved with Ralph, so she knew Ned had the Viagra. Riley wanted Felicia to give him the overdose, threatened to tell the cops about her involvement with the gun scheme.

He told her if she tried to tell them about him, they wouldn't believe her. He was one of them. He knew Ralph was going to roll over on him, and he couldn't take that risk. Felicia was smart, though. She did what he asked, but then decided she needed to disappear, just in case. It saved her life. Not that her life was going to be worth much now.

I picked up my mechanical pencil, poised it above the notebook. "So Felicia shot you after she got you in the Jeep?"

Jack snorted. "She says it was an accident."

"When did you catch Ned watching me?"

"After I left you at your mother's house. He had a camera; he'd been taking pictures of both of us walking."

The pictures at Ralph's weren't the only ones. Tom found pictures at Ned's, even more.

Speak of the devil, Tom stuck his head in the doorway, cocking it at me. "Come here." He gave Jack a short nod before disappearing.

I got up slowly. My leg was wrapped up where the bullet had grazed it, and a large bandage covered up the scrape I'd gotten when I'd fallen on my face. I was told there was nothing to be done for my jaw except muscle relaxers—nothing was broken—and it could take weeks before I could eat anything but soft food.

I'd spent the night at the hospital "for observation," but I stopped into Jack's room while I was waiting for Vinny to pick me up, to make sure he was okay.

"One more question," I said. "How did you know the cops would show up at Ralph's that night?"

"I didn't think they'd show up so quickly. I'd called the feds about the guns. Anonymously. Told them what they'd find."

"You said you were there to get something."

"You."

"What?"

"I had to get you out of there."

"You followed me there."

"I saw you leave the restaurant, which way you were

headed, had a hunch you might end up on Arch Street."
He grinned. "You're very predictable. Anyway, I wanted
you out of there before the feds showed."

"Gee, thanks," I said. "So Shaw was right—you
weren't in on the straw purchases?"

"Not my scene."

No shit. I hobbled past his bed toward the door.

"I hope you're coming back." Jack winked.

"Don't think we've got some sort of goddamn bond
now just because we both got shot," I grumbled through
my clenched jaw.

"I can see why that private dick likes you so much.
You're feisty."

I smirked, trying not to smile. I tell Vinny I love him
and suddenly I'm a soft touch for male strippers.

Tom was leaning against the nurses' station, smiling
in a way I recognized at a good-looking nurse with fiery
red hair and bright blue eyes that twinkled back at him.
He didn't see me as he spoke softly to her, but she
spotted me and took a step back, lifting her chin in my
direction. Her name tag read EILEEN, and I nodded at
her. "Hey," I said.

Tom slipped on his "official" face, but not before the
flush disappeared. I wanted to tell him it was okay; hell,
he'd seen me with Vinny—I didn't care if he dated anyone. But because we'd never been particularly good with
expressing our feelings in any way except the bedroom,
I didn't say anything.

"What's up?" I asked.

"We got those ballistics tests back."

I struggled with the desire to open my notebook,
which I still held loosely by my side. "Yeah?"

"Got something to tell me?"

"My lawyer's not here."

"Do you need her?"

"So I went to the firing range. I practiced shooting. I
didn't empty the magazine and left six bullets in it because I got bored. What did you think?" I cocked my
head and stared at him.

Eileen was openly listening to us. If she was interested

in Tom, then she was going to have to deal with me and Tom, too. Just like Vinny had to.

"Why did you let me find the gun in your car?"

I chuckled. "Jesus, Tom, I didn't let you find anything. How the hell was I supposed to know you were going to reach under the goddamn seat? The flip-flops were on the floor."

"And one of them was stuck under the seat."

Eileen snorted, and we both looked at her at the same time.

"What is it with you two?" she asked, but the gleam in her eye told us she was cool with it. I liked her. Tom did, too, from the way he flushed again.

"Riley is sitting in a lot of shit," Tom said, taking my arm and turning me away from the nurses' station—but not before I caught the wink he gave Eileen.

"He didn't shoot at Ralph with a registered gun, did he?"

"He shot at Ralph with Ralph's gun. One he bought a week ago in Middlefield."

I frowned. "How do you know it was Riley?"

"We found the gun in his apartment. Arrogant asshole thought he'd get away with it." Tom hung his head. "He was a good cop."

"No, Tom, he wasn't," I said softly, touching his arm. "Why have Felicia give Ralph Viagra if he was going to shoot him?"

"Covering his bases," Tom said.

I sighed.

"I'm sorry I had him watching you. If I'd known—"

Vinny walked around the corner, and I took my hand off Tom's arm as he stopped talking. Vinny brushed a curl off my cheek.

"You're pressing charges against Ned Winters for the stalking?" he asked.

I looked at Tom and nodded. "Yeah. That, and kidnapping me and shooting me. I wish I could charge him just for being an asshole and holding fucking grudges."

"Nice to see you're feeling better." Vinny grinned.

"Did Ned tell you why he did this?" I asked Tom, ignoring Vinny. "Because he wouldn't tell me anything."

Tom took a few steps farther from the nurses' station for even more privacy, and I followed. Vinny wasn't far behind.

"Your ex-husband was going to set you up."

"What?"

"That kiss in the bar? Ned Winters was supposed to get pictures of you with your ex. Ralph was going to bring them to your mother and tell her you were involved in the straw purchases. That you were secretly still involved with him. Winters was holding that grudge against you; it wasn't too hard to talk him into it. He knew you'd probably get off, but you'd get bad press and might have even lost your job over it. That was enough incentive for him."

I knew I pissed people off, but this was beyond anything I'd experienced before. "Why did he continue after Ralph was dead? Why did he kidnap me?"

"Felicia told him you were the shooter, that you tried to kill your ex. She wanted to deflect any sense that she was involved, and put it all on you."

"So by telling you all this, Ned's trying to save his ass? That he was justified in kidnapping me, holding a gun on me?"

"He says he didn't mean to shoot you. He just wanted to scare you."

And he thought I deserved it. Our conversation on the way to the cave solidified that for me. If Ned was right, then Shaw had been wrong. Ralph didn't want to try to redeem himself with me. He wanted me to go down with him. He was an asshole to the very end.

"Did Riley kill Ashley?" I wanted to hear what Tom had to say without my own opinion thrown in.

"You'll find out when you see the press release," he said.

"Jesus, Tom, I have no idea if I'll get to see the press release." I'd left a message for Marty to call me, but he hadn't gotten back to me yet. I knew Dick Whitfield was skulking around the hospital somewhere, trying to get information about Jack Hammer and me.

"We found fibers from the condo in his cruiser. And some blood."

I'd told Tom about seeing the cruiser that night.

"So he was really the guy, huh?"

"Shaw and Decker both knew it. And if Ned hadn't gotten to him first, Decker probably would be dead, too," Tom said. "I have to go talk to him again. I'll call you later, see how you're doing." I'd already spent hours giving my statement. I nodded. "Sure. How's Shaw?"

"Ask him yourself."

I turned to see Reggie Shaw approaching. "Hey there," I said.

"Lovely to see you up and about."

I was getting used to his affectations. "Thanks." But then I remembered something. I tugged on Tom's sleeve and pulled him away from Shaw and Vinny, who were talking.

"One thing. Ashley had told Vinny that someone named Reggie would give her shit if she was just talking to someone at the bar without selling any shots." This had bothered me.

Tom grinned. "The club manager's name is Reggie, Annie."

Okay, so I hadn't done my homework, as Shaw had so aptly pointed out earlier—and that reminded me of something else. "Shaw owns the house that Ralph lived in and that condo. What other properties does he own in the city?"

"All you have to do is check land records, Ms. Seymour." Shaw's voice resonated from behind me, and I turned to see him smiling at me. "I have nothing to hide."

He was smooth; I had to give him that.

I made Vinny stop at the paper when we left the hospital. I'd managed to avoid seeing Dick anywhere, but I needed to clear up things with Marty. I needed to know

if Charlie Simmons was taking me off my beat perma-
nently. Dick's comment when I saw him at my mother's
barbecue about "something else" besides his being employee of the month was nagging at me. In a really
bad way.

The newsroom was mostly empty; it wasn't ten a.m.
yet. Only Marty and Jane Ferraro were at their desks.
Kevin Prisley was on the phone. I wanted to ask him to
check into Shaw's properties next time he went to city
hall; I couldn't leave Shaw alone. I needed to know more
about the man.

But I didn't have time to talk to Kevin. Marty cluck-
clucked over me and my bandages when I came in, and
he pulled me into the conference room as Vinny went
off to get a really bad cup of coffee out of the machine.

When we were seated with the door closed, Marty
leaned in toward me, his face dark. "I've got some news
for you."

My stomach lurched, and I took a deep breath. "Don't
tell me I have to cover social services now," I said
grimly. "I don't think I could deal with that."

Marty's face brightened and he smiled. "Oh, Annie,
it's not that bad." He paused. "Charlie's taken a liking
to Dick, as you know. He also knows that you're good
at your job and Dick has a bit to learn yet. He and I
have spoken at length about this." He paused again.
"Dick's going to start blogging."

Blogging?

"We're beefing up the Web site, Internet exposure.
We have to—we have to compete. Blogs are a way to
do that. Dick's going to do a police-beat blog."

"What does that mean, exactly?" I asked slowly.

Marty chuckled. "Don't look so worried. What it
means is, he'll be taking your stories, and any he might
do, and blog about crime stories, trends, do profiles, on
the Web site. I think it'll help his writing. It'll get him
out of your hair a little, but you'll have to work with
him on content. Can you do that?"

As long as he didn't take my beat, I didn't give a shit

what Dick Whitfield had to do. I barely knew what a blog was, much less how to write one, so I could live with this plan. I nodded. "Sure."

Marty grinned and stood. "Great. I'll tell Charlie you're all set. Now that all this is over, take a week off, heal up, and then get back to work next week."

Vinny leaned on his elbow, his face over mine. "You okay? You're not hurting too much, are you? We could wait."

The pillow was soft under my head, the light streaming into the bedroom, warming our bodies despite the cool air from the air conditioner. At least Riley had done something right.

"I think we'll have to abandon the acrobatics for the time being, but I'm fine," I assured him. And as I said it, I knew it was true.

Also Available from

Karen E. Olsen

DEAD OF THE DAY

An Annie Seymour Mystery

A soggy April has hit New Haven, Connecticut—along with an unidentified body in the harbor. The strange fact that there were bee stings on the body gives *New Haven Herald* police reporter Annie Seymour an intriguing excuse to put off her profile of the new police chief—a piece that becomes a lot more interesting when the subject is gunned down.

But this is only the beginning of a killer exposé—because as she connects the dots between the John Doe, the police chief, and the city's struggling immigrant population, Annie's drawing a line between herself and someone who doesn't want her to learn the truth— or live to report it...

Available wherever books are sold or at penguin.com

THE BRAND-NEW SERIES STARRING
FORENSIC HANDWRITING EXPERT
CLAUDIA ROSE

POISON PEN

A Forensic Handwriting Mystery
by
Sheila Lowe

Before her body was found floating in her
Jacuzzi, publicist-to-the-stars Lindsey Alexander
had few friends, but plenty of lovers. To her
ex-friend—forensic handwriting expert Claudia
Rose—she was a ruthless, back-stabbing
manipulator. But even Claudia is shocked by
Lindsey's startling final note:
"It was fun while it lasted!"

It would be easier on the police—and Claudia—to
write it off as suicide. But Claudia's instincts push
her to investigate further, and she quickly finds
herself entangled in a far darker scenario than she
bargained for. Racing to identify a killer, Claudia
soon has a price on her head—and unless she can
read the handwriting on the wall, she'll become
the next victim.

**Available wherever books are sold or
at penguin.com**

BEVERLY CONNOR

The Diane Fallon Forensic Investigation Series

In this absorbing series starring
forensic anthropologist Diane Fallon,
the bones of the dead often reveal
the secrets of the living.

DEAD HUNT

DEAD SECRET

DEAD GUILTY

ONE GRAVE TOO MANY